RAIDERS
ON THE SAINT JOHNS

ISBN:978-0-9821223-7-2
Library of Congress Control Number: 2009941039

Published by Global Authors Publications

Filling the GAP in publishing

Edited by Barbara Sachs Sloan
Interior Design by Kathleen Walls
Cover Design by Kathleen Walls
Front Cover Photo credit: The drawing of "Capture of the Gunboat Columbine" is from *Dickison and His Men*, by Mary Elisabeth Dickison. The map is an 1865 Union Army map of St. Johns County, Florida.

Printed in USA for Global Authors Publications

Raiders on the Saint Johns

Lydia Hawke

To Dustin and Shawn -
Enjoy the adventure!

Lydia Hawke

Dedication:

To my faithful readers with love and respect..

Acknowledgement

Special thanks to: Van Seagraves, curator of the Museum of Southern History in Jacksonville, Florida, for allowing me access to rare books for research purposes.

Also to Mary Kross, for her expertise in the creation of palmetto hats as the Minorcans crafted.

CHAPTER ONE

Palatka, Florida, March 1863

Every bullet must count.

Hiding behind a plank fence near the waterfront, Jack Farrell cocked his hat brim lower to shade his eyes against the glare of the sun rising over the east bank of the St. Johns River. He would not let the dazzle spoil his aim.

Jack and other sharpshooters picked from Captain Dickison's Confederate cavalry company had spent the night in a damp, musty ditch, waiting in ambush for the side-wheeler *Mary Benton*. After unloading a Union raiding party at Orange Mills on the far bank, the Federal transport ship steamed ever closer. Now, his deadly accurate Enfield musketoon ready, Jack watched the vessel glide alongside Teasdale and Reid's wharf. The *Mary Benton's* upper and lower decks teemed with dark-faced Union soldiers and their white officers.

To his left lay Martina's cousin, Ramon Andreu. High-spirited Russell Cates, just beyond, watched the boat with uncharacteristic grimness. Charlie Colee, at eighteen the youngest of the St. Johns County men, covered his right. Other troopers waited behind the fence and dirt fortifications they had dug overnight, ready to fire on the vessel the moment their captain gave the order. The remainder of Company H hid in reserve behind the riverfront warehouses, in case the enemy succeeded in invading the town.

The *Mary Benton* was the same boat that had brought Yankee troops to Picolata. That landing created a disaster for Jack, resulting in an assault on his Minorcan wife, Martina, the wounding of his young brother-in-law Carlo Sanchez, and the loss of their home. The thought of that huge force of Union soldiers marching off that boat, again threatening his loved ones, made Jack's gut tighten with apprehension.

Whispers came down the line to lie still and maintain silence. In a stand-up fight, the hundred or so dismounted cavalrymen would be overwhelmed by four or five times as many Negro soldiers prepared to march off the boat. Jack rubbed his stubbled jaw and flexed his fingers, seeking to settle his nerves.

The *Mary Benton's* crew set a gangplank onto the wharf and a man in civilian clothing stepped onto the wooden dock and walked to the road. He stood in the middle of the street, hands on hips, looking around the deserted town. After a few minutes he strolled back to the boat, apparently satisfied no Confederates lurked in the vicinity.

Down the line to Jack's right one of the Palatka men, Jim Burton, muttered, "That's Tom Driver, a river pilot. Guess we know which side he's on."

"He didn't see us or he woulda run like a scalded cat," Russell whispered.

"Hush," Ramon hissed.

The soldiers on the boat queued up, ready to disembark. The first in line marched across the gangplank and onto the wharf. Jack brought his rifle to his shoulder, steadying it against the fence post. Focused now, confident in his job, he sought a target, aware of his comrades doing the same.

Jack spotted a white officer who stepped onto the wharf and turned to face his men. He followed the officer's movements with the sights. *Shoot the officers first.*

He dismissed a fleeting thought of his brother Dan, a Union lieutenant. Dan couldn't possibly be here. He was far to the north, fighting against Jack's old outfit, the Army of Northern Virginia. Certainly they would never face each other.

A crew of bluecoats wheeled a field piece down the ramp onto the dock. *Best not let them start in with that thing.*

At a blast of Captain Dickison's cow horn, Jack squeezed the trigger. Rifle fire crashed all around. He swiftly reloaded as the breeze off the river wafted the smoke away, then looked up to seek another target among the aroused enemy. He kept his holstered revolver handy in case the fight turned close and personal.

*

Corporal Isaac Farrell, of the 2nd South Carolina United States Colored Regiment, started at the sound of a rifle volley. Lieutenant Colonel Billings let out a grunt and fell against him. Isaac caught his commanding officer and supported him so he wouldn't hit the ground.

Gunfire knocked down another man next to Isaac. Shouting soldiers milled in confusion, some trying to run back to the boat, blocked by soldiers trying to disembark. Still others returned fire toward the hidden rebels. Officers on the ship screamed orders to fire.

Holding up his wounded commander, Isaac yelled for the other soldiers to make way. He felt the warm wetness of the officer's blood soaking into his own uniform. The officer stumbled along with him, swearing and cussing out Tom Driver for letting them fall into a trap. "Dirty damned traitor! I'll have him shot!"

A bullet buzzed past Isaac's ear as he hollered at the men to pick up the dead and wounded. Another man fell nearby. Hands reached down to drag the victim along. Space cleared on the gangplank, and Isaac hauled Colonel Billings onto the deck.

Gently, he laid out the officer on the worn planking. Pale and sweating, no longer yelling, Colonel Billings stared at Isaac with the blankness of shock. Blood poured from a hip wound, and both of his hands were shot through. Lieutenant Owen and knelt beside the stricken colonel, then looked up at Isaac. "Corporal Farrell, don't just stand there! Give those rebels some lead!"

The throaty boom of one of the boat's big guns signaled an answer to the attack. Isaac unslung his rifle and leveled it toward the fence, where he saw a puff of smoke that marked a rebel shooter. Might be his former friend Jack Farrell, whose family name Isaac adopted before strife split up the household. No matter. This was self-defense.

*

Minie balls sang over Jack's head. The colored troops, probably inexperienced in battle, were shooting too high to do any damage. The hastily dug breastworks helped protect him as well. With cool deliberation he picked another target and pulled the trigger. Then a bullet thwacked into the fence post next to his head and sent a splinter into his cheek. He picked it out and wiped off a trickle of blood from the puncture, looking straight ahead. He thought he made out Isaac preparing to take another shot, and ducked.

A shell exploded behind Jack. He flinched and prayed the gunners could not bring the gunboat's artillery to bear downward on such close targets as himself. His wiry body still carried the painful reminders of his earlier encounter with a similar shell. The basic, survival-loving part of him remembered the agony of disabling injuries and wanted to bolt. What kept him in place, loading and firing with outward coolness and mechanical precision, was sheer devotion. *You bastards won't get to my Martina again.*

Captain Dickison called out an order to fall back and take cover. Jack did not need a second invitation. He leaped out of the ditch and raced for the warehouse, knowing he could make a stand there if need be.

Another shell exploded, closer this time. It threw sand onto his clothing. A third shell, bursting even closer, kicked up still more dirt. He heard shouts and a yelp. Jack swerved behind the shelter of the building and peered around the corner. He aimed the Enfield toward the artillery mounted on the boat, trying to find a gunner to pick off, but metal plates shielded them.

To Jack's relief, the bluecoats appeared to have no taste for street fighting. They surged back onto their boat as fast as they could get out of each other's way, hauling the unused field piece up the ramp as well. By shooting that officer, Jack hoped he had cut the head off the beast.

He continued to fire into the mass of men on the deck as the sailors cut the hawsers and powered away. The boat shoved clear of the landing and steamed north out of rifle range, back toward Orange Mills. The shelling ceased. Jack reloaded his rifle, wiped blood from his face and closed his smoke-stung eyes for a moment. He crossed himself, a habit picked up from Martina along with a renewed infusion of faith.

"We won." Ramon, who piled in next to him, crossed himself as well.

Jack brushed dirt off his gray uniform. "Anybody hurt?"

"Russell caught a shell fragment. Nothing serious. Guess he wanted a furlough."

Jack glanced at Russell Cates, who was busy stanching a bloody place in his thigh. "You all right?"

"Does this mean I can get Martina to nurse me?" Cates let out a nervous, no-offense laugh.

"Find your own woman to take care of you," Jack growled.

Captain Dickison called out congratulations to his troops. The successful defense kept the Yankees from marching into Palatka. Martina and Carlo were safe, this day at least.

Jack drank water from his canteen to soothe his parched throat, although he craved something stronger. It was not the first time he vowed those damned Yankees would have to walk over his dead body to get to Martina. He knew it would not be the last.

A week ago Jack had shot a Yankee who threatened his wife, just before he had to evacuate her and her younger brother from their home. It was a pity Captain Prescott was not likely in condition to fight with this landing party. Jack itched to finish what the bluecoat started.

Dickison ordered the men to hold their positions until the *Mary Benton* steamed out of sight. Then he told them they could return to camp. Ramon helped Cates to his feet. Seeing that his friend was in good hands, Jack hefted his rifle and set his steps toward the house, ready to assure his wife she was safe.

*

Martina Sanchez Farrell paced about the front porch, half crazy with worry at the sounds of nearby battle. Trees and buildings obscured the view. *Jack, please be safe.*

Carlo, perched on a rocking chair, did not join her in the pacing, nor did he run to see what was going on. The bullet hole in his thigh still kept him confined, a hard thing for an active fifteen-year-old boy. The cuts and bruises on his face from the beating Captain Prescott gave him were healing, but the gunshot wound was taking longer. "The shooting has stopped, Tina," he told her. "That means the Yankees are gone."

His optimism should have given her cheer, but the nagging thought that the fight might have gone the other way did not leave her mind. Even if the Confederates did prevail, some of them might have died in the effort. She realized Jack's troop was the only opposition against another boatload of Yankees. That placed them in mortal danger every time it happened. Did they shoot or capture Jack?

"I can't stand it. I'm going to go find out," she told Carlo. "If any of our men were wounded, I can help them."

"I'm going with you." Carlo picked up the cane Jack made for him and stood up, holding the weight off his hurt leg. The sun-browned teenager, using a walking cane as an old man might, made an incongruous picture.

It would not be right to leave Carlo alone to wonder what happened. "I'll hitch up Ladybug to the wagon so you can ride." She tied her sunbonnet over her dark, braided hair, gathered up the halter and lines, and went to the paddock. Jack's red hound, Nip, crawled out from under the house and followed at her heels. She led the little marsh tackie to the wagon and hitched her up, leaving behind the cavalry horses belonging to Jack and his friends. Then she helped Carlo climb into the wagon and started toward the waterfront, Nip leading the way.

After the Yankees shelled their home at Picolata, Martina and her wounded brother fled twenty miles south under the protection of the Confederate cavalry and her trooper husband. Most of Palatka's residents had deserted the town after previous Yankee gunboat invasions. To her regret, even the Catholic church was now closed, the priest's congregation having withered away. She and Carlo had moved into this roomy vacant house, rent-free unless the owners showed up. That seemed unlikely, as one of the few civilians left in Palatka told her the owners were Northerners who left on a Union gunboat the year before. They were not likely to return while Palatka remained under Confederate control. The house was within two miles of Camp Call, Captain Dickison's headquarters.

She was content here because Jack had received permission to live at the house with her and Carlo. They were getting along satisfactorily in their new circumstances, provided the enemy didn't break up her home life, as was their habit.

Martina searched the faces of the soldiers walking toward camp. The first man she met told her all was well. When she spotted Jack she let out her breath, hardly aware she held it. He waved and picked up his pace to a jog, rifle slung over his shoulder. Nip ran up to meet him, then turned and fell into a trot alongside his master.

She took in the reassuring sight of her husband. Although he had resumed shaving now that the winter chill had eased, the overnight vigil had roughened his chin with stubble. Burnt powder and a smear of blood streaked his face, and dirt stained his uniform. Despite the shadows and the fading scars on his cheek, she loved the way he looked. His roguish smile and direct, blue-eyed gaze intrigued her from their first meeting. In time she accepted his wild streak as well.

She reined Ladybug to a stop as Jack met the wagon, grinning at her. "We ran 'em off, darlin'! Captain said we could go home for a spell." He glanced at her brother. "Hey, Carlo. We scared 'em good. I'll bet they don't stop 'til they haul into Jacksonville."

Carlo let out a whoop and raised his fist in a triumphant gesture.

Martina sagged with relief.

"They're gone." He set his rifle onto the wagon bed. "For the time being."

Of course it was only for the time being. The Yankees were not going to go away. Not far away, for sure.

"Russell Cates took a hunk of shell in his leg. Think we can give him a ride?" Jack looked over his shoulder. Martina followed his gaze and saw Ramon walking slowly with a limping Cates, who steadied himself by holding onto Ramon's shoulder. Charlie Colee ranged alongside.

"Was anybody else hurt?"

"Don't think so," Jack said. "About the time they started fighting back we'd taken cover behind that brick warehouse."

She greeted the St. Johns County men. They had frequently taken shelter at the Picolata house while scouting near their home turf under Captain Dickison's orders, and now they shared the house.

Ramon lowered the back panel of the wagon so Russell could hoist himself onto the wagon bed, facing backwards. "Want us to take you to Doc Williams?" Jack asked.

"I'd just as soon go to the house. All it needs is to be cleaned and dressed." Russell most likely harbored a dread of doctors and hospitals, a horror shared by many. They noticed how often patients came away worse than when they went in.

Jack climbed onto the seat and took the lines from Martina. She rested her hand on his knee, content to let him take over. Ramon and Charlie said they wanted to walk to the house, working their stiff limbs after a night spent in a ditch.

Martina lifted her hand to Jack's powder-smudged face and wiped away a drop of blood from a cut. "I hope it doesn't leave another scar."

He grinned at her. "Are you afraid I'm starting to look like a tom cat dragging in after a hard night on the town?"

She regarded him, cocking her head to one side. He could make her smile even on the blackest of days. "Is that what you've been up to?"

"I guess you found me out."

"Wicked man." She slapped his knee. He laughed, shook the lines and coaxed Ladybug into her customary plod.

Martina looked out over the waterfront, the empty warehouses, and the quiet streets. "Are the Yankees really gone?"

Jack sobered and dropped his shoulders, finally showing weariness. "We held the advantage in position. They outnumbered us but were mighty exposed while they were trying to disembark. We could have picked them off piecemeal if they stuck it out. I guess they didn't know our strength and didn't want to find out."

"They'll be back," she said.

He did not contradict her.

CHAPTER TWO

St. Augustine, Florida, March 1863

Union Captain Dan Farrell stood on the deck of the supply ship, scanning the still-familiar bay front of the town he had not visited in seven years. St. Augustine was again under control of the United States, although most of the state was in rebellion. He hoped to help set that right.

The ship's pilot guided the vessel alongside the dock in the calm Matanzas River water. Crewmembers tossed lines to the shoremen to secure the boat and ready it for unloading.

"Are you glad to be home, Captain Farrell?" Elizabeth Alexander batted at a horsefly buzzing around her head. "It certainly is a quaint looking place."

Dan smiled at the buxom young woman. "It's the oldest town in the United States. Spaniards built it. St. Augustine isn't New England, you know."

"Captain, I can see that it isn't new, let alone New England. The seawall is crumbling, and those houses look positively blighted." Her supercilious smile irked him, but he forgave her the slur. During the last leg of the voyage from Beaufort, South Carolina, he had admired the pretty redheaded daughter of a garrison officer. Her presence had caused him to pay closer attention to his appearance, making sure the razor took every whisker, and taming the cowlick in his light brown hair with comb and oil. His wool dress coat, tailored to fit his lean, muscular frame, was too heavy for the spring day, but he wanted to present himself well.

"Blame the salt air. It weathers everything." He pointed to the right. "That fort, San Marco, has been there for a couple of centuries. It's built of coquina, cement made out of seashells. Absorbs cannonballs like a sponge. It was always considered impregnable, though our modern weapons could change that."

She darted a quick sideways look at him. "Do you think the rebels can recapture St. Augustine?"

He smiled at her. "I doubt it, Miss Alexander. I understand our soldiers have made the town secure from attack."

"I expect I'll see some excitement." She sighed coquettishly. "Perhaps a brave young officer will save me from those rebel villains."

"Villains." He shook his head, thinking about his brother, Jack. "They're American soldiers, not savages. I doubt they would harm a young lady. Still, it would be prudent for you to stay within our picket lines to avoid inconvenience."

She lifted her chin. "I believe I can do some good here. The Negroes need to be educated so they can make the most of their freedom."

"Did you know a number of them can read and write? The schools in St. Johns County educated some of the Negroes as well as the whites."

"I thought it was illegal to educate slaves in the South. Papa said it's against the law in South Carolina."

"Not here."

"I can add to their knowledge." She gave a self-confident nod.

"I admire your idealism, Miss Alexander. I hope I'm not too idealistic in believing Florida can be readmitted to the Union."

She inclined her head and smiled. "That is a worthy goal, Captain."

"If we can get enough men to renounce the Confederacy and pledge loyalty, it can be done. I believe there's enough Unionist sentiment in the state to bring that about."

"I'm so glad you told me your family never owned slaves." She sniffed her disdain. "I don't think I could be friends with someone who participated in that evil."

"My father objected to the institution, though some of our friends and neighbors suffered no guilt about it. Mostly they considered their servants part of the family."

"Like housedogs?" Her pretty mouth puckered in distaste.

Dan let out his breath. "Maybe something like that." Although he didn't like the practice, he did not appreciate the superior attitude some Northerners took about all things Southern. He was a Unionist, not an abolitionist.

He pointed to the pleasantly shaded plaza, visible from the wharf.

"See that pavilion? That's where the slave traders used to do business. That quaint building facing it is the Catholic cathedral. My father wrote in one of his letters that the priests still hold Mass there every day."

"Papa attends the Presbyterian Church. You aren't Roman Catholic, are you?"

The tone of her voice implied more disapproval. "I am. So are a good number of the townspeople. This was Spanish territory for a long time." He waved his hand along the bay front. "Northerners used to stay in that hotel. They liked the warm winters. The war shut down that business, though."

"Papa said we'll be staying at Mrs. Anderson's boarding house. Where is that, I wonder?" She laid a hand on the railing and peered at the less-than-promising dwellings along the bay.

"I seem to recall it's a few streets west of here, toward the San Sebastian River."

"Why, Captain, you're a regular tour guide."

"If you wish, I can show you around." Although his enthusiasm for her companionship had diminished, duty required him to make the offer.

"Please do." She favored him with a brilliant smile. "What about you? Where will you stay?"

"My father and stepmother live in the old Spanish part of town. The house belongs to my sister-in-law."

"You have a sister-in-law? I'd like to meet her."

"I don't think that's likely," he said dryly. "Not any time soon. I understand she moved away, although it wasn't her idea."

"She's married to your brother?"

Dan nodded, keeping his expression neutral. "If you should venture out of town and encounter rebel scouts, you might have the pleasure of meeting him."

Miss Alexander wrinkled her brow. "Oh, my."

Dan let the subject drop. His little brother always ran against the grain. Now he ran with an especially annoying band of Confederate cavalry somewhere out in the countryside. Most likely he was the most annoying soldier in the lot. Even when they were kids, Jack was a scrapper, a crack shot, and could lick his wiry weight in tigers.

It was now Dan's job to help the Union Army recruit a force of Florida loyalists to kill or capture the Confederates threatening Federal interests, his scapegrace brother among them.

*

After reporting to Colonel Putnam at garrison headquarters, Dan made his way, valise in hand, to his father's residence in the Minorcan quarter near the old city gates. His letter should have preceded him, so his visit would come as no surprise.

Formality no longer necessary, he shed the heavy coat and carried it over his arm. The sun played on his back, pleasant enough this spring afternoon, but predictive of the hot and humid summer to come. He soon stood in front of the house, an old-fashioned Spanish-style tabby-and-timber dwelling, windowless on the street side and bordered by a high wooden fence. He opened the gate, walked inside and rapped on the door.

Leon Farrell threw the door open. "It's about time you came home."

Dan grinned at his father, a trim, graying man, severe of aspect and attitude. "It's been a long time, hasn't it? To make matters worse, the ship had to wait for a strong tide to cross the bar at the inlet."

"You look hardy and well-filled-out. Army life must agree with you."

"You're fit enough yourself, Pop, even though you've been away from the farm."

"Margaret is off visiting friends, so we can have a good talk just between us."

Dan opened his valise and pulled out a bottle of port. "Let's relax with a glass of wine while we catch up."

"Good. We can celebrate your promotion."

"I guess Washington decided I needed more authority to go with the job."

While his father found serving glasses and a corkscrew, Dan sat at the table and looked around. Someone, whether the former inhabitants or his stepmother, had furnished the plain home with yellow curtains over the few windows and a matching upholstered chair. He supposed most of the unfinished pine furniture came with the house, because it smacked of Spartan living and lacked the frills Margaret favored. Stairs led from the modest downstairs to another floor, where he assumed the bedrooms were located.

"Jack's wife used to live here?" he asked his father. Sketchy correspondence had kept Dan informed to an extent, but he wanted to clear up the details of what had gone on with his family while he was away fighting the rebels in Virginia. He was most curious about his brother and his new sister-in-law.

"It's still hers. It's been in her family ever since the Minorcans settled in St. Augustine." Pop poured a glass of the wine and handed it to him. "We live here rent free, though I'll have to pay the taxes. She and Jack sure won't be able to come to town for that purpose, or any other."

"Nice of you to manage it for her, considering."

"Jack is still my blood, no matter he's thrown his disloyalty in my face."

Pop is not a forgiving man. It's a wonder I managed to stay on his good side all these years. But I had an easier time following the rules than Jack ever did.

Dan stretched his legs and rested back in the chair. It was good to free himself of the confining ship. "Last summer I volunteered to come down here and raise a company of Florida men for the Union army." Dan smiled wryly. "When Jack was still somewhere in Virginia."

Pop shook his head. "Now you're going to have to fight him down here instead."

"Unfortunately." Dan took a long sip of the port and savored the sweet bite of alcohol on his tongue. "Who could have expected that?"

"He was hurt pretty bad during the Maryland invasion, so the rebel army discharged him. He came back to heal up at the farm."

"Which he did, I gather."

Pop nodded. "I did my damnedest to keep him from going back to the rebellion."

Dan imagined the browbeating Pop must have employed. "Didn't listen, huh?"

"Never does. He could have come into town to take the loyalty oath, but he refused. Said he wasn't a turncoat. Misguided loyalty. I hoped he would at least stay out of the fighting. But you know how he is. Bull-headed. Once he healed up, he snuck off with Dickison's band."

"And arrested you." Dan grinned. "Wish I'd been able to see that, without getting shot by his friends, of course."

"I was so mad, I could have shot him myself. Just hard enough to put him out of action again. The rebels picketed the roads and held up anybody going in or out of town."

"Guess he was diligent about doing his job."

Pop poured himself another drink. "That boy has always been a trial. Colonel Putnam wanted to arrest Jack while he was still at the farm, but I vouched for him. In effect, he was on parole, though I don't think he ever signed any papers. After he joined Dickison's gang, the colonel suspected me of spying. Can you imagine that?" The older man snorted. "I'm glad you're here in person, to show the colonel I really do have a son who wears a blue coat with a captain's shoulder boards."

Dan glanced at the wool coat hanging across the arm of the chair and laughed.

"Jack has caused me considerable trouble," Pop mused. "Only way I could ever get him to do anything was to tell him to do the opposite."

"You were always pretty hard on him, Pop."

"He deserved it. Never could stay out of trouble, then he left home and got into even more trouble in Lake City when he killed that fellow."

"It was judged self-defense. Anyway, they turned him loose."

"He got in with bad company. Now he's turned completely rogue."

"I guess he figured if he had the name, he might as well have the game." Dan sobered, remembering how it used to be. Pop was a strict disciplinarian, and Jack ran afoul of his wishes so often their father took it for willful disobedience. Dan had an easier time pleasing his sire. Sometimes he tried to run interference between his father and his brother, but it only got him a licking, too.

"Is his wife, Martina – is it – still at the farm?"

Pop shook his head. "I'm lucky the house is still standing. Jack and his gang got into a fight with a gunboat that landed at Picolata and shelled my property, trying to get at the rebels. Damage could have been worse, but it's bad enough. Jack, Martina, and her brother Carlo went upriver to Palatka. I think the rebels have encampments there." He stood up and went to a little desktop, shuffled through some papers, and pulled out one. "This is the letter Martina wrote and left at the house."

Dan quickly read through it, then let out a low whistle. "Who is this Captain Prescott? The one she says attacked her?"

"He used to be stationed here, got assigned to raise a colored company. Isaac joined up about then. Prescott was interested in Martina, but I gather she didn't feel the same way about him. She told me he made improper advances and she was scared of him. She hit him with a pot in front of his men. That must have humiliated him, so he wanted to get rid of her. If her letter is to believed, his intentions from start to finish were less than honorable."

"She wrote the rebs shot this Captain Prescott. Did he live?"

"I inquired and found out he's expected to recover. He claims Jack was about to kill him after he surrendered, but another rebel stopped him from carrying out the coup de grace. Prescott escaped and made it back to the boat."

Dan stared at the letter, biting his lip. "If this is true, I can see Jack wanting to finish off the bastard."

"I have no reason to disbelieve Martina. And I never had a good opinion of Prescott."

"It appears Jack is going to make you a grandfather." Dan gave the letter back and chuckled. "Your first grandchild will be a pure-bred rebel."

"Maybe they'll have a girl." Pop cracked a smile.

"They're the worst rebels of all."

"She and Carlo were meeting with Jack while she was still living in town. The boy passed personal letters through the lines for us. That part was innocent enough. Knowing Jack, he most likely was passing intelligence to his rebel friends as well. She and her kid brother were ordered out of town. Prescott claimed she was spying for the rebels. She said he falsified the evidence." Pop shrugged. "She would have been banished sooner or later anyway. Her older brother, Francisco, was in the rebel army. Last month the army finally got around to deporting people with Secesh ties."

"I remember him, I think, from school. Was?"

"He got killed in the same battle where Jack was wounded."

Dan took another gulp of wine. He was in that fight, too, in Maryland. He would never know whether his command had directly confronted that Florida regiment during the battle. "Sow the wind, reap the whirlwind," he murmured.

"Martina and her brother went to our farm. Seems Jack had told him they could do that if she ever got forced out of town. I think he was sweet on her all along."

"What's she like?"

"Lots of the Minorcan girls are pretty enough, but she's the cream of the lot. Smart, capable. I told Jack she was the best thing he was likely to find. He told me lightning would strike because we agreed on something."

Dan grinned. Pop didn't offer such praise about just anybody. "I gather you approve of her. It's hard to imagine my hard-living brother getting hitched to a nice girl."

"Jack got the better deal."

"Seems he had something to offer." Dan ticked off the assets on his fingers. "Your house, your oranges, your cattle. . . ."

"It was all right with me. Isaac left the place to join that colored regiment soon after Jack came home. Jack and Martina kept it from going to seed with nobody living there. Now the place is abandoned. I fear squatters will move in and ruin it."

"We'll go out there and take a look," Dan said.

"Up to now it's been unsafe for me to live at the farm. Rebel gangs have threatened my life over my beliefs. Maybe that'll change, with the Union Army occupying Jacksonville and controlling the river."

"Our army pulled out of Jacksonville," Dan said.

Pop blinked. "No!"

"The rebs pressed them pretty hard from every direction, and they thought the town would be too much trouble to hold. The Confederates can't stop our boats from steaming past Jacksonville and dominating the St. Johns, anyway."

"The soldiers, both sides, have captured or destroyed every boat they could find up and down the river," Pop said. "They even chopped up our little rowboat. I wasn't too happy about that. Didn't think to hide it before they got to it."

"That isn't all. Colonel Putnam said a transport boat attempted to unload some colored troops at Palatka. Sharpshooters surprised them just as they tried to disembark. They lost some men, and Colonel Billings was wounded. The rebels were well positioned, and our men were under hot fire from their sharpshooters. Retreat was the better part of valor. They returned downriver."

Pop played with his empty glass, spinning it slowly in his hand. "Jack was most likely doing some of the shooting."

"Yeah." Dan sighed. "And I'll be on the hunt for him."

CHAPTER THREE

"We've been ordered east of the St. Johns." Jack delivered the news to Martina bluntly, without softening it. "In the morning, we'll raft our horses across the river and ride to our old outpost on the road between Picolata and St. Augustine."

"All four of you?" Martina's welcoming smile faded as her brow knitted, her only sign of concern. She continued to beat the cornbread batter.

"The surgeon says Russell's well enough to ride along. Russell isn't so sure, but he's coming with us anyway. We're spread thin as it is."

Jack wanted to memorize the sight of Martina's sultry dark eyes and delicate features. Her trim waist had barely thickened, her condition not yet obvious. "I have good news, though. The Yankees have pulled out of Jacksonville again, so maybe we won't see as much of them on the river."

"Thank the Blessed Mother," Martina breathed. "We've had enough of their gun boats." She scraped the batter onto a skillet, her motions deft and well-practiced. "Ramon found me a tough old rooster, so I stewed it for a long time. I hope it's edible."

"Darlin', you could make old shoe leather taste good." The tantalizing aroma had already hinted at what they were having for supper. His messmates contributed their rations and whatever else they could scrounge in return for Martina's cooking for them. Leaving the farm had complicated his ability to provide, but so far they managed.

"The boys and I, we're going to contribute some of our rations so you and Carlo won't have to worry about your next meal. I figure we can stay at the homestead sometimes. Between the provisions we hid and our friends in the county, we should have plenty."

She nodded, not looking up. "How long will you be gone?"

"Beats me." He shrugged, vexed that he had no say in such matters. "I won't be too far away. Maybe I can find a way to slip back to see you now and then."

"I hope so." She glanced at him, then back to her work as she smoothed the batter. "Did Ramon tell Teresa to come stay here?" Her cousin's wife and child had been living as refugees ever since their home fell behind Union lines just outside St. Augustine.

"He believes they're safer where they are, but she wrote him saying she isn't happy in Lake City. She'd rather live closer to him. She'll probably take the rail cars to Waldo and find a ride here. Then you'll have female company. Maybe you won't be so lonesome."

She gave him a fleeting smile. "I'm only lonesome when you're gone. Carlo wants me to take him to the river. He's not steady enough to cast the net, but he can use a line. He's anxious to do something useful."

"Tired of sitting around. I know how he feels." Jack rubbed a deep ache in his arm, which had healed awry. "Maybe you can get some rest with the four of us out of your hair."

"What do I care about rest?" Martina wiped her hands on her apron and looked steadily at him. "I'll miss you something awful."

He closed the space between them and took her into his arms. She sagged against him, her stoic act crumbling. "Be careful," she murmured into his shoulder. "Don't let them hurt you."

"We'll get them instead." He held her close and kissed her forehead, consoling himself that he would have one more night with her before he left. "Keep some things packed in case another gunboat comes and you have to leave in a hurry. Don't wait to be sure. Just leave."

She nodded against him. "I wish we could go with you, stay at the house like we did before."

"Tina, that place has a bulls-eye on it now, and we'll have to keep our guard up whenever we take shelter there. For sure you're safer here."

"I only feel safe when you're with me."

Jack wanted to tell Martina she was his anchor, his solid ground, his purpose beyond mere survival, but the words would not come. He figured she knew.

They had already discussed moving her farther west, to Orange Springs, where some of the Palatka ladies resettled. But she flatly refused. For one thing, she pointed out, it would be too costly because she would have to pay rent. Besides, they would be farther apart. If he stopped a bullet, she wanted to be there to take care of him.

She won the argument.

*

Jack stepped into the house at the family farm, Ramon right behind, Charlie carrying in an armload of firewood. The closed-up interior smelled of dust and old fireplace ashes. Jack was struck by the memories the place held: growing up there with his father and brother, then the happy time when he shared the house with Martina. He swept his gaze around the front room to the door leading to their bedroom. Even after he had recovered from his wounds and joined the cavalry, he was still able to come home from time to time and spend nights with her.

Charlie stacked the wood in the fireplace. Ramon prowled through the house as though expecting something menacing to jump from the shadows.

Jack set down the jar of popskull on the pine table. Dug out of the cache he had hidden by the still in the woods, the outside was wet from his washing off dirt in the spring. He noticed a leaf of paper and recognized his father's strong hand. He picked up the note and read it.

"My father's been here. He wasn't happy with how we left the homestead."

Ramon paused in his pacing and lifted an eyebrow. "We didn't shell that orange grove. The Yanks did."

"Never mind. I'm used to getting the blame."

Jack threw the letter down and picked up the jar, refusing to let his father's predictably hostile attitude worsen his already sour mood. He hated leaving Martina with only her wounded kid brother, a shotgun, and a friendly hound dog for protection.

To make matters worse, the surgeon was wrong about Russell Cates. After Russell had spent a few hours in the saddle his leg wound opened, leaked and showed signs of infection. He could not continue to ride without more pain, bleeding and damage, so they left him at his family's home southwest of St. Augustine. The convenience of leaving him in good hands was offset by the danger of a Yankee patrol catching him.

Jack closed his hand around the jar. "Give me your canteens and I'll pour you a smile."

Ramon and Charlie gladly complied. After Jack filled their canteens, he took a sip straight from the jar, savoring the burn.

"Too bad about Russell," Ramon said. "Hope the Yanks don't find him."

"To Russell." Jack held up the jar in a toast. "We'll just have to drink his share until he gets over his malingering spell."

"He'll be all right, with his mama and sister Sarah fussing over him." Ramon took a pull from his canteen and licked his lips. "They're smart enough to keep the Yanks from finding him."

"There's a lot to be said for scouting close to home." Jack forced a grin. "First we call on the neighbors to find out what the Yanks are up to. They haven't seen a blue coat in a couple of weeks, which is fine with me. Stop at Russell's house and his mother makes us ham sandwiches." He nodded to the youngest trooper in their little band, who was sticking lightwood under the split logs. "Then we show up at Charlie's place and *his* mama feeds us beef stew. We leave there so any Yanks that happen by won't catch Charlie's family giving aid and comfort. We get to sleep in this cozy house, out of the weather. You boys have no idea what real soldiering is like."

"I hear you." Charlie laughed and glanced up from his fire building. "My brother Jim writes home from Virginia. No rations for a week, nothing to eat but snow, fighting off a whole brigade of Yanks with a Bowie knife."

"Charlie, my boy, Jim is not spinning yarns. You have no idea how good you have it. He ought to get a transfer and join us." Jack took another swig. "We're living like outlaws, having a good time doing it. I keep telling myself what fun I'm having."

Charlie sloshed his canteen, sampled a swallow and coughed. The eighteen-year-old, raised by a solid, sober family, probably wasn't used to the taste of raw liquor, but would choke before admitting it.

"Better than nothing, even without sweetening it." Jack took another taste. "Yeah, it'll do." He'd promised Martina he wouldn't get drunk anymore. He hadn't promised not to drink, though, and he knew how to stay out of trouble. He could do without the opium, but a little liquor would soothe the twinges and aches, at least for a little while.

Ramon said, "Charlie, don't overdo that stuff. You've got first watch."

Jack regarded his wife's cousin, who turned to scan the yard through the window. "Ramon, how long has it been since you've seen Teresa?"

"Months. Why?"

"Aren't you going to bring your family to Palatka? Have them move in with Martina. The house is plenty big enough."

Ramon just looked out the window.

Jack's grin came easier this time. "Having your woman handy might improve your cranky disposition. Martina's all for it."

"I don't want them caught in the middle of a fight like Martina and Carlo were."

Jack drummed his fingers on the jar. He tried not to feel uneasy about his wife's situation. Most likely, with the Yanks having abandoned Jacksonville for the third time, they would be more cautious about sending their gunboats upriver. He hoped the recent licking made them wary. "As long as our troop is guarding the roads, the Yanks'll have a hard time invading Palatka by land."

"They can't get to Lake City by gunboat," Ramon pointed out.

"Not directly. They could get pretty close by way of the St. Mary's. You really think one place is safer than another? I sure like having Martina within a day's ride."

"Haven't seen my little Ana so long she probably doesn't even know me anymore." Ramon turned and stared at the flames Charlie had started.

"Maybe the captain will give you time off to see them. You could go over to Waldo, take the cars from there."

"I doubt it." Ramon shook his head. "Our troop is supposed to cover a hundred miles, all the way from Mandarin clear to Volusia. Captain Dickison has asked General Finnegan to send another company from Jacksonville to help us out. I hope they come."

"He ought to be able to turn them loose now that the Yanks have steamed out of there. I heard they burned half the town as a farewell present."

"They burned the Catholic church," Ramon added. "Episcopal, too, just to show they're impartial."

Jack picked up his father's letter again. He considered writing a reply, then changed his mind. He wouldn't bother with it. Nothing he could ever say would make Pop happy. Best not to continue the conversation. He turned the paper over, polished off the remainder of the whiskey, and set the jar on top of the note.

To hell with Pop. Jack liked his new family better than the old one, anyhow.

*

Sarah Cates Phillips spread material for her sewing project on the table. Her younger brother, Russell, sat half-dressed on the couch while their mother removed the bandage from his thigh wound.

"It doesn't look any worse this morning," Emily Cates remarked, relief in her voice. "But I still don't understand why that doctor said you were fit to ride all over creation."

"I thought I'd be all right." Russell poked at the draining puncture in his thigh. "It just kind of broke open on the way here."

"From the look of it, you need to stay out of the saddle for a good while. I don't care what that doctor says." Mama cleaned the area around the wound with a damp cloth. "He cares more about getting soldiers back to duty than he cares about what happens to them."

Sarah smoothed the red-checked gingham in preparation for cutting out the pieces for her father's shirt. She would not be wearing anything but black for another six months, the remainder of the mourning time for her husband, Edward. She glanced at Russell, who had grown a short, sandy-colored beard since joining the cavalry. "It'll be good to have you home, unless the Yankees catch you here."

Her mother nodded. "There's a load of laundry in the back room for you to hide under in case those scoundrels search the house, son."

Russell laughed. "You're going to bury me under a pile of dirty clothes?"

"You should be glad Mama's thinking ahead. We always have to plan for when the Yankees come. If you fight them," Sarah pointed out matter-of-factly, "they will shoot you. I'm already in mourning for Edward. That's too much grief as it is." In six months time she had gotten used to the fact she would never see Edward again, and the tears did not well as quickly. She counted that as progress.

"All right, Sis. I'll be good. I'll go to ground like a scared rabbit." Russell quirked a smile. "And hope they don't stick their swords into the pile and ventilate me again."

"We won't let them do that." Sarah picked up the pincushion and attached a paper pattern to the fabric, careful to minimize the waste of precious cloth.

"How will you stop them? Throw yourself in between and let them stab you instead?"

"How dramatic." Sarah shook her head and rolled her eyes at her brother, who had always been an awful tease and still made fun of everything. She feared he was a careless soldier, and prayed he would have a chance to mature and develop a more responsible attitude.

"I'll think of something dramatic myself. Maybe I'll throw a fit of convulsions to scare them off."

Mama picked up a strip of cotton sheet and wrapped it around Russell's thigh. "The Yankees know we have a son in Dickison's cavalry. Naturally, they figure we're always scheming against them. They keep accusing us of informing on them."

"Never!" Russell barked out a laugh. "You'd never do a thing like that, Mama."

"Once that horrible Captain Prescott forced Papa to walk all the way to St. Augustine at gunpoint," Mama added. "The colonel said if they jailed everybody that helped the Confederates they would triple the population of the town and the soldiers would run out of rations before the next supply boat docked. He finally let Henry go."

"You won't be seeing Prescott around anytime soon," Russell said. "Jack Farrell took care of him."

"I don't like it when people get hurt, but I wouldn't waste any sympathy on Prescott," Sarah said. "That hasn't stopped them, though. The Yankees made it plain they want to evict families with Confederate ties from this side of the St. Johns River. We're thankful they haven't burned us out. Yet."

"If they keep taking our livestock and provisions, they'll starve us out," Mama said. "We have to be smarter."

Papa let the cattle run wild in the woods, hunting them up on horseback with a whip and catch dogs as needed. Hiding food in unlikely places was another tactic they had adopted. "They don't think field peas are real food, so if we put them on top of the meat, they won't bother it." Sarah picked up the scissors and started cutting the fabric.

She heard Papa, who had been planting corn, clump onto the porch. He stuck his head inside and said in a low, warning voice, "Yanks." Then he closed the door and stepped back outside.

Sarah exchanged a worried glance with her mother. Russell reached for his gun belt. Mama said, "Come, on, Russell. Let's go to the back room and hide you."

Obedient for once, he stood and limped into the bedroom, carrying his weapons. At that speed, he would never outrun the slowest Yankee.

Mama grabbed the bloody dressing off the floor and picked up the pan of water. Sarah recalled that Russell's friends had kept his horse with its military equipment, so that evidence was gone. Mama followed her wounded son through the door and shut it behind them.

Sarah carried the scissors to the window and looked out to view the evil coming their way. As Papa had announced, a sizeable number of Union soldiers filed into their yard. A man in civilian clothes rode at their head alongside an officer. The pair reined in and dismounted.

Her mother came back from the bedroom and joined her at the window. Sarah said, "Mama, Mr. Farrell is with the Yankees."

"I'm not surprised. If he were younger, Leon Farrell would be wearing one of those blue uniforms himself." She shook her head. "He as good as disowned poor Jack for fighting on our side."

Sarah studied the captain who handed the reins to another soldier and approached the porch, a paper in his hand. She wrinkled her brow in confusion. "That Yankee officer looks enough like Jack to be his… why, Mama, it's Dan!"

"Are you sure? As I live and breathe… It could be him. We knew he was in the Union Army. It's been years since he left."

The memories flooded back to Sarah, of her fleeting crush on the older boy. She recalled when he and his father joined along with her father to fight the Seminoles. At the time she thought him handsome and dashing in his blue uniform. Times had changed, and now that uniform represented the colors of an oppressor, not a hero.

Aware of her faded black dress, she felt plain and frumpy. Then came a stab of guilt for caring about such frivolity during her time of mourning. Why should she want to look attractive for a Yankee, even the long-absent Dan Farrell?

Wouldn't it be a nasty turn if Dan had returned to inflict ill will on her family? If he made a prisoner of her brother? Or worse. She had already lost a husband. The thought of losing Russell as well was too much to bear.

She stared out the window at the homegrown Yankee. Men were easy to distract, and if she managed to muster enough feminine wiles to divert him despite her widow's weeds, perhaps she could entice him from any destructive plans he had in mind.

"Howdy, neighbor," Mr. Farrell sang out. "You remember my son, Dan? Dan, this is Henry Phillips."

"Good day, Leon. Dan, I hardly recognized you. Haven't seen you since we rode south after those Seminoles. What brings you back to our neck of the woods?" Sarah heard Papa's polite, politic reply distinctly through the window.

She marched to the door and opened it, the scissors still gripped in her hand.

"You'd better stay inside!" Mama hissed.

She ignored her mother's warning and walked onto the porch to stand next to her father. She nodded to the elder Mr. Farrell, who tipped his hat in greeting. Then she turned her attention to the Yankee officer in the person of Dan Farrell.

He smiled and touched his hat-brim. Sarah caught her breath at the sight of the full-grown man. Dan was mostly as she remembered: strongly built, with the same clean-cut, even features as his father and brother. His erect military bearing seemed natural to him, and he exuded Yankee superiority. Did they teach that condescending attitude in the Union Army, or did it just come naturally? Her gaze dropped to the paper he held. What terrible edict did it contain this time?

"Miss Sarah. It's been a long time, and it is so good to see you." Dan smiled as though he were on a friendly social call. "Or should I address you as Mrs. Phillips?"

She stilled a sharp reply and looked down. "Mrs. Phillips. The Yankees killed my husband, but I still carry his name." Her father laid a firm hand on her arm, but she did not feel the need for protection. It was hard to fear Dan, despite the threatening presence of his troops.

"My condolences. My father told me about your loss—"

"Perryville." How could she beguile him while they discussed such a topic?

"I was in the Army of the Potomac. We were not at Perryville."

His denial irritated her, but with her brother's life at stake, she must control her tongue. "I'm so glad to hear you weren't personally responsible." She smiled sweetly and returned her gaze to his face. "I would invite you in for refreshments, but Mama is sick in bed. I do hope you and your soldiers won't disturb her."

"Of course we won't." Dan locked eyes with her, and she feared he would know she lied. "I hope she gets better soon."

"What brings you back to Florida?" Arms crossed, putting on a good show of being unafraid, Papa roved his gaze toward the sizeable force of troopers sitting on their horses and back to Dan. "Are you going to be stationed in St. Augustine now?"

"Yes, sir. I'm on assignment here." Dan offered the paper to Papa.

Slowly the older man uncurled his hand and took it. Sarah stepped closer and read it around his arm. "So...." Papa looked up from the paper to Dan. "You're encouraging our boys to desert, even to join your army."

"It's an opportunity, sir. Not every man in Florida appreciates Confederate rule. If they give up the fight, they can return to their homes and live their lives in peace, unmolested by us. They can join up if they wish, but they won't be conscripted against their will. With the enlistment bounty offered, the Union Army pays well. I'm sure folks will welcome the chance for a sum of greenbacks to leave their families while they earn a decent wage in the army. I'm told your son is in the Confederate Army. I invite him to consider our offer."

Sarah read the effort it took for Papa to stay calm. His silver moustache twitched. He swallowed, slowly folded the paper and stuck it in his shirt pocket.

"As you know, we control this side of the river," Dan continued. "If Russell comes home and renounces the rebellion, we'll offer your entire family protection and he won't have to serve in our army unless he wishes to enlist. It's his call."

Her father's cheeks reddened, but his voice stayed level. "Is that all you came here to say?"

"There's one other thing. Do you ever see my brother, Jack? I understand he's in the same cavalry company as Russell. Does he ever come around here?"

Sarah tamped down her rising panic. It didn't mean he knew Russell was hiding inside. He had said he wouldn't enter the house. Would he change his mind if he suspected? What if he was asking because he knew they helped the Confederates? Would he arrest them after all?

Papa took a deep breath. "Why?"

"If you do see him, tell him I'd like to talk with him. We can meet under a truce flag, of course."

"If we see him," Papa said.

"Are you going to try to get him to desert, too?" Sarah asked.

Dan leveled his gaze at her. "I'd rather not have to fight my brother. I'd rather not have to fight any of my old friends and neighbors, either." His jaw tightened. "But if I must, I will. It's entirely up to them."

Sarah choked back another sharp answer. *Unlike some people, Jack Farrell would never put on a blue coat. Neither would my brother.*

"Just tell him, if you get the chance." Dan offered her a tight smile and a mere suggestion of a bow, nodded to her father, then turned to leave.

Sarah watched him mount his horse, turn its head, and join the rest of the troop.

"They're really leaving." Papa shook his head. "And they didn't steal anything. It's a wonderment."

"Russell is safe for now." Relief drained through her as the Yankee troop rode down the drive, away from their home. "I wonder if Jack knows his brother's in Florida."

Papa touched the handbill in his pocket. "He's about to find out."

CHAPTER FOUR

Jack reined in Choctaw as he and Ramon met Charlie head-on. "Yanks up the road," the young trooper told them in a stage whisper. "Coming from St. Augustine."

"How many?" Ramon leaned forward in the saddle, looking in the direction where the land-based plunder patrols always originated.

Charlie shook his head, talking fast with excitement. "Only spotted a couple of their scouts. More on horseback behind them, but I couldn't get close enough for a good look. They must not have seen me, because they didn't shoot or give chase."

"We could hide here, let them pass by, and make a head count." Jack figured the thick woods' screening the Yanks' passage down Tocoi Road could work to the scouts' advantage as well. "Find out what we're dealing with before we report."

Ramon nodded. "All right, Jack, let's dismount. Charlie, take the horses out of sight, back in the woods, and keep them quiet."

Jack slid off Choctaw and handed the reins to Charlie. Keeping his revolver, he left his Enfield in the boot. He and Ramon ran into the roadside thicket and crouched behind a convenient palmetto stand. The trunk and broad fronds concealed them from view. Charlie trotted the horses away, the hooves drumming softly on the sandy earth. The hardware made no telltale rattles, as the scouts kept the sabers and other accoutrements muffled with rags.

Within minutes Jack heard the approach of horses. He crouched lower and peered between the fronds at two vedettes, the forward scouts, riding by. Close behind them, as though deliberately keeping within sight of the outriders, came the rest of the mounted patrol. No doubt fear of capture kept their formation tight, a tribute to the success of Captain Dickison's troop.

At the head of the main body rode Jack's father astride his mule. Was he serving as a guide? Or had he joined the patrol to take advantage of an escort as he traveled to his farm on the river?

Two blue-coated officers rode alongside Pop. Jack did not expect to recognize either of them. The only Yankee officer he knew was

Prescott, whom he had put out of action, at least for a while.

But there was something about the captain….

Jack stared at the officer, who sat tall on his mount, his hand on his hip near his sidearm, his elbow cocked at a jaunty angle.

Couldn't be.

He felt the blood drain from his face.

What's he doing here?

He hadn't seen Dan in years, but the passage of time seemed to make no difference. He would have known his older brother anywhere.

Jack numbly watched the rest of the patrol file past.

"About forty of them, no wagons, no plunder," Ramon said. "Wasn't that your father riding with them?"

"Yeah." Jack stood and started back to where Charlie held the horses, Ramon walking alongside. "I guess he likes traveling with a pack."

"He'd be better off on his own hook. In that company, he's liable to find himself in the middle of a fight."

Jack ought to tell Ramon about Dan, but what was he supposed to say? Not only was his father at risk when the Confederates attacked the troop, but his brother as well, Dan the Yankee captain. Last time he'd heard, Dan was a lieutenant.

Jack and Dan shared more than the same father. As boys, Jack had looked up to his older brother much as Carlo looked up to him now. They squabbled as brothers do, but they had presented a united front when it counted.

Did they even know each other any more? Was blood thicker than the loyalties each held toward their military ties?

"There's something else." Jack stopped and Ramon turned to face him.

"What's the matter with you, Jack? You don't look so good. Are you sick?"

Was his shock that obvious? Jack took a long breath, wanting to loosen the knot in his gut. "Dan. My brother. He's riding along with that patrol. I thought you might've recognized him, too."

Ramon studied his face, waiting.

"He's probably just here temporarily." Jack looked in the direction the Yankees had gone. "Most likely he's on furlough, and he's just going out to see the homestead. Yeah, that's it."

"I guess we'll find out," Ramon said. "I'll send Charlie to let the lieutenant know about the Yank patrol, and we'll backtrack and see what people have to say about them. We'd better start at the Cates place, make sure they didn't get Russell."

"He wasn't with them, but if they captured him, they would've sent him directly to St. Augustine."

Ramon nodded. "Somebody ought to be able to tell us why your brother is in the neighborhood."

Jack scrubbed his hand over his face. "If Dan came down here looking for a fight, he's sure going to find one."

*

Dan's horse shied, leaped sideways, and banged into Lieutenant Hodges's mount. Dan curbed his rising temper, stifled a curse, and smoothed his hand over the beast's neck, crooning reassurance. The bay tossed its head, chomping at the bit before it settled.

"What's the matter with your horse?" Hodges asked.

"That clump of Spanish moss moved with the wind." Dan pointed toward the offending plant that hung from an oak branch. "The critter figured it was attacking him."

"I'd rather tangle with moss than rebels." The lieutenant chuckled. "Not much horseflesh to pick from, is there? St. Augustine isn't a cavalry garrison, you know."

Dan grunted agreement. The horse could just as well have picked up its case of nerves from the mounted infantrymen in the patrol. Ever since passing the picket outposts he sensed their edginess. They looked around as though they expected a rebel to be lurking behind every bush. No doubt they would have preferred staying within the safer confines of the city.

Heeding Pop's suggestion, the patrol had taken the Palatka Road and swung past the ruins of Fort Peyton, an old Seminole War outpost. From there they headed west toward the river, stopping at every homestead along the way. The terrain was just as he remembered it, flat, sandy, underbrush thick between the pines and oaks interspersed with low, wet stretches. From time to time the road opened to a cultivated field or a tract cleared of timber. Wooden track from a mule-drawn railroad rotted in the middle of the road.

"How do you think your project is going so far?" the lieutenant asked as they rode toward Tocoi, a river landing a few miles south of his old home.

"I'm just getting the word out for now." Dan tried to convey optimism. "We're making progress. It helps that Pop is with us to re-introduce me to people. I've been away a long time." His father still enjoyed standing in the community, even with some of the Confederate sympathizers.

Among those Secesh was Sarah Cates, or Phillips, he reminded himself. The fetching young girl had grown into a lovely woman. She seemed friendly enough, but her ties to the other side ran deep. His army had widowed her, and her brother was a rebel soldier. Her inviting smile no doubt hid her true sentiments.

Hodges nodded toward Dan's father, who led the column. "They seem to be receiving him all right."

"It's too bad we had to come out in force," Dan said. "People are frightened and expect the worst."

"Without a sizeable escort, you'd find out what the worst is. The rebs'd bag you before you got halfway to Picolata. We lost most of a patrol a few weeks ago. Rebs took 'em without firing a shot."

Dan recalled his boast that the Union forces controlled the area east of the river. The soldiers accompanying him did not seem to share that outlook. "If we can deplete their ranks and raise a company of Florida men to oppose the rebels, I'm hoping it'll demoralize them. Weaken their will to fight." Dan shrugged. "Once they find out, I'm sure they'll want to put a stop to what I'm doing."

"At least we know some folks who are already on our side," Hodges said. "If they're telling the truth, we don't have anything but a few rebel scouts to worry about."

"We can't count on that. As soon as they find out we're out here, those scouts will get word to the rest."

Hodges waved his hand toward the cultivated field surrounding the road. "We've come to a clear stretch for the time being. We can breathe easy for a bit."

Dan recalled his Seminole War days. "I gather the rebels in this area fight like Indians. They'll try to surprise us and inflict damage without taking casualties. If things get too hot, they'll disappear into the scrub. We'd better take extra care whenever we pass through the woods and watch for surprises."

"You and your father being loyalists, it's hard to understand how come your brother's a Johnny."

"Most folks around here don't understand how come I'm a Union officer." *They think Jack is on the right side, and I'm the traitor.*

"Do you think he'll come in and talk to you?"

"Could be he's watching us right now." The last family they visited told him they had spotted Jack and a couple of other local men from Dickison's company the day before. "If he does show up, I hope your men remember what to do about it."

"Honor the white flag, bring him to you, and when you say so, surround him and take him prisoner." Hodges shook his head, disgust on his face.

"I don't want him harmed." Dan locked eyes with Hodges. "I hope you've made that plain to every last one of your men."

"What if he starts shooting?" Hodges tensed his jaw. "The people in the neighborhood say he's a pretty hard character. Kind of a local hero for shooting Captain Prescott, who sure wasn't winning any popularity contests. He may not surrender easy."

"Pop and I will take care of it. We won't let it come to that."

"It's bad business." Hodges shook his head. "If we trick him like that, the rebs'll feel justified to use such treachery on us. A truce flag is supposed to mean just that, and ought to be honored."

"That's the order. Besides, if there are going to be any heroes around here, we sure don't want them on the other side." Dan did not bother to explain the importance of removing his biggest obstacle.

*

Jack and Ramon found Russell Cates as they had left him, stretched out, content on the comfortable couch. He grinned up at them without bothering to get up. "The Yanks came by, but I outfoxed them."

Russell's sister, Sarah, said, "Mama hid him under a pile of laundry in case the Yankees forced their way inside the house, but they didn't."

"You weren't supposed to tell them that part." Russell complained. "I like to suffocated."

"Jack, your brother Dan was with them," Sarah said.

"What did he want with you?"

The elder Mr. Cates handed Jack a folded piece of paper. "For once they weren't foraging, but politicking."

Jack read the handbill, wanting to make it and his brother go away. Dan was back in Florida for the worst possible reasons.

"What does it say?" Ramon asked.

Jack resisted the urge to tear the damnable message into confetti and throw the pieces into the fireplace. He handed it to Ramon.

"Can we keep this?" Ramon asked Mr. Cates. "Captain Dickison will want to know what the Yanks are up to."

"That's why I saved it for you."

"Jack, Dan wants you to meet with him," Sarah said softly.

Jack realized all of them, Ramon, Russell, and the rest of the Cates family, were watching his every move. He schooled his expression.

"He said you should bring a truce flag." Her gray eyes sparked. "I wanted to tell him you would never put on a blue coat."

"That's right." Jack stole a sidewise glance at Ramon. At least this neighbor lady didn't believe he would lose his will to fight because his brother was on the other side. He managed a grin. "Where am I going to find a white flag? We don't keep them around. Don't have any use for them. Can you spare a piece of white cloth?"

Nobody said anything for a moment. The silence was as stifling as the pile of laundry that had hidden Russell.

Mrs. Cates said, "I had to tear up a sheet to dress Russell's wound. There's a remnant you can have."

"That should suit."

She reached into a basket beside the couch, picked out a square of white cotton cloth, and handed it to Jack.

"Thanks, Mrs. Cates." He rolled it up and stuck it under his arm. "It's been seven years since I've seen Dan. I guess I ought to find out what he has to say."

"Be careful, son," Mr. Cates said. "It might be a trap."

"Might be, sir." Jack glanced around, noting the concern on their faces. Maybe they suspected his brother could persuade him to turn. "He's been wearing a blue coat a long time. I wouldn't put anything past his kind."

Jack stuffed the white cloth into his saddlebag and rode away from the Cates homestead, deep in thought. It seemed everybody – the neighbors, the enemy, his fellow scouts – knew about his problem. Soon Captain Dickison would know as well.

Riding alongside, Ramon said, "You're going to meet with your Yankee brother? What kind of fool does he think you are?"

"The trusting kind."

"Osceola believed a truce flag, too. He wound up in a dungeon."

"Dan and Pop will try to talk me into deserting."

"Maybe I ought to stop you from meeting them."

"I could have gone into town and made my peace with the Yanks months ago. I didn't then, and I won't now."

Ramon continued to push him. "Your brother wasn't here, then."

"If I took the loyalty oath, I'd have to stay in St. Augustine with my new Yankee friends because otherwise y'all would arrest me for desertion. Martina can't go back to St. Augustine without the Yanks arresting her as a spy. I won't desert her, either." Jack shrugged. "You're stuck with me."

"Suits me." Ramon cracked a rare smile. "Tell you what. We'll take the back trails and get ahead of the Yanks. They're moving slow, stopping at every homestead. I'll stay with you in case you need help."

Jack nodded. "They're changing their tactics. Trying to get our people on their side instead of starving them out."

"For the time being, anyway," Ramon said. "They'll get back to the plundering soon enough."

"He's been away a long time, but Dan could be the best officer they have for the job. He knows the area and the people, and he has Pop to guide him." Jack let out his breath through his teeth. "If he's successful, there'll be hell to pay."

"Deserters and homegrown Yankees?" Ramon snorted. "What kind of soldiers would that riffraff make?"

"Homegrown Yankees know their way around and they know people," Jack said. "They'll be harder to fight than those New Hampshire farm boys. Besides that, they won't be as quick to surrender. If they desert our army and join the Yanks, they won't want to get caught at it. They won't be regular prisoners of war. They'll know there's a noose or a firing squad waiting for them."

Ramon winced.

"We already know some of the folks in the neighborhood are willing to inform on us, just to get on the good side of the Yanks," Jack said.

They rode for a time with only the creak of saddle leather to break the silence.

"How do we figure out who's a traitor and who's a friend?" Ramon asked.

"We know who most of our friends are," Jack said. "Kinfolk of any of our boys. Like the Cates family."

"Mostly. There are exceptions, like your father," Ramon said.

"He's an exception, all right." Jack looked straight ahead. "Charlie's father has four sons in our army. We know he's on our side."

They left the road and struck a trail that would circle them past the Yankee patrol and quietly stalked the enemy.

CHAPTER FIVE

There he is. Dan straightened in the saddle when he spotted the gray-coated rider down the road just beyond the two vedettes, holding a white flag tied to a saber. His rebel brother waited for the Union men to close the space between them. Beyond Jack, just out of range, a second Confederate cavalryman waited.

Dan signaled a halt. Next to him, Hodges whispered, "That your brother?"

"Appears he got our message."

Pop rode alongside and stopped. "It's Jack, all right. Looks like Ramon Andreu is backing him up."

Dan held his position as his brother spoke to the vedettes. Jack looked his way, and Dan raised a hand in greeting. He gestured for Jack to come to him. Jack shook his head, dropped the reins and swept his free arm toward his chest in answer. He exchanged more words with the vedettes. Jack shook his head again. One of the advance riders broke away, rode back to where Dan waited, and saluted.

"Sir, he says he's Jack Farrell. Won't come any closer. Says he wants you to come out to where he is. Just you and your father. Wants us to go away."

"That's Jack for you," the older man said. "Contrary as sin."

He's no fool. This will not be easy. To the vedette, Dan said, "Stay here, then." He turned to his father. "Let's go." Dan urged his horse forward at a walk and reined in next to the second vedette, who had remained with Jack.

Dan sensed a watchful tension underneath Jack's easy posture.

"It's been a long time, big brother." Jack flashed his familiar go-to-hell smile.

"Good seeing you, Jack." Dan nudged his horse closer, bringing its head in line with the neck of Jack's well-groomed chestnut.

Jack's smile soured. He pulled the reins, backing his mount a few steps, creating space between himself and Dan. His saber rested flat against his collarbone. The piece of white cloth drooped in the still, warm air.

Jack glanced toward their father and nodded. "Pop." The obstinate set to his jaw and the defiance in his blue eyes were just as Dan remembered. It bothered him that Jack's distrust was about to be justified.

Jack nodded toward the vedette. "He needs to leave."

The trooper was watching Jack as though he were a coiled rattlesnake. "Wait with the others," Dan ordered, and the soldier obeyed with alacrity.

Dan turned his attention back to Jack. Light and athletic, his kid brother always had been quick, though Dan believed he could probably still best Jack in a contest of sheer might. Scars, appearing as white lines on Jack's tautly drawn cheek, were the only visible signs of the wounds that had disabled him for months. Had those injuries slowed him down? Dan would soon find out.

"We figured you weren't far away." Pop's demeanor was no warmer than Jack's.

"Why are you riding with a bunch of soldiers, Pop?" Jack did not hide his annoyance. "You're better off on your own."

"At least I won't get detained by you and your friends," Pop said.

"Getting detained beats the hell out of getting shot. If there's a fight, I can't do anything to protect you." Jack ran his gaze over Dan. "You're looking fit and sleek. Appears the Yankee army has done all right by you."

"Most likely better than the rebel army has done for you."

The muscle across Jack's jaw tightened. "I don't have any complaints."

Dan regretted his slur. "I hear you have a lovely wife."

Jack's demeanor relaxed a degree. "I'm happy with Martina, and she puts up with me." He shot a sardonic glance at their father. "Even Pop approves of her."

The older man cleared his throat. "Martina is a fine young woman."

"Do you have a likeness of her with you?" Dan asked.

Jack shook his head. "Wish I did. No picture studios where we've been living. She's real pretty."

"And expecting, I hear." Dan nodded. "Congratulations."

"Yeah, late summer, early fall, she thinks. She was a little bit sick, but she's over it." Jack let out a short, self-conscious laugh. "I don't know anything about that female stuff."

"Neither do I. You're finding out, I reckon."

"You're going to be an uncle. Fancy that."

Dan found it difficult to sort through his feelings. He bore fond memories of the rough affection he and his only brother shared. How could they be enemies? Lifelong bonds had become barricaded behind stiff fortifications.

"You've transferred to St. Augustine?" Jack's gaze settled on Dan's shoulder boards. "A captain now? You always did outrank me. I would be so much happier if you weren't wearing that blue coat."

"I'm on extra duty," Dan said.

Jack lifted an eyebrow. "What kind of duty?"

"You haven't found out?"

"I want to hear what you have to say about it."

Dan glanced at Jack's companion, who had not moved from where he waited. Dan considered the saber Jack held, deceptively harmless in its role as a flagpole. He let his horse drift closer to Jack's as though unaware of the movement. "What are you doing prowling around the woods?"

Jack's cocky smile returned. "Giving y'all something to worry about."

"Yeah, we're pretty worried, all right." Dan let out a disarming chuckle. "It's said y'all are hard boys to fight. You're good marksmen and sneaky as sin."

"I notice you've doubled the number of men in your patrols." Jack looked past Dan toward the waiting Union soldiers. "And nobody dares get out of sight of the main body."

"It pays to respect the enemy."

"You're just making it tougher to pick off your boys."

"That's the idea."

"I wish you'd stay in St. Augustine," Jack's grin faded as he locked eyes with Dan. "I don't want to see you shot."

"I don't want to see you shot, either."

"Guess I'm going to have to give another think about my policy of shooting the officers first." Jack's penetrating gaze did not waver.

"Fine with me. Give it up, and we won't have to fight each other."

"You could just as well resign that commission and leave the Yankee army, instead." Jack's good-natured veneer had vanished, his tone sharper.

"You wouldn't face prison or conscription either one," Dan said.

"Is that the latest bait for deserters? Amnesty?"

"We call it coming to one's senses. Think about your wife and the child –"

"Martina didn't marry a stinkin' turncoat." Jack's eyes narrowed. "And I don't believe Yankee promises anyhow."

Pop shot Dan an I-told-you-so look.

Jack snorted. "If you're planning to recruit local Tories, good luck with the sorry lot. At least they'll be good at the plunder parties y'all are so fond of."

"We've run across a number of friendly folks. Not everybody is fond of the Confederacy."

"I've been watching out for backstabbers." Jack cut his eyes at Pop. "Starting with my own family."

Dan moved his horse close enough to make a grab for Jack's reins. Dare he risk it? Jack's saber could strike in an instant. Would Jack use the weapon against him?

Alarm flickered in Jack's eyes, and he started to turn his horse's head.

Dan hadn't anticipated the quick shift, as he hadn't expected Jack to read his mind. He grabbed for the reins on Jack's horse and closed his fingers around the leather strap.

"Let go!" The flat side of Jack's saber smacked across Dan's knuckles before he realized his brother had moved. Pain loosened Dan's grip on the leather as the white flag fluttered to the ground. Jack jerked the rein free. Dan made another lunge for the horse's head, but by that time Jack had wheeled his mount all the way around, yelled for Ramon to run, and took off.

Ignoring his smarting hand, Dan kicked his horse forward and reached for Jack's belt. His fingers slid off his brother's back and grasped air. Regaining his balance over his horse's neck, he urged it to greater speed, hoping to catch Jack and pull him off his horse.

Jack whipped around in the saddle and again lashed out with his saber. Dan shifted sideways to avoid the blow, but this time the broad side caught him in the ribs, throwing him off balance. By the time he regained his seating and control of his plunging horse, Jack and his companion had disappeared into the woods.

Lieutenant Hodges led a handful of troopers past Dan in pursuit but quickly returned. "I won't let my men chase rebs where they can't see them," Hodges said.

Dan stared at the last place he had seen Jack. "Anyway, they're gone."

Pop asked, "Are you hurt? He hit you a couple of good licks."

"I had to chance it." Dan rubbed and flexed his hand, trying to determine whether bones were broken. He gingerly felt his ribs and figured he would have a colorful bruise, at least. I *deserved that.* Jack could have slashed him to ribbons had he used the business edge of the blade. He supposed Jack still held enough brotherly regard not to want to kill him outright. "He always was quick. Your number two son is one tough customer."

"That he is."

Dan could have sworn he saw a gleam of pride in his father's eyes.

"We should have found a better way to take Jack out of the war." Dan shook his head. "That was our only chance. He's finished with us now."

*

To Jack's satisfaction, Captain Dickison had assembled enough troopers near Tocoi Landing to take on the Yankee patrol. To Jack's frustration, his commander assigned him to hold horses instead of joining the fight.

"You have too much of a personal stake in this," Ramon said. "When I told the captain it was your brother we were going up against, he didn't want you in it. And he's right."

"Is he coddling me, or does he think I won't fight? Hell, Ramon. I want a chance to capture Dan, just like he tried to do to me."

"Will you shoot at him?"

"I fetched him a couple of good whacks to keep him off, didn't I? He's going to be mighty sore for a few days. He might as well recuperate in our custody."

Ramon laughed and shook his head.

Jack persisted. "My brother isn't going away unless we put him away. Am I going to be a permanent horse-holder from now on?"

"That would be such a waste of talent." Ramon grinned. "Let's take it up with the captain."

Later, having won the argument, Jack and Ramon rode out again toward Dan, the enemy. Dickison had told them to keep a watch on the patrol's progress and report back at intervals. The Yankees would expect to see two scouts, which would not inform them that more Confederates lay in wait, concealed in the underbrush on either side of the road.

Jack was unsurprised that Dan tried to capture him, truce flag notwithstanding. He had been alert for treachery, just what he had come to expect from his own blood. Those family ties had loosened to the point Jack began to think he would be better off disowning them, as he figured they already had done to him. Now he had a family that accepted him for who he was and did not make impossible demands of him.

Their strained conversation did not count for much of a reunion, but Jack was glad to see his brother anyway. Dan had done well for himself in his Union Army career. Jack wished Dan well, but he did not wish him success in his latest venture. The best solution was for him to turn Dan's plan around on him and capture his Yankee brother. Jack had no illusion Dan would thrive in a prison camp. Still, wasn't a hellhole of a Northern prison exactly what Dan had planned for him?

One dirty trick called for another.

CHAPTER SIX

One of the vedettes rushed back to report to Dan. "Couple of reb cavalry ahead, sir. Same ones as before. They're staying out of pistol range."

Lieutenant Hodges said to Dan. "Should we go after them?"

"Not yet. Let's have the rest of the patrol proceed at a walk while we investigate." Dan urged his horse to a trot, aware of Pop and Hodges coming with him.

Dan spotted his brother, who lifted his hand in a wave. Jack wheeled his horse and rode to rejoin his comrade, who waited farther down the road. Jack then turned to face Dan and his companions.

"Watching us," Dan said. "Wants to see where we're going."

"Are you going to try to capture him again?" Hodges asked.

Dan shook his head. "He's too well mounted. I can't overtake him with this worthless beast. He'd just vanish like he did last time."

"Shoot his horse?" Hodges suggested.

"Too far for a pistol shot. You'd need to bring up a rifle, and he'd see that coming." Besides, if the aim was not dead-on accurate, his brother might take the bullet instead of the horse. Dan clenched and unclenched his sore hand. None of this was turning out as he'd planned.

The two rebel scouts distanced themselves again, slipping out of sight behind roadside scrub.

"We don't know whether there are any more Johnnies around but those two." Dan frowned, noting the road ahead led through a stand of deep forest. "He's sticking with us. Now, why would he do a thing like that?"

"He's mad," Pop said. "Wants to let us know."

"It's more than that." Dan's intuition warned of danger.

"Nothing ahead but woods on either side of the road for about a mile." Pop gave Dan a thoughtful look. "Fine place for Dickison's band to set a trap."

Dan looked at Hodges for confirmation. "That's how they operate, isn't it? Fight like Indians."

Hodges nodded. "It's easy to hide in the scrub, let a column pass through, then catch us in a crossfire."

"I never saw Jack and his accomplices before they stopped me," Pop added.

"That's what I'm thinking." Dan let out his breath and turned to Hodges. "Our mission is to distribute handbills and talk to the local civilians. We're only to engage the enemy if we must."

"You would rather avoid the rebs?" Hodges did not hide his relief. He was just as skittish as the rest of the men.

"I would rather avoid a bad surprise." Dan watched the road ahead for his brother, his enemy, who would no doubt continue to bird-dog them. "Maybe we could do the same thing to him, draw him in and take him." He looked around, but the timbered-out fields they had just passed through offered little cover. "We need to go off in some other direction." He turned to his father. "Any suggestions?"

"Why don't you back up, take the crossroad and head north instead of west?" Pop asked. "You can continue your project, taking your handbills to the folks at Mill Creek. Domingo Pacetti is in Dickison's gang. His house is there, and he has a big family to support. Maybe his wife is sick of his playing soldier and will want to talk him into giving it up and staying home."

"All right. Let's do it." Dan held some hope that Jack would follow and allow a chance to set up an ambush. If Dan pulled the same trick he expected from the Confederates, he and his men could wait in hiding for Jack to ride along and capture him.

*

From behind cover Jack watched Dan, Pop and the Yankee lieutenant turn and file away. He rode forward at a safe distance until he verified the whole troop had made a retrograde movement.

"They didn't take the bait," he told Ramon.

"Let's go back and tell the captain."

Jack nodded toward the retreating Yankees. "Want me to stay with them?"

"Forty horses leave tracks even my little Ana could follow. Besides, they'll figure you're following them. They're liable to set a trap for you. Even if they don't want to kill you, wouldn't be hard for a couple of men to wait in the woods and shoot your horse out from under you, would it?"

Jack stroked Choctaw's neck. "Now, that would *really* make me mad."

*

An hour later, Dan led the patrol away from the Pacetti house after talking with the woman and leaving a handbill with her. The tired-looking wife of a rebel cavalryman had herded her half-dozen children inside and faced him, balancing an infant on her hip. He sensed the raw fear underlying her polite, noncommittal response.

The road led them through a pine forest, where scars on the trees showed someone had been harvesting sap for turpentine. Dan felt more at ease in the cultivated area, where the worst of the undergrowth had been cleared out.

"Who should we see now?" In deferring to his father's familiarity with the country people, Dan had come to realize how much he had forgotten about the area during in seven years. The soldiers certainly had not learned much of the county folk while stuck in their garrison.

"The Solana house isn't far –"

Gunfire, high-pitched yells and shouts from behind them cut off his father's reply. Dan drew his revolver and whirled to face the threat.

"We're under attack!" Hodges yelled.

Dan rushed toward the rear of the column. Most of the men turned to shoot at the oncoming enemy without waiting for orders. One wild-eyed soldier took the example of a riderless horse that galloped away from the fight. Dan pointed his weapon at the trooper's face. "Turn and fight!" he shouted.

His spine-stiffening threat gave the coward pause. He halted and made a show of taking out his carbine and yelled a string of curses at the oncoming rebels. Dan saw the enemy now, mounted, spread out, taking advantage of the roadside thicket, firing into his men with rifles and revolvers. He lifted his sidearm to shoot at the nearest attacker.

A man near him yelped and lurched on his horse. Bleeding, the soldier turned his horse and fled. Another, apparently unhurt, joined him. Dan yelled at him to stay and fight, but the panicked man ignored him and spurred his fleet steed to get away. The fear became contagious. Dan found himself in the middle of a jostling, mixed-up melee as panicked soldiers raced one way or another to avoid the onslaught.

An out-of-control rider headed straight for Dan. He whipped his horse's head around to roll back and avoid a collision, but the uncooperative beast reared instead. The bolting soldier's horse veered and clipped Dan's mount, throwing it off balance. It went down as Dan tried to jump clear.

He did not know how much time elapsed before he opened his eyes and found himself staring into Jack's face, outlined against the sky.

"Hey, Dan. About time you came to. You break anything?"

Dan's ribs and hand smarted, on account of Jack's earlier sword whipping, but the dazzling pain behind his eyes eclipsed the earlier injuries. "I think my head is the only thing that's busted."

"No need to make you get up yet. Just lie still for a while and collect yourself." Jack's voice was unexpectedly gentle. "You came down pretty hard. Can you move your legs and arms?"

Dan discovered he could. He remembered his revolver should have been in his hand. It was missing.

"That's good. I thought you broke your neck."

Reality sank in. His own brother had taken him captive. Jack looked concerned, though he had cause to gloat. "What about my men?" Dan asked.

"We plugged a few, spooked the rest. I saw you trying to rally them. They aren't worth much, are they? Our boys are chasing them. I guess any that can ride fast enough will make it to their picket outposts. The rest are ours."

Dan groped for justification not to be completely humiliated. "You boys have quite the reputation. Besides, the fellows in my patrol were pretty green."

Jack nodded. "They broke quick. Captain Dickison honored my request to stay here and see about you."

"What about Pop?"

"Don't know yet."

"He's a noncombatant."

"Unless he shoots at us. Then he's as much a Yankee soldier as any of y'all."

Dan considered trying to run, but even if he had the wherewithal to gather himself and bolt, Jack would without a doubt catch him. Jack always had been the faster sprinter, even when Dan was not laid low with an aching head.

So much for his first try at recruiting in rebel territory. What a failure. What a disaster. Maybe it was a good thing he had been captured. At least he wouldn't have to turn in a report explaining what happened.

*

Jack figured he ought not give a damn, no matter what befell his treacherous brother and belligerent father. Yet, when he saw Dan take that dangerous fall, he imagined he felt the impact in his own body. Only after Dan opened his eyes and showed he was not paralyzed could Jack begin to enjoy his personal stake in the victory. The burden of fighting his own brother was finished. All he had to do now was make sure Dan did not escape and make more trouble. Fighting strangers was more to his liking.

Ramon led Pop over for Jack to guard as well, unhurt, still riding his mule. Jack felt his second surge of relief, assured that all three of them had survived the skirmish.

Pop stared down at his elder son, who lay on the ground pale, his forehead cut and bruised from his fall. For once their sire was speechless. Pop dismounted and knelt beside his favorite.

Jack could not resist saying, "We captured this Yankee officer fair and square. Didn't violate no stinkin' truce flag, either."

"Yeah, you win," Dan struggled into a sitting position. "For now." He hugged his knees and rested his head on his arms.

"What are you going to do with us?" Pop looked at Jack.

"I don't know what the captain will do about you. As for Dan, we'll take good care of him."

Pop glared at Jack. "Send him to a filthy prison camp to starve?" Clearly, his father had already recovered his bearings and returned to normal.

"How dare you complain about poor, put-upon Dan and his fate?" Jack felt his blood rising. "Isn't that exactly what you planned for me?"

Dan lifted his head. "Jack, I owe you an apology."

"For being what you are? A damned, word-breaking, underhanded, dirty-trick-pulling Yankee."

"Don't hold back, now." Dan quirked a crooked smile. "I wanted you safe, out of the line of fire."

"I'm ever so grateful," Jack snarled.

"You would have done the same to me."

Jack did not reply, because he had to think about whether Dan was right.

*

Dan gulped down water from a canteen Jack gave him. Eventually the pain in his head subsided, though he felt as though he had taken a beating. And he had, in every way possible. The rebels brought back a couple of his unwounded men as prisoners, along with a few wounded, and the body of one dead soldier. Apparently the lieutenant had escaped.

He noted his troops had done little reciprocal damage to the rebels. The rout was complete and disgraceful.

Even if he tried to run, provided he could somehow evade Jack's watchful eye, he was surrounded. Now was not the time to attempt an escape. Later, after he recovered, he would find a way. Pop sat next to him, watchful and sullen, as much a prisoner as he was. Jack and their father finally had quit growling at each other. And at him.

Dan began to pick out familiar faces among the Confederates, as a few were old neighbors he had known as a youth. Charlie Colee was only eleven when Dan left Florida, but he and Jack had been friendly with Charlie's older brothers. Jack mentioned they were serving in the Confederate army outside Florida.

Captain Dickison, a trim man easily identifiable from the gold bars on his collar, walked over. Jack saluted and stepped aside. Dan struggled to his feet, determined to maintain both his dignity and protocol. The commanding officer introduced himself to both Dan and Pop.

"It's an honor to meet you, Captain Dickison," Dan said. "Our boys call you the Swamp Fox. You and your men have been giving our troops considerable trouble."

"Every way we can." Dickison puffed up a bit. Evidently he knew a compliment when he heard one. "How badly are you hurt, Captain Farrell?"

"Just a bump on the head. I see some of my men need attention, though."

"Our surgeon is seeing to them," Dickison said. "We're bringing up a wagon to transport the wounded."

"What are you going to do about my father? He's a noncombatant." Dan glanced at Pop, who seemed overwhelmed and had not said anything tactless. Yet.

Dickison said, "Mr. Farrell, I'm willing to offer you a parole if you swear you will stay in town and refrain from guiding or otherwise aiding the Union soldiers."

"My homestead is on the river," Pop said. "I need to see about it from time to time."

"We can't allow that. I'm convinced you will continue to inform the enemy about our movements."

"The farm is my living. I have to see to my orange grove."

"Everyone is having a hard time making a living with a war going on. That's just the way it is. If we catch you outside Union lines again, it will be a violation of parole. We'll be forced to imprison you." Dickison glanced at Jack. "The only reason I would consider releasing you at this time is because you have a son in my company. "

Pop opened his mouth to speak but must have thought better of it.

Jack said, "Sir, I'd like to have a word with you, if I may."

Dickison turned to him. "Certainly, Private Farrell." He ordered a young soldier to watch the prisoners and walked off with Jack. Dan thought he should recognize the guard, who hefted his Enfield as though he would relish using it, but was not in a mood to ask his name.

"Wonder what he's talking to Dickison about," Pop said.

"Us, no doubt." Dan observed his brother as he conferred with his commander. Jack seemed at ease with Dickison, and Dan sensed a mutual regard. It occurred to him Jack got more respect from just about everybody than he did from Pop. The two of them always had rubbed each other the wrong way.

At length Jack returned and relieved the other guard. "I volunteered for the prisoner detail. Dan, I'm escorting you at least as far as Palatka."

"Fine with me." Dan meant it. Jack would be reluctant to shoot him when he tried to escape.

"The captain didn't want to allow it at first, because he figured you'd take advantage. I told him you might try, but nobody has more reason to keep you in custody than I do."

"This is a hell of a situation, isn't it?" Dan started to shake his head but quit because the movement sent a stab of fresh pain through his skull.

Jack looked away. "Besides, I want to make sure you're treated all right. Whatever has happened between us, we're still brothers."

Dan regarded his wayward kid brother. Perhaps Jack had turned out decent in spite of everything.

CHAPTER SEVEN

"I don't want to ride that devil's spawn," Dan told Jack. "He fought me all the way here." The rebels had captured several other horses along with some of Dan's men. Better mounted, he might be able to make an escape. "You can have that one, and I hope he gives your people just as much grief."

"I've got the perfect critter for you." Jack grinned and pointed to a skinny, swayback roan that stood with its head hanging listlessly, its ears at half-mast. "Gentle enough for a lady."

Dan shot Jack an ironic smile. "No fight in that one, I guess." No flight, either. His wings were clipped for sure.

"We need to clear out. I'll give you a leg up."

"I don't need your help," Dan snapped. He climbed aboard the docile animal and settled into the saddle. The mild exertion aggravated his headache, but he set his jaw and ignored the pain.

Escape appeared unlikely. So did a counterattack that might rescue him. He didn't see how his demoralized patrol could rally after their rout. Perhaps other troops would be sent after the Confederates, but that would take time to organize.

Jack mounted his own horse and took the reins away from Dan. "I'm going to lead you all the way to Palatka."

"Are you a guard, or a nanny?" Dan huffed.

Jack laughed, heeled his chestnut into a walk and hauled Dan's plodding chunk of crow bait alongside. They backtracked over the same road his patrol had come earlier that day, ahead of the ambulance carrying the wounded. The surgeon riding with the rebels had assured Dan he stanched and dressed the wounds of his injured men and made them as comfortable as possible. Four guards, led by a sergeant and a couple of outriders, made up the Confederate side of the party. The captured horses, tethered to the wagon, followed.

The sergeant stood in the stirrups and announced to the mounted prisoners, "I suggest you boys behave yourselves and don't even give us the notion you're trying to get away. We know how to shoot."

"Their hands are tied behind them," Dan said to Jack. "I doubt they can run off."

"We like to remind them." Jack touched his revolver grip. "They're lucky to be alive."

"I'm grateful you didn't truss me up, at least." Dan rubbed his sore knuckles, still smarting from their first encounter.

"Rank has its privileges, I guess. Don't try anything. You won't get far." Jack's sharpened attitude held little warmth. "I don't want the curse of Cain on my head."

Dan looked around at the tough-looking, heavily armed troopers in gray, including his brother. He likely would be in transit for days, and opportunities surely would come up. Maybe the next set of guards, farther behind the lines, would be less competent. He decided to bide his time and remain alert.

"You haven't told me how you ended up here," Jack said. "I thought we wouldn't be facing each other once I left Virginia."

"I put in for the assignment before that," Dan said. "They just got around to sending me to Florida."

"Didn't work out so well," Jack said.

"Appears not." Dan blew out a long breath.

"Those handbills...." Jack shook his head. "Didn't it occur to you anybody that quits our army can't live out here without getting arrested for desertion?"

"We've had a good many come into town and take the oath. Once we have better control over the area, peaceable men will be safe enough anywhere. Too bad you couldn't stay out of the rebel army."

"You and Pop." Jack's jaw tightened. "I'll stand by my decisions."

Dan had touched a nerve, so he tried for a disarming comment. "I guess you have your reasons."

"Seems to me if you hadn't joined the army after the last Seminole War, we'd most likely be on the same side. Fighting for our home state." Jack's tense expression relaxed. "Pop would've disowned both of us."

Jack's comment conjured a mental picture of their irate sire that made Dan smile. "When the war broke out, part of the army resigned and joined up with the Confederates. I couldn't see my way to doing that."

"A matter of honor?"

Dan met his gaze. "I guess we're both pretty well set in our loyalties."

"I came back from Virginia mostly interested in healing up. But the Yanks wouldn't leave us be. I needed to protect my family." Bitterness seeped into Jack's voice. "They meant to hurt my wife. My brother-in-law, Carlo, he's only a boy and no soldier, but the Yanks shot him anyway."

"How is he doing?"

"No bones were broken. He's gimpy but recovering."

"That Captain Prescott you shot. He said you set out to murder him after he surrendered."

"That sonofabitch is still alive?"

"Last I heard."

"Too bad. He needed killing."

"Pop said you had as good a cause as any."

"He told you that?"

"I believe it's a mistake to come down hard on people," Dan mused. "It drives them to the other side."

Jack nodded. "Nobody can stay neutral with both armies contesting the ground. They have to declare one way or the other. Then, maybe at least one side won't bother them."

"It goes both ways. Secessionists forced Pop to leave the farm and move into town."

"I met some of those fellows." Jack grinned. "They made me nervous, too. I joined Captain Dickison's troop, with men I could trust, where I was likely to stay close to home."

"I guess this is a hard place to live these days," Dan said.

"Your army intends to starve people out of this side of the river. I noticed you didn't let this patrol do any thieving. Domingo sure was surprised."

Earlier, Domingo Pacetti had made it a point to meet Dan and tell him he wished all the Yankee officers restrained their men as well as he did. "I guess I should be thankful your friends returned the favor. They haven't gone through my pockets and robbed me yet."

"They won't," Jack shot him a disdainful look. "We leave the looting to the Yanks. But I can't promise anything once we hand you off to the next set of guards."

*

Sarah looked out the window at the odd mix of blue and gray uniformed men filing into the yard ahead of a canvas-covered wagon. "Russell, you'd better get back under that pile of laundry."

"More Yanks?" Her brother limped from the couch to join her.

She made a shooing motion. "They'll see you."

"Quit worrying so much, Sis." He positioned himself so that he could see out with only part of his face exposed.

The situation became clearer as she noticed the Confederates carried guns and the Union soldiers did not. Russell began to laugh, and Sarah's tension drained away. "Looks like our boys bagged that Yank patrol."

Outside, Papa talked with the sergeant who apparently was in charge. Jack Farrell's Yankee brother sat on a horse right next to him. "They took Dan prisoner, too," she told Russell.

Papa came to the door and stuck his head inside. "Russell, they stopped by to take you back to camp. Let's get your things."

Sarah stepped outside and waved a greeting at the soldiers, who removed their hats in return. Dan's disheveled uniform coat, missing some of its buttons, was open at the front. An angry-looking bruise had raised a swelling over his right eyebrow. Jack controlled the reins to Dan's slab-sided mount. Her satisfaction warred with her sympathy for Dan's situation.

Hands on hips, she regarded the two brothers. "I see you two found each other after all."

"We've been getting reacquainted." Jack grinned at his brother.

Dan cast him a sidewise look, then said to Sarah, "It's been an education."

"Where's your father?"

"Captain Dickison paroled him," Jack said. "He went back to town."

She glanced at the wagon. "Did any of our boys get hurt?"

Jack shook his head. "None seriously. We have a couple of wounded prisoners in the wagon. I guess the sergeant will have Russell ride and help guard them, though they probably aren't in any shape to run off."

"Jack tells me one of Dickison's men was right here in your house when we came by this morning." Dan nodded toward Russell, who was making his way to the ambulance. Papa walked with him, carrying his gear.

"We were grateful you didn't force your way inside to search our home," Sarah said. "For once a Yankee came by and acted like a gentleman. I suppose it's because you aren't a real Yankee."

He smiled ironically. "If you meant that as a compliment, I'll be happy to take it that way."

She regarded Dan, her emotions swirling. In a way, she felt sad that he would be going away to a prison camp. She had thought of him often, the youth wearing a shako hat riding off after the Indians. She had moved on to marry another man, who was no far-off dream, but real and present, until he marched away to his death.

In all that time, had Dan ever given her a thought? Did he even know or care that she was alive? Most likely not. Lately he was too busy trying to kill her friends and relatives.

*

The next day Dan still hadn't managed to escape from Jack and his comrades. Even if he broke away from Jack's grip on the reins, the rebels would have no trouble overtaking and subduing him. Besides, although he trusted his brother's forbearance, he could not count on the other Confederates to hold their fire.

The overnight stop for a meal and rest at a planter's home near the Palatka Road had offered some promise. That hope died when, with an apology, Jack tied his hands and feet then reminded him the guards would be on shift duty all night. Later, to his disappointment, his captors finessed the tricky predawn crossing of the St. Johns, which required three trips by flatboat. No one escaped, but no one drowned, either, and the wounded men were still alive.

Although still suffering from an aching head, Dan stayed alert. Along the way he took mental notes of their routes, where Dickison's men hid their rafts, and which rebel sympathizers they encountered. Perhaps someday the information would be of use.

His thoughts returned often to the comely Sarah Cates Phillips. She had treated him with courtesy and had given him a cup of fresh milk. The small kindness magnified in his mind, given his circumstances. He regretted that he likely would not see her again for a very long time.

Finally, Jack led Dan's horse into quiet, unpopulated Palatka. The riverfront was devoid of commerce. No boats were tied at the wharves, and the commercial buildings appeared abandoned.

Jack pointed to the riverfront. "A few months ago the Yankees came in by gunboat, plundered the warehouses and threatened to burn the town. After more visits like that, the businesses closed and most of the people were too frightened to stay in their homes. They left."

"I heard your company ran off the last transport ship that tried to land," Dan said.

"Thank God we succeeded. The Yanks got as far as the wharf before we changed their minds about disembarking." Jack's jaw tightened. "I did what I could to keep them away from Martina."

"Where is she staying?"

"We'll pass right by the house on the way to camp. I want you to meet her. Sergeant Ward won't mind if we tarry for a minute."

"From what you've said about your wife, you want to show her off." Dan smiled despite his general ill humor. Jack was besotted with his Martina and spoke of her often, always in glowing terms. Dan suspected she had a lot to do with keeping Jack from running off the rails.

"Yeah." Jack flashed a grin in return. "And you don't have any choice."

A red hound emerged from under the fine-looking, two-story house and raised a fuss as they neared the yard. A young, dark-haired woman walked onto the porch, the boy alongside supporting himself with a cane.

Jack waved, called their names, and heeled his horse into a trot. Dan's followed, the reluctant mount pulled along by the reins Jack held.

Martina ran down the steps and across the yard to meet them, the dog loping ahead, Carlo making his way more slowly behind her. "You're back!" Joy lit her fine features as she lifted her hand to Jack and he reached down to clasp it. Jack's habitually guarded expression softened when he looked at her. For the first time in his life, Dan envied his ever-on-the-wrong-side-of-things brother.

Martina cast a questioning glance at Dan. Though her clothes were well-worn and make-do, she held herself with thoroughly feminine assurance and her eyes sparkled with intelligence. A rosary dangled from her waist. Dan smiled at her, removed his hat and bowed from the saddle while Jack introduced his wife and brother-in-law and tersely explained to them that he had captured Dan outside St. Augustine.

Dan nodded a greeting to Carlo. The teenager leaned on his cane and glanced from Dan to the other prisoners and their guards, who were progressing along the street. "You licked 'em again, didn't you, Jack?" he said with a satisfied nod.

"We've been lucky," Jack said.

"Smart," Carlo corrected.

"Ramon?" Martina shaded her eyes and looked at the passing horsemen.

"Everybody in our company is all right. Russell's leg gave him trouble, so we brought him back in the wagon. Ramon and Charlie stayed outside St. Augustine on outpost duty."

"Thank God." Martina crossed herself then turned back to Dan. "I knew my husband had a brother, but I didn't expect to meet you so soon." Her manner toward him was restrained but courteous.

"It's a shame we couldn't have met under more pleasant circumstances." Not so devastating for him, at any rate.

Martina, still holding Jack's hand, smiled and said, "Good thing it wasn't the other way around."

Her frank comment forced a chuckle from Dan. "That's a matter of viewpoint."

"If there's anything we can do for you – "

"Distract your husband so I can get away."

"I doubt that!" She shook her head, laughing. "I can fix you a good supper instead. Carlo has been catching a mess of fish." She looked up at Jack. "Will he be able to stay with us?"

Jack shook his head. "I have to deliver the prisoners to the provost guard at camp. I don't know whether they'll want to keep him there or in the town jail. We can take him something to eat later."

"I'm so glad you were able to come home. When do you have to go back?"

"Won't know until I report. I'll come let you know, if they don't keep me there." Jack glanced toward the ambulance and the other guards as they passed by. Sergeant Ward turned in the saddle to look meaningfully their way. "I have to catch up with the detail, darlin'. I'll be home as soon as I can."

*

Awareness that whenever her husband rode away it might be her last sight of him intensified Martina's relief each time he came home. When he returned from camp after delivering Dan to the provost, Jack told her he was permitted to spend the night at the house. This night, at least, she would rest secure in his arms, free from worry.

Tomorrow he must leave her again, continuing with the guard detail escorting the prisoners as far as the railroad station at Waldo. In a few days he would pass through Palatka again on the way back to his post across the river in St. Johns County. She would be granted a few hours of his company, at least.

For now, they sat on the porch, holding hands like the newlyweds they were. He told her and Carlo how Dan had come to Florida to encourage desertion from the Confederate ranks. "He tried to capture me under a truce flag," Jack told Carlo.

"That's against the rules," Carlo said.

"I don't remember him fighting dirty when we were kids. I guess he learned that in the Union Army. They think rules are made for other people. Made me mad, but I understand why he tried. He wanted to take me out of the war so we wouldn't be fighting each other. Anyway, I got away from him."

"You captured him instead," Carlo said.

Jack told them about the skirmish. "His horse fell, and he got knocked out. I thought he was killed at first, but he came to."

"What's going to happen to him now?" Martina asked.

"At Waldo, we'll put him on the train and send him north. All the prisons are pretty far up the road. None in Florida."

"I've heard those prisons are terrible places." Martina searched Jack's face. Certainly this was a hard duty for him. "Aren't you tempted to let him escape?"

The muscle across Jack's cheek tightened and his gaze flicked away. "Like I told the captain, I have the best reasons for making sure Dan stays out of the fight. I'm not happy about sending him to prison, but it beats having to fight him."

"Sometimes prisoners get exchanged, don't they?"

"If he does, I hope he stays far away from Florida."

"Would it be all right to visit with him while he's at Camp Call?"

"He's probably sick to death of me, but I'm sure he wouldn't object to your company." Jack flashed a quick smile. "He has nothing against pretty ladies, from what I've seen."

"I'll give him some smoked fish to eat along the way in case the guards forget to feed him."

Jack gave her hand a squeeze. "You want to feed the whole world, darlin'."

"Not the whole world. Just people I care about. Dan is your brother, even if he is a Yankee officer. We ought to do what we can for him. Once you take him to that train, who knows when you'll have a chance to see him again?"

"Not until the end of the war, I hope," Jack said. "I don't want him coming back down here wearing that blue coat until it's all over with."

CHAPTER EIGHT

Two days later, Jack and the rest of the guard detail escorted Dan and two other prisoners into the village of Waldo. The surgeon had decided the wounded Yankees needed to rest after the first leg of the journey and kept them hospitalized. This part of the trip had gone more smoothly without the ambulance and its passengers slowing progress.

Consisting of a few houses, a general store and a small hotel, Waldo's location at the junction of the railroad and Bellamy Road, the trail that linked Tallahassee with St. Augustine, gave the village strategic importance. Still, no rolling stock waited at the open-air station. The Confederate troops assigned to guard the railroad watched the mixed party of blue and gray-coated soldiers with indolent interest as they rode in.

Jack waited, holding the reins of Dan's horse, while Sergeant Ward, who was in charge of their detail, conferred with the lieutenant commanding the local garrison. Jack pointed to the lines suspended between pine poles alongside the tracks.

"Before the war, when I worked for Samuel Morse's telegraph company, I spent a few weeks in and around Waldo. I shinnied up those poles and strung the wires. Still have my climbing gaffs. I told the captain if he needed any telegraph lines run, I'm his man." His glance at Dan held a challenge. "I suppose your army will want to cut them down."

Dan shrugged. "And burn the rebel cars and tear up the rebel tracks, besides. That's how it is with war."

"It's our job to make sure your vandals don't get to them."

"Men like you are the reason we're having so much trouble winning." Dan's smile was grim. "It isn't right we're on opposing sides."

"It isn't right, but that doesn't change our minds." Mercifully, during their time together Dan had not showed the open disdain for Jack and his comrades Pop had always displayed. Whether Dan truly respected them, or merely thought better of insulting men who had deadly power over him, didn't matter. Dan's conciliatory attitude had helped them stay on warmer terms for the past few days. Jack had enjoyed his Unionist brother's company, despite their difficult guard-and-prisoner roles.

"I suspect you'll keep fighting until you can't do it anymore." Dan's voice held resignation. "I saw that in Virginia, and I see it down here. We're the same way. This war is going to last awhile. I predict in the end we'll reclaim every bit of territory for the Union."

"You're a Yank, so I guess you have to boast. It's what y'all do." Jack shifted the topic. "I had to know Morse code to test the line. Maybe I should brush up and practice, work on my speed so I can qualify as an operator."

"Since when did you get so studious?"

"Since I saw a good reason to make the effort."

"Could be a way to support your family after the war is over," Dan said.

"When I asked Martina to marry me, I told her it wouldn't be easy." Jack rubbed his jaw. "That's one way I haven't disappointed her."

"Your wife seems to be bearing up all right," Dan said.

"She's twice lost her home, but she's been making the best of it." After a couple of days' ride he would be returning to their temporary shelter for a few hours' relief from his military duties. He pictured her loving reception, which brought a fleeting smile to his lips.

"The lady is good for you, and she seems to like you pretty well, too."

"Fancy that. Jack Farrell, a family man."

Jack recalled Martina's question about letting Dan escape. Many times along the way he had run the possibilities around in his mind. Was condemning his brother to prison worse than facing him in direct fighting? He did not know the answer, yet his duty was clear. Besides, Captain Dickison had emphasized that if he got careless and lost a certain Yankee captain along the way, he would make certain the escapee's brother would face a court martial. "Guess I'll be shoving off soon."

Dan extended his hand. "Give Martina my gratitude for her kindness. When she was in charge, I was the best fed Union officer in captivity."

Jack shook the offered hand. "Next time we meet, I hope it's under more peaceable terms." He grinned, wanting to lighten his mood. "I'd apologize for inconveniencing you, but prison is exactly what you had in mind for me."

"We've been treated decently. My only complaint is the damnable vigilance of my guards. Especially my brother, who wouldn't turn his back for a minute."

"Speaking of guards, here they come." Jack nodded toward the primitive depot, where Sergeant Ward led the lieutenant in charge of a quartet of shotgun-armed militiamen.

Jack expected the northbound train to rumble through in a few hours. It ran in that direction every second day, and south on the other days. The provost had verified by telegraph that this was the day to catch the Baldwin-bound cars. "Write to us when you get to wherever you're going, hear?"

"I will."

"Let us know if there's anything we can do to make life easier in prison." Jack continued to keep his face averted, pretending to watch the oncoming guards, lest Dan read his conflicted emotions. "It'll be harder to get a letter through to Pop on the other side of the lines."

"I will." Dan's voice was husky.

Jack wanted to give his brother a farewell embrace but decided that was unwise. Informing the new shift of guards of their relationship and the Union officer's Florida origins could invite extra trouble. They might take Dan for a traitor and treat him like one. He controlled his expression and shifted his gaze back to his older brother. "Take care of yourself."

"Don't get yourself killed, little brother. You have a lot to live for."

"Yeah, I do. You too."

Jack waited while Dan dismounted at Sergeant Ward's order, gathered his blanket roll and slung the full haversack over his shoulder. The other two prisoners dismounted as well and joined Dan in a wary cluster.

The dignified, elderly lieutenant who could have been a veteran of the first Seminole War back in the '30s, a couple of underage boys, a graybeard, and a swaggering corporal stared at Dan and the other Yankees as though they were a sideshow exhibit.

"They'll keep y'all in the town jail until the next Baldwin-bound train comes," Sergeant Ward told Dan. To Jack he said, "We're done with 'em. We'd best feed our horses and start back to Palatka."

Jack exchanged a last look with Dan before the guards, shotguns ready, escorted his brother toward the log house that served as a jail. Jack let out a long breath, turned Choctaw's head, and rode away with the rest of the guard detail.

*

Dan paced the room that served as his cell. The two other Union prisoners had been taken to another room. Guards stood vigil at each door and outside the windows. The lieutenant in charge of this crew of rebel militia apparently thought it prudent to separate an officer from his men. Dan peered out the single window, which gave him a view of the general store next door. Soldiers, apparently off-duty, loitered about the porch smoking and talking. He also could see a small portion of the railroad track, the pavilion, and the platform. The guard stood by the window positioned in such a way he could keep an eye on Dan.

Closely watched by Jack and other experienced troops while riding deeper into rebel territory, Dan had not yet managed an attempt at escape. Surely he would find his chance somewhere during the journey north, the sooner the better. It didn't appear the chance would come sooner. In the middle of a Confederate encampment, in full daylight, he would stand little chance of a successful run for freedom. Best wait until they were on the road before he made his move.

From a memorized map, Dan knew the Florida railroad passed northwest through Starke on the way to a junction at Baldwin. From there the northward track continued to Fernandina, a Union stronghold on the northeast tip of the state. Once the cars reached Baldwin, Dan supposed he and the other prisoners would have to hike into Georgia to catch another railroad leading north through the Confederacy.

However, the south end of the line, at Cedar Keys, was under Union control. The sparsely settled land in that direction would probably hold fewer Confederate troops than the well-guarded northeastward stretch. If only he could escape and find his way to the west coast, he would be among friends. Instead of friendly enemies, like his brother.

Dan recalled his evening at Camp Call, when Jack, Martina, and her brother Carlo had livened a few hours of his captivity. His sister-in-law was a warm-hearted girl, and his immediate liking for her proved justified. She made sure he had a good supper and something more for the road. Along the way his rebel captors provided the same rations they were eating, so he had been able to save the cornbread, cheese and smoked fish she gave him. At some point his handlers might forget to feed him.

Besides, once he escaped, he would need something to sustain him while he was on the run.

Carlo, on the other hand, clearly had little use for Union soldiers, and a gunshot wound had not improved his opinion. Clearly he endured Dan's presence only because his sister insisted, and then he limped off to pal around with the similarly lame Russell Cates.

Watching Jack and Martina together filled Dan with longing. His brother openly adored his woman, and she made no effort to hide her own affection for her husband. Perhaps one day he would find such a life partner, but his near future appeared bleak unless he could avoid imprisonment.

Hours later, the whistle sounding in the distance broke Dan's reverie. Eventually the huff of a steam engine and the clank of driving rods and metal wheels announced the arrival of a train. Dan watched through the window as the engine, lanterns glowing in the deepening dusk, chugged onto the visible portion of track and pulled to a hissing stop. Coming from the south, it would surely take him closer to the final destination the Confederacy planned for him.

Soon after, the elderly lieutenant came to the house and accompanied the guards as they hustled Dan and the two New Hampshire men from the jailhouse to the boarding platform. The same guards were still in charge: the two boys, the old fellow, and the rough-looking corporal. One of the younger guards carried coils of rope over his shoulder.

While a crew filled the engine tanks with water and added wood to the tender, other passengers waited on the platform. An elderly gentleman escorted a pair of young women holding the hands of two small children. The ladies glanced at him then whispered to each other behind their hands. A few Confederate soldiers in worn-out uniforms loitered nearby. Dan expected them to comment or jeer at him and his unfortunate companions, but they merely stared. One grinned and lifted his hand in a good-natured wave.

The train consisted of a tender car, a single passenger car and two boxcars. As soon as the conductor stepped from the train, the lieutenant took him aside, and Dan overheard something about securing the prisoners before the others took their seats.

"Hoof it, Yanks." The corporal lifted his shotgun in a threatening manner and nodded toward the open door of the coach. Dan obeyed, and the privates filed in behind him. The guards closed in after them. Inside the train, the corporal ordered Dan to a rear seat, then made the other two prisoners take separate seats. Lanterns hanging from hooks had little effect on the dimness of the interior. The lieutenant, holding a flickering light, observed from the doorway of the coach.

Once the three of them were seated, the corporal told the boy carrying the ropes to tie the hands and feet of the two privates, who submitted with surly resignation.

After the young soldier bound them, the corporal gestured toward Dan. "Him next?"

"He's an officer," the lieutenant said. "We won't subject him to such treatment."

"Yes, sir." The corporal shot Dan a poisonous look. Dan figured he knew the type: a petty man, eager to enforce his small authority.

"Thank you, lieutenant." Dan gave him a grateful smile.

The lieutenant said to the corporal, "It appears the prisoners are secure. Stay with them until you reach Baldwin. We've telegraphed ahead, so they are expected. After you turn them over to the provost, come back on the next southbound cars."

"Yes, sir." The corporal saluted the officer, who left the train.

Dan studied his guards, and they looked back at him, cradling their shotguns. So far he wasn't impressed. The youngsters and the codger probably knew how to shoot, but the boys might be trigger-happy. The old man appeared dim of eye and partially deaf. Dan had disliked the corporal at first sight and gathered the feeling was mutual.

The ladies, with their children in tow, filed into the train and took their seats at the opposite end of the car. After them, the soldiers boarded, filling the seats nearer where Dan sat, close to the side door of the car. He took stock of his new prison, noting the sagging and worn cushions and general run-down condition of the coach. Wartime shortages were apparent behind Confederate lines.

Typical of most passenger coaches, a door at either end led to the next car. A men's water closet occupied the space between Dan and the back door. The open window next to him presented another possible escape hatch. That was a long shot, because by the time he managed to scramble his whole body through, one of his guards would have time to either grab him or blast him with the shotgun. The rear door offered his best chance.

Dark settled in before the train chugged to a jolting start, headed northward through the night. The car bumped and swayed over the track, which Dan suspected needed maintenance as much as the shabby coach.

Night, he judged, would be his friend. He glanced at the corporal, who had appointed himself Dan's personal guard. Too bad one of the kids hadn't gotten the job, or the rheumy-eyed old man. The corporal was watching him morosely, shotgun ready. If Dan lunged for the back door, by the time he reached it he would be peppered full of buckshot. Death held even less appeal than imprisonment.

He shifted as though uncomfortable, held his belly and said, "I need to use the water closet."

The corporal gave him a sour look. "Plug it up."

"I think I ate bad meat, and I don't want to offend the ladies by having an accident."

One of the young guards giggled.

"How come you didn't take care of that before we boarded?"

"Haven't you noticed we've been sitting on this train for an hour?"

The corporal looked around, then said, "All right. Get up. No funny business. So much as one wrong move, and this shotgun will blow your head clean off."

Dan nodded and stood.

"How come you're wearing that haversack to the privy?" the guard asked. "What's in it?"

"Nothing but food. Don't want it to walk away while I'm gone." Dan gave him a disarming smile.

The militiaman grunted and narrowed his eyes, but made no further objections.

Dan made for the privy, the guard at his back. He opened the door and pretended to unbutton his trousers. The comforting weight of the provisioned haversack pressed his side.

In the dim lantern light admitted from the open doorway he noted the small window above the hollow seat. Cutting his eyes around, looking for an opening, he met the foreshortened shotgun muzzle at eye level. The narrow aisle forced the guard to stand close to him, and the weapon's business end was just a few inches from his face.

A run of bad track made the car lurch and the guard's aim wavered, slipping away from its point-blank aim. Dan took his chance. He whirled, ducked underneath the muzzle of the shotgun and rammed his head against the corporal's chest. The guard crumpled backwards against the wall with an explosive grunt and the gun's load blasted harmlessly upward.

Ears ringing, nostrils filled with smoke, Dan took advantage of the guard's temporary shock. He rushed to the back door, slid it open, and stumbled outside onto the breezeway between the cars.

Dan did not take time to study the dark wooded landscape sweeping by at the speed of a canter. In one move he grabbed the rail, leaped over it, and blindly hurtled himself into space, trusting his luck would hold and he wouldn't kill himself.

He hit the ground on his feet, rolled and tumbled into a ditch. He scrambled up the bank, thanking God he had not broken a leg. Clutching the haversack, which somehow still hung over his shoulder, he staggered into the woods. Vines and scrub tore at his trousers as he ran into the darkness. Behind him, he heard shouts and curses above the receding clatter and roar of the train as it continued north along the track.

He did not look back. It would take the engineer a while to stop the engine. Since the overcast sky showed no stars or moon, he did not believe the guards could find him in the woods if he just kept moving. By morning, when they could set dogs on his trail, he ought to be long gone. Although bruised and scraped by the hard, sliding landing, he did not seem to be seriously hurt.

He planned to continue south, jogging along the track, detouring through the woods whenever he anticipated pickets or towns in his path. The railway line terminated in friendly hands, and he was determined to make it there.

CHAPTER NINE

Despite her sadness over losing her house in St. Augustine and the Picolata homestead, Martina had learned to make a home wherever she landed. Carlo was still with her, and Jack's army duties had not taken him far away. In this she considered herself fortunate.

Her arms ached from the heavy basket of fruit she carried to the wagon. She had discovered a neglected orange grove behind an abandoned house near the river and thought it a shame to let the citrus fall to the ground and rot. The juice brought out the flavor in the fish Carlo brought home every day. Soaked, sweetened and cooked, the sour oranges and lemons yielded fine marmalade and jam. Among the trees she found one that was heavy with sweet oranges, an even more valuable prize.

She skirted a cluster of brambles, which looked deceptively soft with their spray of little white flowers. The bushes sprang up everywhere cleared land went untended. She looked forward to the crop of blackberries they promised.

Satisfied with her harvest for the day, she loaded the oranges onto the wagon, where Ladybug dozed in her traces. Roused, the old marsh tackie pricked her ears, curved her head toward Martina, and swished her tail.

Martina stroked the mare's graying muzzle and looked toward the river for Carlo. Although not yet steady enough on his injured leg to support and cast the mullet net, he sat on the end of the wharf tending several baited lines. Nearby stood a couple of soldiers using cane poles. Another waded in the shallows, a net slung over his shoulder. She did not see Carlo's net on the wagon-bed and speculated the wader had borrowed it.

She picked up a couple of the sweet oranges and set them into the sewing basket atop her palmetto braids and carried the basket across the road to the mostly deserted riverfront. Her shoes tapped along the wooden surface of the pier, and she inhaled the clean freshwater scent of the river. The soldiers, men she knew slightly, spoke and lifted their hats in greeting.

She nodded an acknowledgment and paused. "Do you have any news?"

"It's been quiet along the river since the Yanks left Jacksonville," the red-bearded soldier said. "Quiet enough for us to catch a few fish to flesh out our rations. The river's full of trout, bass, and cat." He pulled up a line of gill-strung fish he had caught.

"This is a good place as long as our enemies stay away." She moved on, secure enough in their presence. Most of the Confederate soldiers in Dickison's troop were respectable family men, and even the rougher element never bothered her. They knew Jack too well to risk such nonsense.

Nip, who had been snoozing beside Carlo, got up, stretched fore and aft, and came up to her, tail waving. She stroked the dog's smooth head and settled down next to Carlo, who wore the straw colored, broad-brimmed palmetto hat she had recently made for him. "Any luck, Chico?"

He grinned and nodded toward the bucket. "See for yourself."

She tipped the heavy bucket and peered inside. Water covered the four good-sized fish he had caught. "As long as we never run out of fish, we'll always have something to eat, won't we?" She pointed to the man who had just thrown the net and was pulling it in. "Isn't that your net?"

"I told him he could use it if as he gives us one in four of the fish he catches."

Martina chuckled. "You are learning to be quite the businessman, little brother."

He smiled and shrugged. "And I won't let him give us nasty toadfish we can't eat, or tiny minnows."

Martina handed Carlo one of the oranges then picked up her hat-making materials. She had learned how to make palmetto hats as a child, and had recently taken up the art in earnest. The cool and lightweight hats made good shade, and she had taken to wearing one herself. Like fish and oranges, the materials cost nothing, but the hats brought a dollar and a quarter each.

After cutting the white shoots from the bases of the plants, she had let them dry on the porch, then sliced them into thin strips. She made long braids from the strips, and was ready for the next step.

"Take off your hat. I'm going to use your head for a model again." She wound the braided material around his crown in overlapping circles and basted them together. Then she took the fragile creation onto her lap to sew it fast.

Even though her hands were occupied, she felt rested, enjoying the peaceful surroundings. These days she tired easily and seemed to need extra sleep, something she attributed to her condition. She expected the child late September if all went as it should. If all went as it should... Would she be able to remain here, where she had shelter suitable for a fragile infant?

For now, she tried not to worry about a future she could not control and gazed across the water to the far side of the St. Johns. Closer to the headwaters, the river was narrower than at Picolata, and she clearly saw the woods on the east shore. Undisturbed by wind or the passage of watercraft, the surface of the water gleamed smooth as a lake. She had not seen a Yankee gunboat since Jack and his comrades drove off the one that attempted to land. If the red-bearded soldier was not mistaken, she had nothing of the sort to fear for the time being. Every night she prayed to the Blessed Mother she had seen the last of the Yankees, though she sensed it was too much to ask.

Certainly it wasn't too much to ask for protection for herself and her loved ones.

*

Jack quelled his anxiety at finding no one home by reminding himself the Yankees were far away, giving Martina no reason to flee. Indoors, everything appeared to be in order. Most likely he would find her with Carlo at the river. Unwilling to wait at the empty house, he mounted Choctaw and headed toward the desolate waterfront.

There he found them, just as he had hoped. As he tied Choctaw near Ladybug and the wagon, Martina met him at the foot of the wharf, her face radiant with delight. He wrapped her in his arms, relishing her soft warmth, unconcerned about scandalizing the others present with their display of heartfelt affection. Then he stepped back to admire her. "New hats?" He glanced from her to Carlo, who rested on his cane and grinned at him from under the wide brim.

"I'm making them," Martina said. "What do you think?"

"Pretty as red shoes." He touched the cool surface of the woven leaves. "Darlin', you could wear a croaker sack and make it look good."

Carlo rolled his eyes, and Jack winked at him.

She said to Carlo, "Are you ready to go home?"

"As soon as I get my net back with my fish."

Jack offered Martina his arm, and they walked along the wharf with Carlo to retrieve his lines and catch. Supporting himself with the cane, Carlo favored his wounded leg as he made his way.

"You're walking a little better," Jack observed.

"Better every day," Carlo said. "No Yankee bullet is going to get the best of me."

"Good man, Carlo." Jack grinned. He helped Carlo haul in his lines, hand over hand. Then he picked up the bucket and carried it back to the wagon while Carlo negotiated with the soldier for his net and fish.

Martina told him about her plans for hat-making, if the soldiers liked them and they sold well. She showed him her harvest of oranges and lemons. "I've been making marmalade, too. If you can stay overnight, you can take some with you. How long…"

"Sergeant Ward gave me the night off. I have to go back to the east side of the river tomorrow. I'll spin it out as long as I can."

"Dan.… how is he?"

"Last time I saw him he was fine." Jack laughed softly. "When I got back to camp I found out he'd escaped."

Martina's smile was tentative. "Escaped? How?"

"The telegraph operator said he slugged his guard and jumped off the train. He got clean away. It was dark, and by the time they braked the engine, he'd slipped into the woods. They couldn't do anything about it until daylight."

"Can he make it back to Yankee lines?"

"If he's clever enough, and if he didn't hurt himself jumping off the train." Jack grinned. "He probably is. I'm glad it didn't happen on my watch, and I hope he finds somewhere else to do his recruiting."

*

Five days after his escape, Dan reached the Gulf Coast. Under cover of darkness he had walked across the railroad trestle connecting the island chain of Cedar Keys with the mainland. Fortunately the Union marines guarding the railroad terminal were not trigger-happy.

The sergeant in charge of the pickets, though suspicious of his account, gave him hardtack and bacon to eat and let him rest by the fire. The next morning, the marines escorted him to the west side of the island and rowed him across a channel to Depot Key. There the

Navy maintained a refueling station at the tiny village of Atena Otie. As in St. Augustine, the tang of salt air mingled with the smell of not-so-freshly-caught fish. The few civilians Dan saw seemed to mingle freely enough with the Union sailors. Either the staunch Secessionists had left, or the inhabitants had swallowed their sympathies to get along with the military.

One of the marines took him to headquarters, where Dan stood before Lieutenant Commander McCauley. Now, instead of the rebels holding his future, his countrymen in charge of this blockading post determined his fate.

Dan shifted on his feet, aware of the disreputable sight he presented: cut, bruised, his face a mass of welts from insect bites. He had long since run out of the food his sister-in-law provided, and he had tightened his belt a notch to accommodate his shrunken waistline. His clothes, stained from his slog through the swamp, hung in tatters. Thorny vines and other predatory vegetation had caught and ripped the fabric during his night travels when he had taken to the woods to avoid towns and picket posts along the railway. The last twenty miles were the worst, as the track between Bronson and the coast led through a mosquito-infested and cypress-knee-riddled lowland. He counted himself lucky he had not stumbled over a water moccasin or an alligator.

"I was assigned to encourage desertion from the rebel army in Florida, and to raise a company of cavalry on the east coast," Dan told the officer on duty. "Dickison – you've heard of the rebel Captain Dickison? – captured me and put me on a train at the Waldo station. I jumped off and avoided recapture. I knew Cedar Keys was under Union control, so I came here."

"How did you manage that?"

"I traveled mostly at night following the tracks. I talked with some Negroes along the way who were able to tell me where the rebel pickets and the towns were located."

The navy officer took a drag on his cigar. "Congratulations on your successful escape, Captain Farrell."

"Thank you, sir. I'm honored to request the cooperation of the navy in returning to St. Augustine," Dan said. "I certainly don't want to backtrack through rebel territory."

"Even so, it will take a while to get you to your post after we make sure you really are a Union officer and not a rebel spy." McCauley stroked his beard, frowning.

Dan drew his weary body tall, mustering all the dignity he could muster in his disheveled condition. "I assure you I am who I say I am, sir."

McCauley raised an eyebrow. "You sure do talk Southern."

"I was born and raised in Florida. I joined the U. S. Army in '55 and have been loyal ever since. I served in Virginia with General McClellan before being reassigned to Florida."

"Commendable. I certainly hope what you say is true."

"As God is my witness. If you can contact Colonel Putnam in St. Augustine, he can vouch for me."

"We have a number of ships operating in the East Gulf Division," the officer said. "They're covering the coastline from the Suwannee River south to Anclote Key. Right now, some of our ships are out in the Gulf hunting blockade-runners. My vessel, the *Fort Henry*, is here taking on coal and supplies. Eventually, we can get you passed down to Key West. If all is well, you can see about getting passage with the South Atlantic Fleet. In the meantime, our pickets will have orders not to let you off the island."

Dan had gone through days and nights of misery and hardship to make it here, only to be placed under an arrest of sorts. He took a deep breath. "I understand, sir."

"You can stay in the officers' quarters, clean up and get some rest until we can check your story." The naval officer gave him a hard stare. "If you turn out to be a liar, we can take care of that as well. Key West has a fine prison facility, and we can arrange a cell with your name on it. Or worse."

After a full meal and a hot, sudsy soak of his exhausted body, Dan crawled into bed and slept into the next day. Later he planned to write a report to send to Colonel Putnam. He imagined the garrison commander's reaction to his failed patrol and was not sorry he would not be present to absorb it.

He resigned himself to a period of idleness, with no command and no hope of one until he could prove his true identity and persuade the navy to transport him back to his rightful post.

CHAPTER TEN

Late December 1863

The summer had proved a time of relative calm. The Yankees had stayed out of Jacksonville and rarely sent their gunboats upriver to Palatka. For Martina, the past months had brought many changes. Ramon's wife and daughter had come from their Lake City refuge to live with her, and Martina's family had grown in another way.

She settled a milk-sated Rosa into her crib and tucked the cotton blanket around the infant. She had positioned the crib close to the hearth, hoping warmth from the frugal fire would ward off a chill. No fever was going to carry off her child, not if she could prevent it.

Ana, Ramon and Teresa's bright-eyed daughter, wrapped one little hand around an upright slat, rose on her tiptoes and peered inside at the drowsy infant. "Let her sleep now," Martina said. "You can play with her later." A compliant child, Ana skipped across the floor. She picked up her slate and chalk. "I'll draw a horse, Mama,' she said to Teresa, who sat on the couch mending one of Ana's white sack dresses.

Teresa's ripening figure showed evidence she and Ramon had productively celebrated their reunion months ago. When her time came, it would be Martina's turn to repay Teresa for taking care of her during her confinement.

Teresa looked up from her task. "A horse like Papa's?"

"Not Papa's." Ana shook her head. "Aunt Tina's. Ladybutt. I'll draw Ladybutt."

"It's bug. Ladybug." Teresa laughed and tweaked her daughter's nose. "You're a bug."

"Am not." Ana giggled and went to work with the chalkboard.

Martina smiled, paying little attention to the exchange as she kept her fascinated vigil over her firstborn. Rosa's eyelids flicked and her pink lips pursed as she suckled in her sleep. Martina marveled at the sweet perfection of the tiny creature, the turn of her cheek, her cap of downy, straw-colored hair. Her fragility. She thanked the Blessed Mother for the gift of a beautiful child. *Please God, let her stay healthy, along with Jack, Carlo and Ramon.*

Carlo's leg wound had healed, and to Martina's distress, he had celebrated his upcoming sixteenth birthday by joining the cavalry last week. A nearby planter, alarmed by the broadening of conscription age, wished to avoid service. He paid Carlo $300 to substitute for him, and the boy talked the gentleman into furnishing him with a good saddle horse as well.

Martina reluctantly gave Carlo permission to enlist because Captain Dickison promised to detail her youthful brother as a courier. She also trusted Jack and Ramon to shield him from trouble. Besides, Carlo pointed out the law would require him to join a militia unit at sixteen, anyway.

Martina heard the tread of hooves on the oyster shell street and rushed to the window. "It's our soldiers," she said, "and some Yankees."

"There must have been a fight." Teresa's voice lost its lighthearted tone, lapsing into dread.

As far as Martina knew, neither of their husbands had fired a shot in earnest for months. Did a skirmish signal an increase in hostilities? Had this fight brought harm to them?

Martina slipped out the door, opening it narrowly to avoid letting in a draft. She stepped onto the porch, aware of Teresa and Ana right behind her. She ignored the cold, damp wind as she searched the faces of the oncoming soldiers.

The gray-clad troopers, some wearing Union greatcoats, rode at a leisurely pace to herd along a sizeable number of Union soldiers in their midst, on foot. The prisoners looked dusty and trudged along without spirit. Dickison's men must have won the fight, but at what cost? Where was her husband? And Carlo?

Her breath came out in a rush when she saw Jack astride Choctaw, veering in her direction. Carlo, riding just behind Jack, waved at her. He looked as soldierly as the others in his confiscated greatcoat and cavalry boots. At the same time she heard Ana call out, "Papa! Papa!" and Martina spotted Ramon as well. She shut her eyes for a moment and crossed herself. Then she waved and rushed down the steps to meet Jack.

He reined in alongside her but did not dismount. "Is everybody all right? The baby?" Anxiety sharpened his features.

"We're fine. Rosa is fat and sassy."

His posture relaxed. "Bet she's grown some."

"What about you? Were you in a fight?"

He shook his head and glanced toward the Yankee prisoners. "Not much of a scrap. We have to take these boys to camp. After we turn them in, I'll be back." He flashed her a grin. "Then we'll get reacquainted."

Jack blew her a kiss and heeled Choctaw back in line. Martina watched him until he rode out of sight.

*

"Without overland telegraphic communications, it took the navy about a month to verify my identity." Finally back in St. Augustine, Dan concluded his report about what had happened to him over the past eight months.

Much had changed during his absence. Colonel Putnam and the 7th New Hampshire had been sent to Hilton Head along with their dependents, among them the lovely Miss Alexander. The colonel, as well as Lieutenant Hodges, had been killed in an assault on Battery Wagner during a failed attempt to take Charleston.

Seated across the desk at headquarters, the present garrison commander, Colonel Osborn, listened with solemn interest as Dan continued his account. "After that, I had to remain at Cedar Keys with the East Gulf Blockading Squadron waiting for transport, then on the *Fort Henry* while the crew intercepted blockade runners and conducted raids. They passed me from depot to depot, ship to ship, south to Key West. In the same manner I worked my way back north with the Atlantic Squadron."

"You've been idle for a long time, Captain Farrell." The Massachusetts officer cocked an eyebrow.

"As a mere army captain among navy officers, my interests held no priority." Dan had expected disapproval over his late arrival, even though he had been unable to exert any control over what the navy did with him. "I made myself useful while I was stuck on the west coast. I continued the work I started here, advising and arming refugees who wanted to fight the rebels. They brought us excellent intelligence and did a little raiding on their own."

Osborn tapped a sheaf of papers on his desk. "Lieutenant Commander McCauley confirmed that. He said you accompanied his marines and put a number of rebel salt works out of business."

Dan nodded. "Yes, sir. I did that as well."

"I also read Colonel Putnam's reports, the ones he left when I relieved him of this command. He mentioned your plan to recruit locals for our army."

"I returned to Florida for that reason and to encourage desertion from the rebel ranks. Unfortunately, I didn't have much time to get the word out before the enterprise came to grief."

"Please understand I am sympathetic to your goals, Captain." The colonel leaned forward on his elbows. "In fact, your return at this time is somewhat fortuitous. I see the advantage in forming a cavalry company from Florida men. Not much has been done about it in your absence, but now that you are back, you can carry on with the project."

Dan suppressed his eagerness. "Have you enlisted any volunteers so far?"

"A handful. That's all. Most in St. Augustine, but other willing men have come into our lines at Fernandina as well."

"That's a start. If we work at it, I know we can bring in more, recruits as well as deserters."

"You'll have to content yourself with dealing with the men within our own lines for the time being. Our primary mission has always been to hold the town and protect it from rebel attack. We don't have enough men to control the countryside. The woods are full of rebels and they know how to take advantage of the terrain. It's dangerous to send our soldiers outside our picket lines."

"If we take out a strong enough force – "

"Like you did last April?"

Dan felt the blood rush to his face. His failure would never be forgotten.

Osborne shook his head. "I don't want to risk more men unnecessarily, especially after our last incident."

Dan had heard talk of the recent rebel attack just outside town. "Sir, what happened, exactly?"

"We've cut down all the trees within a mile of town, so we have to go farther outside our fortifications for firewood. Our scouts reported no sign of rebel cavalry on this side of the river, and we needed the wood. Twenty armed choppers were accompanied by a guard of thirty additional men. Even that proved insufficient." Colonel Osborn let out his breath, fluttering his mutton chop whiskers. "Apparently, their scouts and informers had been observing our movements and expected our men to come out for wood. They were waiting."

Jack and his friends, most likely. Dan wondered how much the colonel knew about his connections with those rebel scouts.

Osborne continued. "Last Wednesday, just as our detail headed into the woods, dismounted rebels sprang out of concealment from behind the palmetto bushes. At the same moment another party appeared in front of our men, completely hemming them in. They commenced firing and yelling for our men to surrender. The rebels mortally wounded Lieutenant Walker, killed another man outright and carried off half the soldiers in the detail."

"Regrettable," Dan murmured.

"It was that swamp fox, Captain Dickison, causing us trouble again." Colonel Osborn leaned forward in his chair. "I understand you have a brother under his command."

There it was. Dan leveled his gaze at Osborn. "Yes, sir. Unfortunately, that is true. Jack is as staunch a rebel as I am a Union man."

"I've met your father."

"A true loyalist," Dan said.

Osborn nodded. "Indeed."

"Sir, I learned a few things while I worked with the refugees on the west coast." He paused, recalling their starving, ragtag condition. "From what I saw, most of them weren't interested in politics or taking sides. A few are loyal Unionists and want to help our cause. Others are fed up with seeing their crops and cattle confiscated by the Confederate commissary or else they hold grudges against the rebel authorities. Whether animated by principle, poverty or revenge, they are willing to fight."

"I haven't seen that sort of passion around here," Osborn said. "Most of the men that have come in are just tired of war and don't want any part of it."

Dan figured it was not the right time to share his theories about why the navy enjoyed more success in organizing Unionists against the Confederacy. He had observed the navy officers offered help and protection to the refugees and did not confiscate their animals or crops. Instead, they traded flour, coffee and guns for the fresh beef, sweet potatoes and oranges the refugees could provide. The alliance proved beneficial to both.

In this part of the state, sympathies seemed to work in the opposite direction. The rebels protected country people from Union raids on their livelihood. Officers like Prescott, who harassed civilians, had soured many of them against the Union army.

"I'd like a chance to turn that around," Dan said.

"After you organize the men in town, take a boat to our base at Fernandina to see what good you can do there," Osborn said. "If you want to venture outside our fortifications, however, you must do so at your own risk." He hesitated. "At least until we have enough men to secure east Florida. There's talk of a substantial east Florida expedition. So far, just politician talk." Colonel Osborn smirked. "I expect we'll be informed after it happens."

*

Dan took a bite from one of the sweet, crisp ginger cookies his stepmother had offered. While he munched he listened to his father's enthusiastic account of the last meeting of the East Florida Unionists.

"Just two weeks ago, Judge Stickney made an announcement that General Gilmore is planning to retake Jacksonville and secure the river." Pop sipped lemonade from his glass. "Once the land along the river is free of rebels, I can return to the farm and see to our interests there. My oranges are most likely rotting on the ground."

"Unless the rebs are eating them. Have you heard from Jack?"

"Not a word."

"You must be a grandfather by now."

"If all went well."

"I finally met my sister-in-law. When I was a prisoner I stayed overnight near Palatka. I can see why you like her." Dan hesitated, then said, "Perhaps you ought to take a more charitable view of Jack. He believes he's doing what he has to do. He has a strong sense of honor and no reason to love our side."

Pop bristled. "He's still wrong."

Right or wrong, he's our blood. Dan turned to a safer subject. "Such an occupation should have an excellent effect on our recruiting efforts, if they make it permanent. Union forces have taken Jacksonville three times so far and abandoned it as many. What are the chances they'll stay this time?"

"With enough troops, the army can occupy the whole area, and with enough gunboats, the navy can protect the riverbanks."

Dan nodded. "If people feel safe, if the rebels can't intimidate them, they might be more willing to declare for the Union."

"We're going to have a convention of delegates in March, right here in St. Augustine. Then we will nullify the rebellion and work to bring Florida back into the Union." Pop sat back and jabbed a thumb toward his chest. "You're looking at one of the delegates."

"Congratulations."

"Once ten percent of the people on the 1860 census declare for the Union, Florida will be readmitted."

"I'll do my part. I still intend to raise a company of Unionists and ex-rebels from our old neighborhood." Dan leaned forward, letting his excitement show. "Colonel Osborne has a few men ready and is willing to let me form a company. Tomorrow I'll get started with them."

"I know a few of those fellows," Pop said. "Let's hope they don't change sides as easily as they change clothes."

*

Dan looked up from the roster at the next recruit, a stranger to him, as were most of the new men. "Jed Tatum?"

"Present, sir." The fellow was thin and leathery as a whip. The blue uniform fit loosely on his spare frame, but his erect bearing gave the impression of military training.

"Says here you're a cattleman."

"Yessir, cows and timber."

"Where are you from, St. Johns County?"

"No, sir. Volusia, down south."

"I understand you left the Confederate Army rather abruptly."

Tatum's light eyes narrowed. "Yessir. Right quick, I did."

"Sit down. Let's talk. I want you to speak freely."

Tatum let himself down onto the campstool and returned Dan's hard scrutiny, a touch of defiance in his expression. Dan read fierce backwoods pride in his face. He recalled his father's suspicion of treachery, as well as Jack's derision about the sort of man who would trade sides.

Dan leaned forward and locked eyes with the man. "Why did you volunteer to fight on the Union side now?"

Tatum's folded his arms across his chest. "I was a good soldier. Good as any."

"What happened to change your mind?"

"I joined up in Captain Graham's cavalry company. He's a fair man, a neighbor man, and we didn't have no trouble. Then he got promoted. He's a major now. Got a new captain. We didn't get along so good."

"It happens," Dan allowed. *Bad officer, or troublesome soldier?*

"I got word my wife was real sick, and had to go see about her. The captain said no, I had to stay in camp. I told him it warn't nothin' but ten miles to my house, but he wouldn't even let me take a day's leave. I went home anyhow."

Dan watched his face, which hardened from leather to stone.

"I took care of things at home, and when my woman got better, I went back to camp. I figured I didn't do no harm. The captain figured different."

"He disciplined you?"

"You might say that, *sir*." Tatum bit off the words. "Bastard made me stand guard in the rain for a day and a half wearin' a sign."

"What sign?"

"Coward. He made me wear a sign sayin' I was a coward for desertin'. A coward! I wasn't out to desert. I came back. I was willing to do my duty. Didn't make no difference to him. Soon as I got a chance I took off for good and never looked back. I get the bastard in my sights, I'll show him who's a coward."

Dan sat back in the chair. Was this the sort of soldier who would back-shoot him if he got on his wrong side? "The Union Army enforces military discipline, too. If you take French leave, you'll face the consequences."

"Nobody calls Jed Tatum a coward."

"Nobody will." Dan tapped his fingers on the desk. Ten recruits. If he turned this one down, he would only have nine left. "You understand, Tatum, you have to follow orders at all times."

"Yes, sir. I told you I was a good soldier."

"Where's your family now."

"I couldn't stay at our place. The captain had men out looking for me, so we came to the Union lines. Left behind my house, my cows, my crops. The wife and little 'uns are here in town."

One excuse for desertion gone, at least, if the family was close by.

"Can't get no work, and I don't mind fightin'."

"Even your old neighbors?"

"They're taking my cows and my crops. To hell with them."

Dan dismissed Tatum, his last interview and looked down at the names composing his microscopic troop. A couple of the men were misplaced Northerners, trapped in Florida after secession, who seemed earnest enough. A few others swore up and down they always were Unionists, never wanted any part of this sorry Confederacy, no sir. A couple, like Tatum, nursed grievances and seemed to think the Union army would help them even the score.

He had to admit some of the fellows did not look promising, but he hoped they could shoot straight, at least.

CHAPTER ELEVEN

Dan hurried to the Colonel Osborn's office in response to a summons from the garrison commander. Captain Gibson, an officer with the 24th Massachusetts, glanced up from his seat across from the colonel's desk. He nodded when Dan entered the room.

After the formal exchange of pleasantries, Dan took a seat at the colonel's invitation in front of a county map spread over the desk. Osborn launched into his purpose for the meeting. "Captain Farrell, how are your men coming along in their training?"

"Sir, I am honored to report my volunteers are progressing nicely. Most of them grew up knowing firearms, and all of them are good riders. In addition to the army horses available, we've rounded up some of the better-looking marsh ponies that roam about loose. We've succeeded in accustoming them to halter and should soon have them saddle broken. In the future we should have plenty of mounts."

The colonel raised an eyebrow. "Are those wild horses strong enough for cavalry service? They aren't very big."

"They're used to living off the land and hardier than the Northern horses, sir. The rebels seem to get around on them pretty well."

Gibson snickered, but Dan favored him with a tolerant smile. He had ridden those ponies throughout his youth and knew them to be intelligent and sound.

"I'll concede that point," Osborn said. "Aren't some of your volunteers reliable local men who know the area?"

"About half, sir. The rest are from Volusia and Duval counties."

"I'm going to give your men a chance for experience outside the picket lines. We need better protection for our woodcutters. We're sending out a reconnaissance in force, led by Captain Gibson, and I've decided to send you and your men along as guides."

Dan hid his rising enthusiasm. "I believe we can be most helpful, sir."

"We've received reports from some of the loyal people passing through the lines that the rebel cavalry has been on the prowl again just outside our perimeter," the colonel continued. "We don't wish to suffer another attack like we did a few weeks ago."

Osborn pushed the map closer to the two captains. Dan recognized the tracings of roads between St. Augustine, Jacksonville, Picolata, Tocoi and Palatka. "We don't know exactly where the rebels are concentrated, if indeed they are," Osborn continued. "I suspect there's a post right here." He pointed to a spot on the Picolata road, just west of St. Augustine. "Other posts are undoubtedly located along the roads. We want to clean them out and keep them cleaned out."

Dan studied the map. *Jack might be manning one of those posts.*

The colonel turned to Gibson. "Pick fifty men from your company, mount them, and ride out first thing in the morning ahead of the firewood crew to take on the rebels."

Gibson nodded. "Yes, sir. I am honored you selected me for the mission. I'll get right on it." He looked thoughtful, as though mentally calculating what he must do to meet the assignment.

"Captain Farrell, you will make arrangements with Captain Gibson to join forces."

"I am honored as well, sir." Dan glanced at Gibson. "I believe my personal experiences when I was a prisoner of war will be helpful. On the way to the railhead, I got a pretty good tour. I also learned a great deal about how this particular command operates."

"Like guerrillas," Gibson said.

"They fight that way, but they are regular enlisted soldiers."

"You give them too much credit." Gibson frowned. "Mostly they hide in the scrub and take pot shots at us. That ambush on our woodcutters last month was a nasty trick."

"Maybe so, but I've learned to respect Dickison's men." Dan quirked a smile. "They use the land to their benefit and ride circles around us on those scrub ponies. I have some ideas about how to combat them."

"I'm listening," Gibson said.

"I agree they'll likely have an outpost on the road past our own pickets, near the place where it forks beyond the San Sebastian bridge. As close as they can get without being exposed by the area we've cleared of trees and brush. If we dash in and rush them, with luck we can surprise them and trap the lot. They won't be able to warn the main force or set up one of their pernicious ambushes."

The colonel nodded. "That sounds practicable."

"They cross the St. Johns on flat boats upriver, near Palatka, where the river narrows." Dan pointed to the location on the map. "If we can keep them from recrossing and trap them on this side of the river, they can't get back to their base or lose themselves in the interior of the state. Given enough men, we could carry that out."

"In time, when our troop strength increases. At present, our priority is keeping the enemy from attacking our work crews." Colonel Osborn regarded Dan with a long look. "I understand you know some of those rebels pretty well."

"Yes, sir, that's no secret. I'd give years of my life to capture my brother alive."

*

The predawn watch was the coldest. Heavy fog obscured Jack's view, and the dampness penetrated the chill all the way into his bones. Dew collected and drizzled off the trees, plopping onto his hat and running off the brim in a slow drip down his back. He shivered inside his greatcoat and watched the road for signs of approaching enemies.

Choctaw snoozed under the saddle, and Jack wanted to nod off as well. He reached into his haversack and pulled out a hunk of venison saved from last night's supper. He gnawed on the stringy meat, hoping it would help him stay awake.

The sky had started to lighten, which gave him hope Russell would emerge from their campsite soon to relieve him. Already he smelled wood smoke from a rebuilt campfire, and the savory aroma of frying bacon tantalized his senses.

For the past few months, outpost duty had bored him with its predictable routine. Low enemy activity in northeast Florida had resulted in a standoff of sorts. Few gunboats ventured upriver from the mouth of the St. Johns, and the Yankees occupying the town had stayed within their own picket lines most of the time. Last month's skirmish with a crew of woodcutters and their guards was the only real action he had seen since his capture of Dan. Jack didn't mind the boredom. He could do without the excitement of trading bullets with the enemy

At present, the bulk of Dickison's troop was about seventy miles away, escorting a blockade-runner's shipment from Mosquito Inlet. Carlo had gone with them in connection with his courier duties. Jack's picket post was one of the few pickets left in the area to keep an eye on the enemy.

Last time he saw Martina, he had warned her of unsettling rumors about a planned Yankee offensive. She agreed to pack and flee to Waldo if gunboats threatened Palatka. He could only hope she was able to do that with their little one to protect. Neither of them wanted the baby exposed to the winter cold throughout a day's wagon ride.

Thoughts of Martina and Rosa warmed him. Whenever he found the little one awake she turned on that radiant smile, made soft noises as though trying to speak, and reached her small fist to clasp his finger in a gesture of pure trust. Although she was named for Martina's mother, the baby's lighter hair and blue eyes reflected his heritage. He vowed to do right by her. She would never know the sting of a razor strop or the pain of rejection he had endured. He was not like his father and was prepared to spoil her shamelessly.

Another rumor held that Dan had returned to St. Augustine. Jack hoped it was untrue. He dreaded another wartime encounter with his brother.

An indistinct sound in the distance jerked him out of his reverie. Hoof beats, muffled on the sandy road and cloaked by the fog? He stopped chewing and attended to the sounds.

Something moved in the direction of the bridge. Another woodcutting crew? He slapped Choctaw's neck to awaken him and studied the movement. Men and horses materialized out of the fog, headed straight toward him.

He drew his revolver and squeezed off a shot into the air. Then he turned Choctaw and dug his heels into the horse's sides to speed him into a hasty retreat.

*

Dan knew the gun's report meant the rebel picket had spotted them and had fired off a warning shot to alert others.

Better mounted this time, he led the charge past the line of trees and scrub into the rebel picket camp just in time to see two men on horseback rush away. Some of his men fired at them, but he doubted they could hit much from the back of a galloping horse.

He spotted another horse nearby, tethered to a line, and veered into the camp clearing, revolver in hand. "Circle around and take that horse!" Dan yelled to the nearest soldier. He saw the head of a man on the other side of the animal. The rebel pulled the rope free and was preparing to mount.

Dan leveled his weapon and yelled, "Surrender, or I'll shoot!"

By that time the other Union trooper had cut off the rebel's escape. The fugitive looked around, realized his hopeless situation, and lifted his hands in defeat.

"Hold your fire," Dan yelled at Tatum, who had the surrendering Confederate in his sights. The hatless prisoner's dark hair dashed Dan's hopes he had caught Jack. Dan ordered Tatum to guard the prisoner and sped away in hopes of adding to his collection. He caught up with the patrol only to find they had given up the chase.

"They hightailed it into the woods," Gibson said.

"Which way?" Dan asked.

"Right about there." The other officer pointed to a trail, obscure in the predawn light, which led from the road. "We'll never catch them in that stuff. All they have to do is turn around and wait for us to ride through singly, then pick off the hindmost."

"I hate to admit you're right." Dan stared at the trail. "They'll ruin any chance for more surprises. I did capture one of the Johnnies, though. I'll take a couple of men back with me, look over their camp, and send our prisoner back to town."

*

Assured the woods-hating Yankees had given up the chase, Jack reined in at a timbered-out patch and turned to face the two men who had joined him after their wild skedaddle. "Where's Ramon?"

"He wasn't with us when you fired the shot. I think he was off gathering wood or something." Russell turned in the saddle to look behind. "I thought I saw him running into camp just as I was mounting my horse. His was still fastened to the line."

Ramon was the careful one. He always took care their little squad had a man on lookout. He made sure his weapons and everyone else's were clean, oiled, rust-free, and ready for use. He also insisted they feed and saddle their horses first thing in the morning, before they settled down at their cook fire. That readiness had saved Russell and Charlie.

"Think they got him?" Charlie asked.

Jack recalled the burst of gunfire as he fled, and his gut clenched. "Either he'll turn up, or he won't."

"They were shooting at us," Charlie said. "I didn't hear any more after we got away. I hope he didn't get shot."

"I left my blankets and breakfast back there." Russell stroked his blowing horse's neck. "I didn't cook that bacon for the Yanks to eat it."

"What do we do now?" Charlie asked.

Jack realized the two of them were looking to him for leadership in Ramon's absence. "We have to let the other pickets know what's going on. Russell, you alert the next outpost that the Yanks are on the move with a good-sized mounted force." He collected his thoughts, realizing too few soldiers were left in the area to provide much resistance. "Tell them a hundred or so, maybe more, are headed toward the river. Charlie and I will keep an eye on them."

"And look for Ramon?" Charlie asked.

"If Ramon escaped, he can take care of himself, and he'll turn up. If they captured him, he's probably halfway to St. Augustine by now. Two men can't do much about rescuing him from that crowd." Jack refused to dwell upon the worst possibilities for Ramon.

*

"Ramon Andreu." Dan studied his prisoner, who sat on a rolled-up blanket next to the dying campfire, between two guards. A spider pan contained a few lumps of cooked bacon amid a puddle of congealed grease, an interrupted meal. The Confederate corporal did not seem to be interested in finishing his breakfast. He lifted his downcast face and a flash of recognition registered in his dark eyes.

Dan told the guards to search the camp for anything of interest and squatted level with Ramon. "I'm glad you decided to surrender when you did. I would have hated to shoot an almost-relative."

Ramon might have allowed a smile if he weren't so busy frowning. "That sounds like something your brother would say."

"Was he one of the fellows with you?"

"He warned us, but I was too far from camp. I should have given up the horse and run the other way instead." His frown deepened. He ran his fingers through his damp hair. "I need to find my hat."

"What were you doing away from your camp?"

Ramon straightened his shoulders. "None of your business."

"Never mind. It isn't important. How many more of your cavalry are infesting the woods?"

"That, too, is none of your business, Farrell."

"The whole troop or just some scattered outposts?"

Ramon shrugged.

"How many men does Dickison have in his command now?"

"Enough."

"Is he still headquartered at Camp Call?"

"You wouldn't answer these questions." Ramon held his gaze. "Neither will I."

Ramon had made it clear he was not going to betray his comrades, unlike less judicious prisoners Dan had interviewed in the past. Most likely if he agreed to talk, he would lie like a politician to protect his friends. Dan lowered his voice. "How is Jack doing?"

"Ornery as ever."

"What about Martina? Don't they have a child by now?"

Ramon nodded. "They named her Rosa. They are doing fine. My wife and daughter are staying with them."

"At that same house in Palatka?"

"As long as we think it's a safe place for them."

Dan nodded and stood. At least he knew Dickison's headquarters were still near Palatka, at Camp Call. To his men he said, "Have the prisoner ride with you back to St. Augustine and turn him over to the provost. Let him look for his hat first." He grinned. "Be sure to hold onto his reins so he can't get away."

*

A northward march up the Jacksonville road located an abandoned camp, the fire still warm. From there, Dan's patrol turned and headed back south toward Palatka, then east to the King's Road to complete their sweep of the perimeter.

That afternoon, although the vedettes reported spotting glimpses of rebel scouts along the way, the long circuit brought neither ambush nor any more captures.

"I wonder where all those Johnnies went," the Captain Gibson mused. "From what the colonel said, I thought we would've engaged the lot of them by now. His informants were either mistaken or lying."

"I'm confident the colonel's report was true enough. Rebel scouts are always on the prowl in these woods." Dan glanced behind him, reassuring himself that the columns of blue coats had not been swallowed up by elusive gray riders.

"All our fishing expedition has caught us so far is one rebel corporal." Gibson waved his hand. "Small fry. I'm beginning to think this Dickison fellow has us fooled into thinking he's more of a threat than he really is. A little man casting a big shadow."

"Maybe the rebels don't want to take us on, if there are only a few in the area right now. Could be the main force is elsewhere." Dan judged Gibson was getting a little too cocky, just as he was right before he got captured. "Dickison will want to show up on his own terms."

"In any case, we're wasting our time. I'm ready to head back toward St. Augustine, since we haven't intercepted the mythical Confederate cavalry. We'll hang around the work detail and make sure no bogey men surprise them."

Dan nodded. "They ought to be about ready to call it a day and come in, too. We should consider our mission a success. We routed the rebel pickets, captured a valuable prisoner, and screened the woodcutters. All at the expense of a few saddle sores." One more thing remained on his list. "I want to pay a visit on a family of my acquaintance. I'll take a few men with me. Perhaps I can learn something of interest from them."

*

Sarah Cates stepped onto the porch, crossed her arms, and regarded the squad of Yankee cavalry that surrounded her house. Then she let her cool gaze rest on Dan Farrell, who stood right in front of her. His smile and doffed hat contradicted the unspoken threat implied by his blue coat and the presence of his men.

"We meet again, Mrs. Phillips." His eyes, the same color as his uniform, sparkled. "You are a lovely vision to behold. May I call you Miss Sarah?"

"You may." She felt her face warm and hoped he did not notice. Out of deep mourning, she had shed the widow's weeds though not the sadness. The muted green dress she wore was more flattering, though her clothes were far from new. She hoped he did not notice that, either. She would have chewed off her arm before admitting her reduced circumstances to this man. "How you go on, Captain Farrell."

His smile widened. "I wouldn't lie to you."

She would have gnawed off her remaining arm before telling Dan she enjoyed the flattery. "Of course not." She shot another glance at the other soldiers, who appeared to be content to sit on their horses, stare at her, chew and spit. "I heard you were back in St. Augustine."

Interest flickered in his eyes. "Who told you that?"

"I thought it was just a rumor." She shrugged to show it mattered not who smuggled tales from behind the lines. "Frankly, I'm surprised you came back for more. Last time I saw you, I seem to recall you were in quite a fix."

"Not for long. I didn't fancy the idea of prison."

She allowed a paltry smile. "I heard you got away from your

guards."

"As soon as I could." Dan lifted an eyebrow. "And I don't intend to repeat the experience. How have you been doing?"

"Haven't seen much of the Yankees lately. Not until now." She stole another appraising look at the column of soldiers with him. "So we've been doing pretty well. To what do I owe the pleasure of a visit from my Yankee friends?"

"I was riding around in the neighborhood and decided to drop by. I didn't mean to make you so nervous."

"Is that so?" She sighed. "Then why did you bring all these soldiers to our house? I hope they don't plan to help themselves at our expense."

"Of course not." He shook his head. "I haven't ever done that, have I? As I recall, you did offer me a glass of milk, which I was grateful to accept."

"Is that why you came? Would you like some milk?"

He laughed. "I don't want to impose on your hospitality. Where's your father?"

She shrugged. "I really don't know."

"What about Russell?" Dan looked past her to the front door.

She gave him a dazzling smile. "Russell isn't here, so he can't come out and play right now."

"Is your mother still pretending to be sick to keep me outside? Are you sure Russell isn't hiding somewhere in your house?"

"Haven't seen him in a while."

"How about Jack. Where is he?"

"Chasing Yankees, I presume."

"Seems it's the other way around." Dan's friendly demeanor shifted, and he turned serious. "We gave him and some of his friends a bad start this morning."

He had mentioned not knowing where Russell and Jack were, so she assumed they were safe. She tried to keep the mood light. "If you intend to inquire about Jack's health, last time I saw him he was bragging about his baby daughter. Says she's the prettiest thing he ever saw. Next to his wife, of course. Doesn't that make you an uncle?"

"That's good news. I already heard about it from Ramon Andreu."

Grasping what he had just said, she tried to keep her voice level. "When did you talk to Ramon?"

"This morning, right after I took him prisoner."

*

Dan watched her face register shock as her hand flew to her mouth. "Poor Ramon," she breathed.

He would love to stand on the porch and spar with this quick-witted woman all day, but his words had put an end to that. The light flirtation over, he must attend to business. It did not give him pleasure to deliver upsetting news to Sarah, but he needed to make a point. She certainly would pass it on to the other Confederate soldiers, including her brother and his.

He realized she was struggling to hide her distress at her friend's plight and tried to reassure her. "We didn't harm him. My men took him to St. Augustine."

"What will you do to him? Where will you send him?"

"He has some control over his fate. If he remains unrepentant, he will go to a prison up north. If he agrees to give up the fight, take the loyalty oath and stay within our lines, I'll see if we can parole him. He told me his wife and child are living in Palatka with Martina. I presume you can get word to them sooner than I can."

Still visibly shaken, she took a deep breath and nodded, face tight with controlled emotion. He wanted to take her hand and console her, but figured she would throw his effort to sympathize right back in his face. "I'll write to her and tell her what happened to him." Her voice was subdued.

"Tell your friends on the other side, the offer I made last year still stands. Confederate soldiers who lay down their arms and take the oath will receive amnesty and won't be forced to fight their old comrades. Or else we continue to make war on them. It's their choice."

"You want me to do your job for you?" she snapped.

"I'm trying desperately to avoid bloodshed."

"Then leave us alone! Why can't you people just leave us alone?" Gone was any effort to hide her anguish.

Dan took a step toward her, then thought better of it. The wall between them was almost a physical force, and circumstances had hardened it. Surely more words would bounce off like raindrops splattering on a hot tin roof.

He put on his hat, nodded, then turned and walked away.

CHAPTER TWELVE

Sarah waited until the Union troops had disappeared down the road before she stepped off the porch. She heard the front door open and close behind her. Mama hurried after her, calling her name, but Sarah ignored her as she headed around the back of the house to the paddock.

The older woman caught up with her just as she reached the gate. "Sarah! Where are you going?"

"I've got to find Russell and Jack and tell them what's going on," Sarah threw the words over her shoulder.

"You shouldn't go off into the woods alone. It's almost dark. Wait for your father, and let him do it. Or at least wait until morning."

"Don't you think they need to know now? Besides, it's more dangerous for Papa," Sarah lifted the latch, slipped into the pasture, and shut the gate behind her. Resting her hand on the top rail, she turned to face her mother. "The Yankees are less likely to arrest a woman."

She walked toward her cow pony, Stripe, not waiting for the older woman to come up with another argument. The animal, probably expecting petting or a treat, obliged Sarah by walking up and nuzzling her shoulder. "Atta boy," Sarah whispered as she grasped the pony's halter. She gave its white-blazed muzzle a perfunctory stroke and led the animal back toward the gate.

Her mother frowned and moved aside as Sarah led Stripe from the pen. "This is foolishness."

"I'm a grown woman, Mama. I'll do as I please."

Sarah shifted her gaze to the road beyond. *More riders*. She shaded her eyes with her hand. When she recognized the Confederates, she let out her breath in relief and waved at the men.

Jack, Charlie and Russell rode to where she stood holding Stripe's halter.

"Thank God you're here," Mama looked flushed and bothered, and Sarah supposed her anxiety showed as well. "Sarah was going to chase off and find y'all. I told her it was too dangerous, to wait for Henry to go instead, but she wouldn't listen to me."

"What's the matter, Mama?" Russell jumped off his horse, and two strides brought him to their mother's side. "What did the Yankees do?"

"Nothing," Sarah broke in. "Dan was here." She glanced at Jack to gauge his reaction. "He said they captured Ramon and sent him to town."

Jack exchanged a glance with Charlie. "It's true, then. Bad and worse." Both of them looked grim.

"I rode around to the other posts to warn them they were about to get overrun," Russell said. "We couldn't get up enough men to whip them."

"What did Dan say?" Jack asked. "Is he still trying to recruit homegrown Yankees? Like him?"

Jack listened in silence while she related her conversation with Dan. "He didn't threaten me in any way. Your brother may be a Unionist scoundrel, but at least he's a gentleman."

"That's one thing in his favor," Jack allowed.

Sarah recalled how much she found herself liking Jack's Yankee brother, against her will, until he delivered the news about Ramon. "He wasn't mean about it," she said. "He wasn't bragging, exactly. He asked me to get word to his wife. Jack, can you make sure she gets the message?"

"Yeah." Jack closed his eyes and let out his breath. "Somebody has to."

"It isn't the worst thing that could have happened," Sarah said. "He said they didn't shoot him. Do you think he can get away?"

Jack shrugged. "Dan escaped. Maybe Ramon can, too."

*

The next morning, Dan paid a visit to Ramon at Fort Marion. The jail reminded Dan of a dungeon, with its cold, gray coquina walls and dim, windowless interior. Ramon was the lone prisoner in his cell. He did not rate special treatment but was segregated from the Union soldiers facing discipline as well as the few civilians being held for spying or civil crimes.

Dan dismissed the guard who had escorted him to Ramon. The rebel corporal, sitting with a blanket wrapped around him, rose from his cot when he spotted Dan. From behind the bars Ramon looked beyond Dan, as though expecting more company.

"How are the guards treating you, Ramon?" Dan asked.

Ramon's gaze returned to Dan's face. "They haven't shot me, yet. But I can't say much in favor of the rations." His shoulders lifted in a resigned shrug. "Did you catch any of my friends?"

Dan shook his head. "Not this time. We'll get around to them in good time."

Ramon cracked a smile. "Might be harder than you think."

"You know as well as I do, you can't win this war."

"Dickison's command hasn't lost a fight yet. We've whipped you every time."

"Not yesterday."

"A few lonely pickets against a whole company," Ramon huffed. "I'm your only trophy."

"Once the rest of the Confederacy falls, Florida will as well. If things go right, Florida will be readmitted to the Union before that happens. You ought to think about yourself. And your family." Dan paused. "Your wife and daughter. How will they fare after we ship you north to a prison camp?"

Ramon's jaw tightened. "Did you come here to taunt me, *Captain* Farrell?"

"I wouldn't do that. I came to make you a better offer."

Ramon didn't say anything.

"Don't you have a homestead and an orange grove just north of town?"

Ramon nodded. "I had to move my family out after your boys in blue took over St. Augustine. The place has been behind your lines ever since." He shook his head in bitter resignation. "I have no idea what's happened to it."

"I talked to Colonel Osborn. He's willing to let you live there with your family if you meet certain conditions."

"Like the ones on that handbill you put out?" Ramon snorted. "Do you expect me to switch sides?"

"Not at all. You'll be on parole. You will have to take the loyalty oath, of course. You can live unmolested inside our lines, but you won't be free to go beyond our picket posts. If you want to return to your home, that's fine, because it's on occupied land. I'll do everything in my power to bring Teresa and your little girl home to you. Nobody will force you to serve in the Union Army, though you could be offered work for wages. You'll be under our protection, so the Confederates won't be able to get to you in case they accuse you of desertion."

Ramon closed his eyes and rubbed his temple.

"Or else we'll send you north on the next ship out of here. You'll be taken to a prison, maybe in New York or Ohio. I've been up north in January. The rivers freeze and winter lasts what seems like a lifetime. So will the war, in my estimation."

Ramon's eyelids slid open, his expression bleak. "Farrell, I already surrendered, but you're still holding a gun to my head."

"I think it's a generous offer." Dan let out his breath. "Ramon, I'm trying to help you out of a tight spot. I believe you're a man of honor and you will keep your word. I took your part with the colonel. He's skeptical, because he believes Dickison's men are a little more pernicious than the average rebel in the ranks."

"How long will I have to think about it?"

"Until the next ship leaves the bay. Either you'll be on it, or you get to go home."

*

Never before had Jack dreaded coming home to his wife. The sergeant in charge of the outposts had assigned him the duty of reporting the latest events to headquarters at Camp Call. He steeled himself to deliver the news of Ramon's capture to Martina and Teresa, whose delicate condition made her especially vulnerable. Knowing for sure Dan was back in St. Augustine, again working against his side, did not help his mood.

As was his custom, he stopped at the house on the way to headquarters. He hitched Choctaw to the porch rail and gave the capering Nip an absent-minded pat. This time he was on his own hook. No sergeant was present to rush him to camp, so he could tarry with Martina for a little while or take the cowardly way out and retreat.

The door opened and Martina stepped out, carrying Rosa. The pink, chubby face, framed with wispy hair, was all that showed of the blanket-wrapped baby. Ana burst past her onto the porch. The little girl looked around. "Where's Papa?" she asked.

It had never occurred to Jack that he would break the upsetting news to the child. "Let's all go inside."

He exchanged a look with Martina. "How is everyone?"

She nodded. "Rosa and I are fine. What's the matter?"

Was he that transparent? He did not answer right away. He put his arms around her, encompassing his daughter as well, and gave his wife a lingering kiss. Then he guided Martina to the door and followed her into the house. Ana rushed past him to her mother. Teresa, seated on the couch, did not rise, but gave Jack a wan smile. At the sight of her inquiring expression he cringed inside. He removed his hat and nodded to her.

"Jack, did Ramon come with you?" Teresa asked as she gathered Ana onto her nonexistent lap.

He shook his head, unable to think of whatever he had planned to say. "He isn't killed or wounded or anything like that."

The women pinned him with startled looks. Martina repeated, "What's the matter? Jack? What happened?"

I'm no good at this. He took a deep breath and started over. "Ramon was captured. They took him to St. Augustine."

Teresa's face drained of color. She crossed herself. "Mother Mary have mercy on us." She hugged Ana, who looked confused and stared at Jack, her brown eyes wide and thunderstruck.

"I don't think they have any reason to harm him." Jack glanced at Martina for support, but the dazed look on her face did not encourage him. He told them what happened. "My brother, Dan is back. He's the one who caught him."

"Ramon will go to prison?" Teresa's voice had gone husky.

"Can we do anything for him?" Martina asked. Rosa started making fretful noises, and Martina patted the baby's back.

Jack knew the impossibility of invading the federally occupied town. "They've got him. That's all there is to it."

"I need to see him." Teresa blinked rapidly, then ran her hand over her eyes. "I need to go to St. Augustine. Jack, will the Yankees let me talk to him?"

"I don't know." Nor did he know if Dan could help her, or if he would.

"But Teresa, you haven't been well." Martina said. "The chills and fever – "

"If it were Jack, you'd run there as fast as you could." Teresa shifted her attention back to him. "Will you let me use the wagon and Ladybug?"

"Of course. But if Martina doesn't think you're up to it...." He took a deep breath to give himself thinking space. "I won't let you go by yourself. I'll be headed back in that direction tomorrow morning. I can't take you as far as the Yankee picket posts, but I can ask the Cates family to try to get you inside town." He tried not to show his panic at the idea of escorting the heavily pregnant woman through an all-day trip, including a river crossing. "You aren't going to have that baby anytime soon, are you?"

Teresa offered a teary smile. "I wouldn't do that to you, Jack."

*

Martina fixed supper while Ana entertained herself with her slate and Rosa napped in her crib. Teresa covered herself with blankets and huddled by the fire, a shivering lump. She had been sick off and on for the past week. At first they attributed her illness to her advanced pregnancy, but finally decided an outbreak of malaria had caused the fevers.

Like most Floridians, Martina and Teresa usually kept a supply of quinine for such emergencies, but they had run out a week ago. The blockade made the medicine difficult to find, and no civilian doctors remained in Palatka. Martina had asked Jack to try to locate a supply while he was at camp.

Finally Jack returned. To her surprise, Carlo came with him, looking worn out after a long ride from the Ocklawaha River region. "They sent me ahead to the telegraph office with a dispatch." Carlo collapsed into a chair. "We have new orders, too. Some of the boys are going down south to help the Cow Cavalry keep the Yanks from rustling our beef."

"Cow Cavalry?" Martina quirked a smile. "What in the world…?"

"They drive the herds north to feed the armies and guard the trail drives along the way," Jack said. "Deserter bands, just the kind of white trash Dan wants to recruit, have been raiding the herds. We need to bust them up and stop the thieving."

"Will you and Carlo have to go?" Martina asked.

"I'm staying at headquarters this time." Carlo shot a meaningful glance at Jack.

Jack laid a bag of cornmeal, a sack of potatoes, a slab of bacon and a small packet on the table. "I got hold of a little quinine. Don't know if it's enough to do any good."

"I knew you could get us some. Any quinine is better than none." Martina slipped into the shelter of Jack's arms. He smelled of wood smoke and horse. "I'm so thankful you're here, even if it's just overnight."

He cast a worried look at Teresa, then settled his gaze on Martina's face and took her hand. "We need to talk." With another glance at the pregnant woman, he led Martina to their bedroom and shut the door. "Is Teresa still set on making the trip?" he asked in a low voice. "She's looking poorly. If something happens to her along the way –"

"I told her she was too sick to go, and you ought to refuse to take her. At first she said if you wouldn't help she would drive the wagon herself. But now she's having another spell of fever. I reminded her how cold it is outside and how close she is to having the baby. She's weak enough to admit she'd better stay in bed."

"Yeah, she needs to stay in bed."

The relief on Jack's face made her smile. "You'd rather face a whole regiment of Yankees."

He drew her to him, grinning. "You know me too well."

Martina gave him a kiss. "I'd better fix her a dose of that quinine now. Then we can eat supper."

"There's something else," Jack said. "The captain ordered me to Fort Meade with the rest."

"They aren't leaving you at your usual post across the river?"

He shook his head. "Not if we're going in force. He wants the experienced sharpshooters. I have to round up our boys over there and give them the word. I'll come back to camp, then we'll be on our way."

Her heart sank. "How long will you be gone?"

He shook his head again. "As long as it takes, I reckon."

The next morning, Teresa showed little improvement despite taking the bitter drug. She wept quietly and refused to eat her breakfast, leaving the cornbread, marmalade and bacon untouched. "Ramon will think I don't care. He won't know why I can't go to him."

"The Yankees probably wouldn't let you into St. Augustine, anyway." Martina stroked Teresa's hot brow with a damp cloth. "He knows that. He knows you're in no condition to travel, too."

Teresa nodded without conviction. Martina suspected Ramon's plight had brought on this latest attack.

"It isn't the worst thing that could have happened. Ramon is alive and well. You will see him again." Martina had little hope her words would have much effect on Teresa's despair.

She heard Jack come in from the yard and looked up at him. He had buckled on his gun belt and held his hat in his hand. "You have to go now?"

He nodded, so she stood and walked outside with him, to where Choctaw cropped grass at the length of his tether, saddled and ready. "Lord, I hope you don't ever get sick like that. I don't want to leave you with all this going on." Jack rubbed his chin. "Carlo can stay with you until he has to go back to camp. He isn't going down south with the troop, so he'll still be close by. At least he has today to rest himself and his horse."

"I'm letting him sleep late." Martina looked toward the house. "Teresa took care of me when Rosa came. I'm doing that for her now." She hesitated, then took his hand. "Stay safe."

"It's been quiet, until that patrol jumped us," Jack said. "Dan made sure we know he's back in town. He talks to Russell's sister, Sarah, it seems, every chance he gets. I'll see if she can find out anything else about Ramon." He let out a low chuckle. "Appears Dan's taken a fancy to her."

Martina managed a smile.

"Tell you what," Jack said. "I'll ask Sarah to come stay with you and help you take care of Teresa and the young 'uns."

"Do you think she would? Please ask her." Sarah had visited from time to time over the past few months, and Martina had taken a liking to the forthright young widow.

He nodded. "I fed Ladybug and Carlo's horse and turned them out. What else do you need done before I go? I could spin it out a little longer."

"I want you to stay forever, but I don't want you to get in trouble over it."

"Darlin', I'm used to getting in one kind of trouble or another. Especially with you."

"Not anymore." Martina cupped his cheek in her hand. "I'm so glad I was able to see into your heart."

"Me, too." His voice was husky. He was better at showing his love for her and Rosa than talking about it. He drew her to him and she rested there, wanting to beg him to stay, knowing he could not.

*

Sarah held Stripe's reins and waited outside the San Sebastian bridge picket post. The Union sergeant on duty would not allow her into St. Augustine without a pass and had ordered her to come no farther until he got word to Captain Farrell that she wished to speak with him.

She had agreed to go to Palatka and help Martina with the ailing Teresa and the two little ones. She had packed and was prepared to join Jack when he swung through Moultrie on his way back to Palatka. In the meantime, perhaps she could find out something about Ramon's fate, or speak with him if the Yankee authorities allowed it. With difficulty she had persuaded the unhelpful guards to get a message to Dan and hoped he would be willing to see her.

Sarah spotted his approach, quick of step, a man in a hurry. She stroked Stripe's muzzle. "That didn't take long," she murmured into the horse's ear. Dan strode across the bridge. She locked eyes with him.

He acknowledged the pickets before he brushed past them, removed his hat and nodded into a slight bow, never taking his attention from her face. "This is truly an unexpected pleasure, Miss Sarah." His slow smile and easy drawl revealed less of his feelings than the lively interest in his blue eyes. She felt the old attraction and wanted to deny her heart's traitorous response to the sight of the homegrown Yankee officer.

"Thank you for coming out to speak with me." She glanced at the guards. "It's a pity I'm not allowed inside my own hometown."

"Ah, Miss Sarah. We both know loyalty is the remedy for that. Did you come to take the oath?"

"Loyalty cuts both ways, Captain Farrell. Not hardly."

"We're friends, aren't we? I wish you would call me Dan."

Sarah lifted a skeptical eyebrow. "As long as you're aiming to destroy my brother and my Confederate friends, I don't know how you expect that."

"A truce, then? Politics and our brothers' affiliations aside."

"A truce, with those considerations, *Dan.* I came to inquire about Ramon Andreu." She patted the saddlebag. "I'd like to see him and give him some things he'll be needing. Socks, a blanket and beef jerky."

Dan shook his head. "I'm sorry, but we can't allow you to visit him right now. I can assure you he's well. We're taking good care of him. If you give me those items I'll see that he gets them." His eyes flashed amusement. "Unless you're trying to smuggle in a weapon."

"So much for our truce. When will he be sent north to prison?"

"On the next boat, unless he agrees to the terms I explained to him, and to you as well."

"Oh, yes. Those terms."

"I can also give him a message from you, provided it's something we can approve."

Sarah did not wish to add to Ramon's burdens by telling him Teresa had taken a turn for the worse. He already knew the baby would be coming soon and that his wife was not having an easy pregnancy. Nor did she think Dan needed to know Sarah was headed to Palatka to assist her friends. "Just tell him I was here, tried to speak with him, and tell him his family knows of his situation."

"I can do that much."

She cocked her hip and planted her fist on it. "Good of you, *Dan*."

"I don't have anything against Ramon, personally. Or your brother. Or mine, for that matter. Their choices are honorably taken. But I disagree with those choices. I disagree strongly – "

"And violently," Sarah added.

"If I am left no other choice." He took on a serious tone. "I want them to lay down their arms and quit fighting the inevitable before they end up dead. I want to be friends with you. With Russell as well. I want Jack to be a brother to me again. I want to be able to ride freely wherever I wish and see whomever I wish without risking my life. I want all of us to reconcile our differences and become one people again."

"Only on your terms," Sarah pointed out. "If y'all would just let us go our own way, there wouldn't be any war, would there, now?"

Dan shook his head. "It's gone too far."

"We agree on that much, at least."

"That's not the sort of thing I wanted you to agree with me about. Nor is it the sort of progress I wanted to make with you." The slow smile returned.

Taken by surprise, Sarah swallowed hard. "Why, Dan, what sort of progress did you want to make?"

"I'd like to see more of you."

Recovering, she nodded toward the picket post. "Then let me come into town. Take me to see Ramon."

He ran his hand over the back of his neck and riffled his hair, releasing a cowlick. "Miss Sarah, perhaps I spoke too freely."

"Why Dan, you can come see me any time you wish." She chuckled. The man was so annoying, yet attractive, for an enemy. "As long as you bring along enough soldiers to keep our brothers from whipping you."

He shook his head, his smile returning. "You are a challenging woman, Miss Sarah."

"I'll take that as a compliment."

"Which is how it's intended."

*

The next day, Dan wrote a letter to Teresa Andreu confirming he would do whatever he could to help her come through the lines and join her husband in St. Augustine. He folded it inside a letter Ramon had written to her, stuffed an envelope and dripped candle wax on the flap to seal it.

His next problem was getting the news to Teresa. It was a shame Ramon's capitulation had taken place after Sarah's visit. She could have carried the news to Teresa, getting the word to Ramon's wife much more quickly. No doubt Sarah would accuse him of blackmailing her friend. He wanted another chance to see the peppery young widow, even though their conversations resembled fencing matches.

The colonel would not authorize a truce-flag delivery to the guerrillas, as he styled Dickison's men. Dan decided to send these copies of the letters through the normal postal channels. He had no idea how long it would take for the envelope to take its circuitous route from boat to an exchange city to find its way behind the rebel lines.

Dan hoped to find a quicker way to deliver the message and fulfill his promise to Ramon. His father had volunteered to take his chances with the rebels, ride to the Cates place and request that they pass it on. Dan told him the risk of capture was too great. He believed Dickison's threat that Pop would be arrested the moment his troopers found him in Confederate territory.

Dan doubted the colonel would authorize another patrol in the direction of Moultrie within the next day or so. He planned to take the next boat to Fernandina, where he could recruit more soldiers from among the Unionist refugees living there and at Mayport Mills. Swelling the ranks of his volunteer force of Florida men would surely damage rebel solidarity.

Another idea occurred to him. Civilians sometimes were permitted to pass through the lines to trade back and forth with the country people. That would be the fastest, safest avenue to deliver the message.

In any case, word would get to Ramon's wife sooner or later, and to the rebels as well. Dan sat back in his desk chair, rested his head against his threaded hands and smiled, imagining the effect the morale-busting news of Ramon's defection would have on Dickison's men, especially Jack.

He pictured his brother's dismay that a soldier close to him had decided to quit the Confederate cause and take the loyalty oath. Dan had stated the options so starkly to Ramon that the man had little choice. Convincing Colonel Osborn leniency was called for in this situation was more difficult. Dan's argument that granting Ramon a parole would help undermine the rebels' will to fight won in the end.

More good news floated on the wind. The expectation of a big invasion had intensified. Perhaps soon, troops would land in East Florida sufficient to occupy all the land between the coast and the St. Johns. Then he would have free rein to travel the neighborhood outside St. Augustine in relative safety. And visit the tantalizing Sarah.

CHAPTER THIRTEEN

Captain Richard Prescott surveyed the northern Florida coastline from the deck of the rolling transport ship. After two days on this tub, redolent with the potent stale-sweat odor of two companies of Negro soldiers packed tight, he longed for solid ground, fresh air, and an end to the queasiness that always plagued his stomach when aboard ship.

He took a final puff from his cigar, removed the chewed stub, and jabbed it toward his first lieutenant. "Owen, once we get off this rust bucket, I believe I shall kiss the sand in blessed relief. I never before thought I would feel that way about the land of traitors, snakes and alligators."

"Ship's captain said we might have a ways to go yet." Owen leaned against the rail, seemingly unconcerned with the pitch of the waves. Prescott envied the man his apparent immunity to seasickness. "Captain has to wait for high tide so the boats can clear the sand bar. Then we can steam across, up the St. Johns, and into Jacksonville." Owen shifted a foot to compensate for the deck's rolling motion. "You'll get your wish for dry land soon after, unless we meet more resistance than the generals seem to expect."

"Resistance or not, we'll surely overwhelm the rebels." Prescott took another drag at his cigar then pointed it at the other troop transport ships waiting for a favorable tide. "Thousands of troops, Owen, thousands. After we retake Jacksonville, the rest of the state will surely follow."

"That's the plan as far as I know, Captain."

Although Prescott had at last healed from the bullet wound suffered during his last stay here, the star-like scar, persistent twinges and deep aches reminded him how close he had come to death. How close he had come to being murdered at the hands of a particular rebel guerilla. "I would enjoy finding that bastard, Jack Farrell, and paying him back for the suffering he caused me."

"Might not be easy to find one particular Johnny in that swamp."

Owen said.

Prescott decided to ignore the barely masked disapproval he heard in Owen's tone. "If we tangle with Dickison's crowd, I'll get my chance." He glanced around at the murmuring crowd of dark-faced soldiers on the deck. His first reactions more than a year ago at being assigned to lead Negro troops were shame and a sense that he had been tagged a failure before being given a fair chance. To his surprise, the former slaves actually made decent soldiers. Accustomed to discipline, they took orders well and were eager to prove themselves in a fight.

Prescott had missed last summer's successful raids up the South Carolina rivers while recuperating from his wound. Perhaps this foray would do more to further his career than his last painful venture.

*

Dan rode from his quarters at Mayport Mills to the beach. He urged his mount to struggle up the deep, sliding sand to the sea-oat-fringed crest. He wanted to see for himself the flotilla headed up the St. Johns River toward Jacksonville.

On his way back to St. Augustine from Fernandina he had taken a boat to the Mayport coaling station, where the base was abuzz with news of the huge expedition preparing to descend upon Jacksonville.

From his vantage point, Dan counted fifteen ships as they passed the mouth of the river. The steamers' funnels wafted smoke into the winter air as they towed sloops with furled sails. In the distance he spotted even more ships waiting their turn to cross the bar. He sat on his horse and enjoyed the sight of many Union soldiers crowding the decks of the passing vessels.

The trip to Fernandina had delivered only a few more recruits. He had forwarded them to join the others at St. Augustine under the authority of a veteran sergeant. Mayport yielded none. Most of the refugees seemed to be more interested in living off the military than contributing to the war effort. He refused to be discouraged, because the invasion would help his project. He hoped the Union Army's move to claim more territory would free more Unionist refugees to relocate into Federal lines and bring in more deserters from the Confederate Army. Soon he hoped to command a force of enough Florida men to go after the rebels and defeat them.

Along with the influx of troops, he had heard of assistance from high places. President Lincoln himself supported the effort to bring Florida back into the Union. Dan had been authorized to move with the army and help register men willing to pledge their loyalty by signature or mark.

He looked forward to the day he could ride the countryside without fear of being shot or captured. A wayward thought of the lovely Sarah Cates Phillips intruded into his mind. He wanted to enjoy the freedom to visit her again, for a purpose other than to gather intelligence about their mutual friends on opposite sides.

Yes, a new day was riding in on the high tide.

*

Isaac stood on the deck looking out at the city's waterfront as the ship glided closer to the wharf. Other transports already had landed, and he heard gunfire as troops poured off and ran down the docks and into the streets to retake the town.

Zeke, at his elbow, said, "That 54th Massachusetts, they get all the fun."

Isaac smiled, keeping his thoughts to himself. Returning to his home state would be sweeter if he had not been forced to leave his wife and little boys back in South Carolina. He guessed he could stand it, though, because one day he wouldn't have to leave them any more. He looked forward to the time he could settle back at the Farrell homestead, free to bring his family with him.

He felt a slight bump as the boat nudged the pilings. While he waited for the order to disembark, he watched with interest as a squad of cavalry rode off another transport and clattered down the wharf onto the streets.

"Yeah, let's get this thing done," he muttered. "The sooner the better."

*

That evening Prescott enjoyed another fragrant cigar while he strolled down the neatly drawn streets of his company's encampment, satisfying himself that all was in order. Most of the Negroes he commanded, off duty at present, busied themselves cooking their suppers, taking care of their equipment, or relaxing. Tomorrow they would return to their task of building and strengthening fortifications around the city.

Three other companies in the 2nd South Carolina had gone upriver while his unit stayed behind here in Jacksonville. He would have enjoyed a raid into the country, where he could round up Secessionists and confiscate livestock and goods. The Massachusetts cavalry had headed west to create havoc in Rebeldom. That would be rewarding as well, except for the fact he loathed horses. For now his command employed shovels and axes instead of rifles.

One of his soldiers, Zeke, met him on his way back to his headquarters tent. The skinny Negro saluted and said, "Sir, there's an officer here wants to see you."

Could his company finally be assigned to something more glorious than digging ditches? "Who might that be?"

"A Captain Farrell, sir."

The name and Zeke's wide grin caught Prescott short. "Is he any relation?"

Zeke nodded. "Yes, sir. He's one of the Picolata Farrells, my old master's neighbors. I knowed him back before he joined the army. Says he wants to talk to Isaac."

"I see." *Damned Farrells*. Prescott cleared his throat. "Very well. Return to your post, private. I'll see what this Captain Farrell has to say for himself."

Prescott had heard that the pestilent Jack Farrell had a brother in the Union army, an officer, no less, but he had never met the man. The fellow waiting for him outside the tent did look unpleasantly familiar, by his annoying resemblance to the bastard who tried to murder him.

Farrell's casual attitude bordered on insolence, making his likeness to his brother more than skin-deep. Farrell wore a new cavalry-style uniform coat, but his broad-brimmed hat looked more like something a Secesh might wear. "Captain Prescott? I'm Captain Dan Farrell." He offered a firm hand and Prescott shook it without conviction.

"What can I do for you?" Prescott didn't like the feeling Farrell was sizing him up with his penetrating blue gaze. Another Farrell trait.

"I heard your regiment came with the occupation, and I wanted to see an old friend, a man from St. Johns County named Isaac. I understand he made corporal."

"Indeed. Indeed. Isaac Farrell, he calls himself." Prescott allowed a smile. "Would the two of you be related in some way? Perhaps by parentage?"

"Good one, Prescott." Farrell laughed softly though his eyes reflected no amusement. "He used to work for my father, but I think you already know that."

"I know your father, and your brother as well." Prescott watched for Farrell's reaction, but the fellow betrayed no surprise.

"Yeah, I think you and Jack had a few disagreements."

"He shot me, then would have killed me if another reb hadn't stopped him."

Farrell's expression hardened. "Fortunes of war, Captain Prescott. Soldiers shoot other soldiers. Sometimes their blood is up, and they keep fighting after they ought to quit. Obviously he had second thoughts, because you're standing here, back in command." After thus dismissing his brother's actions, the impertinent fellow glanced toward the row of tents. "Is Corporal Farrell off duty? I'd like to see him."

Prescott pointed with his cigar. "He's down there somewhere, but I can't be expected to recall which tent is his."

"Thank you."

"Enjoy the family reunion."

Farrell gave him another long look and strode away. Prescott watched him as he made inquires down the row. Isaac eventually emerged from his fly entrance and shook the officer's hand with apparent enthusiasm. Fraternizing with the colored troops was a questionable practice. Prescott resolved to document the incident, in case he ever needed to use it.

*

Dan shook Isaac's hand, appreciating the solid grip after the dishrag Prescott had offered him. Isaac's genuine grin split his face, revealing his strong white teeth. "Mr. Leon wrote me saying you came back to Florida. I'm right pleased to see you again, Mr. Dan. Mighty pleased."

"It's been a long time, Isaac," Dan acknowledged. "Years. You don't hardly look any older, but a lot has happened, hasn't it?"

Dan listened to Isaac's account of how the freedman had joined the Union Army to help him find his wife and children, who had been sold away. After finding them through Jack's inquiries among the Secesh, and bringing them out of bondage, he still wore Union blue and still carried a rifle. "They back in Beaufort," Isaac said. "We free as the army lets us be."

"How do you like army life?" Dan asked.

Isaac's expression closed down. "Ain't so bad, Mr. Dan. I mean, sir. Lieutenant Owen is a good officer, I reckon." Dan noticed he did not mention Prescott. "How is the old place? I ain't seen it since we landed at Picolata and had that tussle with the rebs and Mr. Jack."

"It's been almost a year since Pop has been there, and I haven't at all. Maybe we'll have a chance soon."

After the pleasant visit with his father's former farm hand, Dan strolled back through the streets of Jacksonville, from Market Street to Bay Street. He welcomed the huge presence of Union troops, but he enjoyed less the sight of burnt-out ruins.

Evacuating Confederates had destroyed the lumberyard and sawmill north of town almost two years ago, the first time the Union army took Jacksonville. Later, Federal soldiers razed houses, shops and churches on their way out. He hoped this fourth occupation would be permanent, establishing a firm foothold and undisputed river access. That stability would end the destruction of hapless Jacksonville every time an army evacuated.

Dan had picked up passage from Mayport Mills on one of the tenders bringing coal and supplies to the boats tethered at the wharf. After reporting to General Seymour, he'd taken the liberty to see the sights and look up Isaac. He also met the notorious Captain Prescott, whom he'd immediately sized up as a pompous ass. He smiled at the memory of Jack saying the man needed killing, though Dan would not go quite that far.

He turned to pleasanter thoughts, such as the expected arrival of John Hay, President Lincoln's secretary. From what Dan had learned, both Lincoln and Hay were all for registering a tenth of Florida's free white male population for the Union. That accomplished, Florida could be readmitted, the rebellion reversed in one state, at least.

Of course, the reunion would prove political rather than military in the short term. It would not stop the unrepentant types like his brother from continuing to fight. That would take more convincing, and he was ready to put forth a most forceful argument.

*

Two days later, Dan accompanied Secretary Hay and a swarm of officials to the army guardhouse on Bay Street. "I understand we have about a hundred rebel prisoners in custody," Dan told him. "A few pickets and signalmen were captured as soon as our troops landed. The cavalry caught some outposts unaware, as well as an artillery crew with their guns."

"It will be a tough audience, for sure," Hay said. "A good place to start, though."

Dan considered telling Hay of his success with one rebel, Ramon Andreu, but that seemed paltry compared with the larger vision the President held. "I am honored to assist you with this first step. It's a special passion of mine, because I'm a Florida Unionist, and I am dedicated to seeing my state rejoin its rightful place."

Hay, an intense-looking fellow about Dan's age, smiled through his dark moustache and said, "Captain Farrell, I'm told you've had some success in recruiting Florida men for the army."

"A small success," Dan admitted. "It seems we have hard cases in East Florida. Last year I worked with the Navy in helping the refugees on the west coast. They seem to have less trouble finding Unionists willing to fight the rebels. We're doing what we can to encourage desertion from the Secesh ranks as well. We're getting a few to come in and take the loyalty oath. They are sick of war and ready to quit."

"I've recommended to General Seymour that he send you with the next cavalry expedition. We agree that it would be good to have you meet with refugees we might liberate. We suspect many Unionists are trapped within the rebel lines. Perhaps you can be of some use in helping with deserters, as well."

"I would be honored. That will present a great opportunity."

"General Gilmore believes our occupation of East Florida will be practically unopposed." Hay raised his finger in emphasis. "So far he has been proven correct. Our hope is that the people will voluntarily resume normal relations with the U. S. government."

"Nothing would suit me more," Dan said.

"Some say Florida isn't worth the trouble. No strategic importance." Hay clicked his tongue in derision. "They don't reckon on the effect it would have on morale in the rebel armies."

"Absolutely," Dan said. "It would knock the pins out from under the Florida boys and have the rest looking behind their backs."

Admitted into the guardhouse, the entourage waited in the main lobby for the Confederate prisoners to be brought forward. Dan set his registration book on a table and watched the poor devils file in, accompanied by Negro guards. Most of the rebels had the lank, bony, dispirited look of men who had not eaten well for a long time. Others glared at their Negro guards in subdued rage. All wore uniforms, or patches of uniforms, tattered from overuse. He wondered whether Jack and his friends had sunk to such dire straits as well.

Hay waited until all the prisoners had gathered, then spoke directly and to the point. "Anyone who takes the oath of allegiance and registers his name in these books will be allowed to return to his home, entitled to the rights of citizens of the United States. Those who refuse will be shipped north as prisoners of war."

It seemed to Dan that the tough audience was suddenly paying attention.

Hay continued, "Be assured that the occupation force has come to stay, and if you take the oath, the army will protect you from retribution."

One of the prisoners, who stood with his arms crossed over his chest, spoke up. "We take that so-called oath, ain't you gonna conscript us in the Yankee army?"

"Good question." Hay swept his gaze around the room. "Not one of you will be forced to enlist. You can work your farms or open your shops unmolested, as long as you remain loyal to the Union."

Dan sensed a subtle, favorable shift in the crowd. More of the prisoners spoke up, asking questions about specifics. Finally the first questioner raised his hand. "I'm ready. Let's take the oath."

As those prisoners who were willing lined up for their turn at renouncing the Confederacy, Dan had to restrain himself from grinning during the moment of solemnity. This was what he came back to Florida to accomplish, and the sense of victory was hard to control. Contain it he must, because his triumph was based on the misfortune of these men, and the appearance of gloating would offend them. Hands shaking in eagerness, he opened the register and the inkwell.

Dan looked the first man in the face, sensing a latent resentment behind the capitulation. It mattered not. The fellow's name would appear in the registry, whatever his attitude or true feelings, and that was the goal at this critical time. "State your name, hold up your right hand and repeat after me...."

*

"Looks like there's going to be a fight." Carlo stood in front of the fire, warming his hands. "I'm on my way across the river to tell all the pickets to come in to Camp Call. General Finnegan needs every soldier in the state to report to Lake City."

Martina had heard the alarming news that the Yankees had taken Jacksonville with thousands of soldiers. "You have to go with them?"

"They need every man." Over the past few months Carlo's voice had deepened, a fine growth of moustache shadowed his upper lip, and he had grown half a head taller than her. He wore a gray jacket and carried a revolver on his belt. At sixteen, he was too much a man to suit her, despite his boyish appearance. She wished he were still too young to ride with the cavalry and attract Yankee bullets.

"What about Jack and the rest of Captain Dickison's men? Do you know where they are?"

"Haven't heard a thing. I guess they're still down south with the Cow Cavalry. Jack will want you to move away from the river, in case the Yankee gunboats take Palatka."

She shifted Rosa onto her hip and exchanged a glance with Sarah. "We can't travel right now."

"We're not going anywhere," Sarah added. "Not with Teresa about to have that baby."

Martina nodded, biting her lip. The quinine Jack brought had helped with the fevers, but off-and-on labor pains made it clear Teresa was still in no condition to travel. "She needs a safe place when her time comes. Yankees or no Yankees." Martina stroked Rosa's cheek, recalling how grateful she was to have the shelter of this house, Teresa's experienced guidance, with her husband and Carlo near at hand during her ordeal. "You can leave if you are afraid," she told Sarah, though desperate for her to stay.

"I'm not going anywhere," Sarah repeated. "Unless you're tired of my company. You have your hands full now. With Carlo gone, you'll especially be needing somebody to help take care of things."

"Thank you." Tears sprang to Martina's eyes. The words seemed inadequate for the gratitude she felt. The burden of taking care of the children and the chronically ill Teresa by herself had overwhelmed her. Cooking, feeding, cleaning and changing diapers had consumed her life from the time she crawled out of bed each morning until she fell exhausted onto her mattress. Then Sarah had descended like an angel of efficiency to ease her load.

"I cut lots of wood, and it ought to last a while," Carlo said. "At least until we run off the Yanks and return to Camp Call." He grinned, clearly anticipating a quick victory. "I'll come back through before we head out. It'll probably take a couple of days for us to organize for the trip."

Teresa came to her bedroom door and righted herself with a hand on the frame. "Carlo's here?" Her haggard features and bruised-looking eyes held a degree of interest. "Carlo, have you heard anything about Ramon?"

He shrugged. "Nothing new."

Disappointment showed on Teresa's face. She sagged, supporting her belly with her free hand.

"No news isn't a bad thing," Martina said. A rumor that Ramon had taken the Union loyalty oath had come from a produce trader given permission by the Federals to pass between the lines. Martina hoped it was true, because at least Ramon would be spared the misery of a Northern prison. If Teresa could join him in town once she was able to travel, so much the better. Martina was not sure what Jack would do given the same situation, but the Yankees had forbidden her from going home to St. Augustine. As far as she knew, Teresa was not subject to such a ban.

She suspected the men held a less charitable view of Ramon's apparent capitulation. Carlo had said little to the women about the subject, though his disapproving look made words unnecessary.

It was bad enough that her husband and his brother were enemies. Now that her cousin had joined the other side, she feared her family would never again know peace.

CHAPTER FOURTEEN

"You'll come back faster than you go." Mrs. Parrish's grim smile and narrowed eyes convinced Dan she believed her own words. Riding with the vanguard of the cavalry columns, accompanied by two local guides and another officer, he had stopped at the woman's house at Sanderson. There he hoped to learn something of what lay ahead, and this woman did not restrain her tongue. "Our soldiers'll teach you bluecoats a lesson, that's for sure."

"All we've seen so far is that handful of rebel cavalry running away." Captain Gibson, standing behind Dan, snorted. "If they ever let us get within range, somebody's going to learn a lesson, and it won't be us. Our repeater rifles taught them a thing or two at Gainesville, and it appears they've learned a little respect, at least."

Dan ignored Gibson's scornful remark "Which soldiers are waiting? Are you talking about their cavalry? The Second Florida, I believe."

"Soldiers been comin' down from Georgia all last week." She cackled with malicious glee. "Yep, you blue boys are sure enough in for it."

"We ought to arrest you for your insolence," Gibson said. "That's the kind of lesson somebody wouldn't forget."

Mrs. Parrish paled. "No call for that."

Dan glanced over his shoulder at the Massachusetts officer, hiding his growing dislike, reminding himself they were supposed to be on the same side. "Bad attitude or not, she's giving us information we'd better report."

Dan continued to question the saucy rebel woman, hoping to get more specifics, but concluded she had told him all she knew. Or thought she knew. Like her, most of the civilians saw no reason for secrecy. Perhaps she hoped crowing about Confederate prowess would scare off the Union Army, a mistake on her part.

He and Gibson returned to their horses, where the civilian guides waited. "Some of our cavalry ran into some resistance when they penetrated close to Lake City a few days ago," Gibson said as soon as they were out of Mrs. Parrish's earshot. "Stiffer than we've seen before, but nothing we can't overcome with the force we have. I doubt the rebels could have rounded up enough men to whip our six thousand or so. There aren't that many of them left in the entire state."

"We keep heading to Lake City, we're sure to find out." Dan swung into the saddle. "I'll ride back and tell Colonel Henry what she said."

"He won't credit it much, but I suppose you have to report everything you hear."

"We're advancing into enemy territory like we have not a care in the world, without flankers." Dan shook his head. "Granted it's a beautiful sunny day, a fine day for a ride in the country, but I have this feeling…."

"You and your feelings. Just some skittish Florida cavalry ahead of us." Gibson's smug smile grated on Dan. "All they do is fire a few ineffective shots, then run like deer. We haven't been able to kill or catch a one the past couple of days. Too bad for you. I know you're itching to make converts, but they won't stand still long enough for you to convince them to turn into good Union boys. Or claim they were Unionists all along." Another snort.

"We've had it easy so far. Maybe they're falling back, knowing what they have waiting for us. Drawing us in. We'd best not get complacent."

"You overestimate their brilliance."

Dumb Southerners. Dan had heard the note of contempt before, mostly from the New England men, and had a hard time not taking it personally. He decided not to argue the point, or his misgivings, which Gibson would misconstrue as cowardice.

Dan reported Mrs. Parrish's brag to Colonel Henry. "Do you believe her?" the cavalry commander asked him.

"Sir, I wouldn't discount it. The rebels will expect us to follow the railroad, and they will try to prevent us from capturing Tallahassee. It's only logical they would mass in between."

"I'm confident we can overcome whatever resistance they offer," the colonel said. "The demonstrations our army made toward Charleston and Savannah have surely spread the enemy thin. They can't defend everything at once."

An increase in gunfire to the front caused both men to attend to that direction.

"Well, well," Colonel Henry said. "It sounds as though things are heating up. Let's move forward and see what's going on, shall we?"

Dan urged his horse into a canter and wove through the columns of Massachusetts cavalry.

*

Carlo and Russell Cates fell in with Captain Stevens's company of the Second Florida Cavalry after they arrived at Olustee Station. When Carlo told Stevens they were from Dickison's command, the captain appeared pleased. "Very good. I didn't realize Captain Dickison had made it here yet."

"He hasn't as far as I know, sir." Carlo shook his head. "We were on outpost duty when we were ordered here. I don't know where the main part of our command is right now."

"Too bad. I'd feel better if those boys were along for the ride." Stevens combed his fingers through his dark beard then broke into a wide grin. "At least you're here, aren't you, Privates…?" He glanced from Carlo to Russell, who sat on his horse listening to the conversation.

"Sanchez, sir."

"Private Cates," Russell added.

"Welcome to the party, gentlemen. Glad you could join us."

A frost-laden morning gave way to a sun-warmed late winter day. The light westerly breeze carried the lingering smoke of last night's campfires set by the gathering of several regiments of Florida and Georgia troops entrenched to the west.

Stevens turned in the saddle and ordered his company due east in a skirmish line alongside the railroad track.

Scouts had been watching the Union cavalry and artillery approach all morning, but this was the first real action for Carlo. The railroad and the wagon road that crossed the tracks at several points showed a clear path toward the Yankee approach. On either side of the roads lay an open pine forest, trunks blazed for turpentine collection. Winter-brown grass and clumps of palmetto covered the ground between the trees. No one who knew better dared stray far from the higher ground. Nearby lurked swamps and sloughs that would swallow a soldier's legs or those of his horse.

Carlo found his place at a proper distance from the horsemen on either side. Russell took a position to his right. Carlo kept an eye on Russell, hoping to rely on his longer experience. Carlo's only firefight so far was the raid on the woodcutters several weeks ago, where Captain Dickison had assigned him to hold horses. He had not yet fired his

Enfield or his revolver at the enemy.

The hardtack Carlo ate for lunch sat like a lump in his stomach. He told himself he was not afraid but watchful, paying attention. As one of the few representatives of Dickison's troop, Carlo was determined to make a creditable impression, no matter what the Yankees threw their way.

For the thousandth time Carlo wished Ramon and Jack were present. His cousin's steadiness and his tough brother-in-law's wry outlook made it seem nothing bad could happen. But something bad had happened to Ramon, and Jack had been sent elsewhere.

Carlo did not want to believe the rumor that Ramon took the Unionist oath to avoid prison. He had always admired his cousin but found such a betrayal hard to forgive. When he and Martina lived among the Yankees in St. Augustine, the two of them had refused to take the oath despite the threat of losing their home. They remained true to their convictions and honored their brother, Francisco, for his Confederate allegiance.

Carlo had channeled his determination to avenge Francisco's death at Yankee hands to more practical avenues. The attitudes of Jack and Ramon had rubbed off on him. He now realized it was also important to take care of themselves, each other, and keep those depending on them safe from harm.

*

Teresa paced back and forth across the floor of the front room, holding her belly, perspiration gleaming on her forehead. "It's really coming this time," she gasped.

The strength of Teresa's contractions convinced Martina this was no false alarm. She feared her cousin's wife would give birth earlier than she should.

Sarah said, "I'll take the wagon and fetch the midwife. You can stay with Teresa and the young 'uns."

"Hurry." Martina turned to Ana, who watched her mother, apprehension in her eyes. The child's fears had grown along with Teresa's difficulties. "Ana, you can help. We'll be busy for a while. Can you take care of Rosa for us?"

The child nodded, thumb in mouth. "Yes, Auntie Tina."

"Good girl. Rosa will want a nap soon, so all you have to do is play with her until she's sleepy. I'll take her if she gets hungry or needs her diapers changed."

Ana started a game of peek-a-boo with the baby, who sat on the floor, her back now strong enough to keep her upright.

"Oh," Teresa said, a startled look on her face.

"What's the matter?" Martina asked.

"My water broke."

Later, Rosa's fitful whimpers from the next room intensified into a full-blown howl. Ana ran into Teresa's bedroom and set her hands on her hips, her face set in an exasperated expression. "Rosa won't stop crying. I think she's hungry."

"That's all right, Ana. You've kept her happy for a long time. I'll feed her now." Martina rose from the chair and followed Ana to the front room, where she found Rosa sitting, her face squinched and red, mouth open to let out an ear-splitting squall, small fists clenched "You have your father's temper," Martina chided as she scooped up the baby.

Thoughts of Jack rolled through her mind. How she missed her husband, absent for two weeks now. How she yearned for him to make one of his unannounced visits. She smiled as she pictured her fierce protector at a loss trying to deal with this feminine crisis.

Rosa's cries settled into a fretful whimper. Martina carried her into Teresa's room, sat down, unbuttoned the front of her dress, and offered Rosa her breast. "Now you'd better quiet down."

The fussing settled into blissful grunts and smacks as the baby clamped on for a feeding. Martina arranged her clothing to cover her chest and the infant's face. She was grateful to have an abundance of milk for Rosa. So far she had been able to find enough food to support the baby's nourishment as well as her own.

"Sarah ought to be back soon," Martina said to Teresa.

In between pains, Teresa managed a smile. "Doesn't matter. The baby is going to come anyway, with or without help." Her lips thinned as her belly tightened in another hard contraction.

With her free hand Martina reached for her rosary and fingered the beads. She prayed silently for Teresa, Jack and Carlo.

*

Carlo heeled his horse forward as Stevens's company surged toward the Union vanguard. The Florida cavalrymen fired a few shots, drew fire from the enemy, then fell back a little way. Carlo understood the purpose of this sort of engagement. The Yankees would want to chase their tormentors. Chase them right into the Confederate stronghold, where infantry and artillery waited, ready to welcome them with hot lead.

Carlo braced against the recoil and discharged his rifle at the distant blue-coated men. He did not believe he hit any of them. He stuffed the Enfield back into the boot because it was awkward and time-consuming to reload on horseback. He drew his revolver, but figured the enemy was too far away for its limited range.

He hoped the Yankees had the same problems, but the rapid snap of their rifles proved otherwise. "They're firing mighty quick," the man to Carlo's left observed. "Repeater rifles, I'll bet."

Unused to the noise and confusion, the gelding danced sideways, tossing its head. Carlo kept a tight rein and tried to speak in a soothing manner, but his voice quivered. He looked toward the sound of a horse's pain-scream. Russell's horse sank to its knees, blood spurting from its chest. It sagged into a sad heap as Russell rolled clear, scrambled to his feet, and stared at the dying animal for a moment. He reached down for his rifle and unstrapped his saddlebags, though the Yankees were still shooting. Sand kicked up in front of Carlo's horse's front hooves, which caused the nervous animal to prance.

The rest of the skirmishers in Stevens's company continued to fall back at the enemy's approach, but Russell knelt down and reached for the cinch as though trying to salvage the saddle.

Carlo heard the whack of a bullet's impact. He looked down at himself and his horse, but saw no blood, only a new hole in his saddle. His horse acted no worse than before, so it must not be hurt.

"Leave it!" he yelled at Russell. He kneed his skittish horse closer. "Hurry up! For God's sake get on!" Russell jumped up, threw the saddlebags over his shoulder and sprinted the few yards that separated them. Carlo tried to prevent his dancing mount from knocking Russell to the ground. Carlo offered him a hand, while Russell stepped into the stirrup and swung up behind. Carlo let his horse have its head to catch up with the retreating skirmishers while Russell held onto his belt.

"Thanks, for the ride." Russell's breath grated harsh in Carlo's ear.

"You sure took your time. You trying to get both of us shot?"

Russell made a choked sound that might have been a laugh or a sob.

*

"Colonel I believe we're developing more Johnnies ahead." Captain Gibson turned in the saddle and pointed west. Dan noticed

Gibson had brought the civilian guides away from the vanguard, perhaps in consideration of their safety. Dan sat on his horse next to Colonel Henry, not at all pleased that his premonitions were firming into reality.

"Do you have any idea how many? Any solid information?" Colonel Henry pressed.

"Their cavalry is screening what's there, but one of our scouts worked in close enough to get a clear view along the railway. He counted about a hundred reb infantry jumping across the tracks." Gibson did not look Dan's way.

"Infantry," the colonel mused. He squinted off in the distance, as though trying to see past their own cavalry skirmishers. "I wonder how many he didn't see."

Dan's uneasiness had intensified with the increasing sounds of fighting. "Sir, they might be trying to draw us into something bigger than we expect."

"That's what I'm thinking. Let's call a halt and let the advance infantry catch up with us. Then we'll feel them out in force."

Dan waited with Colonel Henry, and eventually General Seymour joined them. The general ordered two companies of the 7th Connecticut and a portion of the 8th Colored Regiment to proceed ahead in skirmish line. The infantry units moved out in a serrated formation, the New Englanders on the right, repeating rifles loaded and ready; the recently organized Negro regiment on the left. The two forces created a pincer movement.

"We'll find out what they've got," the general said. "Probably not much."

*

Carlo found the captain and saluted him.

Russell said, "Sir, my horse was shot."

"You'll have to requisition one from the Yanks when you get a chance." Captain Stevens waved his hand to the west. "Private Sanchez, take him to the rear, drop him off, then report back to me. Private Cates, report to Colonel Harrison. He'll assign you elsewhere."

Carlo turned his horse toward Olustee station and settled into a canter alongside the railroad tracks. Beyond an abandoned mill, the only landmark in sight, more cavalry stood in readiness.

"Raised him from a colt," Russell muttered. "Sorry, hard-headed horse. I'll miss him. Now I'll have to fight on my feet."

After dropping off Russell with the infantry, Carlo rejoined Stevens's company. The cavalry had drawn up in a skirmish line on the west side of the lumber mill. Carlo halted a respectful distance from Captain Stevens. The officer was conferring with scouts, a Georgia cavalry officer and Colonel Caraway Smith, who commanded the Confederate cavalry in Florida. Carlo recognized him from past courier assignments and an inspection tour the colonel had made to Camp Call.

The officers and scouts intently watched the direction from which the Yankee advance had come while they discussed the situation. Carlo did not see any Yankees and figured they had halted. He overheard the colonel say, "I'm going to take a few men over to the mill and take a look for myself. The roadbed is elevated there, and it should offer a good vantage point."

Colonel Smith glanced around until his gaze rested on Carlo. "You're in Captain Dickison's company, aren't you? Sanchez, is it?"

Pleased the colonel remembered him, Carlo held himself straight in the saddle. "Yes, sir. I carried some dispatches to you."

"Very good. Come with me, Private Sanchez."

Carlo nudged his horse forward and moved along with the colonel, a Georgia trooper, and two Florida scouts.

The little party halted at the mill next to the track. "Let's dismount, tie our horses, climb up yonder, and take a look." Colonel Smith nodded toward the embankment that created a causeway for the roadbed.

Because no one ordered him to stay with the horses, Carlo climbed the elevation with the other soldiers. He stuck close to the affable Georgia trooper who introduced himself as Penniman.

Colonel Smith held a pair of field glasses to his eyes and looked along the railroad track. Carlo peered in that direction but still could not make out any oncoming enemies. Visibility between Olustee station and Sanderson was better than most Florida landscapes because timber and turpentine operations had cleared underbrush from the pine forest, giving the area a park-like appearance. To the south of the roadbed lay a swamp.

Carlo saw movement between the track and the swamp. He pointed it out to Penniman, who said, "Colonel, sir, over there. Yankees."

The officer swung around and peered through the glasses. "They're a little less than a mile away. I believe they are colored troops."

The approaching enemies riveted the colonel's full attention, but Carlo began to fidget and look around. A movement caught his notice.

He gazed to the northwest where a wagon road paralleled the tracks. There he focused on the sight of another squad of Yankees, much closer. The hair rose on the back of his neck when he realized the enemy ranged in skirmish order, jogging unimpeded between the well-spaced trees, their bayonets glinting in the sun.

Carlo nudged Penniman on the arm. "More Yankees! There!"

The Georgian turned to where Carlo pointed and called out, "Sir! We're about to draw fire!"

Colonel Smith lowered his field glasses and glanced in the direction Carlo and Penniman pointed out. "Let's go!"

Carlo ran with the others down the embankment just as a volley sent Minie balls whining overhead. He ran to his horse, whipped the reins free of the pine hitching, and bounded into the saddle.

The scouting party galloped back to relative safety behind the picket line. Colonel Smith drew rein next to Carlo and said, "Private Sanchez, you will deliver a message to General Finnegan."

*

Martina heard the front door open. "That must be Sarah and the midwife," she told Teresa, who was resting between contractions. Relief surged through Martina as she looked toward the bedroom door.

Sarah showed in the ancient, turbaned Negress, who paused, taking in the scene. The sharp bone structure of her face hinted at Indian ancestry. "This is Maum Glorious," Sarah said, "our midwife."

Maum Glorious's hunched back and wrinkled features gave the impression of frailty. Her arthritic, claw-like hands held a carpetbag as though it contained riches. Rheumy eyes, coffee-dark, settled on Teresa. Her smile, revealing long yellow teeth, did not make her face any less fearsome. "That child can come now. Maum Glorious is here," she announced in a creaky voice.

Martina tried to conceal her concern at the old woman's appearance. Teresa stared at the midwife, wide-eyed, clearly sharing Martina's lack of confidence.

The crone turned to Sarah. "You got hot water, honey? I gots to wash up."

Sarah nodded, exchanged a glance with Martina, and left the room. Martina rose to follow, holding the sleepy Rosa carefully, so as not to disturb her. "That's our midwife?" she whispered.

Sarah reached for the bucket of water they kept over the fire. "She's all we have."

They had thoroughly discussed alternatives over the past few days. Dr. Williams was away with the cavalry. The only civilian doctor nearby, at Welaka, liked to sample his own medicinal alcohol to excess. Besides, his women patients had an unfortunate habit of falling ill and dying after delivering. The midwife living on a plantation outside Palatka was convenient and inexpensive. "She looks like a witch." Martina hissed.

"Let's hope she's a good witch, then." Sarah gave her a tired smile. "She comes well recommended."

Martina reminded herself that Sarah had found Maum Glorious through her awe-inspired reputation among the colored folks. Her storied skill at birthing babies had earned her enough money in fees to buy her own freedom, though she still lived in her own cabin on the same property as her former owners.

Martina set Rosa in the crib, thankful the child did not awaken. Sarah lifted the bucket, grabbed a clean towel from a stack they kept on the table, and handed them to her. "I'll look after Ana and Rosa while you stay with Teresa."

Unable to shake her distrust, Martina returned to Teresa's room, determined to watch the midwife closely.

Maum Glorious pulled out a sliver of soap from her bag, dipped her hands in the water, and scrubbed. Then she dried her hands on the towel and squinted at Teresa, whose belly once again knotted into a hard ball.

"Looks like I come just in time."

CHAPTER FIFTEEN

Dan turned his horse in obedience to an order to clear the road and wheel left. Elder's horse battery rushed forward and took its position. The artillerymen unlimbered a cannon and swarmed into action. The big gun cut loose with a deep boom, lobbing a probing shot toward where the Confederate lines ought to be.

"Sending them a message." Captain Gibson stood in the stirrups, gazing in the direction where the rebels had disappeared beyond a slight rise. "We'll see if they respond."

Dan sat on his horse while Elder's men reloaded the piece and fired another shot.

"Nothing." Gibson let out a satisfied huff. "Just some cavalry, most likely."

Dan saw the incoming shell's arc at the same time he heard the enemy's cannon boom. The shell screamed in and landed near the artillery emplacement. An explosion and a different kind of scream, an agonized animal shriek, made Dan cringe. His mount gathered under him as though ready to bolt. Dan murmured softly to the spooked animal and tensed the reins for control.

"They've got artillery, too." Dan nodded toward the unseen enemy. "Sounds like they killed some of our horses."

Dan moved to the position Colonel Henry assigned him, where he commanded a squad of cavalrymen supporting the right of Elder's artillery. To his left, the gunners wheeled three more cannons into place to ply their deadly craft. Connecticut infantry defended the center, well armed with their Spencer seven-shot rifles. Gibson's cavalry squad filled out the area to Dan's right flank.

Dan did not like the look of the terrain, a weed-strewn open field with little cover except for a spacing of pine trees. Just beyond lay the edge of woods where the rebels hid behind trees and in the underbrush. He ordered the men to dismount so they could take advantage of the concealment available and use their repeating rifles more effectively.

He sent the horses to the rear and stationed himself behind a tree, where he could monitor and direct the action without exposure.

Within the next half hour, the pause ended and the confrontation with the enemy escalated. The full-throated boom of cannon punctuated the incessant roll of musketry, swelling and dying and swelling again.

Smoke from the enemy gunfire seemed to catch and hang in the pines. The rattle of rifle shots picked up in intensity. The whistle and spat of bullets filled the air.

Dan heard the twang of a ball hitting one of the cannons. "Ai! Ai!" cried an artillerymen as he spun around, clutching his arm. The Confederate sharpshooters were concentrating their fire on the artillery, trying to knock out the most deadly weapons in the Union arsenal.

Another artilleryman fell, and Dan noted smoke wafting from halfway up a pine tree amid the rebel lines. Sharpshooters had climbed for elevation, finding scant cover in the long, sparse pine needles. Dan made out the form of a man preparing to fire another round.

He pointed out the too-effective enemy to his men. "See if you can hit that fellow up in the tree." Several rifle barrels lifted toward the treed rebel and barked in random sequence. Dan watched the figure plummet. "Good shooting," he called out.

"Swatted that pest," sang a soldier.

An unsettling memory welled up in Dan's mind. *"How did you get disabled bad enough for the Confederate Army to give you a discharge?" he had asked Jack while he was his brother's prisoner.*

"A Yankee artillery battery was causing our men a lot of grief. I was sent with other sharpshooters to put it out of commission. I found a likely position and shinnied up a good oak tree with my gaffs, like climbing a telegraph pole. I opened for business and started potting the artillerymen.

"They spotted me, and I watched them swing the cannon toward me. My belt got caught and it took me too long to get free. Next thing I knew, I was on the ground, the tree was blasted to smithereens, and I was all busted to hell." Jack had grinned with less humor than usual. "I still carry around wood and metal. They don't make good souvenirs."

Dan shook off the recollection and pointed out another rebel sharpshooter for his men to kill. He told himself if Jack was one of the men shooting at him, he had no choice but to shoot back.

*

Trot, canter, walk. Trot, canter, walk. Jack adjusted his numb behind as Choctaw stumbled over a stretch of level road. Jack reached for his canteen, unstopped the cork, and took a mouthful. He sloshed it around his dry mouth before swallowing, then turned to Charlie, riding alongside. "To hell with this. If the captain doesn't call a halt soon, I'm dropping out. Catch up later. I don't want to kill my horse. Damn the consequences."

The younger trooper patted his mount's skinny neck. "Good thing I was able to trade mine for a fresh pony back at that homestead. Old Billy was about to give up, too."

Jack ran his gaze over Charlie's slab-sided steed. "Those folks weren't happy about it, but they've got a better horse, once Billy's rested up."

Choctaw was strong, but the forced march from Fort Myers, covering over two hundred and fifty miles in a few days, was too much. Dickison and his men had accomplished little in southwest Florida before receiving word of the Yankee invasion. An urgent call to turn around and go back north had cut their mission short.

The cavalry column finally halted at a slough for an hour's break. Jack let Choctaw wade fetlock-deep and drink. Then he urged the horse out of the water and onto the bank where he slid out of the saddle, loosened the cinch, dropped the reins and flopped on the ground. He threw his arm over his eyes to shut out the sun, listening to the horse munch grass and leaves near his head.

*

From his post supporting the artillery, Dan watched the confrontation escalate. A New Hampshire Infantry regiment, sent forward to flank the Confederates at the right, rushed through, around, and past Dan's position.

Even without General Seymour's West Point education, he could see the big guns were too close to the enemy and too exposed. The Confederates' shooting continued, deadly and accurate, from positions mostly invisible in the tall grass and woods. The cannon fire, once brisk, slowed as bullets thinned the crews.

Soon remnants of the New Hampshire regiment staggered back. One man holding a shattered arm stumbled toward the rear, but others appeared sound enough. Two men carried a soldier with a bad leg, and Dan confronted them.

"Let him down. The hospital orderly will take care of him. Get your asses back into the fight."

After sending off the self-appointed medics, Dan turned on an empty-handed soldier. "Where's your weapon? What did you do with it?"

The wide-eyed man raised his hands and blathered in a language Dan did not understand.

Dan drew his revolver and grabbed the front of the fellow's shirt. "English. Don't you speak English?" The man sagged in his grip, tears puddling in his eyes.

"He's a Frenchie," panted another retreating soldier paused in his gallop. "Hell, Captain, they took away our Spencers and gave us rifles that don't bloody work. Lookit here." The soldier held up his rifle. "No ramrod, no bayonet. Came like that. Idjit officers had us running into each other while the Johnnies were killin' us. What the hell do you expect?"

Was this going to be a full-scale rout? "Then find a rifle that works! There must be plenty left on the field."

The New Hampshire soldier looked over his shoulder toward the Confederate stronghold, shifted on his feet, and moved, too slowly, to obey. Dan shoved the Frenchman at him. "Show him what to do!"

An infantry lieutenant came after the retreating men, sweating, sword drawn, and turned to Dan. "Captain! Can't we get some help to get these men back into line?"

Dan ordered his men forward to encourage and bully the quitters back into the fight. He noted Gibson was doing the same. "Take advantage of cover," he called out. "Run from tree to tree!" He took his own advice, jumping over branches and through tall grass. He jumped over a bleeding man who crawled away from the fight.

As he approached the rebel lines, the snap of rifle fire continued without a break. Bullets thwacked into trees and clipped through the branches. Shouting, cursing men pushed between the dead and wounded scattered over the ground, past where the rebels had halted the previous Union advance. The smells of smoke, blood and fear filled Dan's nostrils.

The Frenchman seemed dazed. He did not seek to advance under cover but walked in stolid resignation. Dan pointed out a rifle, discarded on the ground. "Pick that up! Take cover and start shooting!" The distinct thud of a ball hitting human flesh coincided with the fellow dropping in a heap.

Dan picked up the rifle, complete with ramrod if no bayonet, and handed it to the man whose weapon did not work. The soldier aimed it and fired, then slipped behind a tree to reload.

A buzzing Minie ball swept off Dan's hat. He snatched the hat from the ground, his finger poking through a hole through the crown, and slapped it back on his head. Peering into the woods, he tried to search out the enemy so he could direct fire. He carried no rifle but squeezed off a pistol shot wherever he saw a puff of smoke rise.

A bullet grazed his shooting arm, but he was too intent to take much notice. From where he crouched, he had limited awareness of how many of his own squad remained with him. He looked around and picked out some of them behind trees and bushes, using their rapid-fire Spencer rifles. *The backup troops are better armed than the men in front.*

The New Hampshire lieutenant strode into the open, herding the infantrymen. He tried to organize them into line, under fire and exposed, waving his sword and shouting orders. Here and there a man fell where he stood. "Load, find your target and fire at – " The lieutenant's voice broke off in a screech and he dropped to one knee.

Someone yelled, "Save yourselves!" Some of the men broke and ran. It was useless for Dan to try to stop those men in full flight. He yelled at the stalwarts still remaining to take cover, hold their positions and keep shooting.

Marching forward would push them right into the teeth of the enemy. Retreating would allow the rebels to press forward and turn the right flank. He just kept firing, reloading and firing. From the noise, the other Union soldiers were doing the same.

*

Maum Glorious pulled the blanket off Teresa. "Get up, honey. You gots to get up and let that child slide on down." The midwife instructed Martina to support Teresa as she walked around the room. All the while Maum Glorious hummed tunelessly. Teresa seemed to relax and settle into her own rhythm of contractions, which appeared to come in a sort of cadence with the humming.

"Squat down, honey," Maum Glorious said. She sat on the floor, Indian-style and ran her hand under Teresa's gown. The old woman grinned broadly. "He's a comin.' An' he's a wigglin'."

Transfixed, Martina steadied Teresa as the midwife told the laboring woman when to breathe, how to breathe, and when to push. Teresa shut her eyes and squeezed them tight. Finally, with a squishy sound and a cry from Teresa, the damp, blood-smeared baby emerged.

The old woman picked up the wet infant by the feet with one hand and held the afterbirth high with the other while she let him dangle. His gender obvious, the boy screwed his purple face into a grimace but made no sound. Fluid dripped from his nose and mouth. He took a gasp then let out his breath in a feeble cry. Martina noted he was smaller than Rosa at birth, more wrinkled, and his wet head appeared bald.

Maum Glorious set him down across her lap and wiped his face with the towel. His breaths began to come regularly, deep and strong. "He needs to rest a spell." She reached into her carpetbag and fished out a length of yarn and a knife. She tied the baby's cord and cut it a few inches away from his body.

Martina picked up the infant, wrapped him in a towel and handed him to his mother, who had collapsed, exhausted, onto the bed.

"A boy," murmured Teresa. "Ramon will be so happy." She studied the infant's face, his fingers and toes. Martina assumed all were present in the correct number.

"He not cooked all the way through," Maum Glorious said. "He a trifle underdone. You got to keep him warm and feed him a little bit here, a little bit there, 'bout every time you think about it. He'll do." She turned her gaze to Martina. "Your young 'un sure is fat and fine. Your milk flowing free?"

Martina nodded. "I always seem to satisfy her."

Maum Glorious smiled, showing her long, strong teeth. "Some of your'n, some of her'n, he get plenty to eat. Let him have his mama for a bit, next time his auntie. He'll do." She wiped off the scissors with a damp rag and placed them along with the yarn back into the carpetbag. Then she braced to her feet and turned her attention to the mother.

The midwife placed a towel under Teresa's legs and massaged the woman's belly. Martina knew what that was about. The doctor had directed Teresa to do the same for her after giving birth, to keep the contractions going and shrink her overstretched midsection.

"I'll name him Ramon," Teresa murmured.

*

From behind, Dan heard a sustained cheer, the heartening sound of reinforcements. An answering shout arose from the troops with him. The New York regiment rushed up, filling in and strengthening the line, announcing their arrival with a series of volleys toward the concealed rebels.

No longer pinned down, Dan pulled out a handkerchief and wrapped it around his bleeding right arm. He pulled the stopper from his canteen and took a long drink to get rid of the burnt powder taste that parched his throat.

A Massachusetts cavalryman ran over to him and threw himself on the ground to avoid the incoming fire. "Sir, Captain Gibson says our job here is done, and we need to return to our stations."

"Tell him we're on our way." Dan watched the soldier dash back to Gibson. Relieved of the responsibility of helping hold the New Hampshire troops in place, Dan gathered his own squad and returned to support the artillery.

He and his men pushed their way through the oncoming New York soldiers. As he settled his squad in position, he realized there was not much artillery left to support. Some of the guns had been drawn off, and a pile of dead and injured men lay across the trails of the abandoned guns. Confederate sharpshooters also had picked off most of the artillery horses. Dead and fatally wounded horses could not pull cannons. The cavalry horses, better protected to the rear, probably fared better.

Dan passed down the order to save ammunition so they would not have to fire ineffectively over the heads of their own infantry. Then yells and the rise and fall of intensifying fighting to the left caught his attention.

Dan ran over to consult with Gibson. "The rebels are trying to turn our left." He nodded toward the action, a half-mile distant.

"We have to sit tight until we get further orders," Gibson said. "Pray the center holds. Those are the Connecticut troops with repeating rifles."

As the afternoon wore on, the New York and New Hampshire regiments on the right retreated piecemeal and in bloodied streams. Few defenders remained to the front, and soon an order came for Dan to withdraw his squad and act as rearguard. He had his men work backwards, firing as they retreated. Finally they reached their horses, fortunately safe behind a stand of trees. He ordered his men to mount. They gave ground slowly and grudgingly as the Confederates advanced, shadows flitting from tree to tree.

"We're whipped, and whipped bad," the trooper closest to Dan muttered.

"Shut up and shoot." Dan feared the soldier had it right.

*

Carlo crouched next to the unresisting body of a Union soldier and removed the cartridge belt. Necessity ordered the macabre act of harvesting supplies from the dead. Following an ominous quieting of rifle fire from the Confederate side, word had come down the line that the Georgia troops were running out of ammunition. To hold the field they had won and defend their advantage, the Confederates needed cartridges and they needed them now. Dead and wounded men from both sides dotting the ground in sad heaps provided a ready source. Colonel Colquitt had sent aides, including Carlo, to fetch whatever they could glean.

Carlo slung the strap over his shoulder along with others he had collected. The five cartridge boxes were starting to weigh him down. He ignored the continuous rattle of gunfire and bullets crackling harmlessly through the overhead branches. The fighting had shifted east, pushing the enemy backwards. The Confederates had succeeded in capturing some of the Yankee artillery pieces and turning them against their former owners.

He moved to the next blood-smeared corpse. Not quite a corpse. When Carlo touched his shoulder strap, the Yankee groaned. His eyes shone through sweaty black powder smears. His thin lips matched the whites of his eyes.

Carlo drew his revolver. “Don’t move.”

The eyes slid shut. “Just shoot me. Please.”

Carlo studied the wounded man. The soldier’s leg, broken and doubled underneath him, seeped blood. Finishing him off didn’t seem right. Killing a Yankee who could not fight back was not a fair way to avenge Francisco.

“I just need your stuff.” Carlo holstered his weapon, removed the man’s cartridge belt and added it to his collection. “I’ll find you some water and fix your position so you aren’t lying on your bad leg. Our surgeons will see to you after a while.”

The Yankee’s weak laugh sounded hopeless. “I’m a dead man.”

Carlo grasped the injured man under his armpits and pulled him straight. The Yankee cried out as his bent leg unfolded. Then the dark blue coat fell open, revealing a loop of purple gut amid a pool of clotted blood. Carlo gasped and jerked his hands away. “I thought you just had a bad leg.”

“One shot. In the head,” moaned the dying man. “I can’t stand it anymore.”

Carlo grappled for his revolver, pointed it behind the Yankee's ear, and cocked it. He looked around. No one seemed to be watching him.

"You're sure?"

"Do it, Johnny." The Yankee squeezed his eyes shut and clenched his jaw.

Carlo's hand wavered. "No."

"Where's your nerve? I'm begging you." The Yankee's eyes sprang open and flickered a warning. "Damn you. I'll kill you instead." His hand reached under his coat skirt.

The Colt barked and bucked in Carlo's hand. The man's head exploded into a red bloom. His legs and arms quivered, then stilled.

Carlo stared at the man he had killed. He flipped the coat for the weapon the Yankee went for but found no sidearm. Not even a knife.

Gagging, Carlo turned away. Brain matter and blood had sprayed his hand, sleeve and jacket front. He tried to wipe the mess off on the grass, then stood and stumbled to his horse. Holding onto the pommel of the saddle, he leaned over to throw up. Then he mounted his horse and rushed to deliver the ammunition.

The staff officer took the cartridge cases from him and passed them to an aide for distribution. He looked at the stains on Carlo's coat, then his face, and asked, "You get shot, private?"

Carlo glanced at his blood-spattered sleeve. "No, sir. Not me."

"Good. Go back and get more. Jump!"

Carlo stared at the officer for a beat, wanting to refuse the order to once again face the horror of pilfering the dead and not-so-dead. Then he wheeled his horse and headed back to the scene of slaughter. He shifted to the Confederate right. Here, most of the Yankee dead and wounded appeared to be Negroes.

This time, he took the canteens as well as the cartridge boxes from the corpses. In that way, perhaps he could atone for the man he had executed, as long as he took care. Wounded men still could be dangerous.

When Carlo returned to the front, a staff officer grabbed the ammunition. "Go to the rear, down the tracks and fetch the cartridges from those stuck rail cars. Fill up everything you have and get it back here on the gallop!"

Carlo rushed to obey, relieved his destination this time would be a railroad car, although he still had to pick his way through a field full of corpses and pain. Other mounted men joined the shuttle, rushing the supplies with hats, pockets, haversacks, saddlebags and cartridge boxes full of ammunition.

Finally a locomotive dragged the cars within reach of the men at the front line. Carlo dismounted, leaped onto the nearest boxcar and lugged a crate outside. He handed it to another soldier and returned for another crate. By the time he brought out the second crate, somebody had broken the first open. A group of soldiers had descended on it like hungry wolves, their powder-blackened hands grabbing the cartridges and feeding them into cartridge boxes and rifles before sprinting to the battle line.

Carlo, ordinance men and rail hands continued pulling the crates from the car and handing them off. The quickened pace of firing and triumphant yells from the resupplied troops told him they not only held the ground previously gained but were driving the Yankees back from where they came.

CHAPTER SIXTEEN

Prescott strode along the breastworks with Lieutenant Owen as they inspected the fortifications his men built just outside Jacksonville. He stood and smoked a fresh cigar while he watched the crew of Negroes work with spade and pickaxe. How was he ever going to earn a promotion as long as he commanded a crew of mere laborers?

"Hrumph. Once again our company's been left behind." Prescott waved his hand toward the project. "Other colored units are headed west. The Eighth North Carolina and the 54th Massachusetts are well on their way to capture Tallahassee with no help from us."

Owen seemed to agree. "Don't seem right. The Eighth don't have near the training our fellows do. Those boys are pretty green."

Prescott sighed. "Seems guarding ditches instead of crossing bayonets with the enemy is our lot these days."

"Seems like."

"Ah, the paths of glory lead but to the shovel." Prescott smiled at his own witticism. Owen wisely chuckled in appreciation.

When Prescott returned to his office with Owen, his orderly handed him an envelope from Colonel Montgomery. He broke the seal and scanned the contents, then broke into a wide smile. "Well, well, well. Owen, we have been awarded a consolation prize. Our company has been chosen to board the *Ottawa* and proceed on a raid up the St. Johns."

"When are we to leave, sir?"

"Tomorrow morning. Toward Palatka, perhaps? Dickison's lair. This is an opportunity for us to shine, Owen."

Prescott smoothed his moustache. He had always found raiding plantations an enjoyable and profitable activity. Perhaps the expedition would bring him a step closer to catching Jack Farrell. As a side benefit, he might locate the luscious Martina, who claimed to be married to that bastard. Yes, this was an opportunity indeed.

*

Hours later, Dan trudged through the chill darkness leading his horse, which carried two wounded New York men. Though sore, his arm wound seemed trivial by comparison. All around he heard the shuffle of feet of the walking wounded and sound men on the brink of exhaustion. An occasional splash and curse marked when someone stepped into a slough.

He stumbled over what he took for a log, but it was a man. The wounded soldier had made it this far before expiring. Dan did not know how many others remained on the field in the possession of a victorious enemy.

At least the shattered army's retreat was orderly. Despite fears and rumors Dan heard little gunfire indicating Confederate pursuit.

Small comfort. A mere captain, he did not know the grand strategy General Seymour employed, if indeed he had one. It seemed to Dan that positioning artillery so close to enemy sharpshooters was not much of a winning hand. Neither was sending regiments one at a time to the front, some of them poorly armed and trained.

At least he had not heard any stupidly optimistic voices try to spin the resounding defeat into a pseudo victory. So much for capturing Florida's capital city. So much for stopping the flow of cattle and supplies northward to the rebel armies. So much for rounding up hundreds of disillusioned Confederate soldiers and taking them out of the fight. As far as Dan knew, the only men snared were those unfortunate Union soldiers left behind.

He took the failed mission as a personal defeat as well as a misfortune for the Union Army. How in blazes was he supposed to persuade anyone to switch sides now?

He had met damn few good Florida Union men since leaving Jacksonville.

*

In the dim predawn light Carlo boiled coffee and ate hardtack and bacon he and his fellow Confederates had gleaned from the enemy. He was growing accustomed to taking what he needed from the battlefield, though he still dreaded finding an apparent corpse that turned out a little short of dead.

Again attached to Captain Stevens's company and sharing their bivouac, Carlo did not know Russell's fate until his friend wandered into the cavalry camp, his clothes torn and dirty, leading a horse as disheveled as himself. Carlo looked up from where he sat. "You saved me the trouble of hunting for you."

"Found you first. Look what else I found." Russell stroked the bay's shoulder. The horse stood easy, though it hung its head and its ears drooped.

"He looks beat," Carlo said, "just like the rest of the Yankees."

"He ain't hurt too bad. Just a little gunshot wound on the rump. Comes with nice new saddle and bridle. You got coffee?"

"You got a cup?"

Russell tied his horse, brought over a tin mug and helped himself to the coffee. He squatted by the fire. "I see you made it through all right."

"I stayed busy. Guess you did too."

"I shot my share of Yankees." Russell took a sip of coffee. "They shot some of our boys, too. I think we gave better than we got, though. Fetched them a sound licking."

"Officers had me running dispatches back and forth." Carlo told him about how he had helped replenish ammunition, but he stopped short of describing the man he finished off. He did not want anyone to know how he killed a helpless Yankee, even though he believed he acted in self-defense.

"The Georgia infantry boys were kind of surprised the cavalry didn't keep after those Yankees all the way back to Jacksonville." Russell lifted an eyebrow. "They think y'all were throwing off."

"Colonel Smith heard the Yanks strung telegraph lines between the trees and set up ambushes in the dark," Carlo said. "Besides, after fighting all day, I guess he figured we were pretty well used up."

"Did you hear the shooting last night?" Russell asked. "About where we did the fighting. I thought the battle was over, but I kept hearing rifles go off. Didn't feel like investigating, though."

An image of the Yankee's exploding head had never quite left Carlo's mind. Maybe more heads had exploded. "Yeah. I heard. Putting horses out of their misery, I guess. The ones hurt too bad." He hoped he spoke the truth.

Russell stared across the campfire and broke into a grin. "Well, look who finally arrived at the ball after the dancing was done."

Carlo followed his gaze and spotted Jack and Charlie making their way to his campsite. He suppressed an urge to run to his brother-in-law. He was not a kid anymore and refused to act like one. He called out and waved them over. Then he stood and clasped hands with the new arrivals.

"We got here a couple of hours ago," Jack explained. "Appears we didn't make it in time to help out with the heavy lifting. We found a few stray Yanks and corralled them. Came looking through the critter camp to see if anybody we knew was around."

"A commotion woke me up. Guess that was y'all." Carlo allowed a big smile to split his face. "I'll make more coffee. Got it off the Yankees."

"We rode hard." Charlie's eyes were shadowed with fatigue. Jack let himself down close to the fire while Carlo poured coffee and added more beans and water to the pot. He gave Jack a mug and settled alongside. Charlie accepted Russell's invitation to inspect the Yankee horse.

Carlo picked up a Spencer rifle he had salvaged and handed it to Jack.

"Always wanted to try out one of these." Jack set down his coffee cup and examined the latest in lethal weaponry. "Do you have any ammunition for it? Ours won't fit."

"I picked up a few boxes." Carlo showed him a tube filled with cartridges.

Jack picked out a cartridge, rolled it around in his fingers and let out a low whistle. "All in one piece. Seven shots, one after another. How in the devil did the Yankees manage to lose?"

"They didn't all have those fancy rifles," Carlo said. "Some of the Springfields we picked up were junk."

"Appears y'all did fine without us, anyway." Jack nodded toward the battlefield. "We rode over the mess. Good thing it was a cold night. It'll keep the stink down until the sun warms things up. I suppose we'll be spending the day following the Yanks to Jacksonville. Or else removing our dead and throwing dirt over dead Yankees. Depends on which straw we draw."

Carlo said in a low voice. "Saw some things… Did some things…." He intended to never speak of yesterday's horrors to anyone, but found himself telling Jack about the wounded man he killed.

Jack listened without interruption until Carlo's throat closed up. Tears welled in his eyes, and he could speak no more.

"I know. I know how it is." Jack pressed a reassuring hand on Carlo's shoulder. "Everybody all right at home?"

Carlo cupped his hands around his tin mug, absorbing the warmth, collecting himself. He wiped his sleeve over his eyes and nodded. "Everybody was fine when I left. Teresa didn't have the baby yet. But I heard something about Ramon."

"Yeah?" Jack picked up his cup and took a swig, watching Carlo over the rim, his blue gaze steady.

"I heard he took the Union oath."

Jack shrugged as though he was not in the least scandalized.

"Heard he wants Teresa to come to St. Augustine."

One side of Jack's mouth quirked up. "Figured he would."

"You wouldn't do that, would you? Take their old oath?"

"Probably not. Even if I did, I still couldn't bring Martina with me into the Yankee lines without her getting arrested as a spy."

"Is that the only reason?"

"Best one I know. Besides that, with no way to make a living, I'd have to stay in St. Augustine with Pop." Jack snorted. "I reckon that would be worse than prison."

Carlo let a soft laugh escape. "Thanks, Jack."

"For what?"

"You know. Making it seem better."

"Ramon probably figured he didn't have much of a choice." Jack's tone had gone serious. "I hope you won't hold it too much against him. One of these days the war will be over, and y'all will still be kin."

"You don't get along so well with your kin."

"Doesn't mean I don't want to. Anyway it's different with Ramon. My folks are on the other side. Ramon just quit fighting before the fighting was over, that's all."

"What if we have to arrest him? Don't they shoot deserters?" There. Carlo applied the ugly word to his cousin and wanted to take it back. But wasn't that what Ramon was?

"I don't think we'll get the chance to arrest Ramon." Jack took another sip of coffee and swallowed it with apparent enjoyment. "Anyway, I'm not going to beat the bushes hunting for him."

"I won't, either. Not unless I have to."

"Tell you what. Let's try to get a little rest before the officers roust us out and put shovels or reins in our hands. We have more rough times coming. You can bet on it."

CHAPTER SEVENTEEN

From his vantage point on the upper deck Prescott watched while the crew of the side-wheeler *Ottawa* secured the vessel to the Palatka wharf. The *Columbine,* a refitted tugboat, nosed in to moor on the other side. "No resistance so far," Prescott told Lieutenant Commander Breese, who was supervising the operation. The ship's captain merely grunted in reply.

No seasickness, either. Prescott much preferred riverboat travel to the pitch of ocean waves. He observed the partly destroyed town, streets strewn with weeds. The stove-in walls of a brick warehouse bearing the sign "Teasdale and Reid" showed evidence of cannon fire. Apparently this was not the first visit from the Union Navy. "Those scows and that broken-down steamer appear to be the only rebel property. No people showing themselves." Prescott pointed with his cigar. "No rebels, either."

"Doesn't mean a thing." The navy man spat over the gunwale. "Last time we sent the *Mary Benton* down here, it ran into an ambush. Rebs played it cagy, stayed quiet, waited for the men to disembark, then opened fire. We lost a number of men and a colonel was shot up pretty bad. We don't want that to happen to us."

"Of course not." Prescott shook his head. "I heard they handled our boys roughly outside Lake City, as well." Just before his company boarded the *Ottawa*, news had trickled to Jacksonville of a stinging defeat suffered by the Union Army. The drive toward Tallahassee had been brought to an abrupt and bloody halt. His regiment could have improved the outcome, given a chance to join the fight.

Or he might have been left moldering on the battlefield, downed by a backwoods ignoramus like Jack Farrell. Prescott touched his shoulder where his coat hid the scar. That gunshot wound had dulled his sense of invincibility, if not his confidence.

No doubt staying away from that battle was all for the best. Now that his company had handed off the shovels for others to utilize, this assignment was more to his liking.

"If you wish, sir, I'll have my men destroy those boats," Prescott told the navy commander.

"Have at it. Before you start, you'd better let a squad scout out the buildings and the ditches for rebel sharpshooters. Tell your men to be quick about it. We don't intend to stay here long before continuing upriver."

Prescott ordered Lieutenant Owen to organize a team equipped with kerosene and matches. He sent another party to feel out the shore for hostile presences.

Soon heavy, choking black smoke from the burning boats forced him off the *Ottawa.* He stepped onto the dock and started toward the riverbank. He noticed a couple of men in ragged civilian garb walking toward the wharf, looking around warily. He met them at the foot of the dock and barred their way. "Who are you, and what do you want?"

"I'm Jason Coker and this is my son Andy," the older man said. "We've been hiding out from Confederate conscription agents. After the soldiers pulled out of Camp Call we moved closer to the river hoping y'all would come along. Our wives and young 'uns are in town." He nodded toward the *Ottawa.* "We want you to take us into Union lines."

"Very well. Come with me." Prescott escorted the refugees to the boat, hand on his revolver butt in case they were liars. Then he turned them over to a provost guard, who could best deal with the layouts, their women and their brats.

Prescott heard no gunfire from the direction of town, so he assumed all was peaceful. When the scouts he had sent out returned, Prescott strode up to Isaac, who led the squad. "Did you see any rebels?"

The Negro corporal saluted. "No, sir, no rebels."

"Very well. Anybody living in this godforsaken town?"

Isaac hesitated and glanced at Zeke, who grinned and nodded.

"Well?"

"House back there looks to be lived in, sir." Isaac pointed down the street.

"Take me there."

Prescott led his squad to the sizeable two-story clapboard house. Clothes of the feminine kind hung on a line beside the front porch. Behind the house, in a paddock, grazed two of the small horses common in Florida.

Perhaps the women hiding within could tell him something useful about Dickison's command, information that might lead him to Jack Farrell. Perhaps they would have more to offer. Some destitute women could be persuaded to give their all in trade for a side of pork or a sack of flour.

"Somebody certainly does live here. Let's see what we can find out." He turned to Isaac. "Have the men remain on the street while I investigate." He strode onto the front porch and rapped at the door.

A woman stepped onto the porch and shut the door behind her. Not just any woman but one he recognized from his patrols throughout St. Johns County. "Ah! Sarah Phillips!" He put on a charming smile. "What brings you to this godforsaken town?"

"I was just going to ask you the same thing, Captain Prescott."

Her bold, impertinent gaze annoyed him. Women ought to show more respect to a man, especially a man who held as much power over her as he did. "Where is old Dixie's troop hiding out these days? Don't you have a brother in that gang of guerillas?"

Her fearless laugh irritated him more. "I'm afraid you'll have to figure that out for yourself."

"I need to inspect the house."

"No. We have a woman inside who just gave birth and her new baby. I won't let you disturb them."

"Let me? We'll see about that." He pushed her aside, flung open the door, and strode inside the front room, temporarily blinded as his eyes adjusted to the darker interior.

"Stop right there!" called out a woman's voice.

He froze, staring into the twin barrels of a shotgun. Behind the weapon stood, of all creatures, Martina Sanchez. The determined look on her face reinforced the deadliness of the scattergun. He took in the sight of her hand poised over the triggers of the cocked weapon. The muzzle did not waver from its aim toward his chest.

"Get out." Despite the tremor in her voice, her fierce expression convinced him she would blast him full of shot before he could draw his own weapon to defend himself. He backed out the door onto the porch. In his haste, he stumbled but caught himself and did not fall.

"And keep going." Sarah Phillips flounced inside and slammed the door so hard the wall shook.

*

Isaac watched Prescott's hasty retreat and clapped his hand over his mouth to prevent the officer from seeing him laugh. He had spotted

Jack's old marsh tackie in the back yard and figured Miss Martina must be inside the house. Captain Prescott likely would not have recognized Ladybug, because the city-bred northern man hardly knew the difference between a horse and a mule. Isaac had pointed out the house, knowing if he did not, that joker Zeke would.

Whatever she did sure put a scare into Captain Prescott. The officer reeled off the porch and shouted to Isaac, "Corporal Farrell! Take the men, go into that house and bring me that Sanchez woman. You know who I mean. She's got a shotgun. Go in with rifles ready and shoot her if you must. Bring out everyone in that house. I'm arresting them all."

Isaac's amusement died. He glanced at his men. Zeke grinned, an expectant look on his face.

Isaac led the men onto the porch and paused at the door. "Miss Martina," he called out. "It's me, Isaac. I'm comin' in, and I'm askin' you not to shoot."

Captain Prescott hollered, "If they don't come out right now, we'll burn them out."

"Please, Miss Martina." Isaac had nothing against Jack's wife, but he figured the boys would consider it great fun to turn the house into a bonfire. He turned the knob and stepped inside. The woman stood trembling and wide-eyed, the shotgun cradled in her arms but not pointed at him. The other lady, Miss Sarah, stood next to her, arms crossed in defiance.

"Isaac, what does he want from us?" Miss Martina whispered.

"Captain Prescott wants everybody outside. You best give me that shotgun, Miss Martina. Don't want no accidents."

"We need to defend ourselves," she said. "Captain Prescott would do us harm."

"You don't come outside, I'll have to burn the house down. Captain says so, I got to do it. That's some kind of harm, ain't it?"

Shoulders drooping, she handed him the weapon. "I'll go. Teresa is too ill. What about the babies?"

"You can tell him about them," Isaac said. "Maybe he change his mind. Meantime, I got orders."

Miss Sarah spoke up. "Isaac, please give us a moment. I'll go with you, Tina. Maybe we can persuade Prescott to leave us be."

*

Martina didn't believe Prescott could be persuaded to leave them be. All the man knew was force. Holding him off with the shotgun might have been a mistake, but what else was she to do?

She would not give him another excuse to destroy the only shelter Teresa and the little ones had. If, indeed, he needed an excuse. She took a deep breath and walked onto the porch to confront him. Heart pounding in her chest, she hugged herself to keep her hands from shaking. She felt weak and unwell. Facing Prescott was harder to do without the shotgun in her hands. Aware of Sarah standing nearby, at least she was not utterly alone this time.

"Ah, Miss Sanchez. Or is it Mrs. Farrell now?" Prescott strode toward her, a smile crossing his face. It was not a good smile. "Where is your man, that worthless renegade? Is he skulking in the bushes, looking for a chance to murder me?"

"What do you want from me, Captain Prescott?"

"You're under arrest for threatening a U. S. officer. You and everybody in that house are under arrest and have to come with us."

"No one else did anything. Just me. Please leave them alone."

Prescott looked past her. "Corporal, didn't I order you to bring the others out? Jump to it, man."

Isaac disappeared inside the house. After a few moments he stuck his head out the door. "Sir, they won't come out. They's a sick lady won't get out a bed, two babies, and a little child."

Sarah said, "I told you Mrs. Andreu just had a baby two days ago. She and the infant can't be moved."

"Search the house, then. See if anybody else is hiding in there." He said to Martina, "I don't care about the rest of them. You're coming with me."

Martina dreaded leaving without Rosa, but she feared telling Prescott one of the babies was hers. And Jack's. Better to leave Rosa with Sarah and Teresa than risk Prescott harming her. Would he stoop to hurt an infant for revenge? She did not want to find out.

Isaac re-emerged after a few minutes. "Sir, that's all they is. Three young 'uns, the sick lady, Miss Sarah and Miss Martina."

Prescott glared at Sarah. "I am arresting you as well."

"Why?" Sarah demanded. "And why are you doing this to Mrs. Farrell? She only threatened you because she was frightened. Seems to me she had good reason."

"Corporal, place both these women under arrest and we'll take them to the boat."

"Sir, I beg of you." Martina felt the hot tears come and hated showing weakness. "We can't leave Mrs. Andreu alone with those babies. Who will take care of them?"

Prescott fished a cigar out of his pocket and took a long moment lighting it. "The spawn of rebels are not my concern."

*

Prescott took a satisfying puff from his cigar and smiled at his captives. They looked terrified, especially Martina, which was exactly how he wanted them to feel. Perhaps by using her as a hostage, he could bring Jack Farrell out into the open to even the score.

A blast from the ship's horn announced it was making ready to leave. He turned to Zeke. "Bring those horses along as well, and hurry it up. We have use for them."

"You're stealing our horses too?" Sarah Phillips fisted her hands, looking more angry than frightened. "Doesn't the Union army have enough horses, without taking ours?"

"I'm confiscating those cavalry horses." Prescott pointed with his cigar. "Depriving the rebel army use of them."

"Those aren't cavalry horses. The gelding is mine, and the old mare is of no use to you."

"I'll let the army make that determination." Prescott laughed. "If it's no good for riding, I'm sure our men will enjoy the horsemeat."

*

Martina walked along the dock to the boat, guarded by two Negro soldiers. Sarah, to her front, was likewise escorted. In front of Martina strolled Captain Prescott. Zeke led Stripe and Ladybug at the rear of the squad. Every clattering footstep of the steel-tapped soldier's shoes on the wooden planks echoed doom.

What would become of Rosa, Ana, Teresa and little Ramon? Never mind what horrors Prescott planned for her and Sarah.

She stepped across the gangplank and onto the deck. There she spotted a navy officer supervising the crew as they prepared to cast off. "Commander!" she called out, thankful she had learned navy rank insignia during their presence in St. Augustine. "May I have a word with you, please, sir?"

"Yes, ma'am?" The navy officer took a step toward her, curiosity on his face.

Prescott imposed himself in between. "Commander Breese, these women are my prisoners."

"Really?" Breese looked over Martina, Sarah, and the horses. "Are the rebels wearing skirts these days?"

"These women may not be in the rebel army, but they are rebels nonetheless." Prescott nodded toward Martina. "This one threatened me with a shotgun. The other one is her accomplice."

"Sir," Martina began, "please listen to our side of the story. May we speak to you in private?"

Sarah spoke up. "Sir, we beg of you. Captain Prescott forcibly removed us from an invalid and infants who are unable to take care of themselves."

Breese cocked an eyebrow at Prescott. "Threatened you with a shotgun, eh?"

"Corporal Farrell has it." Prescott pointed with his cigar. "Exhibit A."

"Don't I have a right to defend myself?" Martina snapped. "Sir, I don't want everyone on the ship to hear what I have to say. Can we please speak in private?"

Breese looked from her to Prescott and grinned. "I always can make time to speak to a young lady in private. Excuse us, Captain Prescott."

"You can't believe her, Commander." Prescott's ears had turned red. "She will do nothing but spin tall tales to deceive you."

The commander inclined his head. "I believe I can discern truth from lies, Captain Prescott."

Martina exchanged a fortifying look with Sarah and followed him into his office. She fingered her rosary and prayed in silence.

Breese left the door to his office open and turned to face her. "What do you have to say for yourself, Miss?"

"My name is Mrs. Farrell," Martina said. "Thank you for letting me speak." She took a deep breath. "I admit I threatened Captain Prescott with a shotgun. I would not have done such a thing if I weren't terrified of the man."

"Terrified? You didn't just meet him?"

Martina shook her head. "No, sir. I've known him for a while." How much should she reveal? "My daughter is just six months old, and I left her back there at our house. There is no one to take care of her and the others Mrs. Phillips told you about."

"You left your baby? Why didn't you bring it along?"

"I was afraid Captain Prescott would harm her."

Breese frowned his disapproval. "He's a Union officer, Mrs. Farrell. Not a monster."

But he is a monster. Martina bit her lip and tried to calm herself.

"Where is your husband?" Breese asked.

"He is in the Confederate Army, sir."

"I'm sorry to hear that."

"His brother is a captain in the Union Army. I'm sure he would vouch for me. Do you know him? Captain Dan Farrell? He's stationed in St. Augustine, last I heard."

"Haven't had the pleasure. What about Captain Prescott's other prisoner? What is her part in this?"

"She didn't do anything wrong. She's helping me care for our sick friend and her newborn. The baby is just two days old, sir. They will perish without us. And so will my baby." Tears flooded her eyes. "Please, sir. Let us go home. You can ask the soldiers. The corporal named Isaac. He searched the house and saw them."

Breese stepped outside the office and told a crewman to fetch Isaac. Soon the sailor reappeared with the Negro.

"Corporal, Mrs. Farrell says you searched her house. Tell me what you saw."

"Sir, I found a lady sick in bed, and three little young 'uns."

"Anybody else?"

"Just Miss Martina here and Miss Sarah."

"That's the other lady your captain arrested?"

"Yes, sir."

"Did this lady threaten to shoot the soldiers?"

"Just the captain when he went into the house, sir. He came out right quick." Isaac's lips curled into an ill-concealed smile.

"Did you see anything else of a hostile nature?"

"Miss Martina gave me her shotgun really nice-like, when I asked for it. I didn't see nothing else military. Only thing was two cow ponies, and we con… confis… we brought 'em with us."

"Thank you corporal. Dismissed."

Hands folded behind his back, the commander watched Isaac leave. He turned to Martina, his neutral expression giving nothing away. "Let's return to the deck, shall we, Mrs. Farrell?"

*

Prescott shifted on his feet and glared at Sarah Phillips, who stood, arms folded, and would not deign to look at him. What was taking so long? Why did Commander Breese ask for Isaac?

Finally Breese emerged with Martina. He told her to stand next to Mrs. Phillips then walked over to Prescott and said in a low voice, "See here, Captain Prescott. We already have a number of refugees and colored contrabands who have come aboard seeking asylum. We have only so much room for passengers. I see no reason to hold these women."

"But Mrs. Farrell's husband is one of Dickison's guerillas." Prescott felt his opportunity slipping away. The commander's word was as good as a deity's on board ship. "I suggest we keep her as a hostage, and perhaps that will help us capture him and the rest of that band as well."

Breese raised a skeptical eyebrow. "I don't see how that would play out. I'll make room for the horses because the army needs remounts, but I will let the ladies return to their home." He leaned closer and lowered his voice. "In the future, Captain Prescott, I suggest you spend more energy fighting soldiers than helpless women and children."

"But, sir," Sarah broke in. "We need our horses. We have no means of transportation without them. And we need the shotgun to defend ourselves."

"To shoot at us?" Prescott restrained his impulse to throttle the woman.

"To defend ourselves." She glanced in his direction, then back to the commander. "From deserters and runaways. Surely you can understand – "

"Madam, I can't do that." At least the softheaded navy man was not going to concede everything to these two Secesh women. "Perhaps you should persuade your men to come home and protect you."

"My husband is dead," Sarah snapped. "At least give us receipts for the horses and the weapon you took from us.

Breese turned to his aide. "Davis, write up the receipts and give them to the ladies."

While they waited, Prescott chewed his moustache in frustration, outranked and outflanked. Others had observed the proceedings as well, as some of his men and the civilian refugees stood within earshot.

Impudent women. Dangerous women. They needed to be controlled, not set free. Damn Breese for being such a lenient fool.

*

"At least they're leaving without us." Martina glanced over her shoulder at the gunboat now pulling away from the wharf. Her pulse still raced after the encounter. Despite their reprieve, she feared Prescott would somehow find a way to pursue her.

"With my pony," Sarah added, "and your old Ladybug. What on earth did they want with her?"

"They just don't want us to have them." Martina's hands finally had quit trembling. She pulled her shawl closer around herself. "We'd better get used to walking everywhere we go. At least we can. It'll be a while before Teresa is up to it."

"They burned the flatboats, so how will I cross the river when it's time to go back to Moultrie?" Sarah kicked an oyster shell out of her path. "Dratted Yankees."

"And my shotgun. I won't feel safe without it. Not until our men return." *If they do.* She touched her rosary and stifled a sob. "Thank God we got away from Prescott."

"The navy commander possesses a shred of humanity, even if that beast Prescott doesn't," Sarah huffed. "But he knows where to find us now. Still, I don't want us to move out of that nice house on his account."

Martina shuddered. "Pray our men come back before Prescott does."

CHAPTER EIGHTEEN

A week after the Union Army's trouncing at Olustee, Dan sought out Captain Prescott at his headquarters in Jacksonville. He bristled with news from a refugee he had recruited into his company. When the aide showed Dan in, Prescott looked up from a mound of paperwork and frowned. "What do you want, Farrell?"

Dan did not waste breath in pleasantries. "I understand you went on the *Ottawa* upriver to Palatka, arrested my sister-in-law, and brought her onto the boat. Is that so?"

Prescott opened a wooden box at the corner of his desk, picked out a cigar, examined it, and bit off the end. "I most certainly did. Had it been up to me, I would have shipped her here and placed her in the guardhouse."

"What was your justification?"

"She aimed a shotgun at me, with intent." Prescott waved his hand toward a weapon propped against the wall. "That shotgun."

"I'm sure she believed she had to protect herself." Dan leaned over the rough wooden desktop and braced his hands on the edges. "I understand you mistreated her in the past, and she's justifiably afraid of you."

"Not so. She's been spreading lies." Prescott snorted as he backed up an inch in his seat. "If a female wants to go around threatening to shoot Union officers, she should be prepared to accept the consequences, same as a man." He struck a match and took his time lighting the cigar. "I'm surprised you claim that little Minorcan she-devil as a relative, Farrell."

"She-devil?" Dan gripped the edges of the desk. "Watch your mouth, Prescott."

Prescott took a drag from his cigar and blew the smoke toward Dan's face. "Mighty protective of that rebel woman, aren't you?"

Damned if Prescott didn't seem to be enjoying himself. "Seems she needs protecting whenever you're around. Who was the lady you arrested with her?"

Prescott lifted a quizzical eyebrow. "Who told you about that incident?"

"Who was the other lady?"

"A Sarah Phillips. I knew her from when I was stationed at St. Augustine, before your rebel brother shot me."

Sarah? Why was she in Palatka?

"There was another woman at the house, too. And some children. I didn't see fit to bring their brats on board." Prescott examined the tip of his cigar. "Messy little beasts."

"Teresa Andreu?"

"Didn't ask."

"Where are their horses? I heard you confiscated their animals."

"That was Lieutenant Commander Breese's decision. We need horses, you know. Don't you want to equip that company of deserters you're cultivating?"

"Martina's old mare isn't fit for service."

"You seem to know a lot about what is what with that rebel's woman. I'm no horse expert, Farrell. Maybe you can find it at the horse depot. A broken-down animal might just suit you. Unless they condemned and put down the sorry beast."

"I'll look into it."

Prescott leaned back farther in his chair and glared at Dan. "Seems to me you're mighty soft on rebels, Farrell. Makes me wonder."

"Wonder what you will. I believe I've made up my mind about you. Stay away from my sister-in-law, or I swear I'll call you out."

Dan left Prescott's office before he lost his grip on his self control and thrashed the man. Assaulting a fellow officer would have jeopardized his commission. He headed for the horse depot.

Prescott's insulting demeanor as well as his mistreatment of Martina infuriated Dan. The little time he had spent with his sister-in-law convinced him that his father's and Jack's high regard for her was well founded. He was more inclined to believe her innocence than Prescott's cool accusations. And if Prescott had also abused Sarah.... How was it he and Prescott were on the same side? The man acted more like an enemy than an ally.

Dan strode the half mile to the horse depot. Had he been a steam engine, he would have overshot the station. He halted at the corral fence and watched the horses as they grazed. The sight of the animals did little to lighten his mood.

The battle was as hard on them as it was on the men. Of the horses that survived Olustee, many were injured or exhausted from overwork. Those expected to recover their usefulness rested in a pasture. Matted hair ringed an oozing wound on one horse's neck. Another suffered a bad cut on its side that someone had stitched together. Most were skinny. Hard use had worn them down.

He had seen the little mare Prescott confiscated from Martina only briefly, during his unwilling sojourn in Palatka. However, among the larger northern horses she should be easy to find. Then he spotted a marsh tackie with a distinctive blaze, like the one Sarah Phillips rode to the San Sebastian bridge when she tried to see Ramon. Nearby was another compact horse with enlarged joints and muzzle frosted with age. Certainly that was the pair Prescott confiscated.

Dan located the sergeant in charge of the horse depot. "I need a couple of fresh horses for my troop," he told the noncom. "I've sent to St. Augustine and Fernandina to have the men brought here, and we need more mounts for them."

The sergeant looked dubious. "Well, sir. Most of them horses ain't fit for duty. Won't be for quite a while."

"I spotted a couple of native horses that don't appear to be injured or run to death. I'll requisition those two as a start, if nobody else has claimed them."

The sergeant checked through a pile of papers on the desk and studied a document. "No, sir. They just came in off the *Ottawa*. Confiscated in a raid upriver."

"I'll take them with me now."

"One of 'em's been condemned. You sure you want that one, sir?"

"I'm willing to take it off your hands. Save you the trouble."

An officer's authority proved useful. The sergeant produced a form, and Dan signed it. He took a couple of halters and lead ropes from the storage room and went to the corral to collect the animals.

They were docile as pets and let him lead them out the gate. The sergeant nodded to Martina's mare. "Sir, that one don't look like she's got much service left to her, if you don't mind my saying."

"She'll do," Dan said. "I'll find a job for her."

"Yes, sir." The sergeant saluted, and Dan returned the gesture as he walked away with his acquisitions.

What on earth am I doing? Am I letting my heart overrule my head? Sentimental foolishness. As the sergeant pointed out, Martina's mare was past usefulness as a cavalry mount, and he figured his sister-in-law only used the nag to pull the wagon.

Sarah's horse presented a problem. It looked fit enough for her rebel brother to ride against the very troop of Unionist Florida men Dan was forming. Although he would like to somehow return the blaze-faced pony and earn the gratitude of its rightful owner, he did not want to allow the animal to be used by his enemies.

He walked the pair to his quarters and picketed them with the bay he had ridden to Olustee and back. The Union-issue horse had not yet recovered from the experience but pricked its ears with interest at the newcomers. Dan fed and watered all of them. He figured he could ride Sarah's horse and let the government issue horse rest for a while. He would hold onto Martina's pony until he decided what to do with it.

*

A week later Dan had consolidated his little command of about twenty men. Besides Coker, he had recruited no troops since the battle at Olustee. He supposed that despite Federal entrenchment in Jacksonville, faith in the ability of the Union Army to prevail in Florida had diminished.

He conducted an inspection and had the recruits drill on horseback to demonstrate their ability. Sergeant Drake, a veteran transferred from a Connecticut regiment, was the only other officer, commissioned or not, the tiny command rated.

Dan sat on Sarah's blaze-faced horse in the chill morning damp and watched the men, mostly mounted on the Florida horses, perform their evolutions under the sergeant's direction. They made a trim, uniform appearance in their new blue jackets and kepis. He was not able to acquire the latest in weaponry for them, but the carbines, revolvers and sabers they had at least matched the rebel firepower.

At length, the demonstration complete, the sergeant rode up to Dan and saluted. "What do you think, sir?"

"Everything seems to be in order. You appear to have instructed the men well in the short time you've worked with them. They can march their horses in formation and follow commands. How is their weapon proficiency coming along?"

The square-jawed noncom puffed out his chest. "Very good, sir. Them boys can shoot. I vow they are ready for action."

"We'll be seeing some directly. General Seymour has ordered us to go upriver aboard the *Columbine*. We're joining the force that's being sent to occupy Palatka."

Drake's eyes flashed. "Now you're talkin', sir."

Dan nodded toward the undersized troop, the men sitting at attention on their horses. He rested his gaze on his newest recruit, who seemed to be taking instruction well enough for a man who had avoided rebel conscription for a year or more. "We picked up Coker at Palatka. He says there are others who would join. The general believes we can find more recruits if we make a strong showing. Of course, we'll be assigned to picket and scouting duty. Think the men are up for that?"

"Ready and eager, sir. When do we report to the boat?"

"This afternoon at five sharp. Have the men prepare their horses and equipment straightaway."

*

Nearby explosions shook the house hard enough to rattle the fireplace hardware. After hanging a bucket of water over the fire to heat, Martina stood up straight and gazed out the window. "The Yankees must be back, shelling the riverbank to run off our pickets."

Sarah headed for the front door. "Let's take a look. If they shoot a cannon our way, at least we'll see the shell coming. Inside the house, we wouldn't know what hit us."

Martina followed and pulled her shawl tighter against the cold drizzle that blew onto the porch and needled her face. Vacant buildings obstructed her view of the wharf, but at least she could see whoever came up the street.

Nip climbed the steps and greeted them, tongue lolling in a canine smile, not the least gun-shy. Martina curled her fingers around the dog's rope collar. "You can go inside the house. Jack wouldn't like it if the Yankees shot you for sport." *Wherever Jack might be.* She opened the door and invited the hound through, just as she had done when the Yankees came two weeks ago.

"I wonder whether Prescott is returning to plague us." The cold seeped through Martina's clothing and she shuddered, as much from fear as the chill.

"Should I feel guilty for wishing Jack's aim had directed the bullet a trifle lower?" Sarah's voice held no levity.

"I don't," Martina murmured.

"At least Teresa's better, and little Ramon is gaining." Sarah cast a longing look toward the west, away from town and the river. "Too bad we can't just leave and take all of us out of reach of those scoundrels."

Martina believed Sarah's steadfastness over these past few trying weeks had brought them all through. In other ways, their situation had deteriorated. Without a horse to pull the wagon, they could not evacuate and take Teresa with them, as she was still too frail to endure a long trek on foot. Without the shotgun, they had only kitchen knives for protection.

The clatter of hoof-beats preceded a trio of Confederate pickets riding away from the river. Sarah called out to them. "Are the Yankees landing?"

The corporal, a militiaman Martina knew slightly, reined in. "Yes, ma'am." His rubber poncho, shiny and wet, rested in folds over his shoulders. He touched his hat and caused more water to drip off the brim onto his gray-stippled beard. "The Yanks are fixing to unload a whole regiment over at the wharf. All we can do is spread the word."

"Thank you for letting us know." Martina exchanged a worried look with Sarah.

The soldier kicked his horse into a canter to catch up with the others. Martina watched the men ride away, envying their ability to flee.

"We've already made up our minds," Sarah said. "It would be better to go to them and throw ourselves at their mercy than to wait for them to find us."

Martina nodded. They had worried the subject to death, and that pathetic plan was the best they could concoct. "If Prescott is with them, most likely he'll think twice about abusing us in front of witnesses, even if they are Yankees. I'll tell Teresa where we're going."

*

Dan led the blaze-faced cow pony down the dock and onto the street fronting the river. Sergeant Drake followed with his mount and the rest of the troop with their horses. The animals seemed to suffer no ill effect from the violent overnight thunderstorm. Dan looked over the portion of the town within view of the riverbank. It appeared deserted and desolate in the gray mist. He said to Drake, "Last time I crossed the river into Palatka, about a year ago, I was a prisoner of the rebels. I much prefer the current circumstances."

"Wonder if there are any hiding in town." Drake scanned the waterfront buildings.

"Commander Breese said they didn't run across any a couple of weeks ago. Coker said most of them pulled out to contest our occupation of Jacksonville. If they aren't here now, they'll be coming back. We're giving them another occupation to dispute."

"Bring it on." Drake spat a stream of tobacco juice onto the dirt.

Dan gestured toward the direction of Martina's house. "We'll start our sweep in this direction. Some people I need to contact live there, or used to."

"Yes, sir. Think they'll give us any information we can use?"

"We shall see. Have the men mount up. We'll keep a sharp lookout in case the rebels are playing possum." Dan swung into the saddle, but when he started forward, he spotted two women walking down the street. They skirted a puddle then righted their course and continued toward him. "Stand by while I see what these ladies want. I believe they could be the very people I'm looking for." He rode to meet the women.

He recognized his sister-in-law despite the wide-brimmed palmetto hat, which shadowed her fine features. Her strained expression relaxed into a brilliant smile. "Dan! It is you! I wasn't sure…"

"I was just going to look for you, and you found me." He turned to the other woman and felt a rush of pleasure. "Miss Sarah. You do have a way of turning up."

"Like a bad penny?" Her cheeks were damp from the drizzle, and her bonnet appeared to be soaked. But her blue eyes sparkled, and he could have sworn she was glad to see him. "So do you, Dan Farrell."

Her gaze shifted to his horse, which took a step forward and extended its head toward her. "Stripe!" She touched the white streak on the muzzle and the animal nudged her shoulder with its nose. "How did you get my horse?"

"He's federal property now."

"My foot." She glared at him. "I have a receipt and I mean to claim him. Where is that beast Captain Prescott?"

"Not on the *Columbine*. I guess he and his company stayed in Jacksonville."

"Thank the Lord," breathed Martina. "Dan, will you stay with us? We have room."

Sarah shot her a disapproving look, then said to Dan, "We also have two babies and a small child. Plus the dog. It isn't a very peaceful household."

"I'm willing to make such dire sacrifices for my country." Dan grinned at her, then turned to Martina. “I’ll be honored to make my headquarters at your house, squalling children and all. Now, ladies, tell me this. Are any of your soldiers still in town?”

Sarah shrugged. “The only soldiers I know of were on the skedaddle. Last I saw of them was the rumps of their horses.” Then she inclined her head. “Do you really trust me to tell you the truth?”

“Would you care a rip if they set up an ambush and shot me?”

Sarah blinked and did not reply. He shifted his attention to Martina. “Where’s Jack?”

“I honestly don’t know.” Her smile faded. “We haven’t had mail for a few weeks.”

“I figure he isn’t much of a correspondent, anyway,” Dan mused. “He wrote me only a handful of letters from the time we left home years ago.”

“We haven’t heard from Carlo or Russell, either,” Martina added. “We’ve been pretty well cut off.”

“Your little brother joined up, eh? Is Teresa Andreu still staying with you?”

Martina nodded. “She has a new baby boy.”

“I have business to discuss with her.” Dan let out his breath. “Ladies, go home and get out of the weather. I’ll assign a guard to make sure nobody bothers you. After I’ve seen to my duties, I’ll be there.”

CHAPTER NINETEEN

Sarah peered through the window into falling darkness, her anxiety tinged with excitement. She watched Dan Farrell dismount from Stripe and loop the reins around a low branch. So far in the service of the Union, Stripe's condition apparently had not suffered. He did not look malnourished or overworked, though Dan had probably been riding him all day in pursuit of anyone opposing the invasion.

She tucked a stray wisp of hair behind her ear as he spoke to the guard stationed in front of the house. The idea of letting Dan live in their household bothered her, but she could not argue against it. Dan's presence and authority would keep them safe from the other soldiers.

"He's alone," she told Martina. "And he's carrying a sack full of something. Do you want to invite him in?

"Of course." Martina laughed, something she did rarely these trying days. "He's Jack's brother, even if he is a Yankee. Would you rather trust our protection to a stranger?"

"He isn't any relation to me," Sarah grumbled. "And he stole my horse."

"Prescott and that navy officer took our horses," Martina pointed out. "Not Dan."

"I'd like to find out how he got hold of Stripe." Sarah watched Dan step onto the porch, pause, and look around as though assessing his surroundings.

"Ask him. And I'll ask about Ladybug as well." Martina opened the door and Dan stepped inside. The dog, darn his hide, greeted Dan like an old friend, wagging his whole body and sniffing the blue trousers.

Dan dropped a hand to rumple Nip's ears, removed his hat and acknowledged Martina and Sarah with a tentative smile. He held up the sack. "I brought a peace offering. Some provisions."

Martina accepted the sack and peeked inside. "Coffee, flour and bacon. Wonderful! We've been running low on everything." She looked up at him and smiled. If she were a dog, she would have wagged her tail.

"Thank you, Dan. I saved you some fish for supper. I'll make coffee to go with it."

Sarah had to give him credit. The man was no fool. After looking around the desolate, unpopulated town, he would have figured out they needed any supplies they could scrounge. She did not want to admit they had been living on catfish and mullet from the river and oranges gleaned from the neglected groves. They had long since run out of corn meal and flour, and she had not tasted coffee in a year.

"I'm paying you back for how kindly you treated me when I was a prisoner." His fond smile seemed genuine as he regarded his sister-in-law. "After I escaped, I lived on the smoked fish and cornbread you packed for me."

"Did you know you have a niece?" Martina smiled back at the Yankee officer, a perfect round of mutual admiration. "We named her Rosa, after my mother. I'll introduce you to your niece, and to Teresa and her family. They're in the back bedroom."

"Of course. As I mentioned, I have business to discuss with Teresa."

"Is it about Ramon? How is he?" Martina fingered the rosary at her waist.

"Ramon is at home, within our lines, and doing fine. He would like to have his wife join him, if she is willing."

"So the rumor is true," Martina mused. "He gave up."

"She didn't get our letters?"

Martina shook her head.

"Unfortunate, but I'm not surprised." Dan turned to Sarah. "Captain Prescott told me you were here. It's just you, Martina, Mrs. Andreu and the children?"

"That's enough, isn't it? We don't have any Confederate soldiers hiding under the bed." Sarah again replaced the loose strand of hair. "Teresa was sick, and Jack asked me to come help out."

"Good for you, and I'm glad you stayed." A genuine smile lit his eyes. "I enjoy your company."

Stop that. She crossed her arms over her chest. "Did you find any of our men to shoot at?"

"Like you said, they seem to have skedaddled."

"See there?" She lifted her shoulders in a shrug. "I told you the truth."

He arched a brow. "Are you afraid I'll shoot your brother?"

"He isn't here. None of our men are here."

"Where are they?"

"We don't have any idea. Just like I said."

"I expect we'll hear from them soon."

"Never soon enough." Sarah looked out the window, past the guard, to where Stripe was tethered. "You didn't tell me how you got hold of my horse."

"Captain Prescott told me he confiscated the ponies. I needed mounts for my troop, so I requisitioned them."

"If he hadn't taken those horses, we wouldn't be stranded." Sarah continued to watch Stripe crop weeds at the length of his reins. "We would have been able to leave, and we wouldn't have to depend on a Yankee officer for protection."

"Fortunes of war, Miss Sarah, but I'll try to be a benevolent despot." Dan turned back to Martina. "I brought your old mare along. The army condemned her because she's too old for service, though I suppose she can pull your wagon. Don't you have a receipt? You can have her because she's of no use to the either cavalry as a war horse."

"Oh, thank you, Dan," Martina said. "We were at such a loss – "

"Yes, that's kind of you," Sarah conceded. "What about Stripe? I have a receipt for him, too."

Dan shook his head, his expression pained. "I'm sorry. He's too fit and strong. We can't risk having him end up in service to the other side. Russell, for instance."

"He's mine, not my brother's."

"We have to deprive your cavalry of every possible mount. If the policy seems harsh, I regret that."

Sarah's rising opinion of Dan plummeted. "I'll bet I regret it more."

"There's plenty to regret all around," he murmured. "When can I talk to Mrs. Andreu? I'd like to speak to her in private, if that's possible."

*

That evening, Dan retired to the porch and sat in the dark. He wanted to give the women privacy, and Lord knew he needed space to think. He had dismissed the guard, because no one would bother the women with him here, and the picket posts would sound an alarm if the enemy showed up. Most of the soldiers had taken over the town's buildings for housing. Military activity on the streets had quieted as the men who were off duty prepared to retire for the night.

After spending the day pursuing the few rebels left in the vicinity, situating his men and settling a few issues with his hostesses, he was free to enjoy the night. During the day the weather had cleared and remained cool, though the west wind had diminished with sundown.

The door opened, and a lithe figure stepped outside. Even in the faint starlight he recognized Sarah's shapely silhouette. "It's a pleasant night," he told her. "We haven't had a chance to talk yet. Come stay awhile."

"Were the children too much for you?" she asked. "Is that why you retreated to the porch?"

"Not at all. I believe Ana is getting over her fear of my blue uniform, and I wish some adults were as easily retrained. As for the babies, they're quiet when they're asleep. What about you?"

"I couldn't stand it indoors, now that your army won't let us light any candles." She walked down the steps and sat on the edge of the porch. "I don't like stumbling around in the dark."

"It's the same in St. Augustine," he said. "They don't want any possibility of signaling to the enemy."

"That's stupid. They wouldn't be able to see our house from beyond your picket posts. Or the river, for that matter."

"I don't make up the rules."

"About my horse – "

"I promise I'll take good care of Stripe."

"So you say. I know how it is. You'll run him to death. Or my friends'll shoot him. Or your friends, by accident."

"I will try very hard not to overuse him or get him shot. Or myself, for that matter." Dan took a deep breath. "Teresa said she'll take the loyalty oath. I can get her passage on the next boat north. Have you decided what you're going to do?"

"I can't do that. Neither will Martina."

He let out his breath. "That's too bad."

"What if I took your oath, and my brother came to me hungry, sick or wounded? Giving him aid and comfort would violate the terms. Or your brother, for that matter. Would you help him?"

"We give proper care to prisoners of war."

"Your rules are harder on us."

"They aren't my rules, but I have to abide by them. You have caused yourself another problem. I don't know how long Colonel Barton will allow rebel women to stay within our lines."

"Will he let me go with Teresa and her little ones on the boat? She needs help to get to St. Augustine safely, then I can go home."

"I'll see what I can do. Teresa says she's feeling better, but she still seems weak. Tomorrow I'll see about getting passes for the lot of you. I'll ask the surgeon to take a look at her, too. He has a stock of quinine if she needs some."

"Now that she's a Union woman, I suppose he'll be willing to treat her. When do you think the boat will leave?"

"I can't say. Right now the *Columbine* is keeping the town within range of those big guns. In case the rebels try to retake Palatka."

"Martina wants to go through the lines and join Jack."

"Yeah, she says that's where she belongs," Dan said. "But I can only give her safe escort as far as our outposts. I won't send out on her own. It's dangerous out there."

"More dangerous for you."

He ignored the taunt. "I don't think Colonel Barton knows about her trouble with the army in St. Augustine."

"You aren't going to tell him, are you?"

"I find it hard to believe she's a threat. She told my father Prescott made improper advances, and when she refused most emphatically, he made false accusations against her. If any of that spying business was going on, probably Carlo was doing the mischief."

"You and Martina have quite the mutual admiration society." Her voice lightened.

He grinned. "It's good to know somebody in this house doesn't despise me."

"It's nothing personal. It isn't you. It's what you do."

"I am what I do, Miss Sarah."

"I have to admit, you're doing right by us. Except for keeping my horse."

"See? I'm not such a villain."

"When we saw you riding toward us, we knew we would be all right," she said. "We were afraid. If Prescott came back, then what?"

"I heard about the shotgun. I would have liked to have seen that. Sweet little Martina backing down Prescott."

"He couldn't get out of the house fast enough." Sarah chuckled. "He knew she meant business."

"Things didn't go well when I met him, either, though nobody drew a weapon."

"Seems to run in the family."

"Yeah. Jack had a few direct and pertinent things to say about Prescott. However, I'm not at liberty to discuss my true feelings regarding a fellow officer."

Sarah laughed harder.

"Nice to know we agree on a few things, Miss Sarah."

*

Jack strapped his climbing gaffs onto his boots, stood and stared straight up into a scattering of pine needles. On a rise near the river, the tree's height ought to allow him to see the river, the streets of Palatka and the surrounding area. Captain Dickison had ordered him to determine the nature and extent of the Federal fortifications.

That was not all he needed to know. He was spoiling to rush into Palatka and bring Martina out, but common sense overrode that impulse. The place was full of Yankees. *I'm no good to her dead.*

"Tall enough?" Captain Dickison asked.

"We'll see, sir." Jack unwound his rope, looped it around the trunk of the pine and began to walk up the tree.

He worked his way up to a branch high enough to provide a good vantage point and that looked strong enough to support his weight. He straddled the branch and tied the rope around himself and the trunk in case the bough gave way. Hands freed, he took from his pocket the field glasses the captain had given him and studied the view.

"A single gunboat tied to the wharf," he called down. "Must be the *Columbine*. Along with an armed launch." Although river-based scouts had been observing the boat traffic, he might as well report everything of importance. "Bluecoats in the street. No horses, all on foot."

Were Martina and Rosa trapped behind enemy lines? He had heard nothing from his family since leaving for Fort Myers, other than Carlo's two-week-old report. What had become of his wife and daughter? If they had left Palatka, he was not sure Martina could have gotten word to him. Yankee raiders had torn down telegraph lines between Waldo and Baldwin. Mail service was unreliable. The hasty march from the outskirts of Jacksonville to Palatka had not allowed him to search for her anywhere else.

Perhaps he could see their house from the top of the tree and learn something, anything.

Jack panned along the streets trying to find the right house, but other buildings and leafy treetops stood in the way. He swore under his breath. Even if Martina waved from outside, he would not be able to see her. He swept his gaze around the perimeter of the town.

"They've already built fortifications. Breastworks and abatis. Lots of troops behind them. Artillery. I can see four cannons from here. They don't intend to make it easy for us."

"All the way around?" Dickison asked.

"Can't say for sure. Too many trees in the way."

"Any openings within view?"

"Only enough to pass their pickets through. They've set out mounted pickets beyond the breastworks." Jack memorized the positions in relation to roads, woods and landmarks. "I'll draw a map."

He studied the layout a little longer to make sure he had figured out everything within view. Then he pocketed the glasses, untied the rope and picked his way down the tree trunk. He jumped off the last couple of feet and turned to face Captain Dickison. Jack handed over the field glasses and accepted a notebook and pencil from the officer. He sat down to sketch a diagram of the Yankee fortifications ringing the town.

After he finished, Jack showed Dickison the map and explained what he had seen. "Sir, I'm afraid they've had time to get themselves pretty well dug in."

Ever since chasing the Yankees from Olustee to Jacksonville, the Confederate forces had concentrated around that city, seeking a way to dislodge the invaders. In the meantime, word that the enemy occupied Palatka prompted General Finnegan to send Dickison's troop here.

While Dickison studied the sketch, Jack looked toward the town, hidden by a screen of forest. He clenched his fists, released them, and clenched them again.

"You don't even know whether your family is still there." Somehow Dickison guessed what he was thinking. "Our standing order is to harass the enemy and trouble them at every opportunity. You'll attend to duty, personal concerns aside."

Jack turned back to Dickison. "Sir, I need to find out."

"Don't do anything on your own. That's an order, Private Farrell. I have a small command and don't want to lose a good sharpshooter unnecessarily. Same goes for Sanchez and Cates."

Jack let out his breath. "Yes, sir. I hear you."

"Very well." Dickison nodded. "Take heart. If they're truly caught behind enemy lines, we'll find a way to get them out."

*

Dan looked toward the woods to the west, where a raid most likely would originate. His men were now stationed on the outer perimeter at a proper distance from the inner line of infantry. Dug in behind fortifications built over the past few days, a third tier of troops guarded the town from attack.

"Everything seems to be in order," he told Sergeant Drake, who rode with him along the line of picket outposts.

"Yes, sir. Not a rebel in sight."

"Colonel Barton requested fifty additional horses with equipment. He plans to mount more of the New York infantrymen. I hope they know how to ride. We sure could use the help."

Dan turned Stripe toward town, steered through the lane between the breastworks and acknowledged the officer in charge of this sector. He looked forward to a peaceful night and enjoyable female company at Martina's house.

He had spent most of the week since landing in Palatka on the move, leading a mounted patrol into the countryside. A search of the area where Dickison's men had crossed the river when he was in their custody did not turn up the hidden flatboats. His efforts in other areas brought more success, as he had netted a few unwary rebel militiamen and a number of refugees who had been hiding from the Confederate conscription agents. Once the word got out that they would not be forced to serve in the Union army, more layouts had drifted into town seeking sanctuary.

Because Dan's duties kept him away from town, he had seen little of the women since that first day and night. But he was not concerned for their safety. The garrison commander, Colonel Barton, had made it clear to the troops that the handful of civilians living within the town were not to be molested.

Although Dan had been able to persuade neither Sarah nor Martina to take the loyalty oath, he had not yet been ordered to evict them from the house and send them outside Union lines. How long the women would be allowed to remain in their home, he could not predict.

Dan recalled telling his father that women were the worst rebels of all, and he hated to admit the enticing and sassy Sarah Phillips fell into that category. He thought of Sarah often, wanting things to be different between them. He suspected as long as the war dragged on, she would continue her defiant attitude and keep him at arm's length.

He understood her divided sense of loyalty, something he knew firsthand. He had no choice but to respect it. All her male relatives, allied with the ghost of her husband, had arrayed against him.

Shots and shouts. Dan whipped his head around toward the racket. "We're under attack!"

*

Jack kicked Choctaw into a gallop, revolver in hand. He burst out of the woods and rushed toward the Union picket post. Around him the other Confederates in Dickison's command surged to the attack, among them Carlo at his right. Jack rushed into the camp yelling. The mounted Union pickets fired a few shots as they rode away. Two dismounted men, left behind at the campfire, ran toward their horses.

Jack bore down on them, calling out, "Stop! Surrender or I'll shoot!" One of the Yankees turned his head to look at him and made a prudent decision. He stumbled to a halt and lifted his hands in defeat. Jack veered his horse around him to cut off his escape while Carlo chased down the other man and brought him back, subdued and crestfallen.

"Hand me your weapon, butt first," Jack snapped. His prisoner gave him a sullen look but complied, as did Carlo's captive. Jack tucked the revolver into his saddlebag and glanced around the picket post to figure out what to do next. Most of all he wanted to question the prisoners, find out if they knew anything of Martina's whereabouts.

A smattering of gunshots told him the fight had pressed forward, in the direction of Palatka. Toward Martina?

Jack turned to Carlo. "Watch these boys. See if you can find out anything about Martina." He rushed back into the fight.

*

Dan and Drake met the retreating pickets where they had dashed behind the safety of the infantry fortifications. "What the hell?" he demanded. "What's going on?"

"Damned Dixie and his boys, sir," called out the New York corporal. "More of 'em than we could take on."

"Dickison? How do you know?"

"This is their territory. I think they got two of our boys."

"Damn."

The pickets had done their job, such as it was, in alerting the garrison to the attack. The men in his troop had ridden into the barricades as well. After accounting for his men, Dan dismounted and observed the infantry form a skirmish line to repel the rebel cavalry. He pulled his field glasses from his saddlebag and looked toward the attackers.

Dan spotted the advance line of rebels, who hesitated a prudent distance from the entrenchments. He focused on a particular rebel on a chestnut horse, but the man was too far away for Dan to be sure it was Jack. An artillery piece came into action, and a shell whistled overhead. It exploded in between the breastworks and the attackers, kicked up a cloud of dirt and debris and obscured his view of the rider.

Within minutes, the Confederates vanished. Already the infantry skirmishers had moved out of the breastworks and were pressing forward to regain the abandoned picket post. Dan scanned the field but did not see any bodies left behind. "They're gone," he said to Sergeant Drake.

"Cowards," the noncom scoffed.

Dan shook his head. "They're just feeling us out. They'll be back."

CHAPTER TWENTY

Jack held Choctaw to a walk along the wooded path. He did not want to startle a nervous bluecoat into shooting at him. Today's raid would have the Yanks' fingers close to their triggers. He held the improvised white flag overhead as he approached the picket outpost.

He hoped he presented a picture of outer calm, although his pulse pounded fast in his ears. The rod that served as a flagpole was slick with sweat. Jack, Carlo and Russell had managed to talk Captain Dickison into agreeing to their plan to locate their missing loved ones.

"You'll be on your own," Dickison had said. "If they shoot you or take you prisoner, it's your bad luck."

"On the other hand, sir, I'll keep my eyes open, and I might find out something useful about their defenses."

The two Yankees he and Carlo captured had told him women still lived in town. He assumed Martina was one of those women. The prisoners also knew of a certain Captain Farrell, whose command of Union Florida cavalry served alongside their mounted infantry, and where he would find the homegrown Yankees.

"Halt!"

Jack reined in and called out, "Truce flag!"

"You surrendering, Johnny?"

"No! Delivering a message."

"Come out and let us see you."

Jack nudged Choctaw into the sunshine and stopped again. Two mounted Yankees, not a hundred feet away, trained their rifles on him. Jack dropped the reins and lifted his free hand to show he held no weapon.

"How many of you are there?" the taller picket asked.

"I'm alone."

"Approach," the Yankee said, "slowly."

Jack picked up the reins and heeled Choctaw in closer.

The taller picket, a sergeant, ordered, "Get off the horse,"

"No. And I'd appreciate it if you'd point those rifles elsewhere."

The sergeant narrowed his eyes and kept his rifle level. "You one of Dixie's men?"

Jack nodded. "I have a message for Captain Farrell."

"What message?" Jack had caught the fellow's curiosity now. "How do you know our captain?"

"The message is in my pocket. I'll give it to you; then I'll leave. I ask that you deliver it to him. I'll come back tomorrow for his answer."

"Hold up a minute, Johnny. Captain ain't far away." The sergeant said to the other soldier, "Coker, go fetch him."

"I'll wait," Jack said as the soldier rode away.

"It's said Captain Farrell has a brother in Dixie's troop." The sergeant lowered his rifle to a less threatening angle. "You do favor our captain. You that brother?"

"If I am?"

"Folks can't choose their relatives." The sergeant chuckled.

Jack adjusted as Choctaw shifted under him. "I sure as hell didn't choose mine."

*

After Coker handed him the note, Dan mounted Stripe and rode to the picket post. Jack sat on his horse and watched his approach with the same outward nonchalance he had affected at their previous truce meeting. This time Jack had tied the white rag to a pole instead of his saber. Dan figured the pole wouldn't hurt as much if Jack whacked him with it.

"Hey." Jack allowed a tense smile.

"Hey, yourself."

"Did you read the letter?" Jack rushed the words, revealing his anxiety.

"Martina and Rosa are fine."

Jack nodded. He seemed to relax a trifle. "It did ease my mind when I found out you were in town."

"I won't let anybody bother them."

"I figured as much, and I thank you. How can we get them through the lines?"

"Martina would like to join you, but I didn't want her to leave without an escort and a proper destination. I couldn't provide either."

"You can send her out now," Jack said. "Unless you're planning another dirty trick."

"No tricks, Jack. I swear. Can I get the same pledge from you?"

"Of course. Dirty tricks are a *Yankee* specialty." Jack grinned. "What about the others? Sarah and Teresa?"

"Teresa and her baby are going to leave when the next boat goes downriver. Sarah will go with them to assist, then she'll go home."

"Sounds like you've got it all worked out."

"I wanted to get word to you, but the only communication we've had lately is hot lead." Dan smiled. "I figured you were in on the fun."

"Captain Dickison doesn't approve of y'all invading Palatka. Neither do I."

"So we noticed. I suppose he'll continue to express his displeasure."

"Until y'all clear out. When will you let my family go?"

"In between attacks?"

"Nobody is attacking you right now," Jack said. "I planned to leave the message and come back tomorrow, but I didn't figure I'd see you in person. There's no need to do this twice."

"No need. It looked to me like she was prepared to leave on short notice, and you sure seem to be in a hurry." Dan lifted an eyebrow. "Once that's done, no more truce. You boys will be free to attack us again."

"We're always up for that."

"Still looking for a fight after the licking we gave you today?"

"Licking?" Jack snorted. "It went just fine. Captured two of your boys, and the coffee and dinner they fixed were extra. We'll do even better next time."

"Where are you taking Martina and the baby?"

"Hell if I know." Jack shook his head. "Someplace safe. Our camp will have to do until we find a house." He flashed a grin. "Did I fool you into thinking I'd grown a sense of responsibility in my old age?"

"I'd do the same thing in your place." Dan took the note from his pocket and wrote on the back. He handed it to Coker and directed him to deliver it to the ladies at his quarters. As the trooper left, Dan told Jack, "I'll wait here with you, just to make sure there's no misunderstanding."

*

Despite Dan's assurance of honor and his disavowal of tricks, Jack remained mounted on Choctaw in case he needed to make a hasty exit. While they waited, he allowed himself to be lulled into a brotherly give and take, news of Pop and Dan's part in the battle at Olustee.

"Rebel sharpshooters were in the trees picking off our artillery crews." Dan's eyes took on a haunted look. "I wondered if one of them was you."

Jack shook his head. "We didn't get there in time to do anything but round up about a hundred head of stray Yankees who were lost in the scrub. It was easier than cow hunting. Carlo was there for the fight, though. Martina will be happy to hear he didn't get hurt. You can tell Sarah that Russell came through all right but his horse got killed. The Yankees replaced it for him."

"Sarah will be relieved." Dan looked relieved as well. "I didn't want to bring her any bad news."

"How are y'all getting along? You and Sarah."

"She resents the fact I have her horse." Dan ran his fingers through the blaze-faced marsh tackie's mane.

"I thought the critter looked familiar."

Dan quirked a smile. "Aside from that, I don't think she hates me too much."

It was Jack's turn to grin. His grin widened when he spotted the wagon approaching. "Here they come."

Aware the Yankees might take violent exception to a sudden move, he resisted the urge to ride forward and meet them. Sarah handled the lines and Nip trotted alongside the wagon. Martina sat on the bench holding a bundled-up Rosa. When she spotted him, the anxiety on her face lightened. The welcome he saw in her dark eyes quelled his wariness and filled him with deep joy. This was his family, the two people he would fight for, even die for if that were required of him.

Sarah stopped the wagon and looked up at Dan. "Didn't take us long, did it? Martina already had the wagon packed."

"Hey, Martina." Jack reined in his urge to jump down from his horse and sweep his wife into his arms. He dared not let down his guard until he brought them safely out of enemy territory. "Sarah." His voice came out hoarse.

"I'm so glad to see you, Jack," Martina said.

Jack nodded, not trusting his voice to remain steady.

"Dan has been a benevolent despot, as he terms it." Sarah nodded to him, her eyes alight. "Solved some of our problems."

Martina turned her warm smile to Dan as well. "Thank you for everything you've done for us."

"My pleasure." Dan appeared pleased with himself. He swung down from his horse and approached the women.

Jack remained mounted, not wanting to add his weight to the wagonload, and moved Choctaw close. He reached down to Martina and touched her hand and the baby's warm little body. Martina whispered, "We heard the shooting this morning."

"Everybody's fine," Jack assured her.

Dan helped Sarah climb down from the bench. "I'll escort you back to the house."

In a lather to get the three of them away from this Yankee stronghold, Jack turned Choctaw alongside Ladybug and gathered her lines in his hand. "Thanks for taking care of my family," he told Dan over his shoulder. "And no dirty tricks this time."

"Go in peace, little brother, until we meet again." Dan touched his hat brim. "Martina, Godspeed to you and my niece."

Jack heeled Choctaw forward, leading Ladybug, wishing the old mare had more pep in her step. With his wife and daughter in tow, he hurried away from the enemy lines.

*

Martina sat quietly in the wagon, holding a wide-eyed Rosa, who jabbered at the landscape as they rolled and bumped past. The tight set of Jack's shoulders betrayed his sense of urgency. Martina knew better than to distract him with conversation until they gained a safe distance from the Federal outposts. She did not share his worry, because she believed Dan's word that they were free to go. Jack did not trust as easily. Affected by his anxiety, she glanced backward and confirmed no one followed.

Within minutes she spotted two men on horseback barring the road ahead. Martina recognized Carlo and Russell, a welcome sight as they rode up to meet the wagon. She allowed herself a sigh of relief. Carlo waved and called out, "Hey, Tina! Hey Jack! Anybody chasing you?"

"Don't think so," Jack said. "Take the rear guard and make sure."

"Where's my sister?" Russell asked.

"Still in town," Martina told him. "She's going home soon. I'll tell you'll about it later."

Russell nodded. He and Carlo let the wagon pass through and rode toward the Yankee picket line. Jack kept the wagon moving forward. Finally he reined in his horse at a cleared stretch of road and let Ladybug stop. Still all business, he turned Choctaw and said, "Hold steady while

I check with the boys."

Martina nodded and grasped the reins with one hand while she balanced the baby on her hip. She looked back as her husband disappeared down the trail. After a few minutes he returned into view at a trot and halted alongside her. "Is anybody following us?" she asked.

From his relaxed posture and easy grin she knew the answer before he said, "Just Carlo and Russell." He bent from the saddle, and she leaned toward him to meet his kiss. "That's more like it," he said. "I'm sorry I was too busy to greet you properly until now." He ran his hand over Rosa's flaxen head. "She's bigger every time I see her. And prettier. Like her mother."

Martina smiled and touched his hand. "Where will you take us?"

"Camp, for now. Then I'll find you something better than a tent." Jack let out his breath. "I'm sorry. I haven't been much of a provider."

Martina shrugged. "You do your best. We're together now, and that makes me happy."

He squeezed her hand. "The boys are coming back. We'd better get to camp before Dan changes his mind and comes after us."

*

Sarah watched the wagon disappear down the road until the woods hid it from view. She could look forward to no such happy reunion with her husband, unless it took place after she joined him in whichever place he had landed in death.

Martina now safe, she became aware of Dan standing close to her. "That was a kind thing you did. I hope it doesn't get you into trouble."

He shook his head. "Colonel Barton told me he wanted to expel anyone who didn't take the oath. I spun it out for Martina's sake. And for yours," he added casually. "As for Jack coming in with his truce flag, that should present no problem. Exchanging family members caught on the wrong side of the lines is done from time to time."

"Of course your colonel will want to get rid of me, too," she said. "That's fine. I'm ready to go home."

"Colonel Barton is a busy man, and you haven't done anything rebellious enough to attract his attention." He grinned. "By the way, Jack said your brother, Russell, is all right, and sends his regards."

"Thank goodness. The gunfire had us worried." With each blast, she feared Russell was in the fight and might be killed. And along with Martina, she felt concern for her friends Jack, Charlie and Carlo. She looked at Dan. Him, too. Not just because he was their protector. Or because her horse might be harmed along with him. Because.... because he was a decent man, and only scum like Prescott should die young.

"Do you want to ride my horse, or shall we walk together?" he asked.

She threw back her head and laughed. "*Your* horse? Just when I was beginning to like you."

"Beginning to like me?" His eyes widened. "Why, Miss Sarah. I do believe I'm making progress."

"Let's walk," she said. "It's a fine spring day. I could use the exercise, and Stripe could use the rest."

Dan offered his arm, and she accepted it. She took guilty pleasure in the strong, reassuring presence of a handsome man and tried to forget the color of his coat. She still missed Edward but had to face the fact he was gone forever. Sometimes forgetfulness was good when it allowed wounds to heal.

Dan led Stripe as he escorted her through the fortifications into town. Sarah noticed he ignored the soldiers watching them. "We're going to be a topic around the campfires," she whispered.

"Does it matter?"

"I'm sure they'll make more of us than a simple walk home deserves."

"I'm going to make as much of it as I can." Dan cast her a sidewise look.

An unexpected thought crept in, a shred of curiosity about what it would be like to allow this man into her bed. It had been such a long time since she had enjoyed intimate male attention. Teresa and her children stayed behind the closed door to their room at night, so no one would have to know....

She shook her head to banish the dangerous fantasy. All she needed was for Dan to get her with a child! Then if he got himself killed...

"What's the matter?" A smile played on his lips.

"I like you," she allowed, "even if you did steal my horse."

"Maybe I could arrange a way for you to get your horse back."

"How?"

"Take me, take my horse."

She knitted her brow. "What do you mean by that, Dan?"

"I've grown fond of you, and I want to keep on seeing you." He grinned. "If I continue to hold your horse hostage, won't that guarantee you'll want to keep seeing me, too?"

Sarah glanced at Stripe. "What an odd suggestion."

"Will it work?"

She sighed. "I just want this war to end."

"I'm doing my best to bring that about."

"I don't suppose you mean you're helping the Union to lose."

He chuckled. "Not by a long shot."

"Are you going to join us for supper?"

"I'll be late. We're on high alert in case our brothers and their friends misbehave again."

"I'll save you something, and you can eat whenever you come in for the night." She considered the food they had on hand, most of it provided by Dan. "I'm mighty tired of fish," she said. "We'll fix the ham you brought us."

"That will be fine."

They stopped in front of the house. He dropped the reins and stepped onto the porch with her, leaving Stripe grazing in the yard. Sarah felt a pang of regret the walk had ended so soon. She turned and lifted her face to him, wondering what it would be like to let him kiss her if he held such a notion.

He slipped his arm around her back and drew her close. His lips brushed hers, then settled into an assertive kiss. She allowed herself to flow with his initiative, satisfying her curiosity but raising her desire.

She broke off and pushed his chest without conviction. "Stop that."

"Why?" His grin was triumphant, and he did not release her. "Weren't you enjoying it?"

Enjoying it too much. "We can't be doing this. It's impossible."

He bent his head and kissed her again. This time she yielded to his demand as her natural longings pushed aside her doubts. She caught his lips hungrily in hers and savored the feel of his strong body through their many layers of clothing.

She fought herself back to sanity and shoved him away. "You. You are...."

"The man of your dreams?"

She socked him on the shoulder. "You conceited thing. I'll bet you say that to all the women."

He laughed and let go of her. "I'll be back for supper, Sarah."

"You'll get nothing for dessert," she snapped.

He laughed harder.

She fled into the house, shut the door and leaned against it. "Men."

"Dan? He's the only man I saw." Sarah realized Teresa was standing at the window, regarding her with a knowing smile.

"You were watching us?" Sarah's face grew hot.

"I wasn't spying on you. I heard someone on the porch and had to see who it was. Anyone passing by would have witnessed your display of affection."

Display of affection? "He caught me by surprise. I didn't realize –"

"If you had refused him, he would have honored that."

"I told him to stop."

Teresa laughed. "I guess he didn't believe you meant it."

Sarah reminded herself she was no young girl caught in an impropriety but an experienced adult. She knew something about men and their wants. Unfortunately, Dan had awakened in her feelings better left asleep. She smoothed her skirts and lifted her chin. "Dan Farrell merely pretends he's a gentleman."

Teresa peered out the window again. "The pretend gentleman just mounted Stripe, and he's riding away with a smile on his face."

"I shouldn't be consorting with an enemy who is determined to harm my brother and my friends." Sarah crossed her arms over her chest. "I need to make that perfectly clear to him."

"You've been consorting plenty, and he's been nothing but helpful to us." Teresa pointed out. "I haven't had a bad spell since that army doctor gave me a supply of quinine. We're eating better than we have for weeks, on account of his contributions. He's going to get us passage to our homes, and he let Martina go with Jack." Teresa hesitated. "Did they get away all right?"

Sarah nodded. "Jack was in a big hurry and I don't blame him."

"I'll miss her," Teresa said. "At least I'm stronger now, and I can do more of my share." Color had returned to Teresa's face, along with a renewal of spirit.

"It's good to see you up and about. We were worried about you." Sarah glanced at the crib by the fire, where little Ramon slept. He had gained steadily in the past three weeks and seemed to want to remain in this world. "And little Ramon."

Teresa followed her gaze, and her expression softened. "Pray he stays well."

Ana, sitting on the rug playing with a rag doll, had been listening to the adult exchange, curiosity on her face. The little girl asked, “Is Uncle Dan coming back?”

“Tonight, sweetie,” Sarah said. “You’ll most likely be asleep by then.” She glanced at the stairs, which led to the room Dan occupied whenever his duties allowed it. Her room was just across the hall, but both of them would continue to sleep alone.

Teresa’s knowing smile returned. “Dan is a fine looking man, and he has a good heart. You could do worse.”

“That’s impossible. He’s a Union officer,” Sarah huffed.

Teresa shrugged. “The war won’t last forever. It’s over for Ramon and me. No Yankee bullet will bring him down.”

"It isn’t over for me.” Sarah moved away from the door, anxious for something to do. If she stayed busy, she wouldn’t have to think about that appealing enemy officer who had the power to rend her heart in two.

CHAPTER TWENTY-ONE

"Come away from the window, Sarah." Teresa's voice betrayed her amusement. "It won't make him arrive any sooner."

Sarah felt her face flush as she turned toward Teresa. "He'd better get here soon. His supper will be hard as a brick." She heard the clop of hooves, and turning back to the window, she watched Dan ride Stripe through the darkness toward the paddock at the rear of the house. "That's him," she told Teresa.

He had arrived safe despite intermittent bursts of gunfire through the evening. Sarah felt glad he had returned unharmed. At the same time, she had dreaded this moment. What was she to say to him? How would he act toward her after their unexpected "display of affection," as Teresa had termed it? Did their kiss lead Dan to believe she was a loose woman to be easily coaxed into his bed?

"He'll be hungry." Teresa's light tone continued.

Sarah glanced back at the young mother, seated on the couch with the sleeping baby on her lap and her little daughter curled up next to her, thumb in mouth. Teresa's placid smile was visible even in the dim firelight. She knew a thing or two about hungry men.

"Then I'd better fix him a good meal, hadn't I?" Sarah busied herself at the fireplace. She added a little water to the pot of meat and sweet potatoes and set it over the flames to reheat.

She heard his boots scrape on the porch. Dan walked in before she reached the door to open it. Of course he did not need an invitation because the house was as much his, by Yankee authority, as it was hers. He closed the door behind him and removed his hat. He swept his gaze over the dimly lit domestic scene and nodded to her and Teresa.

"We saved you some supper, Dan," Teresa said.

"I'll get it for you." Sarah returned to the fireplace.

"Thanks, ladies. I'm famished."

Awakened by his entry, Ana looked at him, then dropped her head back onto her mother's lap, apparently unconcerned.

"I'm glad to see Ana is getting used to me." Dan let himself down on a chair at the big pine table.

"She calls you 'Uncle Dan.'" Teresa stroked the child's dark hair.

"I seem to be collecting nieces." Dan's voice held warmth.

"We heard more shots." Sarah forked a slab of meat onto a plate and glanced at Dan. "Did our boys give you a hard time again?"

"A couple of false alarms. Jumpy pickets shooting at wild hogs. Others discharged their weapons when they came off duty." Dan lifted one side of his mouth in a half smile. "It's nice to know you were worried about me, Miss Sarah."

"Of course I don't want you hurt. I don't want my brother hurt, either." She piled more food onto the plate. "It's dried out because we wanted to keep it warm but didn't know when you would arrive."

"You won't hear me complain. It's still better than my usual rations, I'm sure."

Sarah poked the contents of the plate critically with the fork. "I'm glad you aren't particular."

"I have a bit of news." He looked toward the couch Teresa occupied with her children. "Y'all need to pack. Another boat is supposed to come up from Jacksonville and take the place of the *Columbine* in the next couple of days. It's your best chance to go home."

"Thank God," Teresa said. "Ana, we'll be seeing your papa soon."

"Papa," the child mumbled sleepily around her thumb.

"Oh, good." Sarah tried to sound enthusiastic. She set the plate in front of him and poured water into a cup from a pitcher. He murmured his thanks and tucked into the ham and sweet potatoes. She took the seat across from him and inhaled a deep, calming breath.

"I'm taking the young 'uns to bed." Teresa stood, the baby in her arms, and headed toward her room. Ana followed her, one hand gripping her mother's skirt, thumb plugged into her mouth.

Dan stood as he wished them a good night.

Teresa looked back at Sarah before she disappeared behind the door to her room. *She means to leave me alone with him. Traitor.*

Sarah watched the door close, her pulse quickening. *Nothing is keeping me from retiring as well.* She glanced at the stairs that led to her bedroom, then at Dan, who had reseated himself and regarded her with a smile playing across his lips.

She pushed a stray wisp of hair behind her ear. *I'm not trapped. I can go to my room, too.* She remained seated.

"You don't have to be so nervous. I'm not going to seduce you." Dan set his empty plate aside and met her gaze, his face shadowed in the pale candlelight. "Not unless you want me to." He flashed a grin.

"Why, Dan Farrell! What an outrageous thing to say. I ought to slap you silly." Instead, she let out a tension-relieving laugh.

"I'm glad you won't, Miss Sarah. Now that we've cleared that up, maybe we can relax and enjoy each other's company."

"I would like that," she murmured, grateful he was not trying to corner her. "I would like that just fine."

He reached across the table and laid his hand over hers. She did not snatch her hand away. Instead, she relished the warmth and strength she drew from the contact. When she lifted her eyes to meet his, she could almost forget he had aligned himself against those she held most dear.

Almost. How could she love a man who was out to kill her own brother?

*

Dan stood on the dock with the women as they prepared to board the *Columbine*. Sarah held Ana's hand, and Teresa carried little Ramon in her arms. He hefted Sarah's valise, which carried the few things she had brought with her to Palatka. Teresa's trunk had already been loaded onto the boat.

Teresa turned to him. "We're so grateful for all you've done. I'm going to be with Ramon at last."

"My pleasure." Dan bowed slightly, then turned to Sarah. "That big old house is going to be a lonely place from now on."

Sarah chuckled. "Don't tell such tales. You're going to enjoy the peace and quiet. Besides, you'll invite all your officer friends to share the comfortable quarters."

"Ah, but the present company is so much more stimulating." He grinned at Sarah, who had warmed to him over the past few days.

He squatted to Ana's level, set down the valise and opened his arms. The little girl gave him a quick hug, then retreated to Sarah's skirt folds. He stood and said to Sarah, "Some ladies are easier to win over than others."

"I have to give you credit for persistence." Her eyes sparkled with mischief, but she had given him a glimpse of what lay behind her teasing manner. He wished he had more time to explore those depths.

His gaze wandered, taking in her enticing figure. "You haven't seen the last of me."

"I'm sure." She smiled and offered her hand.

He accepted the invitation and circled his free arm around her waist. She yielded ever so slightly to the pressure. He recalled the taste and feel of her lips on his, and her short-lived responsiveness. It wasn't enough. It would never be enough. He bent down, and when her lips brushed his softly, he wanted to take her back to the house and consummate his desire.

The boat's horn blew a warning of departure. Sarah stepped away from him, her face flushed and radiant. "Stay safe, Dan."

"You, too." His voice was husky. Regretfully, he let her go. He picked up the valise and handed it to her.

She followed Teresa across the gangplank. When she reached the deck of the *Columbine*, she turned, smiled at him, and waved.

Dan watched until the boat pulled away and steamed out of sight around the point. He walked to where he had left Stripe, mounted and turned the horse's head toward the picket post. There awaited his worst fears, that the execution of his duty would require him to end the life of his brother or the brother of the woman he had grown to love.

*

Carlo enjoyed the fine spring afternoon as he rode south on the wood-shadowed trail following the riverbank. The most important part of his mission was complete; he had delivered dispatches and letters along the picket line. All he carried on the return trip to Dickison's headquarters were a few routine reports and a handful of personal letters.

Now that Jack had taken Martina out of harm's way and settled in a nearby town, Carlo felt easier about the situation. His troop, along with other Florida cavalry and allies from Georgia, continued to harass the Yankee outposts outside Palatka. So far they had not succeeded in penetrating the town and dislodging the occupiers, though they certainly kept the enemy spooked.

He let his horse drink from a clear slough as it waded across, and he took a swig from his canteen. Carlo liked his job. He lived well, better than most Confederate soldiers. The pickets at his last stop had let him share some of the wild hog they had roasted, and he brought along a hunk of the meat in his haversack to enjoy later. He rode about the countryside, mostly on his own hook, and rarely drew fire. His experience at Olustee had dimmed his eagerness for combat, though he was still plenty game.

He heard, or thought he heard, a noise behind him and turned to look. His horse turned its head as well and pricked its ears. Carlo did not see a pursuer. Was it a bear, a cow or a deer? Then he recognized the tread of hooves. He dug his heels into his horse's sides, urging it to canter between thick brush on either side of the path.

The trail opened into a more open stretch of pine and scrub oak. He kicked his horse into a gallop to speed through the exposed area, then spotted two men in dark jackets walking their mounts to block his path, their rifles trained on him. "Halt, Johnny!" one of them called out. "We've got you."

Carlo reined in, sick with indecision, knowing he could not get to his weapons before they shot him.

He glanced behind him and caught sight of the bluecoat who followed, pistol drawn. "Don't be stupid," yelled one of the men in front of him.

Trapped, Carlo lifted his hands and surrendered.

They ordered him to dismount and snatched his weapons. Then they searched his pockets and examined the contents of his dispatch pouch. He watched them divide his hunk of pork among them and eat it on the spot. "Captain'll want to see these," the Yankee with the straw-colored beard said. "Might be something important here."

"I doubt that," Carlo muttered. "Unless you like reading other people's mail."

"We been watchin' you for a spell," straw-beard said.

The soldier who had tailed Carlo stared at him while he chewed his last bite of pork. "They're sure takin' 'em young these days. How old are you, boy?"

"Sixteen."

"They'll be robbin' the nursery next."

"I volunteered." Carlo gathered his dignity and glared at the fellow, who didn't appear to be much older than he was.

"Which unit you volunteer for?"

"Company H, 2nd Florida Cavalry."

"Ain't that somethin'." Straw beard grinned. "One of Dixie's boys. That's all right, we're 2nd Florida Cavalry too. Union, that is." He laughed out loud, and the others joined in as though he had made a brilliant joke.

No wonder they knew the area better than the average Yankee, well enough to waylay him. Carlo clenched his fists, wanting to punch the turncoats for making fun of his miserable situation. Then he remembered something that might be important. "Who is your captain?"

"Cap'n Farrell. Mount up, boy. We'll take you to him now."

*

Dan dismissed his scouts and greeted his prisoner, "Well, Carlo. It's good seeing you again, though the circumstances are awkward."

His brother-in-law stood with his arms crossed, silent and frowning. The boy had cultivated a sparse moustache and had grown taller and heavier through the shoulders over the past year. He was turning into a good-looking young man.

Dan opened the dispatch pouch and pulled out the contents. He flipped through the envelopes, sorting out the official ones. "They have you on courier detail these days?"

"Sometimes," Carlo said.

"How are Martina and the baby?"

"Fine." Carlo seemed to let down his guard a trifle. "They stayed in camp for a few days; then Jack found them a house in Orange Springs. She's sharing it with other soldiers' wives."

"Good. I'm glad she's situated. I suppose Jack is one of the fellows giving us trouble, chasing in our pickets at every opportunity."

Carlo cracked a smile. "Count on it."

Dan questioned him further, hoping to gain strategic information, but was not surprised Carlo refused to answer. Dan leaned closer. "You realize I have to turn you over to the provost, who will put you in jail until it's time to ship you off to prison."

Carlo swallowed and looked away.

"I can offer you a better situation." Dan paused, giving Carlo time to stew.

"Let me guess. I desert, take your oath, and I can have everything but my honor." Carlo shot him a defiant look. "I can't do that."

"You could go back to St. Augustine. I'll bet your cousin Ramon would let you live at his farm."

"I already took an oath to my state and to the Confederacy." Carlo set his jaw in a hard line. "I am not a turncoat like the men in your troop."

Dan sighed. What leverage did he have with Carlo, besides self-preservation? The boy had no dependents to worry about, no home to reclaim, and he was as stubborn as a jackass. Or Jack. "I want to help you, Carlo. Think about it."

*

A few days later guards escorted Carlo and three fellow prisoners of war from the Palatka jail to the wharf. Moored at the dock was a side-wheeler, three decks stacked atop one another, shining in the red light of sunset. Twin funnels rose high above the hurricane deck. On the side he read the words "*Maple Leaf*" in bright crimson paint against a white background.

Had the circumstances been different, Carlo would have admired the huge, fine-looking ship, the most elegant he ever had seen, A few civilians, a scruffy-looking man and a couple of women, stood around as though waiting to board as well. Carlo guessed they were Unionists seeking sanctuary in the Yankee haven Jacksonville had become.

So far, despite watching for an opportunity, he had not been able to escape. He had little cause to complain about his treatment, despite the confinement that reminded him his freedom was gone. He had received decent rations, and the guards let him be. Dan had visited him a couple of times to try to persuade him to give up his allegiance. He might as well not have bothered. Carlo would rather face prison than face his friends and family as a traitor.

Carlo walked across the gangplank onto the main deck, which a laborer was sweeping clear of horse manure. Evidently the boat had brought more cavalry to Palatka. That ought to make Dan happy. Now, besides Sarah's horse, he had Carlo's as well.

The guards made him climb a stairway to the saloon deck. As he walked past stateroom doors toward the prow of the boat, he tried to look inside to see what the rooms were like. An open door revealed a rich interior of white and gold paneling. A bedspread, chair and settee of red plush and matching curtains smacked of luxury despite the boat's military use.

One of the guards made it clear he was not destined to enjoy the soft-looking bed. "Sit down, boys. You get to sleep on the deck tonight."

Carlo dropped his blanket roll between two other prisoners and sat on it. He gazed at the river, wishing he were somewhere else. Most likely Jack and Martina, and Captain Dickison for that matter, only knew he had come up missing. That meant dead or captured. Or a deserter. He longed to let them know the truth of his misfortune.

Not that anyone would believe he would consider deserting. He consoled himself with that thought.

*

The boom of an explosion assaulted Carlo's ears as the deck bucked and tossed him upward. He landed with a hard bump and slid sideways. Heart pounding, shocked from the rough awakening, he rolled to his elbow and shrugged off his blanket. Through the ringing in his ears he listened to shouts and the shriek of the ship's whistle. The overwhelming stench of burnt powder made him cough. He felt as much as heard the crack of timbers giving way. The boat shifted, rolling to the right. A haze-covered rising moon offered just enough light for him to make out his surroundings. The walking beam stilled on the down-stroke and the wheels no longer turned. Forward motion slowed then stopped, as the vessel coasted to a halt.

"What the hell?" mumbled the man next to him." Did the boiler explode?"

Carlo shook his head. "Don't you see the smoke and smell the gunpowder? Maybe it was artillery, or ammunition blew up in the hold."

Half-dressed crewmembers and passengers poured out of the staterooms onto the saloon deck. Sailors clambered up the stairs from the main deck. Shouts of "We hit a torpedo!" "Abandon ship! Man the lifeboats," and "We're sinking!" pierced the air. "Get up to the hurricane deck," someone called out, his voice high-pitched and urgent. "The main deck is flooding! Ladies first! Amanda! Where are you?"

The guard, who appeared distracted by the confusion, was not paying attention to him or the other prisoners. Carlo stood and picked up his boots and blanket. He looked toward the dark, wooded shoreline. The hazy moonglow provided enough light for him to make out shapes. The channel apparently edged close to the east bank at this point, within a quarter of a mile. Well rested, he would have no trouble swimming that far, especially after he crossed the channel and gained the shallows.

He sidled closer to the rail. No one looked his way. He peered over the side, where the river had risen to a level within reach. Cold water poured onto the deck as the boat settled deeper, wetness crawling up to his ankles and soaking his trouser cuffs.

The boots would impede him in the water, so he set them down and let them float away, along with the blanket. Despite the chill of the spring night, he shrugged off his jacket as the crewmen herded the passengers up to the hurricane deck, out of reach of the rising water. So far they ignored him and the other prisoners, who stood watching the evacuation.

"Hey, Yank," one of the Confederates said to the guard. "Think we ought to hustle over and get in one of them boats, too? The water's up to my knees, already. They ain't going to leave us here to drown, are they?" Carlo wanted to punch the idiot for getting the guard's attention.

The slow-witted guard looked at the speaker, then toward the stairwell as though weighing his orders to keep the prisoners here against common sense. "Let's go, then. Move it." The prisoners splashed through the rising water toward safety.

Carlo bolted, grabbed the rail and vaulted over it. He heard a yell as he hit the water feet first, sank deep into the cold darkness alongside the boat, then kicked away from it.

He swam underwater for as long as he could hold his breath, his loose fitting trousers slowing his progress. When he popped up and gasped for a lungful of air, he glanced over his shoulder. The boat was just behind him, sitting low on the calm surface. Through the water filling his ears he heard a man's voice shouting "Overboard! There!"

Carlo dived underwater again and kicked as hard as he could toward the shore. He did not hear gunfire and hoped the Yankees were too busy evacuating to bother trying to recapture or shoot him.

At the shoreline a light bobbed and swung with someone's gait. The sound of the blast certainly would have aroused every soul within miles. Yankees? Confederates? The landowner? Or was the lantern-bearer a layout or renegade beholden to neither side?

Instead of heading straight in, he shifted directions and swam parallel to the shoreline with the current, trying to avoid a collision course with the light. He hoped the fellow either did not see him or did not care to intercept him. The light seemed to follow. Carlo's arms and legs grew heavy and his breath came in bursts. He could not tread water in the channel forever. He had no choice but to head for shore.

From time to time he tested the depth and sank without hitting bottom. Finally his feet touched oozing mud. After a few more strokes he set his feet down and settled through the muck onto firmer ground. He walked in the deep silt through chin-deep water up a slow grade toward dry land.

The lantern hovered directly in front of him. In the radiant light he made out four figures. They held rifles. *It's a shame to get recaptured so soon. What else can I do? I can either surrender or drown.*

"Hey!" One of them shouted. "Hey, Yank. We've got you covered. Keep your hands up and come on in."

Yank? At least they weren't Federals.

Even if they weren't friends, they had him anyway. The truth was his best defense. "I'm no Yank," Carlo called out. "I'm a Confederate soldier. Who are you?"

"Come on in."

Carlo stopped, breathing hard, the water still up to his waist, his hands raised to chest height. "I'm Private Sanchez, Company H, 2nd Florida Cavalry. I was a prisoner on that boat, and I got away. Who are you?"

"We're 2nd Florida Battalion. Come out of the drink and let us take a look at you."

Good news if they were telling the truth. Carlo pushed through the cold water until he gained the shore and faced the four men. The lantern light revealed their gray jackets. The man holding the lantern also held a revolver, but he pointed it to the ground. The others carried their rifles at a casual angle. "You came off that boat?"

"I jumped when the guard wasn't looking."

The lantern swung close to his face, dazzling his vision. One of the men said, "I know this young fellow. He's in Captain Dickison's command, all right. He brought us dispatches a time or two."

"Good." The man holding the lantern drew it back. "What happened on that boat, soldier? Didn't they hit one of our torpedoes? I see they're abandoning ship. What kind of damage did it do?"

Carlo turned for another look at the *Maple Leaf*. The silhouette of the highest structures of the steamboat jutted above the water, so the vessel must have finished sinking. Already crewmembers were rowing one of the lifeboats full of passengers north toward Jacksonville. He could make out the smaller boat's progress on the moonlit water.

Carlo told what he had seen and heard, and the men listened intently.

"It worked, then. It worked fine." Whoops and backslapping followed.

"Did y'all do it? Set out the torpedoes?" Carlo asked.

"Sure enough," the lantern-bearer said. "Captain Bryan brought 'em down from Charleston. We took a boat out there and anchored 'em in the channel just two nights ago. We got fast results, all right. We sure did."

"Let's get the boat and take a look," one of the others said. "See what we can get off the boat."

"No use doing that until daylight," lantern-man said.

Carlo started to shiver as his wet clothes sucked the warmth from his body "My boots are still on that boat. Maybe they floated. Maybe y'all can find them."

"We got a fire going at our camp. You can sit by it and dry off while we watch what's doing with that wreck. Good job getting away from them Yanks, Sanchez."

"Good job sinking the boat." Carlo grinned at his new friends, grasping the significance of their project. The Yankees had just lost their freedom to navigate the river unchallenged.

CHAPTER TWENTY-TWO

"Ah, Picolata," Prescott said to Colonel Montgomery as the transport boat changed course and turned into the wide-mouthed cove. "I remember it well. Unfortunately, the memories are all bad."

The commander of the colored regiment glanced at him. "That was where you got shot by one of Dickison's men, wasn't it, Captain?"

"Indeed, sir, indeed." *By a particular one of Dickison's men.*

"Perhaps this assignment will go better for you. For all of us."

"At least Picolata can be supplied and reinforced by land from St. Augustine." Prescott fingered his cigar. "And I suppose the rebels have been too busy on the other side of the river to trouble us here for the time being."

The colonel looked out over the river as though he expected to see a ripple that suggested a torpedo lurked under the surface. So far they had avoided colliding with the explosive devices. "Were it not for those infernal machines blowing up our ships, we could hold and supply Palatka indefinitely. Between the *Maple Lea*f disaster, the sinking of the Hunter, and the daily attacks by the rebel cavalry, we simply had to give it up."

"And the bleating of *The New York Times*," Prescott added. "Reporters who presume to know more than our generals."

Montgomery chuckled. "I believe you have a cogent grasp of the situation, Captain."

Prescott smiled and stroked his moustache. It was good, no, excellent, to receive a compliment from his regimental commander. "Sir, considering I have some experience in this area, I have a recommendation, if I may speak freely."

Montgomery turned to him. "Of course."

"It is our policy to destroy property used by the rebels. I happen to know the abandoned house where I suffered my wounding has been used and, certainly still is being used by Dickison's scouts. It isn't a mile from the landing at Picolata. I suggest I take a party there and burn the house and all the outbuildings."

The colonel nodded without hesitation. "Then see to it, Captain, as soon as practicable."

"Yes, sir. Consider it done. I'll look for other rebel hideouts while I'm at it." Prescott glanced toward a cluster of his men who stood on the deck, rifles in their hands, ready to march off the boat and clear out the enemy as soon as the crew secured the boat to its moorings. He nodded with satisfaction. "I know just the man to carry out the task."

*

Prescott made it his mission to personally supervise the destruction of the Farrell property. The next morning he accompanied his squad, properly armed with rifles and combustibles.

The property appeared more run-down than ever for lack of habitation and upkeep. Rampant weed growth had swallowed the trunks of the orange trees, and his men had to blaze a trail through the undergrowth to get to the house.

He surveyed the Farrell homestead. The two-winged log house connected by a breezeway evoked a spate of unwelcome memories. How the insolent, supposedly disabled Jack Farrell's presence mocked him, under protection of his Unionist father and the late Colonel Putnam. How Prescott discovered that little chit Martina Sanchez had lived with Farrell ever since he got her banished from St. Augustine. He no sooner found her and had her under control than Farrell shot him from a cowardly ambush. Once a rebel, always a rebel. Jack Farrell proved it by joining Dickison's band. The bastard would have murdered him on the spot but for the intervention of a more principled rebel. If, indeed, there were such a thing.

Colonel Montgomery had ordered him to destroy the guerilla hideout. Destroy it he would, with immense satisfaction. It disturbed him not at all that the house was also the property of the elder Farrell and that annoying Union officer, Dan Farrell, who seemed to have more in common with his rebel brother than with his own side.

Upon arrival at Palatka, Prescott had found Farrell had sent the women away. To where, the pestilent officer would not say. He had taken over the comfortable house, invited his officer friends to share it with him, and made it clear Prescott was unwelcome.

Prescott turned to Corporal Isaac Farrell, who had taken on the family name apparently without qualm. Of course, an unschooled

Negro would have no understanding of the finer points of irony. From the sullen look on the fellow's face, he had no appreciation for his assignment, either. Prescott expected the soldier might find his orders distasteful. However, once in a while it was good to demonstrate the reach of a company commander's authority by compelling a man to do something against his will.

"Burn it, corporal." Prescott watched for a mutinous reaction that would warrant summary punishment. Making an example for the other men would serve as another kind of lesson, if necessary. "Burn the house and the outbuildings as well. Burn it all to the ground."

*

Isaac had to follow orders, much as he hated to destroy what he had helped build. Captain Prescott liked his power and seemed to enjoy pushing people around.

It wasn't only for Mr. Farrell's sake he grieved. With the savings he had earned from making popskull and his skill at cultivating the farm, one day he hoped to return with his family to his old home. A free man, he had left his employer on good terms. He expected the Union to prevail and his situation to improve once the war ended.

At least his still, which he hoped remained intact in its hiding place in the woods, would escape Captain Prescott's notice. One day he wanted to return to his old trade, which yielded better profits for easier labor than working the fields.

Isaac hefted a kerosene can from the wagon and handed it to Zeke, who did not share his unhappiness. Zeke would be glad to burn down his old master's neighboring home and would dance while the flames ate it. "Get some dry grass, throw it under the porch, and douse it good," Isaac said.

The outbuildings, too, the captain had commanded. Zeke directed another man in the squad likewise to prime the tool shed. Isaac carried another can of kerosene to his old cabin, which had been blasted by an artillery shell last year, when his company clashed with Jack's. He recalled that day, when he had the drop on his old friend and took him prisoner. Isaac let him go, along with the wounded Carlo. He had told no one and was sure Jack wouldn't open his mouth about it, either.

Isaac piled straw next to the ruins of his cabin, threw kerosene on it, and struck a match. He watched as the straw burned and set the logs afire. Then he turned back to the house to light that fire personally, just as Captain Prescott's order dictated.

He dampened the urge to throw kerosene and a lit match on his captain as well.

*

Because Dan's troop formed part of the rear guard during the Union Army's evacuation of Palatka, he had boarded the last transport ship to leave. His orders to report to St. Augustine required that his men and horses disembark at Picolata and take the stage road east into town. He expected little trouble from the rebels because reports had indicated they were concentrated west of the St. Johns and few remained between the river and the ocean. Scouting the east side of the river and keeping the rebels away from the Picolata-to-St. Augustine supply line no doubt would be part of his job.

Dan enjoyed the trip downriver, contemplating his new assignment, which offered its benefits. He would visit Pop when he reported to St. Augustine. The new security in the area should let Pop visit the Picolata homestead and take care of his orange grove. Perhaps the new freedom would ease Pop's disappointment over the cancellation of the planned Unionist convention. The defeat at Olustee had quashed that endeavor.

Best of all, patrols in the county would allow Dan to see more of Sarah. He assumed she had returned to her family's home, which was located near a main road he would have to travel from time to time.

As the boat steamed into the cove, Dan noticed a smudge of smoke over the trees along the riverbank. He studied the evidence of a fire, his concern building. From his recollection, the smoke originated from about where the Farrell homestead was located. He would find a way to investigate.

After landing, Dan checked in with the officer of the day. He took care of army business, then nodded in the direction of the smoke. "Do you know what's burning over there?"

The officer shrugged, showing little interest. "Rebel property, most likely. I heard Captain Prescott took a squad with combustibles."

"Prescott?" Dan scrubbed his hand over his face. "Prescott, you say?" He stared at the dissipating smoke and hoped his first suspicion was wrong.

The short work of unloading the horses and baggage from the boat seemed to take forever. Finally, the troop mounted, ready to ride to St. Augustine. Dan said to Sergeant Drake, "We're going to take a little detour and check on my family's place."

*

Prescott watched the roof of the house collapse into the fire-engulfed walls, a most satisfying sight. Sparks flew as high as the bare pecan trees in the front yard, and embers caught some of the branches on fire.

He turned to Isaac Farrell, who watched the bonfire with him, sweat beading his dark face. Deprived of the opportunity to enforce discipline on Farrell, Prescott felt a twinge of disappointment, but as a fair and just leader he ought to give credit. "Well done, Corporal. Those old, dry timbers burn quite nicely, don't they?"

"Yes, sir," mumbled the soldier.

Satisfied his orders had been carried out to the letter, Prescott said, "Form the men, and we'll march back to the landing."

"Sir," one of the men called out. "Horses coming." The soldier pointed toward the road.

"Form a skirmish line," Prescott barked. He looked around for cover, anything to decrease his exposure, and drew his revolver as his squad hurried into order, rifles ready. Then he realized the newcomers wore dark blue uniforms. "Hold your fire," he shouted.

He recognized the officer riding at the head of the column, a look of dismay on his face. Prescott smiled. This was going to be delicious.

*

Dan took in the scene of his father's gutted, smoldering house, spotted Prescott and rode up to him. He gripped the reins hard, wanting to use his fists to smash Prescott's smirk. "What the hell is this about?"

"This?" Prescott waved his hand toward the smoking ruins. "Just taking care of business. Orders, you know. Colonel Montgomery commanded me to destroy rebel hideouts and property."

"This house belongs to my father, who is no rebel. You know that, Prescott."

"Dickison's scouts have been using it. One of whom you know pretty well."

Isaac stood nearby, his expression grim. "You know whose house this was, Isaac," Dan snapped.

"Mr. Dan, I mean Captain Farrell," Isaac looked at Prescott. "I had to obey orders."

"He set the fires." Prescott nodded to Isaac. "It's a start. We aim to clean out all the rebel nests on this side of the river. Began to do that last year, before your brother tried to murder me. By the time I'm done, he'll wish he had succeeded."

Too bad he didn't. Dan rejected the unworthy thought. "You make my job that much harder, Prescott. Officers like you drive people to the other side."

"Do they, now?" Prescott's smirk deepened, and he lowered his voice to a confidential level. "I have my suspicions about you, Farrell. You give me cause to wonder about your loyalties."

Dan dismounted and tossed the reins to the nearest of his men. He strode to Prescott, flexing his hands, and stopped within a few inches of him. "I ought to grind you into the dirt, you sorry excuse for a Union officer."

Prescott leaned back, his eyes betraying a touch of fear. "Assault me, and I'll press charges."

"I don't give a damn," Dan growled. He noticed a flicker in Prescott's eyes, then a shift in posture as the treacherous bastard curled his hand around the grip of his pistol. Dan reacted without thought. He brought up his fist in a hard jab to Prescott's jaw. The other officer's teeth clacked together and his head snapped back. He staggered, stumbled, and fell backwards.

Prescott wriggled like an upside-down palmetto bug, spitting blood, but his hand still grappled for the weapon. Dan stepped on his arm, immobilizing it.

"Don't you ever try that stunt again," Dan rubbed his sore knuckles. "Take off the gun and fight like a man, you weasel."

Prescott lay blinking at him, hatred in his eyes, but did not move. "You assaulted a United States officer."

Dan glanced around at the men in his troop. "Sergeant Drake, I believe it was self defense on my part. Do you agree?"

"Definitely, sir. He was trying to draw his pistol on you."

Dan exchanged a look with Isaac, who gave him a furtive smile but did not say anything.

"Are you ready to get up, no foolishness?" Dan did not relieve the pressure on Prescott's gun hand. "Or will I have to take your sidearm away from you in case you want to hurt somebody with it?"

"Let me up," Prescott snapped.

Dan raised a brow. "We can continue to fight. I already told you I want to pound you into the ground. I would enjoy the opportunity. But first take off your sidearm."

"Get off me," Prescott growled.

Dan lifted his foot from Prescott's arm and gave him room, hoping the bastard would come at him swinging. He watched him wipe blood from his mouth and hoist himself up. To his disappointment, Prescott's slow moves did not hold any further threat, but the thunderous look on his face sure did. "I won't forget this, Farrell. And you haven't seen the last of me."

"Sorry to say, I'll probably have to put up with you sooner or later." *I'll watch my back.* "Just stay out of my way." Dan mounted Stripe, rode past Prescott and skirted what was left of the house so he could report the condition of the property to Pop. If nothing else, his father could make a claim against the government, a forlorn hope.

*

"I've selected your company to guard the *Columbine* on its mission up the St. Johns," Colonel Montgomery told Prescott. "The *Columbine* will steam as far as Volusia to deliver orders, ascertain the condition of the post, and render aid as necessary."

"I'm honored, sir. When do we board?" Prescott glanced down at the map spread across his commander's desk. For the past month his company had been stuck at the swampy Picolata camp improving fortifications, their usual occupation. He was beyond tired of supervising picks and shovels. A chance at combat would restore his reputation among his men after the indignity of his disastrous confrontation with Farrell.

"Tomorrow morning. We've had a couple of catastrophes at our distant outposts on the river, and we have to protect our southernmost garrison."

"Catastrophes, sir?" Prescott had heard rumors of whole outposts captured by the rebels. The colonel would know the truth of the matter. "Dickison again?"

Montgomery frowned. "They crossed to the east side of the river and captured the Welaka outpost. If I could get hold of the post commander, I'd prefer charges. As it is, he's a prisoner of the rebels."

"Shameful." Prescott clicked his tongue against his teeth.

"They captured our men at Fort Butler on the west side of the river, as well." Montgomery shook his head and traced the course of the St. Johns with his fingers. "The Volusia outpost is across the river from Fort Butler. It's in jeopardy, and we have no communications with the commander." He drummed a forefinger on the dot that represented Volusia. "It's farther from here than Welaka. Fortunately, we can reach Volusia overland, and we will send reinforcements. The *Columbine* will make the trip much faster."

An unnerving vision of explosions and wrecked boats entered Prescott's mind. "Sir, shouldn't we be concerned about the infernal machines the rebels set in the river?"

"It's a concern, of course. The boats have been equipped with sweeping devices, so they are better protected now."

"Excellent." Prescott could only hope the defenses really worked. He dreaded the possibility of being blown to atoms. Given a choice, he would take the picks and shovels.

*

Spurred by the urgency of the message he bore, Carlo hustled to find Captain Dickison. Reunited with Company H, he had eventually returned to his courier job and secured this horse from the Welaka surrender. Although he rode the same trail as when the Union scouts captured him weeks ago, he did not fear falling into their hands again. The Yankees had abandoned Palatka and, with it, this part of the west bank.

Now the enemy was on the move again.

The Yankee navy's river traffic had slowed since the *Maple Leaf* sank. The night after he escaped from the sinking boat, Carlo had helped row Captain Bryan and his team into the river off Mandarin Point to anchor another deadly charge in the channel. He had watched, nerves stretched to the limit, as the crew handled the wooden barrel full of explosives as though it were made of eggshells. Capped with conical ends, waterproofed and equipped with a percussion fuse, if accidentally set off, the device would have sent them all to Kingdom Come in an instant.

Two weeks later, a torpedo sank the Hunter. Carlo would not mind taking credit for that victory. His personal torpedo might well have done the job.

Carlo inquired of the captain's whereabouts from pickets stationed along the way and finally spotted Captain Dickison in the company of another officer. Carlo called out, "Captain! The river is full of gunboats coming up!"

Dickison exchanged a glance with his companion, and the two rode up to meet him. As Carlo reined in his puffing horse, he noticed the artillery insignia on the lieutenant's jacket. "How many boats, Private?" Dickison asked.

"I'm told six, sir. Two gunboats and four armed transports full of troops."

Dickison said to the artillery lieutenant, "Just as we expected."

"Your boys stirred up a hornet's nest by capturing those posts." The lieutenant stared down the river, although a wooded point hid any possible view of the oncoming boats. "They're coming after us for sure."

"We'd better bring up your guns, Lieutenant Bates." Dickison took out a notepad, penciled a few lines and handed it to Carlo, "Private Sanchez, take this to camp and give it to Lieutenant McEaddy. We'll deploy both companies of cavalry and the artillery, and make good use of the fortifications the Yanks were considerate enough to build."

*

Prescott stood on the deck of the *Columbine* and watched the transports unload two regiments of soldiers at the docks across the river from Palatka. He understood those soldiers were to march south to Volusia and engage the hundreds of rebels who were supposed to be on the east side of the river. As soon as the troops left the transports, the *Columbine* would steam to the same destination. His was the easier job, because he and his men would remain on the gunboat and would not have to trudge miles through the wetlands along the river.

His worries over torpedoes had eased. He did not know whether the rebels had succeeded in planting any of the infernal machines this far upriver. Most likely they had concentrated their fiendish efforts closer to Jacksonville.

He walked around the starboard side of the boat and looked toward Palatka, squinting to avoid the sun, which hung low in the western sky. To his satisfaction, he saw no sign of rebels along the wharf. Could they be concealed in the well-arranged breastworks the Union army left in place?

No matter. The boats were safely out of rifle range on the opposite side of the river, and any rebels lurking in Palatka could only watch in futility.

*

Concealed behind the fortifications along the Palatka riverfront, the afternoon sun hot on his back, Jack watched the transport steamers unload troops across the river. Minutes before, the captain had rousted everyone out of camp and ordered them to position, where they watched the opposite bank.

"They keep on marching off the boats," Jack said to Bill Durrance, a Middleburg man who had hunkered down next to him. "Hundreds of them. Do they think we're still over there?"

"Too bad they got past the torpedoes," Durrance murmured.

"Those torpedoes did seem to change their minds about steaming up and down the river like they owned it, until now." Jack gripped the muzzle of the Spencer repeating rifle he had acquired after Olustee. It would be useful only as long as he could acquire the right ammunition.

Durrance nodded toward Captain Dickison, who watched the Union operations through his field glasses. "The captain's itching to get at them, but our artillery hasn't even bothered to unlimber."

A familiar-looking craft, still loaded with troops, broke away from the pack and resumed its upriver progress. "That's the *Columbine*," Jack told Durrance. "It's a smaller gunboat and can go farther upriver than the *Ottawa*."

Captain Dickison pocketed his field glasses and exchanged words with Lieutenant McEaddy and the artillery officer, both observing with him. "Something's up," Jack said.

McEaddy jogged down the line. "Mount up, men. We're going to intercept that boat at Brown's Landing."

Jack and Durrance left the cozy riverfront fortifications and sprinted with the rest of his troop up the hill to where they had left the horses. He mounted and rushed past Camp Call on a path to Brown's Landing, three miles upstream.

He passed Lieutenant Bates and his artillerymen as they brought up their four field pieces, the sweaty horses dragging the heavy weapons along the sandy trail. Jack and the other cavalrymen arrived at the landing just in time to hear the splash of paddlewheels as the boat glided past. Concealed by a screen of undergrowth that denied the enemy a clear target, Jack watched the smoke billow from the boat's funnels. The grind and clank of iron wheels announced the arrival of the artillery.

Jack said to Durrance, who reined in next to him, "The artillery's too late. They'll never wheel into place in time to shell the boat. We'll get her on the return trip."

*

At sundown, Jack waded into the swamp to the right of the dock, near the field pieces. He and about fifty of Dickison's men had been ordered into the water to support the artillery crews. He did not know what support riflemen would provide against a gunboat as formidable as the *Ottawa*.

The cold water felt good after the hot day's frantic activity. He held his Spencer rifle well out of the waist-deep water and hoped he and the other soldiers made enough commotion to flush out any water moccasins that swam nearby. He slung his rifle over his shoulder and climbed up the wide, flared trunk of a cypress tree to get away from such creatures.

From his perch he peered through the vegetation at the boats anchored in the middle of the river. The *Ottawa*, bristling with heavy cannons, probably dared not follow the smaller *Columbine* farther upstream, where the channel narrowed and a larger vessel could not turn or maneuver. One of the transport ships had anchored not far from the *Ottawa*, and a launch traveled from the gunboat to the transport.

The underbrush served to hide the Confederate activity on the shore. Lieutenant Bate's artillerymen had managed to place their guns without drawing fire from the gunboats. Conversation was prohibited lest their voices carry over the still water.

While he waited for something to happen, Jack's thoughts reverted to Martina. He had enjoyed a couple of nights at camp with his wife and daughter before he tucked them safely away at the Orange Springs house. This time she was farther from the river. He wouldn't be able to see her often, but the Yankees ought to have trouble penetrating that far inland.

Plenty of trouble, if it were up to him.

Graying skies turned dark, and the Yankees lighted their boats, apparently unaware of the field pieces aimed in their direction. As though the enemy had provided a signal for attack, all four of the Confederate cannons fired in rapid sequence. Muzzle flashes split the darkness. Jack clapped his hand over his left ear to protect it against one resounding boom after another.

It appeared the artillery's true aim hit the well-lit targets. Jack saw sailors scurry to battle stations, but he held his fire. The distance was too great for accuracy, and he did not want to waste his precious few bullets.

The artillerymen swiftly reloaded and sent more salvos. Jack braced himself for return fire, but the transport shipped its anchor and made its slow way downstream, like a wounded animal, without retaliating. Finally the *Ottawa* answered the attack.

Jack saw the muzzle flashes and heard the roar of the broadside from the vessel's big guns. He jumped back into the water, figuring he would rather take his chances with snakes than exploding shells, and crouched as far down as he could. The shells blasted behind him and near the field pieces. He felt the concussion like a blow to his upper body, the sensation a bitter reminder of the explosion that had nearly killed him.

Apparently undamaged, the smaller guns on his side got off another series of rounds, attracting a second fearsome broadside from the boat. Through the ringing in his ears Jack heard a call to withdraw.

About damn time. If he had the power, he would have walked on water to get away from the incoming fire.

*

Next day, mission accomplished, the *Columbin*e returned downriver. Prescott said to Lieutenant Owen, "No rebels in sight. This has been a fine excursion. Cool weather and raiding a few plantations are the only things that could have improved it."

Owen nodded. "I was happy to find out the Volusia post was still secure. Once our reinforcements arrive, they should be able to repulse anything the rebels throw their way. I suppose Dickison's men have left this side of the river." He allowed a sarcastic smile. "All four hundred of them."

Prescott chuckled. "Four hundred indeed. Even if they were watching, our gunboats have scared them off." He glanced at the two big guns, the crews protected by sandbags. "The only obstacles I expect on our return trip are those infernal machines." He nodded toward the sweeps, devices resembling garden rakes. The boat had slowed noticeably on the approach toward Palatka as the crew lowered the devices. "And we have the means to counter those. We might as well relax and enjoy our voyage home."

One of the *Columbine's* guns boomed, and a shell exploded on the riverbank. A hundred yards farther, the other gun sent a second message to discourage any rebels who might be lurking in the underbrush. The boat moved closer to the shore, following the channel. Prescott lit a cigar, enjoying the ride, feeling safe and secure on the deck of the mighty gunboat. From this view, he could stand the land of traitors, snakes and alligators.

CHAPTER TWENTY-THREE

Once again Jack readied himself to take on a gunboat. The distant booms of the *Columbine* shelling the woods announced its approach. Bates's artillery crews prepared their guns they had placed at the edge of the woods.

Jack found a likely sweetgum tree and slung the Spencer strap over his shoulder. While he still had a free hand, he crossed himself. He left his Enfield propped against the trunk as a spare, fastened the gaffs onto his boots and climbed into the lower limbs, looping his rope around the trunk as he climbed. He straddled a bough, facing the trunk, and tied himself to the tree so he could use both arms.

Captain Dickison had picked twenty marksmen from his company to take on the *Columbine* on its expected return trip. Jack was one of the first selected, along with Russell. After spending a fitful night interrupted by nightmares consisting of deadly flashes and falling sensations, he feared he was about to relive his night terror. The sting of metal in his side never let him forget his old injuries. He swallowed his dread along with the bile that came up in his throat.

Local men in Dickison's company knew the channel came close to the shore at Horse Landing, which would force the *Columbine* to steam within rifle range. Jack was not pleased with the location because the undergrowth was not as thick here as he would have liked.

He watched Dickison, screened by a cedar tree, look through his field glasses. Jack spotted smoke from the gunboat's stacks and heard another boom and following shell blast, closer this time. Dirt and debris spat into the air a little south of where he waited. He cradled his Spencer in one arm and wiped sweat off his face with his other sleeve. Fellow sharpshooters who were able perched in trees as he did. The rest hid behind whatever cover they could find, their attention focused on the approaching monster.

The artillery crews stood by their loaded cannons, ready to pull the lanyards. Jack did not envy them, because enemy gunners, along with officers, always had been his preferred targets. He steadied the Spencer along the trunk and prepared to shoot.

The boat steamed alongside Jack's position, so close he made out faces among the soldiers on deck. Most of them were Negroes, and his old friend Isaac came to mind. He dismissed unwelcome thoughts that would make his job harder. Instead of aiming for an infantryman, he sought a target among the Yankees who handled the most lethal weapons. Although partially protected by sandbags, the artillerymen showed enough of their upper bodies to invite a bullet.

Dickison signaled with his cow horn, and Jack squeezed the trigger. The sound of his shot was lost in the noise of the cannons firing point-blank into the boat.

*

Prescott shouted an obscenity and flattened himself to the deck. "Owen! Owen!" He looked for his second in command as he jacked into a crouch. The lieutenant had not risen from the deck, still protecting himself from enemy gunfire. Prescott looked through the rails at the puffs of smoke rising from the trees lining the shore. "Owen, get up! Have our men form and shoot back!" Prescott's men grabbed their guns and looked for something to shoot at.

Owen elbowed up halfway then let himself back down flat.

One of the seamen stepped on Prescott's hand as he rushed past. Small arms fire continued to crack and whine around him. Prescott rubbed his bruised hand, swore and screamed, "Get up, Owen! Get up, I say! You bloody coward, get up and form the men!"

Owen turned his face to him, grimaced or snarled, and Prescott saw the blood on his jacket. Owen was of no further use to him.

Another cannonade crashed and one of the navy men yelled, "The chain! They've blown away the rudder chain!"

"Don't just stand there," Prescott shouted at his men. "Shoot the damned rebels!" He drew his sidearm and tried to find a target among the shadows of the trees.

*

The *Columbine* drifted sideways and shambled to a stop. Jack continued to aim and fire through the heavy smoke thrown out by the Spencer. One of the big guns on the boat began to return fire, but the shell rocketed overhead and exploded behind the array of sharpshooters. Remembering how it felt to be blasted out of a tree, he cringed and prayed the enemy artillerymen weren't able to aim the guns any lower.

Jack continued to concentrate his aim on the *Columbine*'s cannon crew while the Confederate artillery pounded the boat. After he used up the first seven-shot tube, Jack untied his rope and jumped down from the sweetgum tree to avoid staying in one place too long and drawing fire. He reloaded, bolted the next shell into place, crouched next to the trunk and sought a new target.

*

One of the Negro soldiers screamed, fell, and sprayed blood on Prescott's jacket where he crouched behind the rail. Another soldier clung to the rail, then sank to his knees, coughing blood. Two more threw down their guns and ran around the deck to the port side. Prescott yelled after them to come back and fight, but they disobeyed.

"The rebs'll slit our throats for sure," one of them threw over his shoulder.

Another cried out, "Rebs don't give no quarter."

Prescott sank behind the rail for the scant protection it offered. His breath came in harsh gasps. His hands shook too hard for him to aim his pistol and hope to hit anything. He watched Lieutenant Owen roll over on his back, gray of face, leaving a smear of blood on the deck where he had lain. Owen's hand moved to the hole in his chest and his eyes rolled upward, showing the whites.

Bullets whined past and pinged off the metal sides of the boat, while the rebel artillery kept up its intermittent pounding. The navy crewmen who were still able-bodied tried to coax the side-wheeler off the sandbar, an impossible task with no steering. Prescott realized the vessel was hopelessly mired on the shallow edge of the channel. The rebel artillery continued to blast the *Columbine* point-blank, and incessant rifle fire from the bank picked off anyone who stuck up his head.

Prescott looked toward the two cannons on the *Columbine*. One was useless, turned the wrong way. The other was out of operation, the crew lying around the gun in varied stages of disability. It took a brave man to stand the concentrated fire on the gunners, and the bravest already had been shot down.

A bullet sang so close to Prescott's ear he felt a puff of air as it passed. He didn't want to die, as it appeared Owen was about to do. He was on his own. Running to the safer side of the boat was the only sane, if ignominious, action to take.

He followed the men who had gone there earlier, yelling at them to rally and return to the fight. When he reached the port side of the deck, he leaned over the rail. It seemed half his company had jumped onto the sandbar, making for the far shore.

*

Isaac stepped over Lieutenant Owen and followed Captain Prescott, thinking to help him keep the men from jumping. He spotted Zeke wading along the sandbar. Then Zeke disappeared under the water. He surged to the surface, sputtering and flailing, then went down again.

Prescott was whiter than Isaac had ever seen him. His pompous bearing had disappeared, leaving him pop-eyed and breathing through his mouth. “Get back here and fight!” Prescott yelled at the men in the river, his voice high and shaky.

“Sir, what you want me to do?” Isaac asked.

Another boom rolled across the river. The ship shook with the impact of a round of solid shot. Prescott stared past Isaac, then turned to look at the water. He climbed over the rail and jumped into the river feet first. Isaac watched in disbelief as his commanding officer surged through the chest-deep brown water toward the other side of the river.

Then, like Zeke, Captain Prescott walked over the edge and sank. Some of the men were swimming through the channel on the other side of the sandbar, but Isaac saw no sign of Zeke. The captain bobbed up, hollering about not being able to swim, yelling for help. Isaac looked around the deck and spotted a wooden powder barrel. He hefted it, found it empty and light, and tossed it toward the captain, hoping he could use it as a float. Instead, the captain kept splashing and floundering.

Prescott appeared as helpless in the deep water as the *Columbine* was on the sandbar. Isaac threw down his rifle and jumped over the side. His feet splashed to the bottom. Righting himself, he waded as far as his feet found riverbed. He could not see the captain. He swam to the place where he had last seen Prescott, dived after him, and bumped into the solid, writhing body of the man. Isaac hooked him from behind, around the waist.

Isaac pulled the struggling officer to the surface. Fortunately, the barrel floated nearby, a good thing, because his sputtering, panicked commander had turned and was trying to climb on top of him. Isaac grabbed onto the rim of the barrel and hollered at Captain Prescott to do the same. Finally Prescott quit fighting him and grasped at the rim. Isaac glanced toward the boat, realizing it would be useless to try to climb back on. Besides, he had sense enough to know the *Columbine* and its crew were done for.

Still, he ought to ask his captain's opinion. "Sir, you want to try to get back on that boat and fight the rebs, or swim for it so we don't get blowed up?"

Prescott, moustache dripping, sopping hair hanging over his forehead and beading droplets of water owing to the load of Macassar oil it held, glared at him. Plainly, Prescott hated him. In saving his hide, Isaac had witnessed Prescott's cowardice, something the officer would hold against him.

"An exploding shell blew me off that boat," Prescott said. "You understand?"

"Yes, sir. I get that."

"Good. Now you're going to help me to the shore."

"Yes, sir." Isaac blew out a noseful of water and wiped his face. "All you got to do is hang onto the barrel, and I'll get you there."

*

When someone on the *Columbine* raised a white flag, the firing stopped. Jack joined his comrades in a shout of triumph. He felt wrung out and empty, as he always did after a fight. His ears rang, and his hands were blackened from burnt powder. Distrustful, he did not lower his weapon. He looked around at his comrades who appeared to be unhurt, and crossed himself again, not in fear this time, but in gratitude. The killing was over, and he was alive.

Dickison cupped his hands around his mouth and called out, "Captain, come ashore in one of your small boats."

"They're riddled with shot," came the reply from the navy officer standing at the deck railing.

"Along with a good part of the crew, I'll bet," Russell muttered. Like Jack, he waited, rifle ready, for a sign of treachery from the Yankees.

"We'll come to you, then," Captain Dickison shouted back. Jack heard him tell Lieutenant Bates to retrieve the flatboats hidden in the brush, take a squad, and accept the surrender. The captain told Bates, "We'd better work fast. I'm surprised that other gunboat hasn't joined the fight."

Jack helped pole and row one of the rafts across the channel to the stranded side-wheeler. He climbed the ladder and clambered over the rail and onto the canted deck, his Enfield slung over his shoulder. Once on deck he held his loaded rifle ready in case one of the enemy failed to honor the surrender. Jack found no familiar faces among the unwounded enemies he and his comrades rounded up and herded into a cluster.

While Lieutenant Bates and the captain of the *Columbine* argued the propriety of a navy captain surrendering to a mere lieutenant, Jack took a position on the gangway, where the unsettling sight and the bloody smell of dead and wounded men confronted him. Bodies lay strewn about in puddles of gore. Those still alive and conscious nursed their wounds as best they could and looked at him with apprehension. One of the Negroes skittered away from him, eyes wide with pain and terror, dragging a bleeding leg. "Don't kill me, master. Please don't kill me."

"I won't. Not if you've surrendered. Tell me what regiment you're in."

"Thank you, master." The wretch stopped trying to edge away and let out a deep breath like a sob. "2nd South Carolina."

Prescott's regiment. "Who's your captain?"

"Cap'n Prescott, master."

Jack gripped his rifle tighter. "Where is that sorry bastard?"

The Negro's eyes widened in surprise. "I don't rightly know, master."

"What about a man named Isaac?"

"Don't know, master. He was here when we was gettin' shot up. Don't see him now."

Jack focused on the other men lying about and spotted a white officer, not Prescott. He recognized the man from past encounters. Prescott's second in command, Owen, watched him with the wary eyes of a trapped animal, his bloodied hand holding a red-soaked rag over his chest. Jack stepped over a corpse and strode to Owen. He confiscated the man's sidearm and asked, "Where's Prescott?"

"Farrell." Ashen-faced, Owen managed a brave smile through bloody lips. "Funny seeing you here."

"Where is he?"

"He ran to the other side. Some of our boys were jumping off. Supposedly he was going to make them fight." Owen coughed and grimaced. "Haven't seen him since."

Jack stalked around the gangway to the port side, where he found no corpses. That was the sheltered side of the boat. He looked over the rail and spotted two bodies floating just underneath the surface, darker of complexion than the Yankee captain. During his quick tour he found no sign of Prescott. The bastard still lived and breathed and had come back to threaten Martina. He was free to do it again. Jack clenched his teeth. Too bad he hadn't spotted the bastard earlier and finished him like he should have done a year ago.

He returned to Owen. "Think he jumped off? Looks like a couple of your colored boys drowned."

"They were more afraid of rebs catching them than they were of drowning," Owen's voice had weakened. "They think you'll murder them."

"That's just something you tell them to keep them in line. What about Isaac? I haven't seen him, either."

Owen shut his eyes and grimaced again. "Look here, Farrell. I got shot in the first volley. Don't ask me where anybody went. I was too busy bleeding to notice."

"All right." Jack let out his breath. "I don't have anything against you. Not personally, anyway. I'll leave you be."

"Before you do, can you find me some water? I'm all dried up."

Jack nodded. "I'll get you a canteen. Anything else you need?"

"Nothing you can provide." Owen coughed up more blood and his eyes slid shut. By the time Jack brought Owen water, the Yankee officer had no use for it.

CHAPTER TWENTY-FOUR

"Somebody's coming." Sarah paused in stirring the boiling laundry, noting the apprehension in her mother's voice. Mama straightened from tending the fire to look down the drive.

A blue-coated man on horseback approached their house at a canter. He slowed as he neared the house. Sarah left the broom handle in the kettle and dried her hands on her apron, sharing her mother's anxiety, until she recognized the rider.

"It's all right, Mama." A thrill of unbidden pleasure replaced Sarah's fear. "That's Dan Farrell." She picked up the edge of her apron and wiped the perspiration off her face, then tried to tidy the strands of hair that had come loose. Why should she care that Dan had caught her flushed and disheveled from doing housework? Besides, he couldn't be so fresh in appearance, either, after a hot day's ride.

Dan dismounted Stripe, dropped the reins and strode to where she and her mother had built the fire to boil the week's load of wash. He removed his hat, nodded to her mother, and looked Sarah over, smiling. "Howdy, Mrs. Cates, Miss Sarah."

"Good afternoon, Captain Farrell." Mama set her hands on her hips. "What brings you out here?"

"I was in the neighborhood and thought I'd stop by."

"You left Palatka?" Sarah looked beyond him. "Where are all your men?"

"We're stationed in St. Augustine now, and we've been assigned to outpost duty on the King's Road. I had some spare time...."

"Our boys chased you out of Palatka?" Sarah did not want him to sense her secret delight at his presence. "Aren't you even a little bit scared, riding around without your troop?"

"With the garrison at Picolata, and St. Augustine well secured, it's safe enough."

Sarah had not seen Russell or Jack in weeks, so Dan was probably right. "Safe for you, I guess. Can't say the same for us, with all the Yankee soldiers nearby."

He ignored the jab. "I wanted to make sure you got home all right."

She lifted her hands, palms up. "I'm here. Have you talked to Teresa and Ramon?"

"Just yesterday." He nodded. "Ramon is busy cleaning up their place. It's been neglected for a long time. Teresa seems to be regaining her health. She is grateful to you for helping her make her way home."

"I won't be seeing much of her," Sarah said. "Now that she's behind your picket line."

"So are you." He smiled wryly. "This is Union territory now."

Mama wiped her brow with the back of her hand. "Are the Yankees going to be giving us more trouble? You know we can't take your oath, with Russell in the Confederate Army. Captain Prescott used to say they were going to clear us out because of that."

Dan's expression darkened. Why would he take offense at Mama's pointing out the obvious? "None of us seem to be exempt from troubles, Mrs. Cates." He turned to Sarah. "Your friend and mine, Captain Prescott, had my father's place burned. Prescott claimed Colonel Montgomery gave the order. My father is as good a Unionist as they come, and they burned his house anyway. The outbuildings, too. When I complained to the colonel about it, he said Prescott assured him the rebels were using the homestead and it had to be destroyed."

"That's despicable. So is Prescott. Can you blame Jack for wanting to use his own house?" Sarah shook her head. "But I don't guess Prescott needed an excuse, from what Martina told me. Is he back in St. Augustine? I hope not."

"He's with the Picolata garrison," Dan said. "Close enough."

An involuntary shudder ran down Sarah's spine. "I hope he stays in that garrison and doesn't come out here to burn our house, too."

Her mother said, "Captain Farrell, Sarah told me how much you helped her and her friends in Palatka. You aren't the kind of Yankee we're used to."

He quirked a smile. "We used to be neighbors, Mrs. Cates. Still are."

"Would you like to stay for supper?"

"I'd be honored." He cut his gaze to Sarah, his good humor restored. "It'll give us a chance to catch up on things."

"We're almost through with the laundry." Sarah nodded toward Stripe. "You can take care of my horse in the meantime."

Dan grinned. “Yes, ma’am.” He collected the reins and led Stripe toward the empty paddock.

As soon as he was out of earshot, Mama said, “I saw the way your face lit up when you recognized him. Are you in love with him?”

Sarah grasped the broom handle and fished out Papa’s trousers. “We’re friends.”

“You told us he practically rescued you and the others in Palatka. He stayed in your house. Was he courting you?”

“I guess he’s fond of me. Maybe like a sister.”

“The look he gave you was not what I’d call brotherly.”

Sarah held the steaming, dripping clothes up to let them drain and cool. “I’m a grown woman, Mama. I can choose my friends as I please.”

“Yes, and he and your brother are mortal enemies. Do you really want to put yourself between them?”

“I won’t betray Russell,” she said. *I won’t betray Dan, either*. She prayed she would never have to make that choice.

“I suppose some good can come of it,” Mama allowed. “If he wants to stay on your good side, he won’t do us any harm.”

“Dan wouldn’t harm us,” Sarah said. “Not on purpose, anyway.”

*

After supper, Sarah’s father lit pine knots to smoke away mosquitoes as Dan and the Cates family settled on the porch to relax. The meal had been a pleasant enough affair, as everyone avoided talk of politics and war. That left few safe topics. Mr. Cates was also reluctant to discuss his cattle or farming operations. No doubt he feared giving Dan too much information might lead to a raid from the Union commissary agents.

Dan sat on the edge of the porch with Sarah a demure arm’s length away. He noticed she had made an effort to make herself presentable after he had caught her showing the effects of hard work. If anything, her flushed, shiny appearance at the washtub had appealed to him as much as if she were turned out in an evening gown, done up for a ball. Fact was, she was just as desirable in any packaging. Better yet, he would like to see her in no packaging at all.

Nor was he fooled by her sass and teasing, which he believed screened her true feelings. If only he could persuade her to let down her guard.

“What’s Leon going to do now that the homestead was burned?”

Henry Cates asked.

"He's still living in St. Augustine, in Martina's house. After I told him about it, he went to take a look for himself. At least nobody cut down his valuable orange trees." Dan did not think it was a good idea to mention his father's rant. Pop insisted if Jack and the other rebels hadn't been using the house, Prescott wouldn't have been able to justify burning it down.

Sarah's father hunched his shoulders. "You think they're going to do that to us?"

"Honestly, sir, with your son in Dickison's troop, you need to be careful."

Sarah shot him a frown. "And if your colonel ordered you to burn us out?"

The fine supper Dan had enjoyed turned to lead in his gut. "I would plead your case."

She locked eyes with him, then turned away. "You'd follow orders."

"Sarah, let's take a walk." He stood up and offered his hand. She hesitated, then accepted his offer. Together they strolled to the paddock, where he set his hand on the top rail. Stripe paused in grazing, lifted his head and made his way to where they stood. The horse stuck his head over the rail, ears pricked.

Sarah rubbed the white hairs of Stripe's muzzle. Dan fished a piece of dried apple from his pocket and offered it to the horse, which delicately lipped the treat from the palm of his hand.

"He seems to like you," Sarah admitted.

Dan grinned at her. "Next time I come, I'll ride my other horse and bring Stripe along. Wouldn't you like to take a ride with me?"

"Is that a bribe? Of course I'd like to ride Stripe."

"Only if I get to come along. I guess that makes it a bribe."

She played with Stripe's forelock, combing the strands with her fingers. "My mother had a fit. She thinks we're sweethearts."

He raised an eyebrow. "Aren't we?"

She shrugged. At least she didn't stamp her foot and deny it. He circled his arm around her waist, and she yielded ever so slightly.

"How can it possibly work?" she whispered.

"We'll make it work." He kissed her forehead, and she turned her face up to him. He pulled her closer for their lips to meet.

"What would Russell say?" she murmured around their kiss.

"Do you care what anybody says?"

She broke off their kiss and buried her face in his chest. "Why do I feel this way about a Yankee officer? It's all wrong."

"Feels right to me." He stroked her hair. "Feels just right to me."

*

Martina sat on the edge of the bed next to Jack, cherishing the sight of her tough husband letting Rosa hold onto his hands so she could pull herself up. "Papa," he said. "Can you say Papa?"

"Zazazaza," The little one pumped up and down, laughing out loud, her mouth and eyes wide with delight at her new abilities.

"Pa. Pa. Smart girl. You've almost got it." Jack's open joy in the gentle play warmed Martina's heart. At one time she had questioned her own judgment in agreeing to marry a man whose flaws seemed to outweigh his virtues.

Now she knew that imbalance was an illusion. As his wounds healed, so did his soul. He had risen to fulfill her belief in him, and she was satisfied with that.

Jack picked up his daughter and gave her a hug. Then he looked at Martina, smiling wryly. He held Rosa at arm's length and wrinkled his nose. "She needs her mother."

Martina sighed and took charge of the baby. While she attended to Rosa's needs, she asked Jack, "How long will you and Carlo get to stay in Orange Springs?"

"Captain Dickison will have a little ceremony tomorrow morning to celebrate our capturing the *Columbine*. You ought to come and watch us parade around and try to perform our drills without running into each other. We're better at real fighting. After that, I guess we'll head back to the river. How do you like Orange Springs?"

"It's good having people around. In Palatka it was mostly soldiers, and your troop seemed to be gone most of the time." Martina bit her lip. Someday, she prayed, their little family would not have to endure the long separations the war caused. The house she shared with three other women was adequate for her and Rosa, but she wanted her husband to live at home as he should.

"By the way, Prescott was on the boat."

Martina caught her breath. "Did he – "

"He got away. Jumped over the side and lit out for the east bank of the river, near as anybody can tell."

Her shoulders slumped. The monster was still out there, free to terrorize her. Jack had found her a shotgun to replace the one Prescott confiscated, but what good had the other one done?

"His company was shot to pieces, and Lieutenant Owen is dead. Too bad it wasn't Prescott, but I doubt he'll be causing us much trouble anytime soon."

"I never wanted anybody dead before." She crossed herself and touched her rosary. She should repent, but how could she change her deepest feelings?

Jack slipped his arm around her back and gave her a reassuring squeeze. "We captured a couple of their outposts and a gunboat. We sank a couple more of their boats with torpedoes. They pulled out of Palatka, too. Yankees call this part of the state Dixie's Land, and they seem to be scared to come this far west of the river. With good reason."

"What about Isaac?"

"He always was handy in the water, so I guess he got away, too. I didn't mind that so much. If we captured him, I was going to claim to own him and save his hide from Andersonville. Try to persuade him not to run back to the Yankee army."

Martina cradled Rosa, now fresh and dry, and settled into Jack's sheltering arms. "I love you," she murmured. "Promise you'll always come back to us."

He laid his rough cheek against hers and whispered, "I always do my best, darlin'. You know I always do my best."

*

News of Dickison's capture of the *Columbine* came with orders for Dan to scout down the Palatka road and look for survivors. Despite intelligence indicating the enemy had quit the east side of the river, he proceeded with a degree of caution. Dickison's bad habit of catching Union soldiers by surprise must be anticipated. Dan had no intention of again falling victim to that sort of catastrophe.

As always, his thoughts meandered back to Sarah. This patrol, despite its worthwhile purpose, kept him from fulfilling his promise to take her for a pleasure ride. No telling when duty would allow him to see her again, though her home was within easy riding distance of his assigned outpost.

He could not deny their opposing loyalties presented a huge barrier. Yet he clung to the belief that their mutual attraction could overcome the problems. Last night they had parted as more than friends, giving him hope he could win her over completely.

One of his vedettes, Tatum, approached and pulled Dan from his reverie. "Sir, we just came across five of our infantrymen. They say they were on the *Columbine* and got away from the rebs."

"Excellent." Dan continued forward with his troop, heartened by the quick success. He spotted the dirty, disheveled, bug-bitten wretches, four colored soldiers and a white officer. The haggard survivors stood or squatted near the other vedette, who sat on his horse nearby. Dan rode up to meet the men and recognized two of them.

He felt his face grow hot at the sight of Prescott. The pleasure of rescuing the men soured. Despite his urge to leap down and give Prescott another thrashing, Dal forced himself to take three deep breaths. He reminded himself that although he would like to throw Prescott back to the alligators, the poor fellows with him deserved better.

"Captain Prescott," he nodded to his fellow officer, then to Isaac and the three other soldiers. "Congratulations on your escape."

Isaac beamed back at him through grime and stubble and threw him a jaunty salute. "You sure a welcome sight, Captain Farrell."

"I need something to eat, Farrell. I haven't eaten in three days," Prescott whined. "I've been drinking from dirty swamps and brackish streams. I've walked far enough. My feet are blistered, and I need to ride."

Prescott's manners had not improved since their last encounter. Dan heeled his horse right up to the other officer, crowding him into taking a step backward. "I'm sure my men will gladly share their rations and their water," Dan said in a pleasant tone, deliberately looking past Prescott to the other soldiers. "We'll let you ride double to our outpost. You can eat and rest a spell before you ride on to St. Augustine."

He let his gaze fall on Prescott. "I'm sure the colonel will be anxious to receive your firsthand report of what happened on that boat."

"A shell blast knocked me overboard." Prescott's peevish tone persisted. "Corporal Farrell saw what happened."

Interesting that the officer called upon a Negro noncom for corroboration. His assertion stank of panic and rang hollow. Dan glanced at Isaac, whose stony face revealed little. Later, he would talk to Isaac in confidence.

"Did any others escape besides your party?" Dan asked Prescott.

"Some of our men drowned trying to get away."

"Regrettable." Dan turned to Sergeant Drake. "See to getting these men mounted. Let's take them home."

CHAPTER TWENTY-FIVE

Drat. Who is it this time? Sarah straightened and hurriedly rubbed her hands on her apron to remove the green stains and dirt. When she recognized Dan, her warring emotions stirred anew. Heaven forbid she should let him know her heart leaped with delight at the sight of him, while common sense whispered a warning.

Dan rode his bay directly to her, leading Stripe. He grinned and indicated her saddled and bridled horse. "Good morning, Miss Sarah. Care for a ride?"

She dropped her apron and tilted her head to one side. "Last time you caught me doing laundry, and this time you find me tending the garden."

"The weeds can wait. Let's have fun."

Fun? It seemed like years since she had done anything purely for enjoyment. "I'll wash up and be right back."

Sarah stopped at the pump and scrubbed, then she hurried into the house. She hadn't felt this excited about an excursion since Edward courted her. "Mama, I'm going for a ride with Dan."

Her mother gave her a speculative look. "Isn't he afraid our scouts will catch him?"

"If they were around, they would've stopped by looking for something to eat by now, like they always do."

"They wouldn't like finding you with a Union officer. And it's even more dangerous for him."

"Mama, he isn't afraid, so why should I be? Besides, our boys know who I am." Sarah opened the pantry door. "Come to think of it, I'd better take some lunch."

"Dried beef." Mama shook her head, still frowning with disapproval. "Corncakes and marmalade."

"Making friends with a Yankee officer isn't such a bad thing, Mama." Sarah stuffed food and utensils into a burlap sack. "If he tells his men not to bother us, they have to follow orders."

"We'll see about that." Mama did not sound convinced.

Sarah went to her room to tame her errant strands of hair. Then she rushed back through the house, picked up the sack and hurried outside, giddy with excitement.

"Where should we go?" Dan asked after he gave her a leg up onto Stripe.

Riding astride was not the most ladylike mode, with her skirts hiked up above her ankles, but the military saddle would make it easy to control her horse. "Do you trust me not to lead you into a trap?"

He quirked a smile. "Do you know something I don't?"

"Lots of things, I expect." She laughed. "For one thing, there's a sand beach on the creek. It's a pretty place for a picnic."

"None of your friends will be waiting for us?"

"I wouldn't do that to you, Dan." She sobered. "Any more than I'd help you ambush them."

"Fair enough. Let's go."

They started at an easy pace, neither in a hurry. It galled Sarah to think she needed Dan's permission to ride Stripe. Yet she could at least enjoy a pleasure ride once in a while, at the expense of Dan's escort. A mixed blessing.

Deferring to the early summer heat, he had taken off his coat and rolled it behind his saddle. She did not have to see the dark blue of his uniform every time she looked his way, and that was fine with her. She admitted to herself that the homegrown Yankee was easy company when she was not tied into nervous knots by his presence.

He told her about the loss of the *Columbine* and about finding Prescott and the other survivors. "Prescott will have to rebuild his company after his losses," Dan said. "He's in Jacksonville now. I don't think he'll be troubling you anytime soon."

"I hope not. He's a small, mean man." Sarah shuddered. "The less I see of him, the better I like it."

"Prescott seems to have that effect on people," Dan said. "I suspect he wasn't blown off that boat as he claims but abandoned his command. Of course that isn't what he'll say in his report. Isaac wouldn't discuss it, and nobody would believe him if he contradicted Prescott. He's only a corporal and colored at that, but he's more of a man than his captain will ever be."

Sarah was surprised by Dan's vehemence. "I thought you weren't supposed to criticize your fellow officers."

Dan lifted an eyebrow. "Who are you going to tell?"

"Nobody." She laughed. "I don't talk to Union soldiers, unless I'm trying to talk them out of stealing our chickens. Except for you."

He sighed. "I'm glad you make an exception in my case."

Sarah took a notion to exercise her sense of freedom. She kicked Stripe into a gallop, threw a glance over her shoulder and called out, "Race you to the creek!" Dan wasted no time catching up to her on his bigger horse. He rode alongside, and she realized he was holding his mount back to keep in stride with Stripe. When they reached the river she let Stripe splash into the shallows up to his hocks, cooling his legs, and Dan's horse did the same. Sarah sat still for a moment, admiring the lush riverscape and the calm, inviting water. "Isn't this a pretty spot?" She patted the sack she had strapped to the saddle. "We can have a picnic, if you want."

After a glance around the area, Dan nodded. They turned back onto the bank, dismounted and tied the horses. Dan spread a wool army blanket in a shady spot while Sarah fetched the sack containing their lunch and set it on the blanket.

"Never mind. I'm not hungry." Still intoxicated with excitement, Sarah took off her shoes and ran down the sandy bank, holding her skirts out of the water.

She laughed at Dan, who followed her to the water's edge and watched, a bemused look on his face. Something gave way inside her, and she wanted to free herself from the pain of her conflicted emotions. She yielded to the reckless urge to loosen the constraints of feminine dignity and act half her age. "You wanted to have fun? Let's have fun! Come on in." She reached down and splashed a double handful of water at him. "I dare you!"

*

Enchanted, Dan took in the enticing sight of Sarah playing tomboy. She had let her skirts drop so the hem dragged in the water, freeing her hands to fling water at him. Laughing, she splattered his trousers, shirt and face, heedless of the loose hair streaming down her neck. She wrinkled her nose and stuck out her tongue at him.

"This is war!" Dan sat down and removed his boots. Then he waded in, surged close to her and splashed her in return, giving her a good soaking. She squealed and redoubled her efforts to get him wet. A torrent of river water smacked into his face, and he retaliated by lunging forward and grabbing her wrists. "Little hellion." He pulled her wet, supple body toward him, barely controlling his desire to make love to her then and there.

Giggling, Sarah struggled to break his grip and succeeded in freeing one hand. She pushed his chest, but he threw his arm around her and drew her into him. When she fell against him, he looped his arms around her waist, gathering her in, savoring her energy as she wriggled, laughing all the while.

"Surrender?" he murmured into her ear. He brushed her soft cheek with his and caught her ear lobe in his lips.

"Never!" She eeled around, slipped out of his grip and splashed him again, then whirled and ran away, holding up her skirts. In a few strides he caught her again. This time he swept her into his arms and picked her up. She kicked and laughed until he bent his face down to hers and planted a kiss on her lips.

Sarah quieted and flung her arms around his neck, giving back every bit as much passion as he delivered. Her slightly salty taste, whether from the brackish water or from her skin, spiced her essence. She nestled against him, and he set her feet down in the creek.

"I said I wouldn't seduce you unless you wanted me to." He took her face in both hands and locked eyes with her. "But you are driving me wild. If we keep this up, I won't be able to stop myself."

She slipped her hand behind his head and tipped it down. She kissed him again and clapped her hips tight to his. He cupped his hands around her rear and snugged her even closer. Then he carried her to the creek bank, where he set her down on the blanket and lay beside her.

*

Sarah sighed, feeling Dan's heartbeat under her ear, physically content, her thoughts in turmoil. In their eagerness they had not even bothered to take off more clothes than necessary to complete the act. "Aren't we wicked?" She lifted her head from Dan's shoulder and grazed his clean-shaven cheek with her lips. How could something forbidden be so wonderful?

"Hardly wicked." He caressed the small of her back underneath the blanket they had wrapped around themselves. "Unless you mean wickedly happy. I am besotted with you, more than ever. I want to keep you."

There it was. The impossibility of their situation. What had she gotten herself into? In a moment of abandon she had involved herself deeply with the enemy by letting her emotions and desires overtake her good sense.

She rolled onto her back with a groan. "How can that be? I must have lost my head."

"No trouble will come of it. You can trust me," he murmured.

"I do trust you." At least Dan's presence of mind did not vacate at the height of passion, as he had taken care not to plant a seed inside her. She was playing with fire, but this time escaped being burnt as badly as she might have been.

He shifted up, planted his elbows on either side of her, and pinned her to the blanket, his face inches from hers. "Marry me."

She stared up at him, taking in the intense way his blue eyes bore into hers, torn. If only it could be. She bit her lip. "Marry a Union officer? How would I explain that to my brother? How would I explain *you*?"

"They'll have to accept your choice."

"Easy for you. My family would never speak to me again. My mother doesn't want me to keep company with you, and my father gives me odd looks whenever you come around. As for Russell.... thank God he doesn't know anything."

"The war won't last forever."

"Then what? Will you go out west and fight Indians?"

"I haven't planned that far ahead."

"That doesn't sound like you, Dan. You're always making plans."

"I didn't plan on falling in love with you."

She pushed him off, sat up and hugged her knees. *Love?* Tears sprang to her eyes. *I must have been crazy to let this happen.* "I can't be in love with you. How can we possibly make it work?"

"Give it time, Sarah. Give me time." He sat up and wrapped his arms around her.

She yielded and rested into his chest. She loved the solid feel of him, his male strength. She loved the way he persisted despite her half-hearted attempts to fend him off. "What would you do with a wife, anyway?"

He nuzzled her neck. "It doesn't take much imagination."

*

Dan held her warm body close to his, thankful a barrier had fallen, and he possessed her at least in a physical way. He understood her refusal to commit wholly to him, though he didn't have to like it. His deepest fear, that he would again confront his brother in a deadly fight, was compounded by the fear that he would meet hers as well.

"I don't know what we can do to change the circumstances," he said. "Your brother hasn't shown any inclination to give up, and I won't, either."

"You are a stubborn man," she murmured.

"I don't run away from a challenge." He chuckled. "I love challenges, like you. Otherwise, you would have scared me off months ago."

"Am I that scary?"

He shook his head. "I'm sure your clever tongue has flayed many a man."

"And how many women have you conquered?"

"Not many at the frontier posts where I spent a few years. And the war.... I'm at home here but not really at home. I feel like a stranger in my own territory. People who used to be my neighbors want to come at me with a pitchfork.... or a pistol...."

"You're one of the invaders," Sarah said. "They see that blue uniform. And you're coming to fight their sons and brothers. Like mine."

"I just want it to be like it was before." He sighed. "People getting along, no more fighting."

"We'd do just fine if the Yankees would leave us alone."

"This is one 'homegrown Yankee,' as you term it, who doesn't plan to leave you alone."

"Maybe someday, when the war is over," she murmured. "At this rate, that will be a long time."

"I guess I'll have to be satisfied with an engagement for now."

She did not disagree, and he took that as assent.

*

The summer passed quickly for Dan. As if by common consent, the opposing armies in Florida tended to stay close to camp and their picket posts rather than invite heat stroke on the march. The occasional patrol turned up no resistance, which convinced him the rebels had ceded St. Johns County to the Union. No one had shot at him for a couple of months, though he knew that was about to change.

His summer assignment, monitoring the St. Augustine-to-Palatka road, enabled him to visit Sarah whenever he could break away from his duties. The barriers between them had eroded further, though the war-related problems had not disappeared. Some topics were best avoided. He considered them secretly engaged, and she allowed that was the case.

Today they rode to a deserted house a few miles from her own. Sarah had swept the cabin floor and made their private hideaway comfortable, a safe haven to escape from mosquitoes, deerflies and prying eyes.

They lay together, contented, on the Spanish moss-stuffed pallet. A refreshing sea breeze drifted through the cabin's open windows. Dan had put off telling her his news, not wanting unpleasantness to mar their happiness. But tell her he must. "I'm going away tomorrow. Don't know how long I'll be gone, so I'll leave Stripe at the horse depot to spare him the hard use."

"You're leaving your outpost? Where are they sending you?"

"I can't tell you that, of course." Nor did he want to tell her news of the recent skirmish, where some of his fellow Union soldiers had tangled with Dickison's men. Such discussion was an unwelcome reminder of their differences. But she would find out eventually. "I heard about a hot little fight near Palatka. Our side lost a few men, and on your side, Captain Dickison's son was killed."

She sat up. "Charlie Dickison?" Her expression clouded. "He's – was – such a nice young man. What about Russell? Jack?" Her voice raised in alarm.

"Dixie's son is the only rebel casualty I know about. Our men didn't hold the ground." Or the bodies. No need to point out that side effect. "They're probably all right."

"You're going after them?"

"I don't think that's the primary objective. It's a raid. That's all I can say." His orders would probably lead to a confrontation with their brothers' troop, and affirming it to her would only pick at an unhealed sore.

"How can you do it? Go after your brother, and mine?" Sarah sat up and hugged herself.

"I have to set aside personal feelings and perform my duties." He looked up at her unhappy face and sighed. "I guess they look at it the same way."

"Men. Men and their stupid, murderous duty." Frowning, she bit her lip.

He sat up and wrapped his arms around her. She settled against him, and he murmured in her ear, "Sarah, I love you, no matter what happens." He prayed her feelings for him were just as unshakable.

*

Subdued and quiet, Sarah rode home beside Dan. Troubled over the danger to her brother, an unshakable feeling of impending disaster weighed down her spirit.

For the past two months the lull in the fighting had also calmed her fears. She told herself the war would have to end someday and then she would be free to declare openly her love for Dan. If her family could reconcile themselves to the fact, so much the better. In the meantime, she kept the depth of their entanglement secret.

Just as Dan would not tell her where his orders were sending him, she kept facts from him as well. She told him nothing of the occasional visits by Confederate scouts, whose knowledge of the countryside allowed them to watch the Union movements undetected. Hers was a careful dance, betraying neither side to the other, and praying her lover and her friends did not show up at the same time.

Despite their uneasiness with Dan's courtship, her mother and father had come to appreciate that his protection kept the Union soldiers from harassing them. They played the same fence-sitting game as she did. No one in her family would let on knowing anything about the presence of either army. Sarah figured closed mouths harmed nobody. So far.

The coming military campaign was not the only thing troubling Sarah, and she finally felt the need to speak out. "You weren't so careful that time."

He did not answer her right away. "I was caught up in the moment. It won't happen again."

"Are you trying to trap me into marrying you sooner than I want to?"

"Do you think I would be that underhanded? I made a mistake, that's all. Don't you trust me by now?"

"Dan, we can only trust each other so far." She blew out her breath in exasperation. "You can't tell me where your orders are taking you, and I can't talk to you about any of my friends or my brother. You're afraid I'll use such information against you, and I know you'd use it against Russell." Tears stung her eyes. "How can we go on like this?"

"Wait." He reined in, and she halted Stripe and turned in the saddle to face him. "Don't throw up more fences, Sarah. Nothing has changed between us."

"You're right. Nothing has changed. I'm carrying on with you like a foolish girl, not paying the least bit of attention to what's going on around us."

"Don't let it poison us, Sarah. Please."

"I'm sick from the poison." She blinked fast, but the tears spilled onto her cheeks. "And I'm afraid. I'm afraid for you, and I'm afraid for Russell. I'm afraid for us."

"How can I fix it, Sarah? What can I do?"

"You could quit fighting, but you won't."

He looked straight ahead, not at her. "I can't."

They rode the rest of the way home in silence.

CHAPTER TWENTY-SIX

Jack clicked an unconnected telegraph key, striving to increase his speed at Morse code. The station operator, Nat Brady, looked up from his watch after Jack tapped out the last word of the message "Seven words a minute, and accurate enough. You're coming along." He allowed a wry smile. "I'm not worried about you taking my job anytime soon, though. Not at that speed."

"I wouldn't mind trading my gun for a key." Jack grinned at Nat, who had been teaching him the science as well as the trade. "Guess I'll have to wait until we whip the Yankees or they whip us."

"Keep practicing, son. Keep practicing."

Jack would rather spend off-duty time with Martina, but at the Waldo headquarters he lived in a tent. She and Rosa were better off at the Orange Springs boarding house. Jack glanced at the silent instrument on Brady's desk. "Seems quiet tonight. I haven't heard any messages come in."

"It's curious," Brady mused. "Nothing from the Starke office all day, and their operator always checks in. I got a message this afternoon from Gainesville asking if a line is down. I had no answer for him."

"I wonder if something's brewing," Jack mused.

He stood and went to the window to investigate a commotion outside the office. A detachment of cavalry, led by an officer he recognized as Captain Rou, galloped their sweaty, blowing horses into the rail yard. "Those fellows have been stationed near Jacksonville," he told Nat. "Wonder what they're doing all the way down here."

Sensing an air of urgency about the officer, Jack stepped outside just as Captain Dickison emerged from his quarters. Jack sauntered closer, followed by Nat, wanting to overhear the conversation.

"....Yankees took Starke, burned our rail cars and supplies, and it appears their cavalry is headed toward Gainesville," Rau said.

"This is the first I've heard of it." Dickison glanced at Brady. "I've received no communications."

Nat lifted his hands, palms up. "Captain, we haven't heard a thing from Starke all day."

"No wonder," Rau said. "The Yankees cut the telegraph lines and tore up the tracks."

Dickison turned to Jack, his expression grim. "Private Farrell, find Lieutenant McEaddy and tell him to report to me. We're going to call in our pickets and ride out with all possible speed. We must put a stop to those vandals." Dickison bit out the words, his eyes hard. Jack knew he would welcome a chance to avenge his son, killed by a dirty Yankee trick less than a week ago.

Jack wasted no time carrying out the order. A Yankee raid this far inland filled him with dread. It sounded as though the bluecoats were still a long way from Orange Springs, but he knew as well as anyone how fast cavalry could travel.

*

After a moonlit all-night march from Starke, the Union cavalry, 300 strong, hit Gainesville and routed the small force of Confederates guarding the town in a bloodless charge. To Dan's relief, Colonel Harris allowed the tired soldiers in his victorious command to feed their horses and rest.

In the yard next to the railroad depot, Dan slipped the bit from his horse's mouth and gave it a nosebag of corn. He smelled coffee brewing and longed for a bracing mugful and a few hours' sleep. Marching at night spared men and horses the merciless sun. Dawn soon would bring the debilitating heat inevitable in a Florida August.

Two days ago he had led his troop to Picolata, where the men loaded their horses and equipment onto a ferry and crossed the river to Green Cove Springs. There they joined Captain Morton's two companies of Massachusetts cavalry and rode to rendezvous at Starke with Colonel Harris's force of cavalry and artillery.

Dan recalled riding at the head of his company into the small town, which consisted of a single tree-lined street, a few houses, and the mill that provided fuel for the locomotives. Harris's men already had begun their work of demolition. Cut telegraph lines dangled from the few poles they did not chop down. Four railroad cars smoldered on the tracks. The stink of scorched corn and sweet potatoes made him sneeze. A crew of soldiers worked on tearing up a section of track with crowbars and axes. If any civilians remained, they cowered behind the closed doors of their homes.

"Looks like we're late to the party," Sergeant Drake had said.

"I'd just as soon leave the fun to those who enjoy it." *Like Prescott.* Fortunately the smug bastard had not joined the expedition with what was left of his company.

On the way to Gainesville, the soldiers had stopped at farms to confiscate animals and valuables, then burn what they could not cart away. At the Lewis plantation they appropriated wagonloads of the woman's belongings, along with her Negroes, although some of them had to be coerced into coming with the army. The column of wagons, horses, and human contraband had come to a halt in the town square.

The thievery of the woman's possessions bothered Dan worse than the destruction of enemy property. He had experienced the bitterness of seeing his father's house burned and was ashamed to be a party to the spread of more misery.

Am I getting too soft for the work? He recalled Prescott's accusation that he was a Southern sympathizer. Although he would never admit such a sentiment, the authorized plunder and waste weighted his spirit. Once the war ended, he expected it would take years for Florida and the rest of the South to recover.

While planning the march, he had suggested to Colonel Harris that the troops bypass Waldo, where intelligence led him to believe Dickison's men were headquartered. Although the decision made sound military sense and Harris readily agreed, Dan wondered at his own motives. He had to admit he was not eager to engage Dickison's men, especially Jack and Russell.

Maybe he never should have volunteered for service in his home state.

After caring for his cavalry-issue horse, Dan wrapped his hands around a steaming mug of coffee. He leaned against a fence rail in front of Beville's Hotel and sipped the strong stuff as he enjoyed the view of the town square. The aroma of sizzling bacon tantalized his nostrils. After a good breakfast, surely his mood would improve. Sergeant Drake stood nearby, enjoying his own cup.

Dan's men behaved as they should, resting or attending to their animals. However, he watched some of the Massachusetts soldiers emerge from a house across the street, their arms laden with plunder. "Hey!" he shouted, but the men scampered away with their booty.

"They're looting a private home," he fumed at Drake. "It's off limits."

Drake shrugged. "Boys are just blowing off steam, Cap'n."

"My eye. They ought to be under stronger discipline."

Dan located Colonel Harris at the railway depot and told him about the incident. "Colonel, besides that, on the way here I noticed a number of the boys are more interested in pilfering houses than holding their positions. Even if we don't respect civilian property, I'm concerned they won't be ready in case the rebels attack us."

"Your concern is duly noted," Harris said. "I've established pickets surrounding the town in case the rebels work up enough nerve to take us on again. We won't have any trouble from the rebels as long as we're in Gainesville. Don't you realize we just whipped Dickison's men?"

Dan stared at the colonel, nonplussed. "Ah, sir, I beg your pardon. I've tangled with Dickison's men maybe a dozen times, and those weren't his. Didn't you notice they were a bunch of kids and old timers? Home guards. Once they caught sight of our numbers, they couldn't get away fast enough."

"I'll speak to the company commanders and have the men brought in line soon enough, Captain." Harris shot him a patronizing smile. "Try to get some rest. We have a lot of work to do here."

A boom from the direction of the Waldo road followed by the nearby crash of an exploding shell caused Dan and the colonel to whip around and look for the source. Moments later Dan spotted a handful of blue-coated soldiers galloping as though the devil were chasing them. "Rebs!" the man in the lead screamed. "Whole bloody regiment right behind us! They got artillery!"

The colonel bolted into action, barking out orders. Assigned to support the artillery, Dan ran to prepare his men for attack. He ordered them to their position to the rear of the single cannon. On the road in front of the hotel, the artillerymen wheeled their howitzer to face the expected onslaught. A dismounted cavalry company rushed to protect each flank. Other units sought cover behind the road fill and fences. Dan felt exposed on his horse despite his troop's reserve position behind the big gun.

A shell screamed in and exploded in the square, throwing up dirt and metal fragments. Another followed, landing closer with a terrific noise. Dan's horse crouched, ready to bolt. He tightened the reins and spoke soothingly to the animal, trying to control his own nerves. The howitzer crew quickly loaded and fired toward the source of the incoming fire.

"Those aren't the same militia we dispatched," Dan told Drake.

"Colonel Harris seemed to think we licked Dickison."

Drake snorted. "Dickison don't quit that easy."

"I told him so." *If that's Dickison, we're in for a real fight.*

In for it they were. Within minutes the ear-pounding artillery duel raged and the small-arms fire snapped to his front. The center defending the road from Waldo managed to hold the rebels in check despite the ferocity of the attack. Then Dan noticed cavalry moving to his right and realized the enemy detachments had swerved. They outflanked his force on both sides.

*

Weariness from the night march forgotten in his excitement, Jack urged his tired mount into a gallop as he followed Lieutenant McEaddy's lead. The hunt was over, and it was time to bag the quarry.

While dismounted troops and Lieutenant Bruton's cannons engaged the Yankees head-on, Jack's platoon cut between a swamp and a field to flank the enemy's left at the edge of town.

Aware of Charlie Colee, Bill Durrance and Russell Cates riding alongside, he saw bluecoats shooting from behind a rail fence at the edge of a yard. Yelling and firing his revolver, he and his comrades charged the enemy, who got off a few more shots before they ran for their lives. A short chase brought down one hapless Yankee, who dropped like a rock. While most of the enemy retreated to the center of town, a handful took cover behind trees, reloaded and fought back.

"Charge!" McEaddy yelled. The platoon fanned out into and rushed the stubborn hangers-on. Puffs of smoke gave away the Yankees' locations as they fired.

Alongside Jack, Russell shouted, "Remember Charlie Dickison!"

The dirty Yankee trick fresh in his mind, Jack took up the cry. Just last week bluecoats had gulled the captain's son into believing they had surrendered, then shot him through the heart.

Jack lay flat over Choctaw's neck and chased a Yankee who broke away and fled toward the nearest house.

Two ladies whose curiosity seemed to overrule their common sense had walked into the yard, one an old woman leaning on a cane. "Go back in the house!" Jack shouted. He pointed his revolver upward because the women were in his line of fire.

They did not react before the man he was chasing vaulted the low fence and ran behind the women. They turned to face the Yankee and seemed confused about what to do about him. Using the women as a shield, the bluecoat whipped out his revolver and pointed it at Jack.

"Move! Get out of the way!" Jack screamed just as the older lady lifted her cane and clubbed the Yankee's arm.

His aim ruined, the fugitive swore and grabbed at her cane, but she would have none of it. She ripped it out of his grasp and whacked him on the side of the head. "Don't you shoot our boys," she shrilled. The soldier reeled but stayed on his feet. The other woman kicked him on the shin then grabbed his gun arm, hampering his aim.

Jack jumped Choctaw over the fence and reined in just as the old lady cracked the fellow on the head again, this time taking him down. He lay stunned. "Get his gun!" Jack hollered as he swung off the horse. The younger woman snatched the pistol from the Yankee's hand and pointed it at him, holding it steady with both hands.

Jack also leveled his revolver at the prostrate soldier, who rolled onto his back and stared up at the steely-eyed lady who held his gun, then at the cane-wielding woman.

"Surrender, or you're dead," Jack snarled.

"Oh, hell," groaned the bluecoat. "I'll surrender if you'll keep that old witch from hitting me again."

"Witch!" She pounded her cane on the ground. The Yankee threw his arm over his head. "Take that back, young man!" She prodded him in the side, and he curled into a ball.

"Serves you right for hiding behind hoop skirts." Relieved the immediate danger had ended, Jack barked out a laugh. "Good work, ladies. I owe you." He nodded at them and tipped his hat. "Yank, raise your hands so I can make sure you're disarmed."

After Jack went through his prisoner's pockets, the older lady gave Jack a wrinkly, toothless smile. "We'll guard him for you, son. Hurry up and lick the rest of 'em."

"Ma'am, are you sure y'all don't want to take 'em on yourselves? You fight better than half the men I know." Still laughing, Jack climbed back on Choctaw and returned to the battle line.

*

Dan watched the fight from his vantage point at a street crossing, growing more anxious by the moment. The rebels had outflanked the Union forces on both right and left, driving them into the center of town. The Massachusetts troops had quit the depot and clustered in the road and the square, defending against the assault from three directions.

A demoralized fellow dropped his rifle and ran underneath the house across the street like a rabbit to ground. Colonel Harris rode his horse back and forth along the line, haranguing staff officers and dispatching couriers to urge the men to stand and fight.

Most of the rebels did not present themselves as targets but darted from one obstacle to another, taking cover and protecting themselves. A deadly crossfire developed as the enemy started to pick off the artillery horses to immobilize the piece. Struggling animals lay down in their harnesses as the crew frantically reloaded and fired the cannon, apparently to little effect. The screams of the poor animals frayed Dan's nerves even more than the bullets zipping close to his head.

Dan had dismounted his men to allow them to shoot from behind what cover they could find. He also had sent his horse to the rear because he did not want to present a conspicuous target for enemy sharpshooters. He noticed the howitzer crew had quit working the gun and took cover behind it instead. They drew their side arms while their sergeant dashed over to the colonel.

Sergeant Drake knelt behind a porch rail next to Dan, clutching his revolver. He nodded toward the cannon and its idle crew. "Think they're out of shot?"

"For pity's sake, let's hope not." Dan wiped stinging sweat away from his eyes. "Though they haven't done much good with what they had."

A renewed round of yells drew his attention to a squad of mounted Confederates charging down the main street, straight for the howitzer. As the rebels closed in on the cannon and its crew, Colonel Harris sent the sergeant scurrying and bellowed, "Save the artillery! For God's sake save the artillery!"

Dan shouted for his men to concentrate their fire on the oncoming cavalry. He saw a horse go down on its knees, throwing its gray-jacketed rider. The resulting collision toward the front of the column blunted the attack. The artillery crew worked to mobilize the field piece with their few surviving horses. To Dan's relief, the rebels backed off, stymied by the defensive fire, at least for the time being.

As the howitzer rumbled past, pulled by bleeding, stumbling horses, Dan looked down the road in the direction it was headed. To his horror, he saw why the Confederate cavalry had quit worrying the artillery. They had swung all the way around and now threatened to close the only escape route.

Dan pointed out the new threat to Drake. "They're going to

surround us! We'd better put a stop to that. Let's get the men mounted and go after those fellows." He ran for his horse, his men at his heels.

By the time he had his troop ready to counterattack, a courier galloped down the line yelling, "Save yourselves! Cut out the best way you can!"

A column of dismounted soldiers already had started running past Dan's squad. Others had mounted their horses and were pounding to escape. He said to his sergeant, "We'll hold off the enemy and give our boys a chance to get away."

Defeat a bitter taste in his mouth, Dan led his men to help salvage what was left of the colonel's command.

*

"After them! Don't let them get away!" Lieutenant McEaddy yelled.

Whipped but still giving fight, the bluecoats poured out of town, trying to make their exit. Jack chased the escapees on his jaded mount, determined to bottle up the Yankees in the streets and finish the job. Sweat stuck his shirt to his back, and lather drenched Choctaw's coat. Jack controlled the horse with his knees as he drew his saber and raised his revolver.

A squad of Yankee cavalry rushed his line, hollering and shooting. McEaddy ordered a countercharge. Jack wheeled to meet the new threat. He sought a target as he pushed to meet the enemy head-on. *Shoot the officers first.*

Once within pistol range, he slowed to steady his aim, picked out a sergeant and fired. The man slumped in the saddle. Through the din Jack heard Russell, an arm's length away, yelp in pain. He glanced at his friend, who clutched his forearm, grimacing.

Pushing forward, Jack spotted an officer amid the Yankee troopers. A conspicuous leader, the man rallied his men, revolver in hand. Jack aimed for the center of his body, then something about the officer's appearance penetrated his mind. He found himself locking eyes with Dan.

Lips drawn back in a snarl, his weapon aimed for a kill, Jack stared at his brother for a heartbeat. Instead of raising his own weapon, Dan froze.

As though by common consent, Dan veered aside at the same time Jack deflected his aim. Jack gave Dan a stiff nod and found another Yankee to shoot.

*

The running fight continued for miles, the pursuing rebels giving Dan little time to reflect on his unnerving encounter with Jack. Nor did he have a chance to count his losses until Colonel Harris called a halt to rest the remnant and their staggering mounts beside a clear, spring-fed stream.

Dan let his exhausted horse drink. He washed his face and hands, soothed his burning throat with the cool water, and filled his canteen. He creaked to his feet, threw an arm over the saddle and propped himself against his sweat-slick horse. The spent animal leaned into him as well, as though they held each other upright.

His earlier encounter with Jack kept playing in his mind. He recalled watching his brother's fierce expression dissolve into confusion that reflected his own inner war. He could not bring himself to shoot his brother, the enemy, even in self-defense. Apparently Jack felt the same way.

How could Dan continue to fight the rebels knowing his brother was among his most formidable foes? The concept of holding the Union intact at any price had worn thin. Was it worth the cost?

He kept finding himself retreating as part of a defeated army. Could the Union hope to prevail against a highly motivated enemy like Dickison's command? This morning while the Union soldiers fought for their lives, the Florida rebels fought for their homes and families. They would not give up easily.

He estimated only about 40 of the approximately 300 Union men who captured Gainesville that morning formed this band of survivors. In the confusion of the running fight, he was unsure which of his own men had escaped.

A handful of men from Dan's company gathered about, their movements weary. Tatum sat nearby nodding off, his back to a tree. "Have you seen Sergeant Drake?" Dan asked Coker, who had waded into the stream to fill his canteen.

"He got shot and fell off his horse," came the grim reply.

"I didn't see." Dan lowered his head and kicked the damp earth. Then he squared his shoulders and pushed away from the saddle. He waved his hand at the little group, fewer than half his command. "Who else in our company made it out?" He knew he would not like the answer.

"Well, sir," Coker shrugged and gave him a crooked smile. "I reckon what you see is it."

Dan reported to Colonel Harris, who sat on a log with his head in his hands. "Sir, are we really the only officers present?"

Harris lifted his head and turned his red-rimmed eyes to Dan. "It appears so, Captain. We lost the Howitzer, after all our efforts to bring it off. The horses gave out, and the rebels got the gun." Harris's sigh sounded like a sob. "I believe the column with Captain Morton rode the wrong way. I went after them but had to turn back. They are certainly prisoners by now. My command…." His voice broke off in a note of despair.

Dan felt the same hopelessness. The only thing that had saved his troop from even worse loss was their aggression in cutting their way out. *The devil took the hindmost*. Perhaps more would evade pursuit and make their way to safety.

"Colonel, one of my men, Coker, is familiar with this part of the country. I suggest we let him guide us to the Bellamy Road. From there we can make our way to our garrison at Magnolia."

Harris flicked his hand in dismissal. "Fine, fine. See to it, Captain."

Gunfire made both of them start. Dan turned his head toward the sound, though he was too numb with exhaustion and grief to give much of a damn what it meant.

"They're still after us," Harris groaned. "Our rear guard will be driven in any moment now. It seems we're stuck between the swamps and Andersonville."

CHAPTER TWENTY-SEVEN

The hotel lobby was well ventilated and clean, free from the stench of blood, vomit and waste Jack remembered from his experience in the Maryland field hospital. He found Russell asleep or in a drugged stupor, stretched out on a mattress in line with three other injured Confederates.

Russell's eyes slid open at Jack's approach, and his tight lips curved into an attempt at a smile. His face, pale and drawn, shined with sweat. A clean sheet concealed the wounded arm, or what was left of it.

"Hey," Jack said. "You doing all right?"

Russell grimaced. "As long as they give me enough opium."

"Too bad we're fresh out of popskull."

"Just my luck."

Jack's gaze wandered down the sheet. He could imagine what it covered. The visit brought home vivid recollections of his own extended stay at the Florida hospital in Richmond two years ago. "Captain is sending Carlo, Charlie Colee and me to St. Johns County on a scout. I guess you'll want me to give a message to your folks."

"Yeah. That'd be good. Tell 'em I'm still alive. Most of me, that is." Russell pulled down the sheet to reveal the huge bandage covering the shortened arm. Blood had seeped through the dressing, leaving a red stain. "Doc said the bone was smashed and it was either the arm or my life."

Jack swallowed hard and sat down at the edge of the mattress to hide an unexpected spell of wooziness. "Do you want me to ask Sarah or your mother to come take care of you?"

Russell touched the edge of the bandage where it covered the stump. "If they can. Yeah. I'd like that."

"We can take your horse so one of them can ride back. You won't be able to ride him for a day or two, at least."

"A day or two," Russell murmured.

"You'll be better off having somebody who gives a damn taking care of you. I expect you'd bring Martina if it was me."

"When you dig up your popskull, bring me some, will you?" Russell forced a smile. "Hey, we sure gave the Yanks a licking."

"I think we avenged Charlie Dickison pretty well. Killed some, rounded up a slew of prisoners, chased the rest for a ways. Took back most of their plunder. We had to break off before we rode our poor horses to death." Jack smiled grimly. "If I told anybody about the licking we gave the Yanks, he'd accuse me of lying. The captured Yanks give us the proof."

"Did you catch Dan?"

"You saw him?"

Russell nodded. "You had the drop on him."

Who else watched him fail to bring down his brother? "We didn't pick him up, but we got his sergeant. I shot him in the chest, but the Yankee surgeon said he might live. He's taking care of his own over in the courthouse. The militia's beating the bushes for Yankees right now. Maybe they'll bring in Dan."

"Alive, you hope."

Jack looked off, not wanting Russell to read his eyes. "Yeah. Alive."

*

Hearing the dreaded words that Russell was wounded, Sarah stared at Jack, reliving the day a letter informed her of Edward's death. *Not again.*

Mama gasped and clutched Sarah's arm. "How bad is he hurt?"

Sarah folded her hand over her mother's, blinking back the hot tears that stung her eyes. Dan wouldn't tell her where he was going. Was he in the Gainesville battle, too? What if he were killed? What if he shot Russell? Horrible possibilities chased each other through her mind like evil varmints.

"Doctor had to take off his arm." Jack indicated his own forearm. "Below the elbow. When I talked to him, he seemed to be doing as well as he could." Jack pulled a folded paper out of his pocket and handed it to Mama, who leaned on Sarah for support. "He asked me to give this to you."

"Mama, he's wounded, not dead." Sarah wanted to console herself as well as her mother, who held the letter so she could read it through her watery eyes.

"They cut off his arm," Mama mumbled as though the realty were just sinking in.

"I brought his horse so one of y'all can go to him. That's what he wants." Jack rubbed the side of his jaw. "He'll do better."

Sarah lifted her gaze to Jack. His resemblance to Dan tightened her throat. She wanted to ask.... would Jack even know? She forced out the words. "Was Dan there?"

Jack nodded. "We tangled with his company. That's when Russell was hit."

"I knew it." Sarah shuddered. "I just knew it. I wonder if he's all right."

Jack locked eyes with her. He was no fool, and she sensed he knew more about her feelings for Dan than he would let on. "Not many of the Yankees got away, but he must've."

A hurricane of conflicting emotions swept though Sarah's heart. Dan most likely was unhurt, but her brother was maimed and still could die. Wounded men often did not survive. *Loving Dan is wrong.* She rested her hand on her belly, praying she would suffer no penalty from their last indiscretion. *Dan is a Yankee, an enemy invader who was out to destroy my brother and finally succeeded. First Edward, and now Russell. I can't continue to betray my family, no matter how much it hurts.*

"One of us has to go take care of Russell," Mama said.

"I will." Sarah snapped out the words. "Mama, you'd best stay home with Papa. If Dan comes around, tell him he won't be seeing any more of me."

"You shouldn't blame him." Jack shook his head. "People on both sides get shot in a fight."

She hardened her resolve. "When do we leave?"

"Charlie Colee, Carlo and I have to nose around and see what the Yanks are doing around here. It would help if y'all tell us anything you know. We'll come by on our way back tomorrow."

Sarah lifted her chin. "I'll be ready."

*

Dan turned his horse toward the Cates farm, looking forward to finding comfort in Sarah's arms. More than ever he was determined to convince her to accept him as her husband. He was not averse to marrying in secret, an extension of their clandestine affair. This time he would overcome her doubts and fears.

If only he could overcome his own. In the wake of the last debacle, he had considered resigning his commission and giving up his dreams of seeing Florida return to the Union.

The worthiness of the cause had begun to wear thin. He detested the tactics of looting and destruction the Union Army had adopted. He wanted no part of it. Harassing women and old men, confiscating their animals and property, and arresting people for their political leanings seemed a wicked way to conduct a war. The resounding defeats his army had suffered made him consider the possibility of divine retribution.

He had lost half of his command, and that grieved him deeply. Although the responsibility had been laid at the feet of Colonel Harris, Dan shared in the humiliation. Harris likely faced a court martial for allowing his men to make mischief instead of preparing for possible attack. Dan did not expect to be held liable, though many of his command had suffered death or would be imprisoned in a Confederate hellhole. The only thing that kept him from ripping his shoulder boards off and handing them to General Seymour was the realization that he would denigrate his men's sacrifice.

One of the lucky forty, Dan had straggled into the Federal post at Magnolia the day after being driven out of Gainesville. His superiors had granted him a two-day furlough, time to collect himself and prepare for the effort of rebuilding his company.

He intended to take full advantage of the free time. During the Gainesville ordeal, he had often thought of Sarah and whether God and the rebels would allow him to see her ever again. She had become a bright light in the darkness of his despair. Perhaps a better cause than his precious Union.

Sarah's father met him in the yard. Always reserved in his presence, Henry Cates seemed even more distant than usual. As Dan dismounted, he sensed a wrongness in the man's demeanor, a bad news sort of expression on his face.

"I've come to see Sarah." Dan wanted to make a bolder statement, then decided he was sick of secrets. "And to ask you for permission to make her my wife."

Mr. Cates's silver moustache quivered, a sign of tension Dan had learned to recognize. "Son, I can give or refuse you all the permission in the world, but you'll have to convince her first."

"I intend to do just that, sir."

"You'll have to go behind our lines to do it." Dan listened with growing unease as Henry Cates told him about how she had gone to nurse Russell deep in rebel territory. "She left something for you. I'll get it from the house."

Dan waited on the porch, feeling like a stranger at the familiar homestead. Finally Sarah's mother and father both stepped outside. Dan accepted the envelope from Mr. Cates and pocketed it. He preferred to read the letter in private.

"When do you expect her to return?" he asked Cates.

"I guess that depends on how well Russell does."

"For your sake, I hope he recovers." *And mine, too.*

"Anyway, it's up to her," Cates said. "Girl's got a mind of her own."

Dan gave him a bleak smile. "That she does, sir. That she does."

He bade Sarah's parents goodbye and rode out of sight of the house before he opened the envelope and read. Sarah wished him well, but what Russell suffered at the hands of the Yankees had made up her mind. She no longer could see her way clear to keeping company with a Union officer. Sarah requested that he not try to contact her.

Dan stared at the letter, absorbing the bitter words. The woman he loved still considered him an enemy, despite their intimacy and the understanding between them. If it were possible, he would have tried to reason with her, but Sarah was out of his reach.

*

Sarah held up her hand to help Russell out of the wagon, but he refused assistance. "I can get down by myself, Sis." She stood nearby, ready to catch him if he stumbled. He swung his legs over the side and planted both feet on the ground, holding onto the sideboard with his remaining hand. He smiled in triumph although his face was drawn with the effort. "Told you."

She smiled back at him. "I wasn't trying to baby you." For the past few weeks she had stayed by his side to bring him through infections and weakness. All-night vigils, bathing his face to cool the fevers, cleaning his suppurating stump, and making sure he ate life-sustaining nourishment had left her drained. As the fevers cooled, his stump began to heal, and he showed renewed interest in his surroundings. She believed her persistence had saved his life.

Finally Russell's surgeon deemed him strong enough to make the trip from Gainesville to the boarding house in Orange Springs. There they could stay with Martina while he convalesced. Sarah looked forward to the change of scenery and renewal of friendship with Jack's wife.

Martina met them in the yard and greeted her with a hug.

"Where's mine?" Russell gave Martina a wolfish grin.

"You must be feeling better." Martina looked him over and shook her head, smiling. "It's a good thing, because the young girls in this town will not let you rest."

Russell glanced at the empty sleeve, doubt clouding his face.

"Nobody will care about that." Martina patted his good arm. "As long as it won't keep you from dancing. Come on inside. I'll introduce you to our landlady and show you to your room."

Despite his bravado, the two-day wagon trip had tired Russell. After drinking a glass of lemonade, he settled into his bed for a nap. Sarah unhitched the horse and took care of it; then Martina helped her bring in the few belongings she and Russell had brought.

Sarah sat on the porch with Martina and took a few moments to sip lemonade and chat before unpacking. She rested her head on the chair back and enjoyed the view of splendid pecan, oak and citrus trees leading to the crystalline lake. She reveled in the fall breeze that had banished the suffocating summer heat. Rosa wandered about the shaded yard with the dog while Martina watched her.

"I'm glad a vacancy opened and we were able to bring him here," Sarah said. "It's a pretty place. Peaceful."

"Peaceful," Martina repeated. "Haven't seen a Yankee yet."

Sarah pictured Dan in her mind, an image she could not seem to shake. Even her preoccupation with her brother's welfare had not crowded out her thoughts of the man. Her longing to hear his easy laugh and feel his loving touch left her empty. No matter how hard she tried, she could not fill the hole in her heart.

Rosa picked up a stick and whacked it against a tree trunk. When the stick fell from her hand, Nip picked it up and scampered a few feet away, then turned and faced her. The dog crouched into a play bow, tail wagging.

"She's a beautiful child," Sarah murmured. A little one of hers and Dan's could have turned out just as pretty and smart as Rosa, the fathers being brothers. Fortunately, that was not to be. Her monthly curse had washed away her fears that Dan had gotten her into trouble. An unbidden pang of regret had come with the liberation. *Maybe I ought to get a puppy.*

"Rosa looks like Jack's side of the family." Martina let out a laugh. "She didn't get that tow head from me. I tell Jack she has his temper, too."

Sarah managed a smile. "Temper or not, he's been a good friend to Russell."

"Have you heard from your folks lately?"

"They're doing fine. The Yankees haven't been bothering them."

"Have they seen Dan? Is he all right?"

Sarah nodded. "He came around. Once." She focused on Rosa, who had taken the stick from the hound's willing jaws. She threw it down, the dog picked it up, and the child squealed in delight. Rosa took several unsteady steps toward Nip, who backed off slowly as he played keep-away.

"Jack said he almost shot Dan." Martina said softly. "Did you know that?"

"Russell told me."

"I'm glad they recognized each other in time. For all our sakes."

Sarah did not want to admit just how glad she was. The conversation was tilting into dangerous territory. Time to put a stop to it. She stood and stretched. "I'd better check on Russell and unpack our things."

"Russell is going to be all right. He's out of the fighting for good. And you can always change your mind about Dan if you wish."

"Martina, Teresa tried to play matchmaker. I don't want you doing it, too."

The other woman laughed. "I won't say another word about Dan. I promise."

Sarah gave her a quick hug then retreated. Sarah knew she could not contain her tears if the other woman said anything more.

*

As Russell slowly recovered his strength, Sarah busied herself over the next few months nursing other ill or wounded soldiers who convalesced at Orange Springs. Jack and his friends passed through often, to Martina and Rosa's delight.

Jack and Carlo came for a visit in mid-December. For an early Christmas present Jack gave his daughter a rag doll and brought Martina a supply of coffee, flour and quinine taken from the Yankees. Martina showed pride in his recent promotion to corporal, though Jack shrugged off the honor as of little importance.

Watching Dan's brother with his happy little family always caused a ripple of discontent in Sarah. She longed to return to her parents' home in case Dan happened by, but that path led to danger. She sensed that once she laid eyes on the man, she would not be able to resist, yet resist she must.

When Jack and Carlo went outside to saddle their horses, Martina and Rosa accompanied them to say their goodbyes. To Sarah's alarm, when Russell came down the stairs, she saw he had somehow fastened his gun belt. She followed him outside, where she discovered Carlo had brought out Russell's horse and saddle as well.

The sisterly instinct to thrash Russell and tie him to his bed turned into clenched fists, which she placed on her hips. "Russell, tell me you aren't going with them."

He flashed his grin. "Sis, I'm bored stupid around here. I can see and I can ride well enough to help the boys scout St. Johns County."

Jack looked up from tightening his cinch. "You didn't tell her?"

"Didn't want to worry her." Russell shrugged. "I'll be fine, Sis. Anything you want me to tell Pa and Mama?"

"I don't need to tell them you're being foolish. Haven't you risked your neck enough? There's no reason you need to do this."

Russell turned serious. "You said you like being useful. So do I. I'm sick of sitting around this town. I'm sick of being an invalid."

"Russell...."

Sarah looked at Martina, who shook her head. "I didn't know, either,"

"Do you want to go home with us? I expect we can give you a ride." Russell's voice was tentative, as though he didn't really want her to come.

Jack gave Russell an exasperated look. "You could have given her some notice, time to pack."

"I just this morning made up my own mind." Russell shrugged. "What about it, Sis? You want to get your things and go home?"

Home would bring her closer to Dan, and she could not risk seeing him. "If it's all right with Martina, I'll stay here for a while longer."

"Of course." Martina smiled at her. "You know that. But you can't avoid him forever."

Sarah stifled a sharp comeback and reminded herself Martina was her friend. Helpless to stop Russell, she watched him check his equipment.

As usual upon departure, Jack embraced his wife and daughter. The child raised her chubby arms to her father and chanted "Zazaza." Jack seemed delighted with her effort to say Papa. Next Carlo gave his sister a hug. Martina touched her rosary, and her lips moved as her men climbed onto their horses.

Sarah's throat tightened. She fisted her hands, fighting back tears.

Russell gave the saddle a satisfied thump and turned to Sarah. "You're going to tell me to be careful, and I'll say I will."

She nodded, the tears overflowing, and gave him a lingering hug. Russell said, "Thanks for all you've done for me, Sis. I'm fine now."

Russell mounted his horse with surprising grace. He gathered the reins in his one hand and settled into the saddle. The old confidence seemed to return to him, along with his careless grin. "See you later, Sis. Martina." His wink at Rosa brought a giggle in response.

Sarah stood close to Martina, who balanced Rosa on one hip and wouldn't meet her eyes, as though tears were contagious and she feared a breakdown of her own.

CHAPTER TWENTY-EIGHT

Jack figured the rifle would make a bigger impression than his revolver. He held his Spencer rifle ready as he nudged Choctaw into the swamp water.

A reduction in the number of hungry mosquitoes compensated in part for the December chill. Although fall weather had thinned the rank vegetation, the vines and palmettos were still thick enough to provide cover. Choctaw's hooves sank hock-deep in the shallow brown slough.

Jack nodded to Charlie and Russell as they positioned themselves in the brush along the edges of the causeway. Jack drifted behind a stand of Spanish moss-laden cypress trees, listening to the incautious approach of horses and the creak of buggy wheels. The scouts had spotted a man on horseback accompanying two men in a buggy headed down the Jacksonville road toward St. Augustine.

Sometimes the Yankees weren't careful what they told people. Folks friendly to the scouts happened to mention that the commander of the 17th Connecticut would be making the overland trip to preside at a court marshal in St. Augustine. Lately the Yankees had been cavorting around the county as though they owned it, unchecked and unafraid. Jack figured it was high time to teach them a lesson.

He urged Choctaw into a quick splash through the slough onto the road. He blocked the buggy's path and trained his Spencer on the occupants. At the same time, Charlie rode up behind their quarry and Russell appeared just to the left of the carriage. Russell pointed his revolver at the mounted man, a Yankee captain. As the driver reined in to avoid a collision, Jack hissed, "Surrender! Keep your hands in sight."

"By the way, Merry Christmas," Russell sang out.

Jack had to chuckle as he watched the astonishment on his captives' faces. They glanced at each other and at the weapons pointed at them. Slowly their hands came up. The younger man driving the buggy, a lieutenant, said in a disgusted tone, "Don't shoot. I surrender." Jack turned his attention to the other officer, a pompous-looking fellow with a gray-stippled beard and a how-dare-you expression. Jack judged the man to be about the same age as his father.

"Colonel Noble." Jack grinned. "I guess that court marshal is going to have to convene without you. You'll be spending Christmas Day as our guests. Personally, I'd rather spend the holiday with my wife and daughter than with a Yankee officer, but I guess I'll have to make do."

The enemy officer sat ramrod straight and glared at him. "I refuse to surrender to a corporal. A guerilla, no doubt." Noble whipped his head around at Charlie and Russell, the picture of indignation. "Where is an officer?"

Jack laughed out loud. "Colonel, this rifle pointed at your head gives me all the authority I need. Charlie, let's go through these gentlemen and make damned sure they're disarmed. Then you can take over driving that buggy. By and by we'll find us an officer so our prisoners can finish surrendering."

*

Colonel Noble's capture sent soldiers swarming out of their St. Johns County garrisons like ants from a kicked mound. Prescott and his command set out from Picolata to hunt down the rebel brigands who snatched the senior officer. Returning the missing colonel to the 27th Connecticut would make an excellent Christmas gift for the regiment, and an even better one for Prescott's career. He hardly could contain his delight at the prospect.

He had spent the past six months in Jacksonville rebuilding his shattered company, most of them killed or captured during the rebel attack on the *Columbine*. As Negroes drifted into the Union lines, he continued his recruitment activities and had swelled the ranks of his company to more than fifty men. Still not full strength nor fully trained, they would have to suffice.

Only a few days ago he had transferred with his little command to the river base at Picolata, fortuitously landing him at the right time and place to take advantage of this opportunity. He had a few ideas of his own about how to find the colonel.

Surely local spies had informed the rebels about the anticipated arrival of Colonel Noble and his companions at St. Augustine. Those same spies no doubt would be able to lead him to the men responsible for the hostage taking. All they needed was a little incentive to tell him everything they knew.

The territory east of the river had not proven especially dangerous despite this latest incident. Prescott believed only a few rebel scouts, such as those responsible for nabbing the colonel, roved this side of the river, and they were not present in force.

Although he detested horses, the assignment required speed. Prescott selected ten men, including the recently promoted Sergeant Isaac Farrell, to utilize the available horses. The rebels and the soggy climate had taken a toll on the animals. Just two months ago Dickison's men swallowed whole a company of cavalry near Middleburg, on the other side of the river. That more livestock succumbed to various equine maladies interested Prescott hardly at all.

Just as he set out with his company past the picket posts, a man met him on horseback and waved him down. Prescott recognized the fellow from his previous patrols through the area before Jack Farrell shot him. Dawson claimed Union sympathies, though Prescott suspected the farmer's loyalties shifted with the tide.

"Well, Dawson," Prescott said as he halted his beast. "What do you have to say for yourself?"

The deeply tanned Florida man, probably younger than he appeared from his weather-grooved face, spat onto the ground. "I got information about the boys that bagged your big colonel."

What luck! Prescott tried not to let his eagerness show. "Out with it, man."

Dawson's eyes narrowed. "Where's my reward?"

Of course the greedy fellow wanted money. "I'll see you get something. Only if we catch them."

"Maybe I ought to go into the post and see your colonel instead."

Prescott drew his pistol and pointed it at the man's arm. "You'll tell me. Now. Or your reward will be a painful one."

Dawson stared at the gun and swallowed. "That ain't right, Captain."

"Just tell me, then you can report to whomever you wish."

The farmer rubbed his arm as though he anticipated the bullet piercing his flesh. "Well, then. I know who two of the reb scouts are. Local boys. Not so sure of the third."

Prescott jabbed the pistol at him, impatient.

"Russell Cates and Jack Farrell."

Jack Farrell. Prescott let out his breath. "Where'd they take him?"

"I expect they're long gone by now. They intercepted your colonel up north of here, so they probably took him by boat up Julington Creek to the St. Johns. Across to Black Creek. I hear y'all gave up your garrison at Magnolia after the rebs whipped your critter soldiers at Middleburg."

If the man was correct, the colonel was far away by now, along with that cockroach Jack Farrell. If he was on the west side of the river, he was as good as gone. "They wouldn't have taken him on south to cross at Palatka?"

"Begging your pardon, Captain, I'd sure appreciate it if you'd point that gun somewheres else."

Prescott lowered the pistol, realizing his chances of rescuing the colonel and putting away Farrell were next to nothing. "Couldn't they have gone down the Palatka road?" He realized his voice held a pleading note and cleared his throat. "Are you sure they didn't do that?"

"The rebs don't confide in me. That's just what I'd do if I was them. Not that I'd do nothin' like them boys did." Dawson shook his head vigorously. "No sir, not in a thousand years."

"Who informed the rebs about the colonel's movements? Surely they knew when and where to intercept him."

Dawson shrugged. "Coulda been anybody. Or maybe them boys just had their eyes open."

"What about Henry Cates? Think he did it?"

"He's pretty tight with the rebs, seein' how his boy is one of them. Most likely he tells them whatever he knows."

"Very well, then. You're free to go." Prescott holstered his pistol and let Dawson hurry off toward the picket post. He started his squad forward again, deep in thought. Perhaps he could wring some success out of the new information. Farrell had no one within reach besides his off-limits Unionist father and his brother, the so-called Union officer. Cates held no such immunity.

Prescott led his party to the Cates homestead and surrounded the house with his squad, weapons ready. He shouted, "Cates, come out here!"

After a short interval the door cracked open and out stepped Henry Cates. Prescott turned to Sergeant Farrell, who sat on his horse nearby, "Bring him to me."

After the noncom dismounted and did as directed, Prescott looked down at the silver-haired Secesh, who regarded him, arms folded. The fellow's gaze roved about from one of Prescott's soldiers to another. If Cates was nervous, he had cause. "Where's that rebel son of yours? The one in Dickison's band. Russell."

"Russell lost an arm over at the Gainesville fight. He's disabled."

Prescott snorted. "I've heard that story before. He and Jack Farrell and another rebel scout captured Colonel Noble. We're going to find them."

"Did they now?" Cates' moustache twitched as though he had the gall to be amused. "First I've heard of it."

"Where'd they go?" Prescott drew his revolver and regarded it thoughtfully.

"I haven't seen Russell in days."

"Don't bother sticking to your lies. Beats me how a Secesh like you has been allowed to remain within our lines. You ought to be sitting in prison." Prescott turned to Farrell. "Take a couple of men and go into the house. Bring out anybody else that's hiding in there."

Cates looked over his shoulder at the house, then back at Prescott. "Just my wife. Leave her be."

"You're not the one giving orders here, Cates." Prescott stroked his moustache and smiled. "Where's that good-looking daughter of yours? Sarah, is it?"

"She ain't here."

"Where is she?"

"Safe in Dixie's Land. Go after her if you dare."

"Defiance will get you nowhere," Prescott snapped.

Escorted by the three soldiers Mrs. Cates came out of the house and stood next to her husband. Prescott holstered his pistol and tipped his hat pleasantly. "Good morning, Mrs. Cates. I trust you've had a pleasant Christmas."

"Up until now." The woman gave him a sour look. "What do you want with us?"

Prescott dismounted, tossed the reins to one of the soldiers, and moved into Cates, forcing him to take a step back. "Tell me what you know about the whereabouts of Russell and the colonel the scouts captured."

"Look for Dickison, if you have the nerve. I expect he can tell you."

Prescott slapped Cates, hard. The man reeled with the impact then glared at him.

"I told you not to give me backtalk." Prescott rubbed his stinging hand.

"Stop that, Captain Prescott." Mrs. Cates slipped her hand onto her husband's arm. "Even if we wanted to tell you where our son is, we can't."

Prescott again pulled out his pistol and pointed it at Cates. The threat got results from Dawson, and he expected it would give Cates belief as well. "One more time. I need to find them, and I need to find them now."

Cates continued looking him in the eye. "Is this the sort of tactic your Grand Army of the Union prefers? Bullying civilians?"

"Leave us be." The woman's voice shook with fear. Prescott turned his attention to her. The old girl looked good for her age. He glanced at his sergeant, whose expression did not entirely mask his disapproval. If his men weren't present….

Prescott slashed Cates on the side of the head with the pistol. Cates staggered, then righted himself and lifted his hand to the long, bleeding welt cut by the sight. "It's said our son saved your life, Captain Prescott."

"That's the only reason I haven't burned your house or shot you on the spot, Cates. Instead, I'm arresting you as an enemy informant, suitable for hanging." Prescott turned to Farrell. "Sergeant, pick two men to escort this spy to St. Augustine and turn him in to the provost."

*

This January morning's chill north wind discouraged Sarah from spending more time outside than she needed to feed the few chickens and hogs hidden in pens in the woods. She had rushed home after Carlo relayed news of Papa's imprisonment, believing Mama shouldn't be alone in her distress. So far her mother's efforts to get Papa released had come up empty.

Alerted by the drumbeat of a cantering horse, Sarah looked out the window. "Rider coming. Not ours. A Yankee." She shivered and drew her shawl tighter around her shoulders. Was Prescott returning to plague her mother again? As he rode up to the house she recognized him. Not Prescott. The man who approached brought a different brand of danger. "It's Dan."

"Maybe he has news of Henry." Mama's posture relaxed and she smiled, a relief Sarah did not share. While Mama believed she had less to fear from a family friend among their enemies, Sarah dreaded facing him and risking a rekindling of old feelings she had managed to bury. She was better off without Dan and his complications.

Sarah moved to the edge of the window so she could continue to see out without being seen. Yes, it was Dan, no mistake, and he was alone. Considering the recent turmoil in the county, was he fearless or just arrogant?

Mama had mentioned he had not visited for months after coming to see Sarah and announcing to her father he intended to marry her. Until now. During her stay in Orange Springs Sarah heard that Dickison's men had destroyed a Union cavalry troop near Middleburg. She was terrified for Dan until Jack mentioned the Yankees were part of the 4th Massachusetts, and Dan's company was not involved in the incident.

So far Dan had honored her request not to try to contact her, but here he was. How could he know she had come home? Only her family and the St. Johns County scouts knew, and they sure weren't talking to any Yankees. Sarah clicked her tongue. "Good thing he didn't stop by last night, when Russell and his friends came for supper."

Mama's brow furrowed. "I hope Dan's not here on any sort of official business. That's never good."

"He wasn't in St. Augustine when I went to inquire after Papa. He's been away somewhere. You talk to him, Mama. Please don't tell him I'm here."

Mama gave her a searching look. "If he asks, I won't lie to him."

"I'm not asking you to lie. Just don't tell him, hear?" Sarah hugged herself. "You ought to be glad I don't want to see him. You didn't like me being friends with that Yankee officer anyway, except it kept us a little bit safer."

"He's a good man. Too bad he's one of *them*." Mama threw on her shawl and wrapped it around her shoulders. "I'll be careful what I tell him, and I'll do my best to keep him outside."

Sarah's throat caught as she watched Dan's easy dismount. She pictured his muscular body hidden beneath the greatcoat, a sight she earnestly believed few other women had enjoyed. He tethered his horse to a tree and looked toward the house for a long moment before striding onto the porch.

Sarah pressed herself against the wall, her heart racing as Mama slipped outside, letting in a sluice of freezing air. Mama said, "Dan, what a pleasant surprise," as she closed the door behind her. "Are you alone? Is this a social call?"

"Purely social, but I left some of my men watching the road and around back in case your boys decide to pay us a visit." Sarah closed her eyes as she heard the sound of Dan's warm chuckle. *Please go away.*

"It's cold out. May I come inside?" Dan asked.

"I believe we can talk just as well on the porch, if you don't mind." Mama's voice was firm.

Sarah heard the scrape of a chair as Mama took her seat. She hardly dared breathe, wanting to catch every word he said.

*

"As you wish." Forced to accept that relations had chilled between the Cates family and himself, Dan leaned against the porch support. He didn't want Sarah's mother to see him as pathetic and needy, so he planned to play it cagy, wait and get around to a casual inquiry about her daughter at some later point. "I saw Mr. Cates at the fort. He told me about Prescott's accusations."

"They won't let me into town to see him." Mrs. Cates's voice tightened with indignation and worry. "They stop me at the bridge and won't let me go any farther. What are they going to do with him? I can't find out anything. Is he well?"

"He's all right, and I don't think he's in any immediate danger." At least he could deliver a bit of good news. "I believe they just want to keep him under arrest so he can't assist the enemy. He isn't the only one they've rounded up for informing the rebels. There's talk of sending the civilian prisoners north, but they haven't done anything official about it so far."

"I pray they don't." Some of the anxiety smoothed from her face. "Is there anything you can do?"

"I'll see about getting you a pass so you can visit him."

"Oh, would you?"

"Prescott had no call to handle him so roughly." Dan shook his head. "I wish I had been here to prevent it."

Mrs. Cates's eyes hardened. "He likes to hurt people."

"I'd like to take him down a peg, myself." He took a deep breath before dealing with the hard truth. "We have to be honest about what's going on. You and I both know your husband would do anything to help Russell and the rest of Dickison's men. So would you. It's only natural."

Her hands folded in her lap, and she pursed her lips.

Dan raised a brow. "The Confederate scouts sure seemed to be in the right place at the right time. Got away clean, too. Our people think they knew exactly what they were after."

"Henry and I couldn't have told anybody about Colonel Noble's plans. We can't tell what we don't know."

"Somebody did." Dan quirked a smile. "Of course, if our men are talking too much, they ought to be considered just as liable."

Mrs. Cates cleared her throat. "Would you please take my husband some warm clothes? He left with nothing but what he wore on his back."

"Of course." Dan reached into his pocket and handed her the envelope. "He gave me a letter for you."

Mrs. Cates read the short note, blinking rapidly. Then she wiped her eyes and looked up at Dan, her eyes reddened. "It's good to hear from him." Her voice wavered. "I've been so worried."

"I'll try to keep you informed. About your husband, of course." He smiled at the need to clarify.

She folded the letter and gave him a watery smile. "We've missed you, Dan. In spite of the goings-on with the war and all."

"My orders kept me at Jacksonville for the past few months." No need to mention he stayed there to rebuild his troop after the Gainesville fight. The larger city offered more prospects for recruitment. Besides, with Sarah gone, he had little incentive to make the trip below St. Augustine.

"You're back for a while?"

"I'm sorry, Mrs. Cates. I can't discuss my future assignments." He hesitated. "But I ought to be able to stop by now and then."

Mrs. Cates sighed. "I guess there are a lot of things we can't talk about."

*

Sarah poked a lock of hair behind her ear and shifted on her feet. So far Dan hadn't even bothered to ask about her. Did that mean she mattered nothing to him after all his persuasions, proposals and their lovemaking? How narrowly she had escaped him getting her in a family way. Surely she had fallen in love with the wrong man. If only falling out of love were as easy.

She continued to listen to the two of them make small talk, Mama at her tactful best. It was good policy not to insult a Yankee officer. Any Yankee officer.

Finally she heard him ask, "What do you hear from Sarah?" She held her breath, waiting for Mama's reply.

"She's been keeping herself busy." Sarah exhaled slowly. Mama's non-answer was just fine.

"I was hoping she'd come back home, so I could talk to her. She's been out of reach in Dixie's Land, as our soldiers term it. Maybe I can give you a letter for her." His voice softened so much she had to strain to hear. "I think about her all the time and want to let her know how much I miss her."

"I miss you, too," Sarah whispered.

"I'll see that she gets the letter," Mama said.

"Thank you," Dan said.

"Excuse me while I gather up Henry's things and get paper and a pencil." Mama came inside and handed Sarah the letter on her way to the bedroom.

Torn, Sarah stared down at the unopened envelope. Her heart urged her to go out on the porch and let Dan wrap his arms around her. Her head reminded her one of his men likely shot Russell, and no doubt he would have arrested Papa if given the order.

She slunk to her room, distancing herself from Dan as far as possible. She dared not read the letter until he rode away.

CHAPTER TWENTY-NINE

"Sir, any closer, and the pickets will hear us." Jack rubbed his gritty eyes and turned to Captain Dickison, who had halted with him. Behind them, hooves thudded to a stop and several other horses crowded up close. Ahead in the shadowed darkness, nothing appeared to disturb the deep night quiet.

He and the other scouts had spent the day and most of night guiding Dickison's force around the Union picket posts. The grueling march had followed a tricky all-night river crossing near Palatka, shuttling men and horses a dozen at a time on a single raft. Now they waited about a mile from the Yankee garrison at Picolata, not far from his old home.

The commander peered along the dark road ahead. "Suggestions?"

"Last we heard, about 400 Yanks were there, mostly colored. Boats go back and forth between here and Jacksonville all the time. We ought to get fresh information, though." Jack nodded toward Charlie Colee, who lay over his horse's neck, napping during the halt. "His daddy lives behind the lines, and Charlie slips through all the time. Mr. Colee probably can tell us something."

Dickison nodded. "Very good. Farrell. You go with him."

Jack roused Charlie, and the two of them nudged their horses forward. Jack let Charlie take the lead, even though he was also familiar with the backwoods path that would take them to the Colee homestead undetected.

He waited in front of the house, holding Charlie's horse, while the younger man went inside. Lit candles soon flickered through the windows. After a few minutes, Charlie came outside, his aging parents walking onto the porch with him. Mrs. Colee held a lantern.

Charlie returned and said in a low voice, "Father is coming with us. He wants to talk to Captain Dickison himself."

A few minutes later George Colee had his horse saddled and rode along with them. Jack felt special respect for the older man, who had tutored him after the Catholic academy expelled him for fighting. Missing an eye from an injury sustained during the first Seminole War, George Colee still had plenty of steel in his spine. He managed to remain on his property despite the Yankee occupation even though all four of his sons served in the Confederate Army.

After picking their way back to where the troop rested, Mr. Colee greeted Captain Dickison. "Thank you for coming to give those Yankees a lesson."

"We've been hearing about them stealing livestock and harassing people," Dickison said. "We want to put a stop to it."

"The officers are just as bad as the common soldiers. I've been lucky. Since I live within their picket lines, they figure I can't inform our boys, so they haven't arrested me yet." George Colee chuckled and nodded toward his son. "They don't reckon on Charlie knowing how to slip back and forth under their noses."

"We need to know the strength of the post and the best way to approach it," Dickison said. "If you can help us with any recent information, we'd be greatly obliged, sir."

"They just reinforced the garrison. Doubled the strength. I'd say now eight hundred men are housed in the old hotel and in tents. Besides that, they brought in several pieces of artillery."

Dickison rubbed his chin, obviously figuring odds.

Colee continued, "I'm thinking if you attack that stronghold you're liable to get my boy killed."

"This is not a suicide mission," Dickison said.

"Sir, if the garrison is too strong, we can still capture a picket station down the road," Jack added. "I kind of coveted those fine horses of theirs."

"I heard something else today." Colee pointed east toward St. Augustine. "Every Friday night there's a dance at the Solana house. Charlie and his friends know where it is. I heard there's a big affair tonight, with a regimental string band, so officers will surely attend. They'll be spending the night, seeing as how the party is a long way from their posts and they won't want to ride home in the dark. Maybe you can join the festivities."

Dickison smiled. "Any of you boys want to go to a dance?"

"Those folks are Yankee sympathizers, sir." Charlie's voice had lightened with anticipation. "So are the girls who don't mind entertaining them."

Russell snickered. “I think I’ll capture one of those gals while I’m at it. See if she’d rather entertain me.”

*

Only the urgency of nature’s call forced Prescott out of the warm house and into the chilly predawn air. He stumbled through the dew-wet weeds to where a stand of trees and underbrush offered privacy. There he unbuttoned his trousers and sighed with relief as he emptied his bladder.

He shut his eyes against the pain of his headache. His brain still swam in an alcoholic fog, and his mouth tasted like a ditch. The dance had lasted well into the small hours, but to his disappointment most of the other officers had staked out the few pretty girls before he arrived. The only woman who seemed interested in him beyond a do-si-do was a fat, snuff-dipping wench with brown teeth. He was not that hard up for female companionship. His standards remained higher, even if sometimes he had to pay for his satisfaction.

Hearing the tread of hooves on sand, Prescott did not look up right away. The military string band already had stowed their instruments onto the ambulance and had started toward their quarters in St. Augustine. Other soldiers, most of whom had spent the entire night kicking up their heels, reluctantly straggled out to their horses or carriages.

Finally Prescott’s wine-fuzzed brain registered the riders were coming from the wrong direction. He buttoned his pants back together and parted the brush for a better view. Two columns of horsemen approached at a walk. Breath from the wiry men and the skinny animals rose like steam in the still air. Even in the dim light, he realized the soldiers did not have the look of a Union troop. Although their greatcoats covered their uniforms, their keen expressions, stalking attitude, and drawn weapons made the hair on the back of his neck rise.

He stared at one of the riders at the head of the column. Recognition hit him like a blow to the stomach. Jack Farrell. Prescott was glad he had already relieved himself. He slid his hand down his hip for his sidearm, then thought better of drawing their attention by shooting at them.

Don’t panic. He crept deeper into the brush, clenching his teeth so they wouldn’t chatter. It seemed to take forever for the rebels to stream down the road and surround the house. He cowered down as far as he could, terrified Jack Farrell would find him.

Shouts, orders to surrender and galloping hooves assailed Prescott’s ears. His breath came in gulps as he listened to the rebels round up the partygoers. Lucky for him nature had called when it did, and he was not among the prisoners, or worse, under that double-damned rebel Jack Farrell's control. If only his luck continued to hold.

*

Along with a half dozen other troopers, Jack split from the main force and overtook the four-horse ambulance, weapons drawn. "Surrender!" Sergeant Ward demanded. The driver halted the vehicle and lifted his hands.

"Give us that carriage. We want to take a ride," Russell hooted.

"Don't shoot, boys. All we got is musicians." The teamster appeared unarmed, but Jack concerned himself with who and what was hidden under the canvas wagon-top.

"Everybody out!" Jack ordered. "Now!"

A young soldier stuck his head out from the canvas. Seeing Jack's revolver, he retreated back beneath the cover. Shuffling and bumping, one by one the scared occupants crawled into view and jumped down from the ambulance. Russell looked into the wagon. "No guns, just fiddles and bows."

Charlie Colee laughed. "Our turn to have a party. Musicians, instruments, everything but the young ladies and the punch."

"The ladies and the refreshments are back at the house," Russell reminded him. "Unless the Yanks already drank everything."

Who else was at the house? Jack knew a couple of Yankee officers he would especially like to put out of business.

*

Prescott burrowed deeper into the leaves and wished himself invisible as he listened to the rebels secure their bloodless victory. Neither side had fired a single shot.

Again riders approached his hiding place. Prescott could not see them, but the squeak of leather and the thump of hooves gave him warning. They halted a few feet from him. He hardly dared breathe lest they see or hear his exhalations.

"Guess he got away." Prescott recognized Jack Farrell's voice, the accents of a semi-illiterate Florida Cracker.

"Seems he couldn't have gone far, unless he got wind and snatched a horse before we got here," the other rebel said.

"Must have. Damn. We just missed catching that bastard."

"He had no call to arrest my father. He's still rotting in the old fort."

Cates. It must be Cates.

"Bastard," Farrell repeated. "Too bad we weren't there to put a stop to that."

Prescott calculated whether he could drag out his pistol and shoot both of them before they realized where he was. He started to inch his hand toward the grip of his revolver. Could he kill them and still escape from the rest of the rebels?

The house was no more than a hundred feet away and crawling with graybacks. He would not last two minutes after he shot Farrell and Cates. Squashing two lice was not worth losing his life. His hand stilled.

"Sure was an easy capture." Farrell snorted a laugh. "The Yanks hear Dickison's around, and they're in such a hurry to surrender they wet all over themselves."

Cates snickered. "They said your brother wasn't here. Don't he like to dance?"

"Let's finish the circuit and get back to the house," Farrell growled.

Prescott let out his breath when he heard the horses' retreating hoof-beats.

*

After Jack conferred with Captain Dickison, he sought out Carlo, whom he found chatting with a pretty Minorcan girl on the porch. Jack nodded to the young lady, who gave him a demure smile. She seemed not at all intimidated by the arrest of her former dance partners.

Jack took Carlo aside and said in a low voice, "The captain got wind of a Yankee plunder party headed south. He's going to split the command and go after them with the bulk of the force. He's having Lieutenant McCardell take charge of the prisoners. We'll hang back, cut the telegraph wires and watch the road for a while. Then we'll catch up with Lieutenant McCardell's detachment and help them get the Yanks across the river."

Carlo cut his eyes back toward the girl.

"You fancy that young lady?"

Carlo's face reddened. "I was just passing the time, and she was real nice. She gave me some cake."

Jack decided not to embarrass Carlo further by pointing out he should not trust a girl who socialized with the enemy. Yet, he trusted

Sarah, although he suspected her involvement with his Yankee brother used to run deeper than she would admit. "Did you know Prescott was at the party?"

His brother-in-law's eyes narrowed. "Did we capture him? Where is he?"

"Russell and I hunted around for him, but he got away."

"Too bad." Carlo shook his head, his mouth a grim line. "After what he did to Martina and me."

"Maybe next time he'll stand and fight so we'll have our chance to even the score." Jack nodded toward the house. "Tell your lady friend goodbye, and let's get moving."

*

Prescott huddled in his hiding place for what seemed like a lifetime before muffled commands, the drum of many hooves and the creak of wagon wheels signaled an end to his siege. Finally the only sounds were the hooting of an owl and a rooster crowing in the distance. He nerved himself to unfold his body and peer through the vegetation that had saved his hide. No one moved on the road, not a soldier of either persuasion.

Feeling bolder, he crept closer to the open yard and looked toward the house. He took a deep breath and congratulated himself on his narrow escape.

No doubt the rebels had taken all the horses along with the buggy he had ridden on from Picolata. A furtive look around confirmed his assumption, unless both he and the enemy had overlooked something. He considered looking inside the house to see if anyone remained there. No one the rebels might have left unmolested in the house was of the least interest to him. However, they might know something useful.

Prescott made a cautious circle around the house. The front door opened when he approached, and two women stepped onto the porch. The prettier one ducked back inside, but the fat, brown-toothed woman squealed his name, ran to him and gave him a hug. "You're safe!" she cried. He endured her embrace with as much grace as he could muster. After a moment he pried her away and stepped back from the miasma of stale odors that clung to her clothes.

"They didn't catch you," she gushed. "Oh, Dick, I'm so glad you were clever enough to escape. Wasn't that horrible?"

"Indeed." He forced a grim smile to acknowledge her happiness. "Those were Dickison's men."

She nodded furiously. "I know a few of those fellows, too. They're from around here. That Jack Farrell. The Cates boy. Did you see he's missing a hand? Charlie Colee's folks live at Picolata. I didn't know the rest of 'em, though. They must not be St. Johns County boys."

"Those men and their families need to pay for this outrage." Prescott considered ways he might accomplish that end. "Did they really get all the men? That is, all the men but me? Am I the only one left?"

"Sure did. They even took old Mr. Solana with them. Said he was a Yankee same as the rest."

"I need to go to headquarters with all possible speed and report what happened. Do you have any horses the rebels didn't take?"

Brown-tooth shrugged. "Best you look around. I'll ask the Solana girls if they have any hid away."

"Yes. Do that. Or I'll have to walk." Prescott dreaded the long trudge, especially with his worst enemies on the hunt for him.

*

"Wait up!" The call came from somewhere behind Dan's column.

Dan lifted his hand to stop his men and turned in the saddle to see what was amiss. He spotted an aide jogging up the street from headquarters, his breath blowing white in the cold morning air.

The corporal puffed up to him and saluted. "I apologize for stopping you, sir, but Colonel Osborn requests you investigate a certain matter."

"I'd be honored to do whatever he asks. What does he want?"

"The regimental string band hasn't returned from that dance at the Solana house. The one on the Picolata road? They're overdue, along with Lieutenant Carney and a number of men from his company. The colonel wants you to go up that way and find out if anything is wrong."

Dan smiled. "They probably had too much fun, and they're sleeping it off."

The aide chuckled. "Let's hope so, sir."

"Tell Colonel Osborn we'll roust them out."

"Thank you, sir." The aide stepped away from the horsemen to let them pass.

Dan again headed his troop toward the San Sebastian bridge. The men had enjoyed a short rest in town, but it was time to relieve the Massachusetts troops manning their old duty post down King's Road. He calculated a small detour would add several hours to the trip, depending upon what he found.

*

Jack positioned himself at the edge of the woods across the road from Carlo. The Yankees had felled every tree and shrub within a couple of miles of St. Augustine. "They don't want us sneaking up on them," he told Carlo. "But they can't sneak up on us, either."

With Carlo's help, he had finished cutting the telegraph wires in several locations along the road. The enemy would restore the lines as soon as they discovered the breaks, but for the time being couriers would have to carry communication between St. Augustine and Picolata. Couriers he and his comrades could intercept at will.

Jack saw movement. Riders. He forced his burning, sleep-deprived eyes to focus. "Here they come," he told Carlo. "If it's just a few, we'll bag them and add them to Lieutenant McCardell's collection."

His brother-in-law stood up in the stirrups. "More than a few."

"Yeah." Jack squinted at the riders. "I'd say twenty or so. That what you think?"

Carlo nodded, dragged out his revolver, and held it with the muzzle pointing skyward.

"You don't need that." Jack waved his hand at Carlo's drawn weapon. "I don't intend to let them get within range."

Carlo shrugged but did not put away his weapon. *If having it handy makes him feel better, fine.*

"They don't seem to be in a big rush. Probably a routine patrol," Jack mused. "We'll just watch those boys for a while and see what they're up to. See if we need to warn Lieutenant McCardell."

*

Prescott interrupted his hike and slipped back into hiding. His headache had worsened, if anything, and his fine new boots, designed more for style than for walking, had turned his feet into a mass of blisters. He had hoped to encounter friendly soldiers who could offer him a ride instead of this menace. The underbrush here was sparse, but he dared not seek out a better spot. Moving would invite detection. He drew his sidearm and checked the caps. All appeared to be in order, so he was equipped to defend himself.

Fortunately, the two mounted men had not spotted him. Their attention seemed to be directed elsewhere. He knew they were rebels. Dangling telegraph lines and fresh hoof prints leading along the route to St. Augustine had warned him not all the enemy had left with their prizes.

Through his paltry screen of vegetation he watched the horsemen ride a little closer, turn and face the other way. They repeated the action. Their behavior puzzled him at first, then he speculated they were falling back before the approach of Union troops.

As the rebels neared, recognition chilled Prescott deeper than the cold morning air. For the second time that morning Jack Farrell came along like a plague to threaten his existence. If the two men spotted him, surrender was out of the question. He harbored no doubt Farrell would want to finish what he started and shoot him on sight. Prescott consoled himself with the assurance his loaded Colt offered a degree of protection.

The rebel scouts worked their way ever closer. Prescott shifted his attention to the second man, who looked vaguely familiar. Two years had passed since Prescott held Martina Sanchez's brother Carlo under his power. The deeply tanned young tough very well could be the same boy.

Farrell's distraction was an unexpected gift. Prescott began to believe he could strike first and eliminate his worst enemy. This time, no force of vengeful rebels was at hand. Singlehandedly killing two enemy scouts would do much to enhance his reputation. Many a political career was built on a lesser exploit.

Wouldn't it be delicious to turn the rebels' ambush tactics back on them? Slowly, stealthily, he raised his revolver and thumbed back the hammer. The metallic snick crackled in his ears. Farrell and Sanchez, still out of earshot, did not react.

Prescott waited until the scouts rode so close he could not miss. He aimed the revolver at Farrell's chest and pulled the trigger. The shot rang out and the revolver bucked in his hands. He quickly got off a second shot. Through the muzzle smoke he saw Farrell jerk in the saddle. *Got him.*

He shifted his aim to Sanchez.

CHAPTER THIRTY

At the sound of the gun's report, Carlo caught sight of the muzzle flash and heard the thwack of a bullet hitting its mark. At the blast of the second shot, his startled horse sidestepped. A third rang out and a bullet zipped past his head. He pulled hard on the reins with one hand and brought down his gun in a hasty aim toward the revealing muzzle smoke. He fired, then fired again.

The attacker hiding in the roadside thicket shrieked and fell forward out of the roadside bushes. He rolled onto his back, clutching his pistol, still dangerous. Carlo pulled the trigger one more time. The bluecoat grunted and twitched, then quieted. When Carlo recognized his old tormentor Prescott, he controlled the temptation to keep shooting until he emptied his revolver.

Then he glanced at his brother-in-law. *Jack!* Forgetting about the enemy crumpled at their feet, Carlo shoved his gun into his holster.

Jack slumped in the saddle, his lips compressed to a thin line. A red stain spread between his fingers, pressed to his side. Another bloody patch bloomed on his shoulder.

Carlo nudged his horse next to Jack's and fumbled for Choctaw's reins. "Those Feds heard the shots for sure. We need to get out of here." He dug his heels into his horse's flanks, determined to lead Jack out of danger.

*

Dan knelt beside Prescott, who blinked up at him, eyes glazed and terror-filled. Apparently the Union captain was the loser of the gunfight Dan had heard. "He's still alive." Dan glanced up at the man who held his horse. "Coker, hand off my horse. Go back to town on the gallop and bring an ambulance and a surgeon."

"Farrell," Prescott rasped through bloody teeth.

"What happened here?" Dan unbuttoned Prescott's gore-soaked coat. One bullet had entered his chest, the other his belly. Either wound could be fatal. "Rebel scouts? How many?"

"Two." Prescott's eyes focused. He seemed to gather his wits and dispel his confusion. "Your brother, the bastard."

"Jack?" Questions filled Dan's mind, but he feared Prescott was in no shape to answer them.

"I shot him. I got him first." Prescott's bitter laugh turned into gagging. His eyes rolled upward.

Was this the moment Dan had dreaded most? "Where'd he go?" Prescott's breaths came in rales. Blood bubbled from his nose and mouth. He convulsed and grimaced as though fighting the inevitable.

Dan turned away, knowing he could do nothing for the other officer. Running through possibilities in his mind, he walked along the road, seeking tracks and other clues, hoping he would not find his brother in the same dire condition as Prescott.

Although yesterday's traffic had cut wagon and horse tracks in the dirt, his men had not ridden over this part of the road yet. The fresh prints of shod horses went in each direction atop the older impressions. Not many horses. Maybe two, just as Prescott implied. Down the road, he noticed a telegraph wire hanging loose. The rebel scouts had done more than shoot Prescott.

"Sergeant Tatum, take ten men and see what happened at the Solana house. I suspect our men didn't just oversleep. Feel your way along and don't get yourselves ambushed. After you find out, send a man back to St. Augustine to report, and take the rest of the squad to relieve the picket post per our original orders."

After the sergeant picked his men and rode away, Dan turned to the others. "The rest of y'all follow me. We're going after those scouts. I believe we can track them."

Dan knelt beside the dying man, who had quit moving and didn't seem to be breathing. Dan felt the floppy wrist for a pulse and found none. The surgeon could deal with Prescott's body.

*

When he looked back and saw Jack wobble in the saddle, Carlo slowed alongside to grip his brother-in-law's arm. His leg bumped against Jack's as they rode in lockstep. Choctaw's easy canter did not miss a beat, as though the horse was doing his best to help his injured partner remain seated.

"Don't fall off," Carlo begged. "God help us, don't fall."

Looking straight ahead, Jack held a handful of mane with one hand while he pressed the bullet hole in his side with the other. "Did you kill him?" he asked through clenched teeth.

"I hit him twice but didn't waste time checking."

"You did right. Saved us both."

Carlo glanced behind, fearful of pursuit. The Yankees without doubt heard the gunfire, found Prescott, and were coming after them. Jack's wounds frightened Carlo even worse than the threat of capture. His sister's husband had stepped into the place left vacant by the deaths of his own father and brother. He was terrified he would lose Jack, too.

They must find help. Lieutenant McCardell's detail guarding the prisoners, complete with an ambulance, had several hours' head start on them, but Carlo feared Jack would bleed to death before they reached the detachment.

"I'm taking you to the Cates place," Carlo told him. "It isn't far."

"Better leave me there," Jack whispered.

Carlo hated the idea of abandoning him, although Sarah and her mother offered the best help within reach.

*

Sarah and Carlo helped Jack off his horse. Between them, they half-carried the wounded man into the house. "The couch." Sarah indicated the settee across the room with her chin.

"I'll bleed all over it," Jack mumbled.

"Let us worry about that." Sarah's mother spread a towel over the fabric under Jack as she and Carlo eased him down on his back. Jack's eyes fluttered shut, but his face remained tense, his lips tight over clenched teeth. "Rest easy, Jack," she said softly. "Think about Martina and Rosa. We'll patch you up."

"I'll get some water and tear up a sheet. I think we have a little whiskey." Mama hurried away, on a mission.

"Get the scissors, too." Sarah bent over Jack and unbuttoned his jacket while she listened to Carlo tell her how Prescott ambushed them. She fought down her fear as he mentioned his suspicion a Yankee patrol would come after them.

"You'd better go, then. You've done all you can." Sarah peeled the blood-soaked wool cloth away from the holes in Jack's torso. Mama set down a bucket and gave her the scissors and another towel. Sarah cut away Jack's cotton shirt and cleaned clotted blood away from the wounds, fearing what she would find.

She glanced up at Carlo, who stared at his brother-in-law, his expression bleak. "Don't you think you'd better skedaddle? Do you want the Yankees to get you, too?"

Carlo wiped his sleeve across his eyes but seemed rooted to the spot. Sarah knew the teenager idolized his brother-in-law, and she understood his grief. She felt almost as sorry for him as she did for Jack.

Sarah wiped away the gore from the bullet hole in Jack's shoulder and picked out bits of cloth the bullet had carried into his flesh. She realized the wound was not as serious as it looked except for the bleeding. Jack's ribs had diverted the slug, which tunneled under his collarbone and came out at the top of his shoulder without entering his chest, thank goodness. She was not so sure about the wound in his side, which had stitched him through and out his back. Whether it had hit anything vital, she did not know, but she knew she had to stop the bleeding. She pressed the cloth to the worst bleeder, the exit wound at his shoulder.

"I lived through worse," Jack murmured.

Mama slipped a hand behind Jack's head to lift it so he could drink from a cup. "He'll need lots of water." Sarah counted her experience with wounded men at Waldo and Orange Springs as useful. "The bleeding will dry him out."

"I put some whiskey in it," Mama said.

Jack shifted his gaze to Carlo. "You still here? Leave. That's an order, Private Sanchez." Jack spoke with obvious effort. "Find Lieutenant McCardell. Tell him what's up and watch your rear. Git."

Carlo nodded but did not move. "I'll tell Martina." His face worked.

"Tell her..." Jack's voice faltered. "Tell her not to worry. Take Choctaw so the Yankees won't get him." He lifted his hand. "Now git."

Sarah heard the receding hoof beats as the young soldier left. A few minutes later, the thump of many hooves and the clank of weaponry announced the arrival of more soldiers. She exchanged a glance with her mother. "Press on his wounds while I see who's here."

Jack said, "If it's Yanks, don't make trouble for yourselves. Give me up."

Sarah bit her lip and nodded. She didn't see how they had a choice.

*

Dan halted his squad in the Cates yard, where instinct had guided him more surely than the obscure tracks. If Jack were seriously hurt, as Prescott implied, he might have sought help from Sarah's mother. "I'm going to inquire at this house," he told his men. He handed his reins to the closest trooper. "Wait here and watch for any sign of the rebels."

"You want some of us to go with you to back you up, Captain?" the soldier asked.

Dan shook his head. "I know these people." That seemed an understatement. He looked over the house, overcome by an overwhelming sadness. Six months' separation from Sarah had not diminished his sense of deprivation. *Did she ever receive my letter? Does she think of me? She told me she loved me. Did her feelings for me die?* If only she were home so he could talk sense into her and somehow win back her affection. If only.

He had done what he could for Sarah's father and mother, arranging for a pass for Mrs. Cates to visit her husband at the old fort. The lady seemed grateful for the favor, but she would not say when Sarah would come home.

He dismounted and walked up the steps to the porch. There he noticed a suspicious red smear on the wall next to the door. Dan sidled next to the window and peered inside. The curtains hid only part of his view of the couch, where a male figure, stripped to the waist, lay on his side. Dan could not see his face but assumed he was one of the rebel scouts he had been tracking. Could be Jack. Mrs. Cates sat in a chair next to him, her hands on his upper body, apparently ministering aid. Although she probably heard his boot steps on the wooden porch, she appeared too busy to look his way.

Dan was unsure of the situation: whether the man, though wounded, would offer to fight, or whether other rebels waited inside, prepared to subdue him. He drew his revolver in case he needed it, stepped to the door and put his hand on the knob.

The door opened, and he found a resolute Sarah blocking his path. He sucked in a surprised breath. His shock of pleasure at the sight of her evaporated when he saw her face, her expression as fierce as a mother bear's.

She nodded to his weapon. "Put the gun away, Dan. I won't let you harm Jack."

"I wasn't going to – good Lord, Sarah." He holstered his weapon and tried to look past her at his brother.

Sarah's posture relaxed a trifle. "Carlo said Prescott shot him."

"How bad?"

"He's shot twice. We're trying to stop the bleeding."

"Where's Carlo?"

"Long gone." She crossed her arms over her chest in defiance. "You'll never catch him."

Most likely she was right. Sending his men on a futile chase after one man, now unencumbered by a wounded companion, would be a waste of effort. He would have to settle for capturing Jack, whose opposition had been a thorn in his side for the past two years.

"Let me by, Sarah. You know I have to accept his surrender."

"Is that how you think of it? He's your brother, and he's hurt bad. Real bad."

"Sarah." He reached for her arm to move her aside. "He needs medical attention, and I'll get that for him."

She looked down at his hand and back to his face. "I know you don't want him to die." Her voice broke as she stepped back to let him pass.

Dan cleared the few steps to the couch, aware of Sarah following at his elbow. He looked down at his brother. Jack, fully conscious, regarded him without fear, though pain hollowed his eyes and tension marked his ashen face.

Mrs. Cates looked up. "Hey, Dan," she said in a preoccupied manner while she continued to press bloody pieces of towel onto Jack's shoulder and back. A heap of reddened clothes lay on the floor. Dan spotted Jack's holstered revolver with its belt on a nearby table and picked it up.

"Well, Dan." Resignation was heavy in Jack's voice. "You finally got me fair."

"Fair and square," Dan murmured.

"Better you than any other damned Yankee."

"Prescott's dead," Dan said. "In case that makes you feel any better."

"Our women are safer with him gone."

"He shot you twice?"

"Yeah. I guess he got me double for old times' sake."

"I need to get you to a doctor in St. Augustine."

"Doctor, bah." Jack glanced from Sarah to her mother. "I like my nurses better."

Same old Jack. Dan smiled. His brother's vital spirit and general cussedness might be enough to pull him through. "Remember, you're a married man." He looked over his shoulder at Sarah. Her expression had softened, but when her eyes met his, her guarded look reasserted itself.

Dan returned his gaze to Jack, considering options. He could send for another ambulance and a surgeon as he did for Prescott. The back-and-forth would take hours, even if they were willing to rush for the sake of a wounded Confederate corporal. Jack needed more medical resources than either he or the well-intentioned women could offer.

He was overdue relieving the Massachusetts soldiers at the outpost. To hell with that. They could wait. He would have his squad report to the picket post, while he personally transported Jack to St. Augustine. He couldn't trust anyone else with the job. His order to investigate the missing partygoers gave him a certain amount of latitude. Nonetheless, he would take a setback in his career to give his brother a fighting chance. "I need to use your wagon," he told Mrs. Cates.

"For Jack?" Sarah's mother looked doubtful. "Are you sure you ought to move him?"

"Still bleeding bad?" Dan asked. "Show me."

She lifted the compresses from Jack's shoulder and side. Dan leaned over to examine the wounds. The blood did not flow freely, a good sign. "How many Confederates besides you and Carlo are in the area?" he asked Jack.

Jack eyes flicked away as though he were calculating, then back to meet Dan's. "Nobody'll bother you."

Dan sensed that although Jack wouldn't reveal much, he was not lying. "Tell you what, Mrs. Cates. Keep it up while I tell my men what's going on."

Behind him, Sarah said, "I'm going, too. He needs somebody to take care of him along the way."

Dan turned to face her, touched by her determination to fight for a friend. "Good for you. I can get you a pass to enter town with me." He wanted to tell her how much he desired her company for his own sake but did not push his luck.

*

Sarah watched Dan walk out the door. "Thank God it was him and not some other Yankee officer," she told her mother. Despite the defensive attitude she had taken with Dan, she knew he would not harm them or allow any meanness from his men. She had recognized his concern for his brother's life and shared the worry. In trying to save Jack, they were on the same side and had to work together.

His presence affected her just as she knew it would, and spending more time with him would further sap her will. He could be so persuasive. She recalled the heartfelt letter he had written to her and how much it had stirred her affections, no matter how hard she tried to suppress them. Maybe she wanted to be persuaded. She picked up the sheet Mama had brought out and started a cut with the scissors, ripped off a strip, and made more strips. With those strips she and her mother dressed Jack's wounds.

When they finished, Sarah looked out the window. Dan's men had brought around the wagon, had found the tack, and were hitching up one of the cavalry horses. "Dan isn't taking Papa's horse. That's good. They'd most likely keep it. Just like Stripe."

"Dan didn't take Stripe, Prescott did," Mama reminded her.

"Details," Sarah breezed. "Dan kept him, anyway." She gathered a blanket, a pillow, a towel, and a supply of drinking water for the trip. Wounded men were always thirsty, and it was important to keep Jack warm and control his bleeding.

Not trustful of Dan's troops, she made sure he was close at hand before she took the supplies outside and set them into the wagon. "I'll get a couple of pillows to cushion his ride," she told Dan.

"Jack will appreciate your kindness." Dan caressed her with a long look and grinned. "I sure would. It'd almost be worth it to get myself shot."

She shuddered. "Don't say that. I don't want you hurt, either."

"I know." His smile disappeared. He looked away, then back at her. "Would you fight as hard for me?"

"Jack is my friend, but I love you." The words just slipped out. "Oh." She clapped her hand over her mouth. It was too late to take back the admission.

Aha." Dan regarded her with a triumphant smile. "My feelings for you haven't changed, either, even if you did rip out my heart."

"I need to get those pillows." She turned to flee back into the house.

"Sarah." Dan caught her arm, stopping her in mid-flight. "Quit running away. Promise me, once we get Jack situated, you'll hear me out."

She looked down at his restraining hand, swallowed hard and nodded.

"Good girl. Now, let's take my brother to the hospital."

CHAPTER THIRTY-ONE

Dan stayed in the hospital room while the surgeon examined Jack. He had refused to leave until he was satisfied his brother received medical attention. The doctor, though businesslike, was not unkind. After he re-dressed the wounds, he said to his patient, "Looks like the bullets didn't nick your vitals. You are one lucky rebel."

"Thanks, Doc." Jack's eyes slid shut. Dan supposed the stiff dose of brandy the doctor administered had taken effect. Despite his pallor and clenched teeth during the bumpy wagon ride, Jack had not complained.

Sarah's presence surely helped Jack endure the trip. It warmed Dan's heart to see how fiercely she fought for his brother. He had to leave her in the lobby while the doctor worked on Jack. He longed to be with her and had to curb his impatience.

The surgeon packed up his kit and turned to Dan. "Why all the fuss? Who is this prisoner? An officer?"

"He's my brother," Dan said. "In my haste I failed to mention it."

The surgeon's eyebrows shot up, and he looked from Jack back to Dan and nodded. "I see. You command that Florida cavalry company, don't you, Captain? This is a sad war." He clicked his tongue. "Did he have anything to do with the rebels snatching the string band and some of our officers at the Solana house? That sure caused an uproar."

"He probably did. Didn't you, Jack?"

Dan noticed his brother's lips curve into a faint smile, but his eyes remained closed. "Without firing a shot." Though weak, his voice conveyed pride.

Dan figured Jack had earned the bragging rights. "On the way into town we met a squad galloping in pursuit. I doubt they'll be able to catch the rebels and their captures. Dickison's men are pretty slippery. I have to give them their due."

"Never been whipped yet." Jack's voice strengthened, and his eyelids flicked open.

Dan recalled his disastrous encounters with Dickison's troop and could not disagree. "My duties won't allow me to stay in town, but I've sent for Pop."

Jack rolled his eyes. "Damn. Getting shot and captured is bad enough."

"Pop needs a hobby." Dan grinned. "He'll want to keep you around so he has somebody to complain about."

The surgeon took his leave and walked by the shotgun-toting provost guard, who stood at the door as though Jack were capable of making trouble.

"I need to take Sarah home and report to my post," Dan said. "You need to rest, so I'll leave you be. Can I do anything else for you before I go?"

"I think y'all have done everything you can." Jack gave him a tired smile. "She's some lady, isn't she? Don't let her get away from you."

"If I have to carry her off kicking and screaming."

Dan acknowledged the guard's salute as he passed and strode to the lobby where Sarah waited. Her bloodstained skirt and her hair falling from its restraints in untidy golden strands marked her labors on his brother's behalf. He found her all the more desirable for it. She rose to meet him. "How is he?"

"The surgeon said he has a fighting chance, and we both know he's a fighter. He also mentioned you and your mother did the right things for him." Dan offered her his arm and he gave her a hand up onto the wagon. After climbing onto the bench next to her, he picked up the lines.

"I'd like to see my father." Sarah looked off in the direction of the fort, then back at Dan. "Is that possible?"

Already long overdue at his post, he weighed the possibility of Colonel Osborn demanding his head on a platter, against the chance to please Sarah and enjoy more time with her. No contest. "It'll have to be a short visit, but I'll see if I can arrange it."

She turned and looked at the quilt and pillow she had brought along to ease Jack's ride to town and keep him warm. "I'd like to give my father that quilt, but it's all bloody."

"He has plenty of blankets. I made sure he's comfortable."

"I should have known," she murmured. "You have a way of fixing things."

"I do my best for my family. After all, he's going to be my father-in-law."

She glared at him, then broke out in a laugh. She punched him on the arm. "You're mighty sure of yourself, Dan Farrell."

He grinned, gave the reins a flick, and headed for the fort.

*

The short visit with her father at the fort assured Sarah he was all right for the time being and left her hopeful that he would be allowed to come home soon. She conceded the Yankee hospital was the best place for Jack at present, especially after Dan convinced her even prisoners of war received decent treatment. Sarah knew what it was like to lose the man she loved, and she prayed Martina's man would not die.

On the way to town, their common cause of saving Jack's life had left little room for the other issues between them, but she drew confidence from Dan's calm leadership. In a way she was relieved her admission came out in the open. No matter how hard she tried to deny it, she still loved Dan.

Jack had surrendered to him because he had no choice; she, on the other hand, could choose to surrender or continue to run away, as Dan had accused.

She sat close to him on the bench, not quite touching, though she would not object if he rested his hand on hers. The wagon rolled across the bridge and past the picket post into the open field surrounding the town. "What will they do with Jack? Will they throw him into that dungeon like they did to my father? Or ship him north to prison?"

"They won't move him until he's fit to travel. I'll try to get him paroled and keep him inside our lines. Maybe there's a way for him to convalesce with Pop. Of course, then I have to hope they don't murder each other." He blew out a long breath. "The Confederacy can't hold out much longer. Their armies are losing on every front up north. The war will be over soon, then we can get on with our lives."

"I want it to be over now," she admitted.

He cut his eyes sidewise at her. "Did you read my letter?"

"It was.... eloquent." She tucked a wisp of hair behind her ear. "I didn't want to cause you distress." *I've had enough distress for both of us.*

"Are you angry with me?"

She shook her head. "Loving you has always felt like a betrayal of my family."

"If you were angry, it would be easier to fix."

"Jack told me not to blame you for Russell getting shot, but you were there, giving the orders." Sarah recalled what the Union soldiers in Dan's troop were like. All Florida men like Dan. Like Jack, Russell and Carlo, wearing different uniforms, holding different views. "I thought I could get over you."

"Like a case of the sniffles?"

"Worse," she huffed. "More like consumption."

He slipped his arm around her back. She yielded to the slight pressure, nestling against him. How she had missed Dan, his strength, his solidity, and his easygoing nature. Working with him to save Jack had underscored his compassion and generosity. Maybe she could find it in her heart to forgive his overriding fault, the color of his uniform. Her family would just have to accept it. Or not.

"Marry me, Sarah," he murmured into her ear.

She shivered, tickled by his warm breath, and turned her face to him. "Convince me."

He grinned as though he never had any doubt. "My pleasure."

She found his kisses most persuasive.

*

Jack figured he ought to be flattered by the presence of a shotgun-toting guard at the door. Apparently the Yanks considered him a prize capture. It was not often they caught one of Dickison's men. Except for the implied threat of the guard's vigilance, captivity made little difference to Jack, because weakness chained him to his cot as surely as manacles.

The hefty dose of medicinal spirits dulled the worst of the pain and allowed Jack to doze. Weighted by weariness, he welcomed the drifting sense of peace until voices at the edge of his awareness intruded. The mention of his name aroused him. He heard Pop's voice telling the guard he had permission to see the prisoner. Jack focused on his father's face looming over him. Did he come to gloat?

"Hey, Pop." Speaking sapped his energy.

"Dan told me where to find you, son." Pop's Adam's apple bobbed as he swallowed. "Then he had to take Sarah Phillips home and report to his post."

Jack tried to nod but decided moving his head was as difficult as talking. Despite his dulled perception, he realized Pop had called him "son," an affectionate address he had always reserved for Dan.

"We've had our differences. I regret your casting your lot with

Rebeldom." Pop cleared his throat. "What's done is done. It's time to rebuild and put that behind us."

Finding it hard to give a damn what Pop thought, Jack closed his heavy eyelids, wanting his sire to go away and leave him be.

"You've done your duty as you saw it," Pop's voice was low and filled with feeling Jack had never heard before. "I respect that."

Jack forced his eyes open, realizing what it cost his father to admit that much.

Pop's stern features registered concern, something Jack was not accustomed to seeing. "Is there anything I can do for you right now?"

Freedom? Recovery? Bringing Martina and Rosa to his side? "Nothing, Pop. Thanks."

His father seemed to study him, his usual reserve intact. "I'll be back from time to time; make sure the military authorities treat you all right."

As Jack watched Pop walk away, he wondered whether his father had gone soft in his old age. Or maybe the entire conversation was merely a fever-driven dream.

*

Escorted by Dan, Martina passed the guard into the room where his captors held Jack apart from the sick and convalescing Union soldiers. Unsure of what she might find despite Dan's assurances, she fingered her rosary and prayed silently. The possibility of finding an empty bed where Jack should be had haunted her throughout the nightmarish two-day journey to St. Augustine.

Instead, he lay on the cot, his head resting on a pillow, a blanket covering him to his chin. Dan excused himself and left her alone with her husband. Awake, Jack locked his gaze on her. His lips curved into that familiar roguish grin she loved. "Darlin," he breathed. "You are a beautiful sight. How did you get into town?"

She bent to kiss him, prickling her cheeks on several days' worth of stubble. His hand crept out from under the blanket and gripped hers with comforting firmness. Martina straightened and blinked through the blur of tears, cherishing the sight of his face, gaunt and pale as it was. "Dan worked it out." She did not want to tell him Dan had placed her under arrest so he could bring her through the picket post. "How are you, my love?" she asked, her voice thick.

"Better, for seeing you." Jack's eyes were clear and lucid. "Prescott added a few new scars to my collection."

"My poor, dear husband." She smiled, blinking back tears. "I will kiss every one."

"Yeah, I know you will, darlin'." He squeezed her hand. "Did Carlo tell you what happened?"

She nodded. "He stayed close after he left you and saw Dan take you in the wagon, then he doubled back and talked to Mrs. Cates. When he told me, I packed up our things and came right away." She glanced at the guard and lowered her voice. "Carlo came with me as far as the Cates place."

"Where's Rosa?"

"Outside with Sarah."

"I'd like to see her, too." He swallowed hard. "Darlin', you don't know how glad I am you're here."

"Are the Yankees treating you all right?"

He nodded. "They don't bother me much. Pop brings me orangeade and eggs. He brought Father Aulance, too. I told him I wouldn't be needing last rites." Jack chuckled. "He wanted to hear my confession, so I entertained him for a while."

Hearing Jack's light tone, Martina's anxiety melted away. "You're going to be fine," she murmured. "You really are."

He squeezed her hand. "Stay with me until they run you off."

She cut her eyes at the guard, then back at her husband and set her jaw. "Let them try."

*

Late May 1865

Uneasy, Carlo held his horse to a walk as he approached the Union picket post at the Sebastian River bridge. Stripped of weapons when he lined up for surrender at Waldo, he distrusted the well-armed bluecoats. He had removed his gray jacket and rolled it with his blanket, but he did not feel like a civilian, and the Yankees were not likely to take him for one. He felt much older than seventeen and figured he looked it.

A burly, rifle-toting Yankee stepped into his path, suspicion on his face. "Papers. You got papers?"

Carlo held himself erect. "I'm as good a citizen as you are now." He handed the guard his signed parole and the certificate stating he owned his mare. Fearing confiscation, he had left Jack's U. S. branded horse at the Cates place.

While the guard looked through the papers, Carlo studied the river, inhaling the musty scent of marsh. A low tide had exposed mud and oyster beds. A mullet broke water in the channel, gleamed in the sun, and fell back with a splash. Later, maybe he could go fishing. Eventually, he wanted to own a shrimp boat and run it offshore. Maybe a steam-driven propeller boat.

Hidden in his socks, the gold coins lay hard against his ankles. He hoped they did not jingle in case his former enemies went through his clothes in a thieving expedition. Dickison's men had demanded long-overdue back pay as part of the price for helping John Breckenridge, the Confederate Secretary of War, escape to Cuba. Carlo had collected Jack's share as well and wanted to be able to deliver it.

The guard nodded. "The papers seem to be in order. I guess all is forgiven, Johnny."

Carlo knew better than to say what he really thought, that he was not ready to forgive or forget.

The Yankee handed back the documents. "You have business in town?"

"I used to live there." Carlo glanced toward his boyhood home, which he could not see from the post. "Looking for my sister and brother-in-law." As if it were any of the Yankee's business.

The guard stepped aside and let him pass. Carlo crossed the bridge and headed toward the Minorcan quarter, where he expected to find Jack and Martina at the old house. Not wishing to encounter more Union troops than necessary, he took back streets to avoid the plaza and the barracks on the south end of town.

He reined in and looked over the fence at the house before dismounting. The windowless tabby exterior facing the street had changed little since Jack's father and stepmother had taken residence. He did not know whose house it was now, or if he had a home at all. If worse came to worst, maybe Cousin Ramon would let him live on his property.

At the sound of his name, Carlo turned and spotted a Yankee officer walking toward him. He reined his horse's head around and faced Dan, unsure of how he was supposed to act. The only times he had associated with Jack's brother, one or the other was a prisoner.

"Hey, Carlo." Dan's voice sounded subdued, and he appeared to have the same doubts. "Martina isn't here."

Carlo knitted his brows in worry. "I thought she was still staying at the house."

"Not today. They're all at the homestead. I'd be out there helping rebuild if I weren't on duty today. There's a lot to do."

"I expect so." Fortunately, Carlo had taken a meal and fed his horse at the Cates place, as he, Charlie and Russell had ridden homeward together. "I hear you bought a house in town."

"Yeah, the army is leaving me here for a while, to help keep the peace." Dan grinned. "I guess you heard the rest of my news, too."

Carlo dredged up a wry smile. "Russell is fit to be tied."

"He'll get used to the idea."

"Maybe." Russell had not taken the engagement calmly. "One of these days he might start speaking to her again. And you."

"I can't help what he thinks about it." Dan shrugged. "Sarah's done right by him, and he ought to be grateful."

"He had a right to be mad. He's proud, and he gave up a lot."

"Y'all have earned your pride. But you have to bend a little, now."

"A lot, I expect." Carlo swallowed his bitterness. "Is Jack over at Picolata, too?"

"He's able to do a little light work at the homestead. He's talking about getting on with the telegraph business, like he did before the war. Says he's been practicing his Morse code, and he'll be fit to climb poles before long."

"Lots of wires to repair. Guess we've both torn down a few." Sarah had kept Carlo informed of Jack's condition, as she could pass through the lines unmolested even before the fighting ended. It paid to have a fiancé with a little influence. "You did right by him, too," he allowed.

"Managed to spin it out long enough to keep him from going to prison up north." Dan appeared self-satisfied and content. The look of a victor. "When Isaac musters out, he's going to bring his family down from Beaufort and help Pop run the farm."

Carlo smiled at the thought of Isaac running the whiskey-making business as well. As far as he knew, neither the elder Mr. Farrell nor the Yankees had discovered the still deep in the woods. Maybe Isaac and Jack would go into a partnership, unless Jack's father and Martina found out about it.

"Thanks for letting me know what's going on. I guess I'd better head over that way." Carlo touched his hat brim in a jaunty salute. Back straight, head high, he set off toward Picolata. On the way, he could stop by the Solana house and pay his respects to a young Minorcan lady. See if she wanted to see more of him from time to time.

Although the Confederacy was defeated, he took satisfaction in knowing Dickison's command had never been whipped. Severe testing over the past four years had left him sure of his abilities. His future was out there somewhere, and he was ready to meet it.

Afterword

When I wrote **Raiders on the St. Johns**, I endeavored to dramatize the tensions between warring factions in northeast Florida during the War Between the States. Confederate Captain John J. Dickison commanded Company H, 2nd Florida cavalry which operated mostly in the interior of the state. Other companies were added to his force at times. Most historians credit him and his men for making it too hazardous for the Union troops to gain a foothold in the area west of the St. Johns River and east of Cedar Key. In fact, nearly every time they tried to invade, the Union troops were soundly defeated.

The Union forces did organize two regiments of cavalry from Florida men who had their reasons for wanting to fight against the Confederacy. Most of those recruited were from the west coast. The recruitment efforts were not as successful on the east coast, and I suspect, as have other historians, that the Union Army's heavy-handed tactics in this area alienated many folks. On the west coast, the Union blockade squadron achieved more success, as they protected the Florida Unionists, armed them, and traded with them. Records show that in early 1864 a few Union recruits were signed up in St. Augustine, but as to whether someone like Dan Farrell experienced further success is not clear.

I tried to replicate the engagements depicted as faithfully as possible. It may seem curious that the Confederates won all of them, but that is what the record states. The Union suffered a huge setback at Olustee, which also torpedoed plans for readmission of the state until after the surrender.

The Maple Leaf, which was sunk off Mandarin Point just south of Jacksonville, has provided intrepid divers with wonderfully preserved artifacts that were saved from deterioration by the same mud that hid the wreck.

Confederate scouts captured Colonel Noble and his companions soon after the colonel boasted he could travel between Jacksonville and St. Augustine in perfect safety. That Christmas Eve, he discovered he could not.

The capture of the dance party actually occurred in much the manner portrayed. Although the young soldier who infiltrated behind the lines to gather intelligence from his father is not identified in Dickison's writings, I assert that it very likely was my uncle, Charles Colee, who brought out his father, George, to talk with his commander.

Dickison and his men achieved two amazing exploits that almost defy belief. The capture of the gunboat *Columbine*, achieved with a few artillery pieces and a dozen sharpshooters, was a unique feat. Cavalry is not supposed to be able to take on a heavily fortified gunship and win! But it happened just south of Palatka.

The inconclusive first Battle of Gainesville did not involve Dickison's troop, though the Union reports made those claims. The second Battle of Gainesville was so one-sided that I spent a lot of time scratching my head and analyzing how it could be possible. The opposing forces were about equal in strength, and in fact, some of Dickison's men were untrained recruits. The Union troops had just taken the town and should have been in position to resist the attack. Instead, the Confederates crushed them with very few casualties. Of the 300 Union troops involved, only about 40 made it out with the main column, though a number of others managed to straggle to safety. Dickison admitted to only six casualties, two dead and four wounded. This compares to an inconclusive but much larger number of Union dead, many wounded, and over a hundred prisoners. The only explanation I found was that the Union troops were busy looting, were caught off guard, and suffered the consequences.

Since the publication of **Exiles on the St. Johns**, I have found two more Confederate ancestors previously unknown to me. John J. Irwin, the father-in-law of my great, great grandfather James L. Colee, served as a lieutenant in the same company, Baya's Artillery, 8th Florida. Alexander J. Wells served in Company D, 54th Georgia regiment. He was the father-in-law of John Hardy Bolton, my great, great grandfather. I turned up a single, lonely Union soldier in my background William Boor, who served in an Ohio regiment.

I hope I have illustrated northeast Florida's much-overlooked role in the War Between the States in an informative and entertaining manner. It is my belief that accurate historical fiction is the most interesting way to learn about those sad but fascinating times.

About the Author:

Lydia Hawke has written four Civil War novels, FIRETRAIL, PERFECT DISGUISE, EXILES ON THE ST JOHNS, and RAIDERS ON THE ST. JOHNS. FIRETRAIL and PERFECT DISGUISE have been adapted into feature movies. She also wrote SILENT WITNESS, a suspense novel set in the world of dog agility trials, under the name Lydia C. Filzen. Her non-fiction work and photographs appear frequently in *Clay Today* and *Civil War News* with the byline Lydia Filzen. She is an avid history buff and lurks about Civil War reenactments trolling for stories and great pictures. Also, she shows champion Collies in conformation and agility. Lydia is a member of various writing organizations, United Daughters of the Confederacy, Orange Park Amateur Radio Club, Collie Club of America, Pals and Paws Agility Club, Greater Jacksonville Collie Club and Greater Orange Park Dog Club. She owns DesJardin Electrical Service with her husband, Larry. In her spare time she… Spare time???

LaVergne, TN USA
22 November 2009

164947LV00003B/7/P